Praise for
Alliance Rising:

"Cherryh and Fancher expand Cherryh's extensive Alliance-Union universe (which is fast approaching its 40th birthday) with this taut drama set aboard the star-orbiting Alpha Station. . . . Rather than rely on pyrotechnics, Cherryh and Fancher ground this fine work in the difficult choices that their characters must make in the face of an uncertain future. The economics and sociopolitics are as riveting as space battles, enhancing this welcome addition to the Alliance-Union saga." —*Publishers Weekly*

"This is a measured, compelling work that's clearly leading in to a wider arc. . . . The conclusion drops the reader off with cliff-hanging verve." —*Locus*

"Another exciting entry in Cherryh's extensive Alliance-Union Universe. . . . Well-imagined far future." —*Kirkus*

"I enjoy and respect [Cherryh and Fancher's] writing; I get a bit smarter each time I read something they've written, which does nothing to get in the way of stories both exciting and hope-inspiring. I recommend *Alliance Rising* in the strongest terms." —Book Review Crew

"Fascinating reading. The details of ship operations, station politics and family relationships are intricately interwoven, realistically rendered." —SFcrowsnest

"*Alliance Rising* is a long, slow burn of a novel . . . but in the hands of Cherryh and Fancher, this is gripping stuff." —Nerds of a Feather

C. J. CHERRYH AND JANE S. FANCHER

ALLIANCE RISING

The Hinder Stars I

DAW BOOKS, INC.

DONALD A. WOLLHEIM, FOUNDER

1745 Broadway, New York, NY 10019

ELIZABETH R. WOLLHEIM
SHEILA E. GILBERT
PUBLISHERS

www.dawbooks.com

To Betsy, for making this book possible.

Rosie's Pub was Alpha-based spacer turf. It was where you went on the Strip to spend time, to talk with shipmates, friends, and other ships' crew who were regulars at Alpha Station.

And like other bars on the Strip, Rosie's maintained, half-lost in the glassware and the bottles of liquor on the shelves above the bar, a schedule board—a list of ships coming in, ships leaving, ships currently in dock. Wide-screen, three separate displays: interstation FTLers, maintenance insystemers, and on the far left, the sub-lighters, those two remaining links to Sol Station and Earth, one ship coming, one going, on their ten-year-long voyages— Sol being the only star outside the jump range of the faster-than-light ships: ironic proof, some said, that there was a god.

That part of the screen rarely changed: two ships, two destinations, no surprises there. The other two sections, with FTLers listed in the center and insystemers on the right, ebbed and flowed with the tides of commerce— shifting but generally predictable.

Until three hours ago, when the words *in arrival* had flashed above the listing of FTL ships and assigned berths.

In arrival. With no name or origin, just an ominous blank where both ought to appear.

Three hours and counting, and still no update.

Nobody remembered that happening. Ever. FTL ships dropped in at system zenith and sent ID before the first vane pulse, so ID arrived nearly simultaneously with the entry wavefront. *In arrival* always, *always*, came with a ship name attached. Period. That information kept honest folk from flashing on Beta Station . . . and the ghosts of stationers who had just *disappeared*, back at the dawn of all the star-stations, when the sub-lighter *Santa Maria* had come into Beta Station, at Proxima Centauri, and found . . . nothing. No remains, no explanation, no clue.

No one visited Proxima, ever, after that. Alpha Station, at Barnard's Star, the first station outside Sol system itself, developed daughter stations in the opposite direction, and thrived.

Until FTL changed everything.

Alpha still maintained its unique sub-light trade with Earth, over a twenty-year round trip, a distance only pusher-ships could travel without a break. But one of Alpha's own daughter stations, Bryant's, farther on in a direction opposite to the Centauri stars, was close enough to Alpha for modern FTLers to one-hop it, and it was close enough to Glory and Venture to do the same. With those stations, Alpha maintained a modern traffic, always the same ships, generally on a schedule. And give or take the age of Alpha's systems and the occasional glitches, citizen nerves and the futures market stayed fairly steady.

But who was this inbound now? Locals and spacers alike wanted to know. And they wanted an answer a lot sooner than three hours with no ID.

Malfunction in the display? If so, it was a station-wide malfunction. Crew from bars up and down the strip poked their heads in, asking was Rosie's display frozen, too?

In Rosie's, the early assumption had been that it *was* just a glitch, that the screen was frozen—except, as various people immediately pointed out, the *time* kept ticking away in the corner of the display.

And over on another display, behind the blue neon sign for Beloit's Premium Vodka, the news screen and the station information screen ran on as usual, unglitched. Likewise an entertainment channel at the back of the bar was running smoothly.

God knew, malfunctions were no stranger to Alpha. The station being the oldest of all star-stations, breakdowns happened now and again, though usually not so long-lasting in a system so basic and critical to a station's well-being. Consolation was that, over near the hand-printed *Rosie's Special Ale*, the local market board ticker, that other heartbeat of commerce, was still running. Its clock marked a steady flow of time above the list of current prices for goods on Alpha, and last-known prices for the same goods on other stations. Every ship that came in caused a cascade of changes in those prices—and not only as their cargo went on offer. Along with physical cargo, every ship also brought information safely stowed in its black box, untouchable information vital to every aspect of interstellar trade. And as an arriving ship's black box fed its last gulp of data from afar into the station's systems, that data joined the data every other ship had fed in from every other station, some of it way out of current date and from the other end of civilization, some near enough to be use-ful. The station's computer would rapidly sort out the rel-evant market information, and that screen would stabilize, reacting only to in-station trade—until the next ship ar-rived.

That information flow affected the markets. It affected plans. It was the routine pulse of trade and business. But in the last three hours since the arrival screen had frozen, local prices had begun to react, wildly, unpredictably, for internal reasons. Uncertainty did that. Movement in the market meant people shifting their bets, freeing money, prepared to draw back and hope to buy in low.

Betting on changes in prices, whatever that incoming ship carried.

People with money at stake were not happy. Spacers and station customers with agreements ready to sign, now put on hold, would be pissed as hell.

Dammitall, was the frequent comment. With *In Arrival* lit up, there *should* be a ship name, not a frozen screen. A manifest should arrive to settle those fluctuating numbers.

Hours on—with no announcement from admin—it was insane. Did admin *want* a riot on the Strip?

Big question was: what ship was it? Had to be incoming from Bryant's Star. There was nowhere else for it to origi-nate, sanely speaking. There were a few Alpha regulars not in port, ships who *might* have changed their mind, done a quick turnaround at Bryant's, but how would *that* warrant this silence? And why would they, with their regulars at Venture and Glory waiting?

Unless it had to do with the strangers currently in port: three of them, all from routes farther up the line, from Pell and beyond. Three ships trading in foodstuffs and metals, and not saying *why* they'd come all the way out here, or when they planned on leaving.

This problem with the schedule boards was downright embarrassing, something major as this malfunctioning in front of these fancy, state-of-the-art outsider ships.

Spacers began to speculate in low tones about, well, maybe station had shut down the flow deliberately. Maybe it was an accident in the jump zone. A mistake could fling a ship into Alpha's small red sun. Miscalibration of a too-old nav system could send it on a comet's path, outbound for a million years or so, nobody able to catch it—a cheerful suggestion that came from one of *Firenze*'s stranded crew. Station might not be getting any information from the arrival and station might still be without any answer.

Maybe it was just a damaged antenna. That had happened. Station might be trying, in the fierce output of a sun, to find a very tiny signal.

So why didn't they just *say?* A breakdown? A glitch?

Maybe a ship in serious trouble.

Maybe, nervous-making thought, a ship that *chose* to run incognito.

The *Santiago* captain, word came down the strip, had queried Alpha Central—what's going on with the board? What ship's coming in?

And gotten just a, "System is down. Be patient." That . . . to a captain's direct question about an incoming ship. No denial or confirmation that *something* was out there, which anyone with half a brain *knew* was the significant part of that question. Central could have set that concern right with four simple words: *There is no ship.*

So maybe there was and maybe there wasn't. Secrets ran deep on Alpha. Maybe station was withholding that information for some good reason. But they'd damned well better say something soon.

Speculation began to run amok, quietly spoken, so as not to jinx the possibility, that, God, maybe it was finally an FTL arrival from Sol. That came from a stationer mouth, first, a waiter—no spacer really thought that. Even if Sol had found that long-sought jump-point to get them here, a sim-trained crew would be dead crazy to be the first to test it.

But it *could* be, the speculator insisted, a robot probe. It could mean that FTL to Sol was on the horizon, and they would all soon be living in luxury.

Stationer-thinking.

Practical speculation said *dream on, stationer,* and moved on to another, more realistic possibility. Realistic and a bit ominous. Was it *another* outsider—and this one not saying its business?

In the last ten days, Alpha had had *three* ships come in, two of which had never visited Alpha before, none of the three admitting any connection with the other two—and they had sent metal and food prices down. A temporary dip, that—canny traders didn't panic. But the arriving out-sider crews were standoffish and sticking to a ship-speak nobody could penetrate, and not anything like the same ship-speak, either. Alpha crews might welcome one ship—charitably. There was barely enough trade in the First Stars to keep Alpha-based ships moving on very limited routes. Some ship that generally operated the other side of Venture Station *might* drop in, oh, every half-decade or so, with some new item unique enough to warrant the cost, and it could be welcome. Two such at once, yes . . . once in living memory, when two had jumped in at the same opportunity and destroyed their own profit margin.

But *three?* They'd undercut Alpha-based ships' barely break-even margins on two vital commodities. They'd made ships reassess their own plans and scramble for cargo that wouldn't be affected by some similar dump of goods at Bryant's, which these ships would have visited, coming here.

Questions on *that* topic had started to fly up and down the Strip, to which "Don't know," and "Bob down in cargo said that his cousin Sam heard that one of the newcomers said . . ." weren't highly informative answers.

Station, on the other hand, wasn't complaining about the influx of foodstuffs or metals. And when that third ship had showed up within five hours of the second, bars and sleepovers mothballed since the last pusher-ship departure had been pressed into operation, fast as personnel could be pulled in from the residency side of the station. The newcomers might use a ship-speak nobody could understand, but they had pidgin enough when it came to food and drink and lodging, and ship's scrip began to flow into stationer hands. Two newly reopened bars were routinely full of the outsiders.

And now might a fourth have arrived? Maybe in trouble and unable to send the standard identification? Thoughts of "What could be wrong?" began to extend to "something wrong further away than Bryant's?"

Something going on between Pell and Cyteen, the two mega-stations that thus far had managed a relatively peaceful co-existence?

Not a happy thought at all, but a possibility that always lurked in the shadows of every Alpha-based mind.

Not surprising, then, that for the last three hours speculation had drawn local spacers from bar to bar up and down the Strip, waiting—hoping—for some flasher to come up on-screen to say it was all a false alarm, that the input was screwed, that some fool had pushed the wrong button, and there *was* no ship.

Because even if that incoming ship wasn't in trouble, one more crew crowding the Strip, one more bar opening to take favored, experienced station staff away from the regular Alpha crews' watering holes, one more ship's requests for accommodations and services stacking up in the already-scrambled administrative queue, with *more* goods flooding into a small market . . . well, tempers already on edge were going to snap, no way not, and damned if they'd feel guilty if a little furniture got broken, not after this too-damned-long silent treatment by admin.

"Did you hear?" a newcomer said. "They're opening the Olympian. They're calling in staff."

"No way," somebody said.

But a check of listings proved it was true. And it stopped being a question of "is it a ship?" and became a question of "just how big *is* it?" The Olympian, old and regal, was the palace that housed pusher crews during their extended sleepovers. Big crews. Favored crews.

But it couldn't be a pusher. There were only two serving Alpha. You wouldn't ordinarily mistake their arrival signature for an FTLer's, not to mention their vector. Sol began to be in question again. And Station ops *had* to know more than they were saying, damn straight.

47.3 minutes into the fourth hour—the screen flashed.

And all eyes turned.

Up came the Alpha Station logo, the Greek lower-case alpha in blue supered over the Earth Company's round gold EC, a portentous change that drew instant mutterings of relief and the sound of bodies pushing back chairs to get a better view at the bar.

"Well?" somebody asked of the unresponsive screen.

The image persisted. There was a moment of hushed silence in Rosie's.

Then the standard message crawl appeared, saying: . . . *Berths number B-12 and B-14 are being reassigned . . .*

"*Crap!*" someone exclaimed.

. . . *Ships are being moved back by service craft at this time. There is no need for crew to report. The stationmaster offers apologies to* Qarib *and* Firenze *crew. There will be no charges for the extended wait or for the pushback.*

The bar broke out in profanities and a predominant, "*Charges?* What friggin' charges? For pushing our ship out? For stranding us? They got no right!" and from a Firenze: "What the hell? Repair already forgets about us, stuck out on the end. Dammit, they're going to move a repair crew out *to* us, or Abrezio's gonna get himself a new one!"

And: "Dammit, put the fucker up on A-mast! Let *Rights* fuckin' move over!"

Followed by a chorused: "*Dream on.*"

Nobody, but nobody intruded on A-mast. *The Rights of Man,* Alpha station's own bloody huge albatross, was too precious to be put at risk.

"Guess that settles it," Fallan Monahan said quietly. "That spook incoming must be real."

"But why two berths?" Ross, also Monahan, of *Galway*, was having the same uneasy feeling. "Security?"

"Maybe it's just that damn *big.*"

"Pusher?" Ross asked, and Fallan shrugged.

"Sol *could've* built another pusher without telling us. Can't imagine them throwin' us resource like that. But it'd be helpful if they put another pusher on the route, providin' they sent something *not* earmarked for *Rights.*"

Ross, only a time-lagged two decades and a half, hadn't lived long enough to see an Alpha-based pusher-ship in dock but once in his life, and he was hard put to recall if it had needed two berths. All he remembered was that it was *huge.* A ship designed to push the mass of a station core between stars.

And thinking of that, he wondered . . . would two berths be enough?

"F' God's sake, *is* it a friggin' pusher comin' in?" someone asked his question aloud. "From where? And what's it doin' on *our* list?"

"Could be an inbound with a problem." A new voice in the crowd. "Maybe leavin' room for repair modules. Humanitarian takes precedence."

Any incoming with an emergency situation had a right to immediate access, to dock, offload and onload and stay at dock as long as they had to: that was a law ancient as they came. Alpha would have to make room enough to grant that.

"Precedence my ass! We got a *schedule* to keep."

That was temper talking; no one in Rosie's would point fingers. Still, it seemed a prudent time to keep quiet, seeing as how at B-10, *Galway* had not been affected by the reshuffling, and neither had the Rodriguezes' *Santiago*, at B-8. Maybe it was just timing: *Galway* had finished her loading and was in the final stages of resupply and fueling; *Santiago* was in the onloading process. *Qarib* and *Firenze* were endmost on the B-mast. *Qarib* had refueling and cargo yet to go, so she would have to be moved in again— which she could be as soon as *Galway* headed out. But unlucky *Firenze*—not even operable—had been undergoing yet another repair at dock. If this incoming ship also had problems, where did *humanitarian precedence* leave them?

No matter what, all those operations lost precious time. An unguessable extent of time. Time for the numbers to flux, time for the expectant customers on the far end of the run to get nervous and start looking elsewhere for their goods.

Station populations depended on timely arrivals of those goods. Ships' *reputations* depended on keeping their routes reliable. All of that meant real, tangible, economic damage to the ships being moved out, but *beyond* all that, being displaced by a ship only starting its process was—well, that was outright *disrespect,* dammit. That incoming ship should be the one to wait. Ships' reputations were touchy matters, their priorities and prerogatives with stations were jealously guarded, no matter their relative size or importance. Priority rested with the first-in unless a life was at stake.

And the reaction to that disrespect would be gathering on the Strip right now.

Four spacers certainly left Rosie's with fury in their stride, headed out to confer with family seniors, and you could bet the captains involved would be headed for station offices to raise merry hell about whatever was going on—and bent on getting every compensation and concession they could squeeze out of admin.

Everyone else just stared at the screen, waiting for . . . something. Anything.

So what the hell was going on that station couldn't give a name to?

Maybe station had balked. Maybe the delay in response was station telling somebody off. Maybe station had been hoping not to have to clear those legitimate and loyal ships to make room, only to lose the argument.

But who could have that kind of pull? With what leverage?

EC. Earth Company. That was the obvious answer. The EC *owned* the station, owned the station and all the ships that came into dock. But that would mean a pusher . . . a new one, as Fallan said. Maybe even one with supply to bolster their foundering station. And if not a pusher . . . well, there remained the ever-hopeful fantasy that the phantom jump-point between Alpha and Sol had finally been found, that they finally had a reachable point of mass that would make the potentially lucrative Sol route an FTL run, not a twenty-year expedition.

Neither of which seemed remotely likely.

The practical bet was still on another outsider.

The three outsider ships they already had, *Little Bear, Mumtaz,* and *Nomad,* were all Venture registry, generally on the Venture-Pell run, with a dogleg up to Viking, maybe Mariner or even beyond. If Venture was looking to expand Venture-Alpha trade . . . that might offer station something it very badly needed. That incoming ship might carry an offer they *couldn't* refuse.

Station, already running lean thanks to that monster on A-mast eating up every damned gram of cargo that came in from Sol, was desperate for everything from flour to iron. If Venture was willing to expand trade, if granting Venture ships a regular berth here was the price of that increase, then station had to be tempted. Fools not to be.

But . . . *damn.* The economics didn't work out for little ships, the ships that, dammitall, had *resisted* the allure of the Farther Star routes and remained loyal to the First Stars. The ships that, dammitall again, had kept those First Star stations alive for generations.

Beyond doubt, station was already benefitting from the increased crew traffic on the Strip. Spacers from outside the normal routes were spending scrip. Sleepovers were booked as they hadn't been in living memory, and on the second arrival, station had invoked bar assignments, meaning that ships were assigned certain bars for their crew and put on notice of good behavior if they strayed into another ship's territory.

And not a one of those establishments that wasn't packed, most of the time. Ordinary eateries, where empty tables were the rule, had called up staff, for God's sake. The influx of scrip might have been roaring good news—if these outsiders hadn't been so damned uncommunicative about their reasons for being here; and *nobody* believed ship-speak was all they could use. When strange things happened this close to the edge of nowhere, with the economy so fragile, people got anxious.

When ships got disrespected in the process, spacers got angry. Damn straight, they did.

As for the ships they were moving off the mast—which meant undocking from the mast and pushing out and away, to let them sit unmanned, unattended except for a robot pusher maintaining attitude and relative position—you did that for a hulk or a construction part, but for a working ship? It was unprecedented anywhere, in Ross's memory. It was an insult, dammit, and there was clearly no consideration of moving anybody up to A-mast, oh, no. *The Rights of Man* sat up there, *loomed* up there, the Earth Company's pet project, a monster of a ship designed to challenge the likes of Pell's *Finity's End* and Cyteen's *Dublin*, the mega-ship merchant ships that were, everyone said, the future of trade for the Farther Stars, built for ring-docking and cans, for a volume of cargo that Alpha or Glory or Bryant's couldn't even conceive of.

Oh, yes . . . *The Rights of Man* got all the room she needed, plus a security perimeter, which meant that all of A-mast was off limits and had been for seven years and more, ever since they'd moved *Rights* in from her construction area.

"My bet," Fallan said quietly, just to Ross, "is that *Rights* is the reason for this sudden flood of outsiders. She had her engine test, oh, long enough ago that word could have traveled far enough and brought a visit back again. Spies is probably what we got, ships from Pell just comin' to have a look-see."

She sits, is what she does. That was Ross's jaundiced thought. *She can't move.* But saying that out loud wasn't politic, even here, in the heart of what had been *Galway*'s home port and home bar for as long as he'd been allowed to leave the minders. *Rights* sat up there and sopped up resources. Everything for the *Rights* build, from engineers to plumbers to massive pusher-loads of resources from Sol—all went for *Rights,* and real coffee, once actually affordable on Alpha every decade or so, was something only Fallan—old and time-dilated as hell—had ever tasted. Sol said build, and Alpha built, even while the pipes leaked a puddle in Rosie's kitchen, who couldn't even do his own repairs because he couldn't get resources. Put it on a work order, they'd say, and it would get fixed. But it wouldn't, until it flooded the place and *then* it'd be a priority, with Rosie charged a premium for overtime labor. If it wasn't a high-pressure line (and Rosie's kitchen drain and toilet weren't) it could wait.

Seven years ago, *Rights* had moved out of her construction frame and docked at the top of A-mast, not under her own power, but pushed and tugged ever-so-gently by service craft.

Five of them. Big day.

The rest of the universe hadn't cared that much.

But maybe someone had been watching, last year, when, to a lot of hype, *Rights* had moved out of dock and run under her own power, tested her engines to system limits, come back, docked, *very* slowly . . . and gone back to sitting.

That hesitant and aborted performance was downright scary—to any self-respecting spacer. An FTL out of control was a threat to themselves and anything in their vicinity. It was no secret that the EC had *stationers* manning that ship, stationers who'd trained on sims. *Stationers* who were supposedly going to take that ship FTL. Station-born crew who were putting on the blue EC uniform and expecting it all would work.

And the sum total of that crew's actual experience? *Rights'* ops crew *had* done shadow-training—once—in a run to Bryant's Star on another ship. They'd sat at boards that looked and responded just like the real thing, made decisions, input instructions to the ship . . . just as if they were actually running it. Fortunately, from what *Qarib* crew said after, their calculations had not, thank God, been what actually *had* gone into the ship's computer. Thanks to instructions from the ship's real crew, they had *not* dropped *Qarib* into the heart of the star.

That was it, as far as *Rights'* training went: sims, that

one run shadowing a working crew on the smallest hauler out there, and a single in-system jaunt which had included one pulse of the vanes, a test that, rumor said, had shut down prematurely.

Maybe Fallan was right. Maybe that run *had* scared people and these stranger ships were here to assess the progress first hand, not trusting rumor or Alpha's official word.

But spies, if it was just spying, were quiet. One ship was quiet. Three . . . maybe now four . . . ships? That wasn't quiet. That was a push.

The screen stayed steady, except that running time-stamp. Four hours, eight minutes. Tension could only hold so long. People ordered beers, Rosie and his waitstaff drew them, and spacers drifted back to tables.

"Want to sit?" Ross asked, scanning the large premises for a vacant table.

"We got the view here at the bar," Fallan said. Fallan was time-dilated as hell, pale, thin skin, not so many wrinkles as one might expect, grey-haired—he wore it shagged about his ears. How old *was* Fallan? Hell, he'd say, it's complicated.

Pusher before he was a merchant spacer, oldest of the Monahans, and great-grandfather to one of the Monahan lines, great-uncle to a good few more, from the days before, from the time when babies were conceived and born in the long decades between stations, when youngers grew up knowing both parents. These days, like all FTLers, they relied on the Monahan women to bring new life aboard, and scattered their own offspring unguessed and untracked, from Venture to Glory and Alpha and back.

Fallan was Nav 1 on *Galway,* oldest crewman aboard, probably oldest of any spacer that walked the deck on Alpha. Ross Monahan, at a mere twenty-four shipboard years, was Nav 1.3—meaning on *Galway* he shadowed the navigation boards, reading the data, making judgement calls the computer noted without implementing . . . first shift backup to first shift nav, backup and trainee, but he worked right beside Fallan.

He shadowed Fallan on the Strip, too—for one thing, to

learn something, because Fallan dropped gems now and again; but for another, because Fallan was *Galway*'s treasure, and a little fragile in a press. Captain Niall Monahan had said, after a certain donnybrook on Glory's Strip, "You stay with him, Ross. You just stay right with him. He doesn't know, sometimes, how fragile he is. And he'll fight, the fool, if *Galway*'s fighting."

So, well, it was an excuse to stay close and hear Fallan's stories, and to ask him questions that, God, kept him thinking, kept him dreaming of things few people living had seen or experienced, kept him asking himself how long until he knew a tenth of what Fallan Monahan knew.

Fallan took the next beer served and shoved it at him across the wet bar surface. Standing room only, and Fallan didn't opt to sit down, so Ross leaned on the bar and watched the unchanging display.

"What's your best guess?" he asked Fallan. "Who's behind this?"

"Pell," Fallan said flatly. "Pell."

"The three we have are Venture registry."

Fallan glanced at him. "So's *Galway,* isn't she? Registry's nothin' but where a ship's built." And gazing into his beer. "It's been coming. Long time it's been coming. Ever since Venture built that station module without so much as a by-your-leave from Sol—this has been coming."

That was a far stretch for a connection, ancient history, even for Fallan. "You mean way back when they set out to Pell's Star?"

"Mmm. Set the numbers in motion, they did. Been fillin' the unknowns ever since. A jump waitin' for a mass point . . ." A blink, and another glance. "You weren't there for the original fuss. Me mum and gran . . . they were."

Ross recognized Fallan in one of his moods, relaxed and just listened. No matter how many times he heard Fallan's stories, he always, *always* learned something new.

"When they built Pell's Station," Fallan said, "it was just like old *Gaia* tellin' the EC where they could stick their replacement crew—on that very first sublight run, when *Gaia* come back to Sol an' told the EC they were stayin' aboard forever an' claimin' the ship for their own, and there was nothin' the EC could do about it. Just the doin' of it changed everything. Same when Cap'n Pell organized to take that station core Venture Station had sittin' around, waiting for someplace to go. The EC was saying cranky old UV Ceti, sittin' so close an' all, was going to cut loose and fry any life at Tau Ceti. The EC was all 'wait on better shielding.' Word at *Venture* was that Sol damned well knew it was looking at a potential biostuffs gold mine in that sweet-zone planet that was hell and away closer to Venture than Sol. Word was the EC didn't *want* a station at that star. No more ex-clu-sivity. No more Earth as the sole source. So rather than waiting for a go-ahead that likely wouldn't come from Sol for decades, if it came at all, Cap'n Pell and Venture Station just said screw you and did what they knew was right. It was a risk. A big one. The EC could've cut Venture Station itself right out of the loop and starved 'em into compliance before they could really set up. But they took the risk and pushed that core on to the next star. *His* star. Tau Ceti. An' *his* planet. Pell's World. *Downbelow*. They just *did*. Just like *Gaia*."

"And it paid off," Ross said, "just like *Gaia*."

Fallan shrugged. "You could say."

That shrug perplexed Ross. Of *course* it had paid off. If that expansion to Tau Ceti had never happened, the First Stars would be helpless now against the EC's every whim. Hard to imagine, being *that* dependent on Sol. Hard to imagine there only being *one* source of biostuffs besides the tanks. But that was the way it had been before they built Pell Station.

True, Alpha was hurting these years, thanks to the EC's obsession with *Rights*, but it still wasn't starving. Biostuffs came from Pell, some even from Cyteen. Heavy metals, to expand, repair, and upgrade ships and station alike . . . those were a different matter, and why *Firenze* made every jump with crossed fingers and why Rosie plugged the leaks with duct tape. Venture had heavy metals—the only one of the First Stars that did—but the supply was limited and Venture used it up as fast as their belters could mine it. From the beginning, Alpha had had Sol to supply the heavies . . . until it all started going into *Rights*.

"Mixed blessing," Fallan said, with a little nod. "It's the numbers, Ross-lad. The mass shift. Pell was just the beginning. Pell's Star had resources, but Pell alone couldn't change the universe. It didn't have the numbers. On its own, it could only make the whole system richer. But beyond Pell there was Viking, rich with heavies. Then Mariner. And Cyteen . . . hell, Cyteen took a page from Cap'n Pell's book. A bunch of geeks went and hijacked another station core that was supposed to be Mariner. They stole that core *and* a pusher, and just kept goin'."

"Geeks?"

"With the souls of pirates," Fallan said, without explaining. "And that's when everything began to accelerate. They steal a core, take them a star and the next viable planet with nobody's permission, then turn about and tell the EC *and* Pell to go to hell."

"So really, it started with Cyteen," Ross said, but Fallan shook his head.

"Without Pell doin' it first, they wouldn't've thought of it, bein' pirates. Pell, he was an explorer, a colonizer. Those eggheads just wanted to develop their tech without any checks or balances. Pell bein' there gave them a buffer between them and Sol. Gave them a chance to jack up their birth rate with birthlabs, terrifying every sane person from Mariner to Sol, and then they went and capped it all with a magic pill that keeps the lot of them alive indefinitely. Not content with personal immortality, no, they smuggle rejuv to the highest bidders, who find out the hard way that they got to keep takin' it or die. And the Cyteeners, they claim—oh so innocent—that only their planet produces the stuff, oh, they'll try hard to supply it . . . but it'll cost. So they make themselves richer than God. Then, *then*, toppin' all, they go an' invent FTL and just hand the tech out for free."

"Except," Ross said, "except to Sol."

"Oh, they don't give a damn if Sol's got the tech. Givin' it to the stations, however, that skewered Sol good and proper, that did. FTL, free for one and all, and Cyteen'll even convert the old pushers to FTL for *free* an' train the crew while they wait. They have nav charts, also free, that

includes everybody *but* Sol, because there's Sol—and the
EC—way off in all that clutter with no good jump point
available. Least so far as Cyteen cared to check. Long as
the entire system ran only on pushers, Sol was equal to
everybody, and a mite more equal, in their own reckoning.
With FTL linking everybody *but* Sol, Sol was screwed. You
think those Cyteen eggheads didn't see that comin'? Pell
now, gotta wonder if they're not keepin' us alive as somethin' of an afterthought, maybe as insurance against Cyteen, seein' as how gettin' in bed with pirates can get your
throat slit."

That was a new slant on what Ross had always thought
of as ancient history. A scary one.

"Or maybe they're playin' nice because they're seein'
pirates on the other side. EC pirates. An' maybe they just
want us on *their* side when those EC pirates escape their
sublight prison."

Definitely scary.

"'Course it could be just because we're a market." Fallan gave him a half-wink, seeming to read his mind as Fallan could sometimes do. "So—how does the EC deal with
this? Instead of talking to Pell and changin' its ways, instead of sending us more of the good stuff to trade with
Pell and becoming part of what *is*, the EC pirates in the EC
offices on Pell steal the plans for Pell's top secret mega-
ship, then the EC pirates back at Sol order Alpha to use
those plans to build them a mega-ship of their own, and to
throw all subsequent pusher loads into that damn monster.
It's like they never even considered that Pell might take
exception to that theft and cut us off entirely—which they
still could—like maybe they don't care if only Alpha sur-
vives and that, only so they finish that damned ship. Early
on, maybe they could justify it. Early gossip said those
monster ships could maybe one-hop it to Sol, which would
make them real tempting to those folks just itchin' to get
out here and get hands-on control. I never saw it, myself.
Couldn't make the numbers work, no matter what. And far
as we know now—I was right. But the good ol' EC just kept
buildin', didn't they? Even after *Finity* was operational and
her performance numbers became official. They kept

building and they'll keep building, pusher load after pusher load, until that ship runs, and when it does . . ." Fallan shrugged. "We're killing ourselves here, Ross-me-lad, and for what reason? A ship that, if it ever does jump, could replace the lot of us. A ship that, even if it never leaves dock, has likely already screwed us all. Just by existin'."

"What you're saying is," Ross said, watching condensation run down the side of his mug and join a set of circles on the scarred countertop, "we stay alive here because of foodstuffs we can only get from Pell—while we build that monster to compete with Pell. You think maybe Pell's finally out of humor about it and these ships are here to put the lot of us out of business?"

"Honestly?" Fallan rubbed his chin, took a sip of beer, and stared at the screen. "No. More likely they just want to get a look at that honking great ship up there. Pell's *got* to know it's been crewing-up and making trials. And no way in hell Pell's not a mite-bit curious about that. Maybe wondering if Sol *has* finally got a jump-point."

Pell definitely had a proprietary connection to that build, however unwillingly, and it was no secret. *Those* were the stolen plans taking shape.

Time was, the EC had had offices at all the stations this side of Cyteen, including Pell. Station *directors* had all been EC-appointed—except for Pell's, and the stations Pell had built. From the start, in defiance of EC directives, Pell had carried on a highly lucrative business with Cyteen, and it was toward Cyteen Pell looked these days for economic expansion and competition. That was why, when Cyteen built a monster ship, *Dublin,* at *their* station, Pell had stripped down old *Gaia* for her steel and built one to match her: *Finity's End.*

The EC had been upset. Sol read Pell right enough: Pell wasn't going to turn over that ship or send it where Sol wanted: Pell was in a head-to-head contest with Cyteen, and they weren't handing *this* design out for free.

So early on, before construction of *Finity* had even begun, the EC office at Pell had gotten their hands on the files, and EC couriers had carried the plans up the line to

Alpha. Alpha in turn had transmitted the information via the Stream at light speed to Sol, the way information had to travel that route; and twelve years later, had gotten orders back up the Stream to build the EC's own mega-ship based on those plans, on a priority above everything. On the next pusher-ship, Andrew Jackson Cruz had arrived, with a pusher-load of materials and a mandate: to make certain *The Rights of Man* became a reality.

From the start, the question every Alpha ship had asked was: To what purpose had Alpha been ordered to build such a ship? To haul what? There wasn't that much trade to move out of here. And most importantly: once that monster did move, where did Alpha's own ships—small and centuries old, most of them—fit into that economy?

But then, and like every plan the EC made, that ship had been slow to take shape, waiting on supply from Sol and a lightspeed dataflow that took twelve years to round-trip. Concerns ebbed and ships and stations alike adjusted to the new flow of goods, such as they got from Pell.

Nobody had been that surprised earlier this year, either, when *Rights* had failed its first trial. Early apprehensions first that it would jump to Sol and second, that it would drive them all out of business . . . had sunk down to a sigh and a business-as-usual for the EC: grand plan, flawed mess of an execution. Sol's monster ship would have been a local joke, if it weren't so disruptive of everything Alpha should be doing. It was a notorious embarrassment clear to Venture.

But could that ship really worry Pell? Could it give Pell ideas about establishing control here—*before* it became viable?

"You think Pell wants their plans back?" Ross said it as a joke.

"Little late for that, in't it?"

"So maybe they're sending us a repair crew. Might be afraid of a mass that big popping into their system out of control."

A dry laugh. "Possible," Fallan said. "Anything's possible. I tell you something. The EC at Sol has always had notions they have a natural-born right to everything out here. And what worries *me* about that ship up there on A-mast—"

Fallan stopped there. Some things *were* dangerous to say, even in Rosie's.

But the ambient was noisy, somebody had put the music on, and Fallan went on. "You see all these blue-coats runnin' around the Strip that weren't there five years ago? Those stationer hires of *Rights* aren't all training for ops crew. They're enforcer-types. Watch their eyes, note how they look sharper the longer they've worn those blue coats. Note how they're poppin' into bars and out again on the Strip. Note that batch that was just now in the doorway. And now they aren't."

Ross *had* noticed that batch looking in and leaving. It was always that way on Alpha. But more so lately.

"Watching the strangers."

"Looking for the strangers on the station, wanting to know where they are, where we are, who's talking to whom. Watching us. Watching, because that's what they do."

"The blue-coats are still Alpha-born."

"Ross, lad, the EC's stupid, but it's not asleep. There's high-level admin come in to build that ship up there. And remember, Sol has the *Finity* plans same as we do. Original theory was, yeah, a mega-ship could one-hop six, seven lights and it'd get to Sol easy with *no* jump-point. That's all slid back to, well, probably not. So what *else* do they do with it, with no jump-point in that direction? They're hiring every unemployed stationer who passes the enforcement physical. They're running sims to train ops crew. That's maybe a hundred on a ship that big. But how many blue uniforms do we have walking around out there, looking into spacer business?"

"Too damn many."

"Enforcement, is what. A lot of it. Like they're bracing themselves to hold onto Alpha. Like it was valuable. And maybe they're seeing a threat."

"Those ships?"

"Maybe something's heating up. Could be they're here to offer something. I don't know. Maybe they want to deal.

When the giants want to dance, the likes of us just stands and watches. Stations have their politics. For us, it's just survival. Some damn bureaucrat comes in with a sweetheart deal, Alpha admin agrees—and we're not a high consideration. We're the little folk, we."

Scary thought. Venture-Alpha was *Galway*'s territory, and *Galway,* though no larger than *Little Bear,* was the largest ship plying the Venture to Alpha routes, and barely breaking even. Pell-based ships deciding to run that route would cut directly into *Galway* profits. The three here had already made a minor stir in the luxury market just bringing in flour and oil and a small store of rare earth metals.

Why? *Why,* dammit. It didn't make sense. A huge profit just wasn't there. Alpha didn't *produce* anything but data, science, and basic foodstuffs off its tanks. Its hope was all *when Sol breaks out.* Alpha-based ships ran the Great Circle routes, to Bryant's, to Glory, Alpha and Venture. Same rules, same market system, same rights and laws, mostly. They got along, mostly. To *have* goods to trade, they had to get those from Sol.

But if Pell wanted to change that . . .

"What I bet," Fallan said, "is that station's not talkin' because it doesn't have a plan yet. *Something* came in on one of those stranger-ship's feeds that station's been keepin' to themselves, and now station's takin' their time telling people what's going on because they don't friggin' *know* what they're going to do."

Ship's feed. The black boxes that talked, ship to station, the moment a ship docked, station downloading to a departing ship before it left—a comprehensive data-dump in both cases, every tick and blip of information, civil and commercial and operational, discoveries and contracts, actions and intentions, births, deaths, publications, markets, and the state of supply.

That was one Cyteen rule that had come in with the gift of FTL, no ifs ands or buts. Sped by ships, it was communication faster than the lightspeed Stream that still connected Alpha to Sol, but that no one past Alpha even thought about using anymore. Current prices of goods, as per the ship's last port, politics, news, entertainment . . .

that black box data was a vital part of every ship's cargo. There were times it was *all* that paid for fueling and sleepover. A big load of new information . . . getting there first could pay, really pay.

"Not much they can do, is there?" he asked. "They got to let that ship dock. And they pretty well got to let it suck up the station feed."

That was a rule older than anything: a ship came in, you gave it a place to dock. And how did they say no to a fourth ship, when three other outsiders had come in and linked up?

"Stationer minds. The EC just doesn't like to admit they're not in control," Fallan said, and gave a near-silent rap on the counter, old superstition, older than Fallan himself. "These visitors, they'll dock and suck up all the data Alpha'll give 'em in the feed—she can squirm all she likes, but that data *will* feed out. Then these visitors will kite out to various interested places, but only *after* sharing what *they* know. So whatever's going on out in the Beyond, Pell doesn't mind us knowing. But maybe the EC *does* mind sharing what they've got. Whatever the first three outsiders brought in—you can bet station's been digesting that for days, and I'd wager something in there has admin really sweating this incoming rig."

A ship couldn't read its own black box, had no idea what information had streamed into it or out of it. Theoretically the station couldn't tamper with ships' black boxes, either, or adjust what import/export and market statistics a station automatically gave out. Station wasn't supposed to censor elections or published items, either, but that was a big theoretical, in Ross's own estimation. There wouldn't possibly be details about *Rights* floating around in Alpha's feed—would there?

New flasher on the largest screen, the EC logo. Special bulletin, the vid said, and this time it went to image, not just a crawl. Thanks to Fallan, they two, Galways, held prime spots at the bar, as tables emptied and fellow Galways and Santiagos and the insystem folk crowded close again.

Ben Abrezio himself appeared on the screen. Station-master. White-haired, ordinary-looking fellow. Executive authority.

"We regret the need to reposition the two ships. We have confirmed the identity of the incoming ship as Finity's End, *Pell registry."*

"Oh, my God," was one murmur from up at the bar.

And a distinct voice, mid-room: *"Bloody. Hell.* This is really getting worrisome."

Ross's own heart had skipped a beat. *Finity's End.*

Of all ships, *that* one.

He caught a corner-eye look from Fallan, who raised a brow as if to say: *Told you so.* And Fallan *had* called it: the outsider visitation *was* about *Rights.*

Finity's End—the monster hauler built by Pell and handed over to the Neiharts of old *Gaia*—was a creature of the Farther Stars and the massive payloads that traveled between those stations. A creature the likes of which he'd never expected to set eyes on—except in the form of Alpha's non-operational copy parked at the top of A-mast.

"Incoming event vid is released on channel 1, followed by the ship's first V-dump. Even following that dump, this ship is carrying an abnormally high velocity, but we are assured it is safe, and, in point of fact, normal for this ship. Mind the following vid is nearly four hours old. She will be braking again in ten minutes, which we will broadcast live. She will be arriving at B-13 at shift-change. Starting now we are issuing a station breach alert. All persons should seek a designated shelter within ten minutes. There is no need to run. Go to the nearest available. We are not worried, fellow citizens, but she does not habitually mast-dock, and we're simply taking sensible precautions. We will have a further statement once she has docked safely."

Rosie's was a designated shelter. They *were* in a place with take-holds and vacuum seals *should* the station take damage.

That was saying nothing about their ships docked to the mast that speeding monster was aimed at. Abrezio might have done *Qarib* and *Firenze* a favor, moving them out, if a ship large as anything going was coming in too hot . . . a ship built for ring-docking that was going to attempt to dock at B-mast.

"Station breach, hell." Ross said. "They friggin' comin' in with a mechanical, or what? They can slow the fuck—"

The screen flashed up, showing a schematic, point of entry, velocity, and timeclock.

"What the hell?"

"Godamighty," somebody said. Which under-described the numbers. *Fast* didn't begin to describe it.

And still another voice:

"Three, four fuckin' hours ago—*Where* are they right now? Station's known about this for *four hours*. They knew what was coming in? Why the *hell* didn't they tell us?"

"Shit! That mother's still haulin' a quarter C. That's got to be *close!* Shit-all!"

"That *V's* not real-time. Three hours ago! Easy!"

V-dump happened almost immediately on entry on automation and again generally twice more, but that ship had come in beyond hot. He couldn't believe anything could dump that much, that fast. He hazarded a glance at Fallan, saw *Galway's* Nav 1 staring calmly at those numbers, and his heart rate slowed. Fallan felt things in his gut in ways Ross didn't . . . couldn't . . . not yet. Fallan had watched it all, could run the jump numbers and place himself at the nav boards without half trying. If Fallan thought it was okay . . .

The blip vanished and reentered. Half the outrageous speed and a good deal closer to Alpha still.

. . . and his heart raced again.

Half the speed and still too damn fast.

"Shit," he said, "is anybody alive on there?"

Did it again.

Dammit, how could any mind take that kind of reality-warp and stay sane?

"Bot at helm, got to be," someone said.

"Or they're fuckin' showin' off." That from a Firenze. *"Damn* them!"

Ross knew, rationally, that the mega-ships *weren't* slower. Their oversized engines threw a lot of energy into the interface. They reputedly did things little ships didn't. Couldn't.

His mind knew, but his nerves twitched. Reflexes trained for years said that things should be done at certain intervals. A regular hauler could take *days* coming in this close. You got to system, you dumped *V*, you settled in for a crew-change, drank stuff to settle your electrolytes and maybe had a sandwich. You then went face down on your bunk to let next-shift talk to station and the markets, all routine, plenty of time to do routine housekeeping and clean-up before the pre-dock.

Sensible. *Polite!* Coming in at that rate didn't give station-folk the willies.

Ross found himself gripping his beer mug white-knuckled. All they had for comfort was a distorted-scale schematic on what was ordinarily the arrival screen. They watched the numbers run, still damned fast. Another glance at Fallan found the old man's eyes on him now, rather than on the readout. Fallan gave him that half-wink, a hint of a smile, before turning back to the screen, and Ross's hand relaxed.

They can't be hauling, Ross thought, trying to think, not react. No way they were hauling. They couldn't dump that much velocity at maximum mass. Not in real space. Not in time. And another part of him thought: God, what was it to sit as crew on that creature, throwing energy off that, if thrown toward station, would take them all out. Energy that, even slightly misdirected, could make the sun itself quake and maybe toss an ugly lot of mass.

Spacetime healed itself. *Had* healed itself, when it spat that monster out into the nearest gravity well it could find.

Plain old here-and-now space . . . was another matter.

Rosie was still serving, still running tabs, all alcohol, nobody ordering from the kitchen, and new people, strays from off the Strip, shouldered their way to the bar and a view of the screens. Bodies pressed tight. Two *Rights* crew in blue uniforms, looking not much different from the blue-coated station cops and about as welcome in Rosie's, kept together, prudently, near the door and not saying much, but watching the screen, the same as everybody.

Also among the incoming were a handful of late-come

spacer types in nondescript green and blue that were new to Rosie's.

"God," somebody said, when new numbers flashed up and the blinking dot kept coming, scarily close and still fast, by the run of those numbers on the sidebar.

One green and blue jacket said quietly, "She's fine. No worry."

That pronouncement got a dozen cold stares. "Who're you?" a Santiago asked. The jam was close, the lights were dim. Sleeve patches weren't that clear, and the vid was delivering background chatter. The man who'd spoken had Asia somewhere in the ancestry, a ship-accent unfamiliar to Alpha.

There were six of them in that dull green.

"*Little Bear,*" the speaker said in accented Standard.

"Wrong bar," Santiago said. "Out!"

"We're under a shelter order," Fallan said. "Give 'em grace, 'Rique."

"They can keep quiet," Santiago said. "We got a damn fool headed at us."

"Only way," another Little Bear said, "in a small system like this, that's how the big ones come out. Deep in the well. No way not. But don't worry. JR . . . he's as good as they come."

"The hell!" someone shouted. "Friggin' James Robert Neihart's no different from the rest of us mortals, and that fuckin' ship's comin' in with hell on its tail."

JR. James Robert Neihart. *Finity's* Senior Captain. Like his ship, a legend before he was thirty. A legend named *after* a legend—the first ever starship's first captain—a man bumped straight to Senior Captain of the newly commissioned megaship, because he'd been just that much faster, that much better than those technically seeded ahead of him.

A part of Ross's brain meanwhile wondered if the Little Bear was right, that this was *how* the big ships would have to come in, and his mind began to run the numbers, and felt a shiver just figuring the mass. Then he thought about the sim-trained *Rights* crew coming in like that and went icy cold.

"Maybe we know, all right," the first Little Bear began, and another Little Bear raised a hand to stop him.

"Station order says go to shelter. So we come in where first we could. Didn't have a sign out there saying who owns this bar."

"*We* own it," a Firenze woman said. "And we're full up. So take your business elsewhere."

"And get a red ticket out there? No, thanks, Alpha. Station calls a stupid take-hold, we take hold, so back off."

"What are any of you here for, anyway?" New voice in the argument, another Firenze, male. "One of your ships is an all-right, okay, no problem, two's a coincidence, but three and now *this? What in hell's going on?*"

"Come on," another Little Bear said, taking the first by the arm. "This take-hold's nonsense in the first place. Let's just go."

"Running?" Santiago asked.

"Like hell!" First Little Bear took a pose.

Just as the vid changed display and showed real-time, vid from the mast.

"Hold, hold, hold!" Fallan said, and interposed an arm. "We got realtime up, here. Lay off! They can't go out there! Vid is up—we got image, here!"

Attention swung to the screen. For the first time the vid focused on a ship still moving fast.

"Damn!" Ross breathed. *Reason* for the take-hold. The image came like a nightmare.

"They brake," one of the *Little Bear* crew said, a calm voice. "They brake."

And right then the image whited out, ghostlike.

And reappeared closer.

When the camera found focus again, *Finity's End* appeared moving sanely as any ship, by the numbers on the side.

"Told you," Little Bear said. "About three more hours to dock. Everything fine."

"You smug sumbitch," Santiago said. "Out!"

It stung, that *told you,* from another small-ship FTLer, from one of the visitors who'd piled up over the last few

days . . . a visitor who, contrary to report, suddenly spoke
perfectly adequate Standard.

And as quick as the thought, somebody at the bar had
bumped somebody and somebody had shoved back.

Barware flew—and bounced. Rosie's stocked plastic
mugs, not glass. Beer spattered, a plate hit the floor, and
the whole bar became a heaving mass of bodies bent on
ejecting the outsiders, who were bent on resisting.

Ross had his own inclinations, but Fallan was by him,
and Fallan was too old and brittle for what came next,
which was short lengths of roller chain out of pockets and
blood mixing with the beer.

"Fal," Ross said, heaved himself atop the bar, sitting,
and helped Fallan up and over. Rosie himself, who massed
about a hundred thirty kilos, braced himself between wall
and bar, trying to keep the bar from being rocked off its
bolts.

No need to call the blue-coats. Two of them, those two
Rights men, were already in the bar, involved in the mess.
It was sure enough more were on the way; and equally sure
other crews were getting the word same as the blue-coats.

Without warning, the overhead lights started flashing,
the door pressure-sealed itself, and the public address said:
*"You will cease and desist immediately. The door will open
only when the incident stops. At that time, officers will be
at the door to take complaints."*

"Hell," Fallan said. "Damned fools."

Worse, they were upset fools. Real upset, not just at the
insult, but at everything that had been going on, ever. Sol
had built Alpha to be its connection to the stars, and Alpha was being left behind, *laughed* at because of a ship
built on stolen plans that not only couldn't do what that
outsider ship was doing, it couldn't even leave dock without
a tug.

But *Rights* wasn't Alpha's ship, not the way *Galway* and
the others were. *Rights* was a newcomer. The others had
history, had been loyal to Alpha, kept it alive. They deserved, dammit, respect.

Hell, Ross thought, Alpha was still as fine a place as the
First Stars had. Maybe not as big as Venture and its high

ambitions, but still, Alpha was how Sol goods got anywhere, the sole link to the pushers. Alpha still had a lot of
people. Goods moved to here and from here. They *had* a
commerce here. They *had* a value to the universe.

For now. And that was the true pain every spacer here
felt. Because all that would change the day they found viable jump points to Sol—and if the useable point lay between Sol and Alpha, Alpha would survive. If it did not, if
they found a jump-point that bypassed Alpha, to, say, Bryant's or Venture, Alpha would become just one more isolated, insignificant First Star station, fading fast and
doomed. Feast or famine, life or death . . . and it could happen tomorrow, or a hundred years from now.

It was scary, and Ross wasn't immune from the feeling
that ship out there brought. The sense of being left behind,
of being mocked for being loyal and honorable to the system that had made their lives possible. If not for Fallan's
presence to restrain him, he feared he'd be just one more
damned fool.

The chaos slowed, sorted itself out. The chains disappeared into pockets, and shouts became narrow-eyed
glares. The blue-coats inside managed contact with blue-
coats outside, and—finally—they began opening the doors.

"*Galway*'s innocent," Rosie muttered, standing beside
them. "Onliest action from the Galways out there was trying to get to you two, and we got the *Rights* guys to witness
it. Just stand pat till the blue-boys sort it out. You all right,
Fallan?"

"Fine," Fallan said, but he was hurting a bit. Ross could
tell, no matter Fallan was good at masking it. Fallan
bruised easily—he'd probably gotten any number of bruises,
being dragged across the bar, and Ross was sorry for that,
sorry, and damned mad about it. You talked about the
glory days, about the pusher-ships, and that was *Galway*'s
Nav 1, *his* Nav 1. Fallan Monahan was off the old pusher
Atlas, whose steel and fiber was the bones of *Santiago* and
Qarib. Fallan had seen it all come down, and he was
damned good, *damned* good at his post. Best navigator in
the Great Circle, *including* whatever attitudinal ass was
bringing that monster ship in too damned fast. Fallan

didn't deserve to see Alpha disrespected by outsiders bent on God-knew-what business.

But there wasn't a damned thing to do about it.

Bottles had gotten knocked down. Empties had bounced all over the place. Somebody was going to get the bill. There'd be charges for cleanup and business interruption sent to every ship present.

Ought to be a big one sent to *Finity's End,* as Ross Monahan saw it.

A really . . . *really* big bill.

Chapter 1   Section ii

"I said *no citations,* sergeant," Stationmaster Ben Abrezio stared across his desk at his two unwanted visitors. Got a grudging nod from Hewitt as he talked to an enforcer on the scene. "*Everyone's* upset, with good reason. Once it's quiet, just let them out. Your chief is here with me and he concurs."

Assent from the far end of the com, and Abrezio sat back in his padded chair, trying not to show his concern.

Alpha was under attack—not armed attack, but it was a message they were getting from Pell, no doubting it, and the repercussions had already begun.

Andrew J. Cruz, Vice Admiral Andrew Cruz, Director of the EC's mega-ship project, had messaged concern when the second Farther Stars ship had come into system. Cruz had phoned in that concern when *Mumtaz* had arrived, making it three such ships docked at Alpha.

And Cruz had blazed a fast passage around to EC offices when they'd gotten the wavefront of *Finity's End* entering system.

His own fault, Abrezio supposed. He himself had panicked. He couldn't deny it. But for good reason. For two agonizing minutes they hadn't *known* what had entered, just that it was unexpected and *large*—and coming in on the FTL zenith vector with a hellish mass. He'd sent that initial data to Cruz, along with the emergency code that *should* have had Cruz and all *Rights* ops crew headed up the mast for *Rights*, prepping for possible evacuation of citizens.

Instead, before that next wavefront had brought them *Finity's* ID, he'd had not only Cruz, but Cruz's second in command, Project Security Chief Enzio Hewitt, at his office door, Cruz demanding entry, *demanding* details directly from him, and Hewitt suggesting they all just calm down—*damn* the man's arrogance—and shut down access to station control points.

Hell if! Only a fool cut off all his escape routes.

But these two didn't think that way, not even after years of station living. Sol-system born, both of them—hell, Cruz could trace back to the first generation on EC's precious number one: Earth-bound Sol Station itself. Worse, both had been *personally appointed* by the head office to handle anything and everything that had to do with *Rights*. Endorsement like that created at-ti-tude. Not to mention competition within their own elite position. Hewitt, latest come and determinedly staking out his territory, had pushed to extend his administrative functions outside A-mast and onto the Strip, as the place where ships' crews could get rowdy and "foreign influence" could slip in.

Endorsement notwithstanding, neither of these silver spooners had any inkling what kind of nerves were involved in what was happening right now. Sitting where Alpha did, near mysteriously abandoned Beta, at the mere mention of which spacers knocked on whatever was available and made whoever had mentioned the unlucky name go out of the room and come back again—Alpha had reason to dislike inbound anomalies.

Like strange ships entering system with off-the-chart numbers.

Rights of Man might have spent most of her life docked on A-mast, but she *was* crewed, she had had a shakedown, they *thought* they had identified the problem that had caused a premature end to that run, and she *could* launch—

at least in-system—if she had to. The plan was, as Cruz damn-well knew, that if they saw anything, *anything,* that looked like doomsday arriving, they were to cram everybody they could into *The Rights of Man* and run like hell for Bryant's, *hoping* that navigator and helm got it right this time and the FTL engines didn't shut down or blow at their first real test.

That measure wasn't the Earth Company's order. It was Ben Abrezio's. Key personnel knew there was an outright evac notice ready and waiting to send at the push of a button, in a determination not to have his people end up . . . *gone*, the way Beta's had disappeared. In Abrezio's mind, in his occasional nightmares in this job, it was how he would leave this station—just load everybody on and jump for the nearest best hope—Bryant's Star.

As happened, it hadn't been necessary. This time. Next time . . . next time the general alarm rang, if Cruz showed up in his office instead of on *Rights* . . . damned if he wouldn't have the man arrested and abandoned on the station for whatever spook wanted him.

Fifteen minutes, *fifteen damned minutes* of heart-racing alarm before that leviathan had announced herself as a known ship who didn't damnwell belong here, a ship coming in hot—so damned hot he had, for the last half hour, still seriously considered issuing that evacuation notice.

But Andy Cruz—after consulting with Hewitt, who had watched the telemetry in his office with great interest—had assured him it was within parameters, barely, and made it clear he had no intention of leaving this office, let alone evacuating.

Arrogant. But Cruz's attitude was nothing, really, to Hewitt's, who'd waltzed off *Santa Maria* seven years ago, and, EC orders in hand, ordered A-mast cleared and *Rights* to be brought into dock, as he assumed control of A-mast security, Strip security, and any other damn thing he'd decided might impact the safety of the *Rights* project. Hewitt hadn't usurped Andy Cruz, oh no. He was just there to support Cruz, who was head of the project and administrator. Procuring materials, equipment, personnel and resources . . . Cruz did that very well.

No, Hewitt's ambitions lay elsewhere and Abrezio wondered, at times like this, did Cruz appreciate that? Hewitt had trained as helm on FTL sims all the way from Sol. Not enough to qualify him for a license: sims were sims, and they *had* none for a mega-ship like *Rights*—or *Finity's End*. But ten years of sims had given Hewitt operational knowledge, knowledge he was *more* than happy to spread around, and now they had Hewitt lecturing Cruz on the physics of their small red star and bowshocks, and just how close that ship *could* cut it.

Hard to tell how Cruz actually felt about that not-always-requested input. Cruz *had* sent Hewitt on the training voyage, in which *Rights* crew shadowed the boards of little *Qarib* to get realtime jump experience—which none of the trainees nor Hewitt himself had ever had, the former never having traveled anywhere outside the system, and Hewitt having come in on a pusher. One had to wonder, in retrospect: had that choice been calculated to bring Hewitt down a notch?

Because it had not been a happy voyage, and Aki Rahman, captain of *Qarib,* had flatly said, Never again.

Cruz, meanwhile, had used the months of Hewitt's absence to make changes in operations, changes Hewitt was *still* trying to roll back to *his* rules. And Hewitt had been *vastly* put out when *Rights'* problem-ridden shakedown cruise had *not* included the Project Security Chief. Cruz had taken personal control of that one—*after* ensuring a similar restructuring of protocols could not take place in his absence.

And all this accumulated discord was parked in *his* office as a whole new problem arrived—this one from Pell Station, on the far side of EC-controlled space, beyond which, past Pell's few daughter stations, lay Cyteen, as great a threat to human civilization as any in history. Cyteen, who ran where it liked, did what it liked, and had no love at all for Mother Earth or Sol or anything the Company had to offer. The problems that could be incoming with these Pell-based ships, whose *declared* business was just trade—were myriad, and on those problems—no, Enzio Hewitt was *not* the expert.

The very identification of the arriving ship represented a serious concern, all on its own. A damned legend arriving without warning—a ship with which this station and the EC had specific and notorious history. Damn those plans. Damn the EC's obsession that had turned his entire career into a logistical nightmare. This after a week of outsider arrivals, who declared their business was just trade.

Ben Abrezio poured a short midday Scotch and offered it to Andy Cruz, who declined it, being technically on duty. So was Ben Abrezio on duty, but they were a long way from other authority, and *Finity's* last braking had been—

Well, not the final straw, but something damned close. Granted that ship's bowshock didn't wreck them all, he'd bet it brought a shitload of other problems to cap a week of coincidental arrivals. At the very least, it meant hundreds more people flooding an already over-taxed station that rarely saw more than two or three ships in port at once. Just recycling was going to be a nightmare. Any ship would be a logistical problem, but to have *Finity*, of all ships, come crashing in, scaring hell out of him and his station . . .

Not to mention the psychological effects that entry could have on the *Rights of Man* ops crew, whose confidence might well be the intended target of this entry. A Family crew shoving the reality of their stolen ship design down their sim-trained gullets.

Damned if his nerves hadn't earned a dram of single malt.

He took up his glass . . . froze at a grunt from Hewitt, who had momentarily found something of greater interest to him than *Finity's* telemetry. Abrezio handed the original snifter to Hewitt, poured a second . . . *not* short . . . for himself, then returned the bottle to the cabinet and thumbed the lock, Hewitt having an unpleasant habit of helping himself to expensive seconds, damn the man.

"I'm going to continue the shelter order until that ship's done whatever it's going to do," Abrezio said. "Where does it think we're going to put it?"

"No way it goes on A-mast," Hewitt said. "That lot won't be allowed anywhere near that ship."

Idiot.

"Never considered it," Abrezio said, trying hard not to patronize. "Mass distribution. I've ordered the end of B cleared, but can it even dock here?"

"Should be possible," Cruz said, and, having poured himself a cup of black coffee, continued calmly: "Obviously *Rights* can. It was in the design, of which that ship out there is the prototype. I'm far more concerned about that approach. It's *not* standard by anything we know. Nothing in any of our records supports it. We have no idea what she intends, coming in that close and that fast."

"That's obvious," Hewitt said. "They're showing out. And since they've been so up front with their demonstration, I want that telemetry worked into the sims, thank you very much."

"If we can," Cruz said.

"I'm not hearing *if.* I want the vid preserved, I want the numbers preserved, I want an analysis, and I want *Rights* crew running the revised sims with the last three hours fresh in their minds. Decision-making on the far side of jump isn't easy. *This* is what this design can do, all-out. *This* is realtime. This is current. This is something we have to match. Something we *will* match."

Hewitt tossed back the Scotch as if it was shots on Stripside, and turned back to the readout.

"I'm sure ops is recording," Abrezio stared at that screen, watching the numbers, sipping his own glass. "It's standard procedure." Hewitt was talking about physics. *He* was thinking about the psychology of it. The deliberate, potentially debilitating psychology of it. "Hell of a risk, no matter how you look at it."

"Finity's End was the first of her kind," Cruz said. "And they probably still update her manual. Neihart undoubtedly tests her limits regularly, off the record, maybe at unregistered jump-points we'd like to know more about."

"Outright *given* a ship like this," Hewitt said. *"What* did the Neiharts pay? That's what I ask. *What* did they pay?"

"They were *Gaia's* crew," Cruz said with a shrug. "They used *Gaia's* core when they built that ship. That name's downright royalty to this lot."

"Royalty? Crew that disobeyed orders on its very first

mission? Crew that refused to step down and hand the ship
back over to the rightful owners? Not my idea of royal
blood. And the attitude's still there, isn't it?" Hewitt lifted
his glass suggestively, Abrezio pretended not to notice, and
Hewitt set the glass down with rather more force than necessary. "Back at Sol, they aren't so reverential about the
Neiharts. Tin gods, ship and crew. Besides, these are the
whatever-degree grandchildren and genetic amalgamation
with God-knows-what ships. Nothing in common with the
originals. *Nothing.*"

Not a fan of the Family ships . . . Hewitt had made that
clear within hours of his arrival at Alpha, and Abrezio had
learned not to fight it.

But out here, to Family ships and stations alike, it *was*
legend how the first starship crew, more than a quarter of
a century on their initial round trip, had defied the birth
ban on the way out and then defied the Company order to
stand down and surrender *Gaia* to a new crew when they
returned to Sol. The Neiharts—another James Robert Neihart in command—had told the Earth Company go build
them another ship. This one was their home and they were
keeping it.

Gaia had made the loop back to Alpha, which they'd
founded. And kept doing it, decade after decade, Alpha's
first pusher, Alpha's life source, all those centuries ago,
before FTL had come along and changed everything.

"*Original* crew on the *original* pusher," Surprisingly,
Cruz stepped in. "This ship—the Neihart name—do matter out here, Mr. Hewitt. It's something you have yet to
fully comprehend, and something you had best keep in
mind for as long as that ship is in port."

Or perhaps not surprisingly. Original. As Cruz himself
was "original." *Sol* original, descended directly from the
first Sol station admin, a fact Cruz managed to drop on
anyone he met, and definitely held over Hewitt. That was
its own variety of aristocracy—originals traced things like
that.

Sol originals got entrusted with important projects.
Originals knew other originals, contacts upon contacts,
insider ways of getting things done. At least back at Sol.

Coming up through the ranks of Sol Station, Hewitt had been a newcomer, a man without antecedents, pushing himself forward, grabbing every handhold he could get. He'd arrived at Alpha thinking his Sol origins alone would mean something, only to discover it didn't work here, where everyone had to prove their worth.

And Hewitt's face said he was *not* happy with Cruz's reminder of his less than spectacular connections back at Sol, but for once Hewitt kept quiet.

Abrezio held his own peace. Cruz had it wrong as well.

Time was, original *had* meant something out here at Alpha. Time was, common stationers, folks who'd come out to Alpha and Glory on the fifteenth, twentieth run—after all the hard and dangerous work was done—had a hard time of it. No one used terms like second class, but it had amounted to the same thing. But that prejudice ennobling the first-arrived had died out long ago. His own ancestry traced back to Abrezios on that same first trip on *Gaia*. His ancestors had been pioneers in discovery. But generations on, so could everyone else born on Alpha Station these days claim a similar link.

On the other hand, those born out here did maintain a serious reverence for the old pushers, and stations kept the ancient bargain with the two pusher-ships that still served, who not only maintained Alpha's contact with Sol, but with the past as well.

And as the first of all pusher-ships, *Gaia* was more than just an Original. Far more. The name James Robert Neihart, the captain of the mission that had founded Alpha, *happened* to be on a plaque in the heart of station ops. On stations from here to Pell, where the old ship had finally been broken down, *Gaia* and the Neihart name *did* mean something. A whole lot of Something.

Something Cruz, sitting there all relaxed and expecting his contacts back at Sol to work and his name to mean something wherever he went, would discover soon enough. Cruz would expect a certain acknowledgment from the crew of the incoming ship. Question was whether the high and mighty Neiharts would know who Cruz was, and who *his* family had been—or give a damn if they did.

"I don't care who they are," Hewitt said into the protracted silence. "Doesn't mean they don't still owe the station that built that ship and handed it over to them, and *that's* Pell. They're working for the Konstantins, don't think they aren't. Here they are, making that splashy entrance, not sending ID for fifteen damn minutes. Sure, they got the attention they wanted. Everybody saw. Everybody watched in awe. *This* is the revelation. Pell's *challenging* us."

"I don't doubt that," Abrezio said. Pell's very existence challenged everything remotely EC. Pell was where the star-stations had changed. Pell was the first of several stations founded on a breakaway operation, with stealth, ambition, and outright defiance of EC authority. Pell was the point beyond which stationmasters were not EC. Pell had its own Family, the Konstantins, who had run Pell Station from its beginnings, same way the Carnaths and Emorys ran Cyteen.

Attitude. Any and all contact with Pell reeked of it. Attitude that would not change until Sol entered the FTL age and arrived, personally, to inform the Konstantins—and perhaps even Cyteen—there were still older powers in the universe.

A momentous occasion that might be closer than most people thought.

"So?" Cruz said, eyes on the schematic. "You're going to confront *that ship* with EC rules? We haven't pushed points with the first three outsiders to arrive here. I *really* wouldn't recommend starting with this one."

"Hell, yes, they'll toe the—"

"We'll deal with them," Abrezio said. "We'll need to put a right spin on whatever they want, reassure the citizens. That's paramount. I'll call a personnel meeting and brief the departments. I'm assuming at this point that it can and will mast dock and that we're going to have to accommodate that crew on the Strip. Somehow. I've already taken the preliminary steps. We'll take this unannounced arrival as a diplomatic approach. Maybe a trade opportunity. Regardless, Mr. Hewitt, until something different develops, we *will* need security to keep a quiet and *optimistic* profile. *No* incidents. No incidents with these outsiders. It seems likely Pell *is* chal-

lenging us. So they've just put on their show. Fine. We'll applaud politely and move on. But the fact is, they've *also* just demonstrated to everybody on Alpha what *Rights* can be once she's in operation. Perhaps we should thank them as well. Either way, we'll *welcome* these visitors same as any ship, and remind them about something they might have forgotten: this is where Sol meets the rest of space, and Pell *needs* the First Stars on their side as much as they ever did. Otherwise, sooner or later, Pell will find itself face to face with Cyteen expansionism all on their own, and they really won't want that. It's even possible these ships are here because Pell sees such a move coming and wants to ensure its position in the human political scheme."

"You think so?" Clearly Hewitt didn't believe it.

"Match Cyteen's manpower? No. Pell can't. But *Sol* can. Match Cyteen's resources? Near-term, yes, *Sol* can. And damn right Sol *will* get here, and the game *will* change. Pell may be thinking of that, too."

"You go right on kidding yourself." Hewitt jerked to his feet and headed for the door. "I'm going over to Central Ops and make sure we preserve that data."

"Do that," Abrezio said, glad to see the back of him.

Hewitt left. Cruz let go a deep breath, with a glance at the closing door, then said, with clear exasperation, "I'll take that scotch, now, Stationmaster, if you don't mind."

Chapter 1   Section iii

They'd come in fast and deep in the gravity well.

And arriving at zenith of Barnard's Star, an unstable red dwarf that could choose that moment to misbehave, they'd taken no chances. *Finity* had a policy—no lingering in the jump zone in such a system, no handoff to next shift until they'd dumped V if there was no traffic restriction. Senior Captain and Helm 1 took her down all the way to a still-brisk traveling speed, flared off more *V* and crossed an ungodly lot of space doing it.

There was not the development and traffic here at Alpha that there was at Venture, no question of hitting anything on their entry heading, and with each *V*-dump, they angled toward the only manmade structure there *was* here at Alpha, until they were on course. They still needed to do another small *V*-dump, but that was for fourth-shift.

First-shift took over the step-down lounge, a vast long cavern of a compartment where bulkheads and take-holds and net rigging were the decor, and where they could draw breath and get real food, could settle nerves that were still operating at hyperspeeds. Here they could be on call, but with hands off controls. They could watch telemetry and image, now, and get station transmissions.

They had a good view. They'd kept scan and longscan busy from *V*-dump on, getting the feel of the place, confirming that Alpha *was* as simple and basic as its reputation. They looked closely, because the whole station was EC-run, and because there was, as expected, the apparent sole occupant of the A-mast, a ship outwardly very like their own—at least in terms of size.

They'd seen that ship before, but only in vids. *That ship* was one of their problems: the ship and the reasoning under which it had been built. Sol's attempt to escape its pusher-prison, perhaps. There'd been that extravagant claim of a plus-seven-light jump early in the planning of *Finity's End* and *Dublin* alike. But that had been a bit of over-sell: *Finity* couldn't do it, and Captain JR Neihart knew it for a fact. *Finity* could jump further than other ships—how far they *thought* it could jump was not information they shared about—but no ship yet built could one-hop it from Alpha to Sol.

Yet Sol kept building its own mega-ship, perhaps refusing to accept reality, perhaps with altered purpose. If escaping the well were their only goal, they could have built that ship at Sol with far less trouble and expense.

That ship out there, constructed from stolen plans, lacked *Finity's* extensive post-trial refinements—Pell's heightened security had made certain of that. JR was relatively sure Alpha was aware now that running a ship this size was no easy walkover. Rumor said the ship had glitched on an easy jump for Bryant's, and the crew was lucky to be in one piece. It wasn't worth a laugh: it was too serious a thing, too great a risk of converting ship and personnel into a plasma stream headed nowhere. Or bow-shocking Bryant's Star into an outburst as extreme energy plowed into that red dwarf sun.

From the moment Cyteen had spread the wealth of FTL for everyone, Sol had had a problem. A big one. Sol was not only an awkward just-out-of-reach gravity well, it had a great abundance of orbiting bodies—too great an abundance. In its multi-billion year career, it had pulled a lot of meaningful mass into its well—a vast cloud of unused and stolen bits that presented a major traffic hazard to any incoming ship.

But sooner or later Sol *would* find a way, and the decision that made Alpha undertake to build a ship to match *Finity's End* was going to play out to its conclusion. Sooner or later, some ship would find a way to Sol. Sooner or later a jump-point would be discovered or some engineer would find some way to tweak the field so a seven-light jump *would* be possible. Change was the rule, not the exception, when it came to technology.

In the meantime, from reports, the only real use Sol was getting out of the immense build was keeping its nearest stepping-stone running and maintaining a contact with civilization past Alpha. Alpha could reach *one* other station, Bryant's, by FTL; it could reach Sol by pusher-ship; and continuing that build provided jobs and kept the Earth Company in touch with points beyond, with EC offices on Bryant's, Glory, Venture, and marginally on Pell.

So the ship had *some* function. And *if* it could solve its problem and go translight, it might be useful locally, but only at the expense of other ships that served the station, which couldn't make local ships happy. As the extended situation, decades of build, with all available resources being sucked into the project, couldn't make the station happy. By all reports, the station was neglecting repairs, calling *optional* items that might impact health and well-being, and was in general on the decline, right along with Glory, off in its own bag-end of nowhere. But—viable or not, building that pilfered ship had provided a lot of jobs, an artificially inflated economy fed by Sol so long as construction lasted. The EC was still big here.

And now, winding down the construction phase, the project was offering other jobs, and handing out uniforms. Training crew—lots of crew—stationer crew—on sims.

That was a problem.

Would it have been better just to have multiple pushers coming with consumable goods, to keep following the age-old EC pattern of paying their stations with vital supply? Sol and its two operating pushers were in direct competition with Pell on that score, and they couldn't possibly win. One year versus ten years to fill a need—when Pell could manufacture local biostuffs into edibility for humans and have regular shipments moving out to the Hinder Stars and elsewhere. Not the exotic variety of product Sol could provide, but even that was changing. It was amazing what the food engineers could do with what Pell's world produced. The Hinder Stars, the stars left behind in mankind's outward push, needed supply Sol was failing to give them. Goods moved. Pell prospered. The Hinder Stars were fed, supplied, and alive.

So maybe that huge project *had* served a useful purpose, simply by making Alpha dependent on Pell's goods long enough to bring them firmly into the Beyond's economy, which was also long enough to build that ship and long enough to preserve Sol's hope of getting back into some economic relevance to its offspring.

But now that that ship existed, viable or not, now that the crew had begun to form, another, far more problematic possibility had begun to suggest itself. Observations indicated that that ship had way more uniformed personnel than required for a full four-by-four ops crew. It didn't require a particularly suspicious mind to realize that if it merely stood off from its station, it became an independent platform firmly under EC control—maybe capable of jump; maybe not—but a platform which, from reports, could hold more enforcement personnel than any single station in the Beyond currently had serving.

If it *did* eventually work out its problems and prove capable of FTL . . . one had to wonder what sort of *goods* it planned to carry, because the images they had of it showed no adaptation to ring-docking, and, more significant, too much personnel room and not enough cargo space.

And they'd named it *The Rights of Man*. Didn't *that* say something?

And if *The Rights of Man* existed only to keep Alpha alive for Sol's reasons . . . one had to wonder whether Sol itself was also building ships of that design—in anticipation of jump points yet to be found. *Maybe* Sol had turned sensible, realized there was no one-hopping their way to Alpha, and decided that somewhere, in some direction, in all that moving real estate, there had to be a jump-point to bridge the gap.

The smart bet assumed the worst. Sol had the material resources to build endlessly. And likely they *were* using instruments and currently sending out probes—unmanned, one hoped—trying to find a route to Alpha. The success rate thus far seemed to have been zero—witness the fact no ship from Sol had ever shown up at any station on their side of that gulf of stars—but that didn't mean that such a visit couldn't happen at any moment, without warning, since such ships traveled faster than any message they could send.

Interesting times they lived in.

JR took a second drink packet—magnesium, sugar, and salt, flavored with almost-fruit, which tasted awful, unless you needed it—pulled the tab and propped his feet up. Fourth shift was on the job. Second and third were still in quarters. They hadn't gotten another takehold, so things were going well up there, but first shift wasn't budging from the safe, comfortable reclining chairs. Fourth shift, the seniormost seniors, the almost-retireds—they generally handled approach. Mum was in charge up there, and things were well under control.

He stared at the drink packet. Remembered to take a sip. Not too bad.

Mum. Lisa-Marie, but Mum to every man, woman and child aboard. JR was JR to the bridge crews; Captain, sir, to the cousins and such while they were on duty, and Senior Captain, sir, to the junior-juniors.

First shift had settled in the lounge in their working teams—habit, after years together on the bridge. JR was solo, sole captain on first shift. Beside JR was Helm 1.1, Jim B; then Shane, who was Helm 1.2, and so on, to the number of four. And so it went, through Nav, Shortscan, Longscan, Systems, Communications, Support, Technical, Medical, Cargomaster. Four of each, all the seated crew of first shift—lifelong Family, all Neiharts; and extensions of one another, old and young.

Elsewhere in the lounge, trainees to the posts gathered in their own groups, the next-in-lines who manned the back rows of consoles, the 1.5 and 1.6 posts, shadowing the main boards. They had boards that worked, but their decisions never reached the actual controls. The ship's computer compared and scored those decisions against what senior crew did.

That brought first shift to sixty-some before one even counted, at the extreme end of the lounge space, the sixteen or so runners, trainees not yet allowed on any boards, but available as hands and feet for whatever seated crew or shadows wanted—usually trivial errands, not always. It was training in patience, training in resourcefulness; a test of nerves, occasionally; and duties kept the bored and talented senior-juniors out of trouble.

Unlike old sub-light *Gaia's* leisurely system entries, where a handful of crew manned the bridge, drinking and playing cards while the engines continued their steady, years-long decel, one day being little different from the next, *Finity* exited jump and dropped into the system between one drugged heartbeat and the next, and the seconds after that entry were by far the most critical of any journey. Most everything *Finity* did was automated, working faster than human thought. But it took human beings to watch multiple readouts and assemble details—more, to know what those details *meant*—and it took years of shadowing and comparing decisions at the boards. It took a concentration far exceeding ordinary limits, it was grueling, and in the end, only the best of the best survived, and those who did survive became seamless lifelong teams.

Finity was a four by four, that was to say, four at every post and four shifts, prioritized; and right now first shift was done with duty, which was why there were, at optimum, long silences in the stand-down lounge, as minds ticked down to human speeds. Bodies, stressed from jump drugs and over-hyped by system entry, processed normal things, the need to move, to blink, to shift in a seat—the sheer luxury of lateral thoughts and the simple pleasure of breathing. Synesthesia was a problem, exiting jump. Sounds had taste and the mind formed unique symbologies into which only the medics and psychs inquired—shortcuts to thought, where thought was too long or normal pathways seemed occupied. Navigators, helm, and longscanners were notoriously rare mindsets, personalities that stationers called beyond strange, and that ship's crew carefully insulated from outside contact. JR had trained for all three before necessity and the senior-seniors' awareness of what a four by four mega-ship was going to demand had dropped him into the senior captaincy.

He'd been all of twenty-five shipboard years.

Hours from handling the last jump, and they were still feeling it, sipping that almost-fruit concoction, a handful daring crumbs of real food, and risking gut spasms. Talking little. Still not ready for complex human interaction.

But they didn't need to talk. They were one creature: first-shift. It was safe here, comfortable here, and Mum was in charge up there—again.

Gaia's last first captain, Mum was, born in *Gaia's* sublight days, before *Gaia* had thrown off the old pusher-engine, rebuilt the bridge, and gone FTL.

Gaia was gone. Almost all the first ships were gone, some still fit to handle high-mass cargos over a short sublight crawl; but old *Gaia*, first of all sublighters, had had a nobler fate. She'd been broken down and broken up, surrendering her precious elements to the ambitious new Green Dock of Pell, and a bit of her, too, to *Finity,* first of all purpose-built mega-ships, the longhaulers, as they were beginning to be called. That plaque on the lounge bulk-head, that stylized blue Earth, in a bronze solar system—that plaque was worn shiny by generations of children's fingers, and of crew touching that emblem for luck before a dicey bit of maneuvering. It had been on *Gaia's* bridge, touched then for luck at every launch.

The whole Neihart family had agreed to a bargain—a new ship, the first of her kind, to drive a whole new, fast-moving commerce—which had entailed an unprecedented shakeup of seniority. *Gaia* had been a trailblazer, and *Finity* carried on that legacy. When *Gaia's* senior FTL crew had stepped down to fourth shift, they'd scrambled the other three shifts, promoting the ones who excelled in the sims of the as-of-then unproven ship, the quick and the young, from all four shifts. The skills were, by their training, a given—but the reflexes and stamina—they'd been the deciding factor.

And years, now, of testing *Finity* to her limits, had molded them into the tightest crew the Neihart ships—possibly any ship—had ever known.

Up there now with Mum was, notably, Vickie, who was fourth shift Helm 1, and always in charge in any risky docking.

Mast-docking *Finity* at this oldest of all star-stations was going to have its moments. Locks and hoses would fit. They were assured of that, at least. They wouldn't be allowed routine and constant access to their ship while at dock. That was typical of mast docking: a station didn't have ample resources to have people traveling up and down the mast. Work crews and bots needed the transport and they understood that.

A reasonable rule was not something with which *Finity* argued.

Alpha went so far, however, as to require the ship be vacated completely, even of infants in the loft, and to leave the hatch unlocked for inspection at Station's whim.

That . . . was not reasonable.

Still, they'd conform to a point. Babies—there were three—would go to sleepover with assigned minders in the station's reliable one-g. It was safer for them anyway. Junior-juniors—there were twelve—would go to sleepover also with minders in charge, and behave themselves, and not be larking about outside the premises, not at Alpha. JR had laid down the law, and the junior-juniors would damned well keep to the rules this time of all times. *If I have to come find you,* he'd said on general address, *you'll be on biohazard cleanup for the next year of your lives.* To help keep them in line, their minders were breaking out some new video games, plus offering prizes. Holiday, so far as the youngsters would see it.

Letting inspection crews wander about was, however, a definite no.

Dealing with the EC administration was bound to have its tense moments, and that was JR's particular problem. But he was not going to deal with them solo. *Little Bear, Mumtaz,* and *Nomad* all showed as in dock, as expected. They had all agreed to the same policy: leave a maintenance crew aboard their ships, lock up, keep quiet about it; and if Alpha decided to pull a random customs inspection, as EC regulations provided, the automatic and firm answer was—again—no. Would they want to inspect *Little Bear?* Probably not. There was only one of the four visiting ships station was likely to want a look at, and no, they would *not* get access to *Finity's End,* no way in hell.

Word came down: they had a berth. End of B-mast. No surprise: mast-end offered room enough. There were also Alpha ships docked on the B-mast, as well as their three allies: Fletcher sat opposite him now, ready to answer questions he might have, silent until those questions came. Fletcher understood. Fletcher was almost as close to him as his shift crew. They'd been rivals once, as junior-juniors, until Fletcher had decided to take his skill at shipboard mischief and put it to a very different use. These days Fletcher was head of *Finity* security, and, depend on it, behind those names on Fletcher's list would be files ranging down to minutiae, ship's characteristics, personnel, recent routes, cargo lists, legal records—everything.

According to Fletcher's list, *Little Bear, Mumtaz,* and *Nomad* were in the closest-in berths; of EC ships, besides the one sitting at A-mast, there was *Galway,* next up from *Finity's* assigned berth at the far end of B-mast, with

Santiago the other side of *Galway.* The other two locals, *Firenze* and *Qarib,* once outermost from *Galway,* were moving out to standoff, both under tow, not likely to the delight of the two crews or anybody else.

That was unfortunate. Clearly *Rights* maintained A-mast all to itself, the mast apparently consecrated to that sole user, no matter the necessity *Finity* presented them. But they'd expected to have B-mast. There was no way for a mega-ship to dock at this station *except* at the mast end, where the pushers docked, and two such masses on one side of the main station was asking for trouble.

Still . . . they could have put those two locals on A-mast. Putting them on standoff was downright insulting. Station's doing, not *Finity's,* still, an apology to the dislodged crews would be politic as well as polite. And JR would have no hesitation about making the apology concrete—*Finity* had some trade items that could slip easily into the hands of the affected crew, the sort of thing one did for favors, ship to ship, family to family—items that a station and especially an EC station, with its notions of rigid control— didn't need to know about.

What was still more unfortunate in the list, however, was the fact that there were *just* those ships. That was *not* as expected, not the way they had charted likely shippresence, from black box reports and usual schedules. *Come Lately* was missing; so was *Miriam B.* Intel had had them as routed *here* from Bryant's. They weren't here. *That* was upsetting. The fog of jump might not be entirely lifted, but it was clear enough for instincts to say—

Two ships missing, and one here that wasn't predicted to be here . . .

"We're missing *Miriam B,* and *Come Lately,*" JR said. "And we've got *Firenze,* as a surprise presence."

"*Firenze* may have lingered on a mechanical," Fletcher said. "She's had notable problems."

"A bonus. But *Miriam B*—that's a puzzle."

Black boxes didn't lie. Couldn't. *Somebody* might have changed plans. But violating the route you'd filed with station was a good way for bad things to happen, not to mention a way to upset your shippers.

They'd find out the story when they docked.

Nothing traveled faster than *Finity's End,* unless it was Cyteen-built *Dublin,* and potentially, *The Rights of Man,* but so far, that ship wasn't in the calculations. *Dublin* didn't visit the Hinder Stars. She was far off at the moment, the other side of the Beyond, probably at Eversnow.

Little *Miriam B* was a low-mass ship, and paradoxically, in the illogic of jump space, was a quiet, slow little presence. A quick check of records showed no other shadow in jump, but then, she was just that slow, and she might yet turn up: they'd left word where they'd been. They *could* overjump a ship in transit, an ability they hadn't advertised. But it wasn't likely they had.

"We're assigned B-13, mast-end," John D, Helm 4.2 said over general address. Vickie, Helm 4.1, would be busy, preparing to finesse them in with no docking arm to assist, nothing but Helm's skill. *Finity's* structure was adapted for ring-docking, which Alpha didn't have; and her cargo-handling was, except for exotics and biostuffs in breachable containers, designed to be temperature-controlled canisters, which required machinery the mast-docking stations didn't have. They weren't linking the docking probe. They were using the forward E-hatch, connecting to the station mast via magnetic grapples and a bare-basics flexible tube connection secured to the airlock. "The market is requesting our manifest," John D said. "Mary's sending."

Mary Salem Neihart was Com 4.2. All that was ordinary. Market wanted to know what they had. The goods would be posted on the boards and trading would begin, ordinary enough, but the offering would be far smaller numbers than *Finity* was accustomed to post. Commerce here was basic, mainly foodstuffs and essentials, and the last thing they wanted was to upset the local ships' trading.

But there were goods that Alpha might not expect. Liquor from Pell and Cyteen, jewelry from Viking, bulk copper from Viking. And, routine but always welcome at remote places, flour from Cyteen and Pell, along with processed fruit. Fruit and exotic alcohol sold high—very high.

Artwork might sell well here. Handmade things of exotic materials. Not that Alpha needed to bedeck its ancient corporate walls in yet one more tapestry, but Earth would be interested, and pay. Such things, tucked away in cabin-storage during a pusher's long sublight run, were a good investment item—always betting that the route stayed sublight, and that the cork stayed in the bottle.

Publications—they had in great abundance, but the other ships had beat them in with those.

"They'll deal hard," Fletcher said, "being the bag end run and all."

Which went without saying. Alpha was the end of the line for regular trade. If goods had gotten to Alpha and been rejected, they only had to be carried back again. No ship could reach Glory except through Bryant's, and they *hoped* not to have to go that far.

"We're not here to make money," JR said, and closed his eyes against a suddenly unstable view. Post-jump could do that to you. And no, they weren't conning anybody. The cargo they carried couldn't profit enough for *Finity* to run clear to Alpha, as was. Nor was there any prospect to bring in three other merchanters clear from Venture runs and the Beyond. No way was there sufficient profit here.

"They're not fools," Fletcher put in quietly. "They'll know the minute that manifest hits the boards that we're here for some other reason."

"Probably assume we're here for the A-mast view," JR said, and, after a test through slitted eyes, met Fletcher's amused gaze.

"Bets on how long before someone asks us directly?"

"Likely too embarrassed," Fletcher said. "The damned thing looks like *Finity*'s half-starved twin, and they can't very well pretend it's not there."

"We don't mention it," JR said firmly. "Not our problem. They bring it up, we're politely curious, as seems appropriate, but we don't point fingers. Just let them worry down that track for a bit."

JR had some sympathy for the Alpha EC's situation. But only a little. No few years ago, following the theft of the *Finity* plans, Pell had deported the officials and staff of the Pell EC office, graciously releasing even the chief cul-

prits from detention, and suggesting that they could find
their way to Alpha at the EC's expense—one of that office
having already made that trip with the stolen files.

It was also true that in their eagerness to impress EC's
top brass, the thieves had jumped a bit prematurely. The
sight of *Rights* at close range—*Finity* as originally designed—
would be interesting, and of course they were capturing
image, but beyond that, the design plans it was based on
were woefully incomplete. They lacked the downside corridor, offices, and docking probe for the new ring-docking
system, for the most obvious change, but far more signifi-
cantly, those stolen plans had nothing of the post-test programming and mechanical tweaks that made *Finity* the
fastest, most stable ship yet built, surpassing, they were
sure, even Cyteen's *Dublin*.

Alpha's engineers, no matter how competent, had never,
ever built an FTLer, let alone something like *Finity*. Alpha
couldn't begin to match the experience of Pell's best, and
considering that aborted first run . . .

Truth was, the theft, while Pell used the incident to give
itself a few years without a well-staffed EC presence on the
station, just had not been that troubling. JR actually suspected Pell security of setting the whole thing up to give
Pell an excuse to boot the EC office and allow them back
again only on condition. The policy all along had been to
give the FTL tech to Sol—for exactly the reasons Cyteen,
who had built the first FTL engines, had sent the design to
Pell. *Do what you can with it when you can. Let's have
trade, not war.*

Well, yes, all the while knowing they were cutting Sol
out of the picture, because in the plans and data Cyteen
had sent to Pell, and that Pell had sent to Sol, the map of
jump points didn't extend beyond Venture.

Cyteen was nothing if not forward thinking.

The jump limit for the smaller-scale FTLers was about
4.69 lightyears, in safety, give or take relative motion, a
major issue; and the Hinder Stars beyond Venture all lay at
a convenient three and four lights from each other. Venture itself was too far from Pell to single-hop . . . but there

was an intervening point at 3.7 lights, a nice, safe, clean point of mass that for the next, oh, ten thousand years, would be comfortably within small-ship range.

So there was traffic all the way to Alpha, though most of Alpha's shipping was just a hop from Bryant's to Glory, Glory to Bryant's to Alpha, old places, old sub-lighter routes. The direct Glory-to-Alpha run was a shade too far for Alpha's ships. *Finity* might do it, *Dublin* might, and *Rights of Man* might make it, if it was ever more than an ornament, but there was hardly profit to be had there. Glory was moribund, a drain on Alpha's resources, and with no station reachable but Bryant's and haunted Beta.

That was the crux of things. Within the scheme of FTL trade, the Hinder Stars were dying. The old trade with Sol was sustenance from Sol in return for labor on the station and information sent back; and gradually, shorting themselves on luxuries from Sol had given the Hinder Stars something to trade with the Beyond markets, which functioned far more directly on exchange of goods. Now . . . even that little trade was gone. Everything that came in from Sol funneled straight into that ship. *Rights of Man* had cost Alpha too much, way too much for a display project. It was a good bet Sol, which had the materials *and* the design, was doing its best to get out of its bottle with a sizeable and authoritarian EC presence.

But so far, it wasn't working.

For the ships that depended on the Hinder Star trade, FTL from Alpha to Sol could be the answer to their prayers. Direct, on-demand trade for raw materials that could be turned, by the local creative types, into station-specific trade items . . . the way it worked in the Beyond . . . that could be the saving of the Hinder Stars, both stations and merchanters. Alpha could go from outermost of the Hinder Stars to main gateway to Sol.

Presupposing the EC let it happen. That . . . was the underlying question. Where it came to regulating authority and policy-setting, the EC *was* Sol. When the EC could get here in a timely manner, with ships and personnel to back their demands . . . well . . . the star-stations beyond Alpha just had to be ready to maintain their own positions, that was what. The question was . . . just how loyal were the locals of this key system to the Earth Company that claimed to own them?

If the EC at Sol was building FTL ships on a more sensible scale, and working up sims to crew them—how long would it be before the fools that populated EC boardrooms at Sol ran out of patience, decided that it must be safe by now, and tried the one sure route: Beta Station, over at Proxima? That was the truly worrisome thought in the minds of those whose business it was to worry about Sol's moves. Proxima, at a remove of slightly more than 4 lights from Sol, *was* reachable even by a small FTL—while Alpha, at something closer to 6, was not. A ship from Sol could hop to Beta, *then* to Glory, following the old pusher route, but that was *not* a route anybody wanted Sol to take. No one, *no one* remotely in their right mind, would tempt the region of space around Beta. An entire station emptied of people virtually overnight, without a hint of the reason? No. Whatever lurked there was best left alone. That route was a no-go.

But no one had ever accused EC Central as being in their right mind where it came to corporate power and infighting.

There was another possibility, almost as unthinkable. One had to wonder if the problems *Rights* had encountered were not due to design changes made by engineers under pressure from Sol to scale up to a six-light jump, exceeding *Finity's* jump capability with a lighter mass ship. And that was . . . insanity, pure and simple. A ship in jump accelerated. The longer it was in jump, the greater the energy— essentially borrowed mass—you had to throw off on exit. Exceed what your target point of mass could pull down? Exceed what you could then throw off? No. Not a good idea.

And the farther you jumped, and the bigger the energy you could throw, little factors became bigger ones. The bowshock was massive. You ran a risk of a less stable star— like the Hinder Stars in general—spitting back. Alpha's red dwarf star was that sort, which was *why* they'd skipped out a bit further on entry, and fast. The potential effect of a hyper-accelerated ship entering a thickly populated and developed system like Sol was inconceivable. Better, *far* better, to have Sol as the tail end of a relatively short hop.

All in all, Sol appeared at least to acknowledge the dangers so far. So far, contact with Sol—through the EC offices on the various Hinder Star stations—was still friendly, still cooperative. Of *course* Pell wanted to see Sol solve its problem. Of course probes would be launched from Pell, hunting for that all-important jump point. Of course if they discovered it, they would share. Absolutely. It took years to have a complete lightspeed conversation, but yes, of course, they were concerned. They'd get right back to you.

Feed Sol information, that was Pell's tactic. Feed them. Talk to them. Make them feel they were still a part of things. Assure them that no, Cyteen was not at this point a threat, but Pell was keeping a watchful eye on them.

Had those probes truly been deployed? Not his problem, though Emilio Konstantin, Pell's stationmaster, would be a fool to risk being caught in a lie. Pell's future depended on trade and peace and cooperation with the stations closest, and on their expertise in a region Sol had no way to understand. A probe or two in Sol's direction would be a small price to pay.

So one could call that ship on A-mast a return message from the EC. We're coming. One way or another, Sol was going to arrive and inject its own orders into the situation, and every station, every ship, every planet would do well to be prepared.

A message named *Rights of Man*, with its unreasonably large crew and limited cargo space. Not an autonomous, generations-deep family such as *Finity* had, or that ran any other cargo-moving FTL going, but a handful of imported officers from Sol and a mass of jobless stationers grateful for the steady paycheck. The EC intended to break the Family ship tradition. That . . . was the second truly ominous message being sent by *The Rights of Man*.

Even Cyteen respected the capital-f Families that had grown up on the old pushers: eleven original Families that had fissioned into sixty-three, and more if one counted the secondaries. If goods moved even in Cyteen's space, it used those same sixty-three ships. Family ships that could talk to other Families, that could make sense to each other for reasons grounded in trade and common necessities and shared knowledge.

The Families had begun with small populations destined for decades of isolation in the sub-lighters. With FTL a reality, a ship-Family meant the common experience of people who *knew* what it meant to lose contact with reality and return again, ready to make life and death hindbrain decisions. Time passed differently for them, and station years and station politics were just irrelevant to shipboard lives. They were the only ones who lived *exactly* in their time: everybody else—did not.

Now the EC, who had resented the Families since *Gaia's* crew had refused to give her up, was going to entrust that expensive monster, *Finity's* unrefined cousin, to a bunch of sim-trained stationers who had no experience in deep space at all.

Never mind the insult to the handful of ship-Families who had remained loyal to Alpha, who had kept the Hinder Stars alive for decades. Never mind the neglect those Families' ships had had to endure because of the priorities given to *that* ship. There'd be no link for *Rights* into the web of connections and shared history that informed and connected every other ship this side of Cyteen. *Rights* was the property of the EC, and anyone who thought the EC would stop at one ship . . . was a fool.

So now the universe had *this* huge creature ready to back EC notions that an EC committee could issue orders and policies and make it all work. Of course a committee could hire a stationer crew and train them in a few months to do what the Families had selected and trained to do for generations.

It had been possible for everybody in deep space to ignore EC's ideas so long as it had taken over a decade to exchange messages that were ultimately irrelevant to each other. Since FTL, they'd all had Cyteen on one side, going way too fast, Sol slogging along sublight on the other, and Pell trying to keep peace in the middle and modernize trade, create markets, *match* Cyteen's expansion, and negotiate with them as equals—everything in delicate balance.

But Sol wouldn't stay in its bottle forever. Cyteen's population was expanding like a yeast culture, but by artificial means, and they were living . . . well, not forever, but *long*. There was going to be a meeting, and one hell of a culture shock—and humanity that didn't come from Sol system or Cyteen birthlabs had everything at stake.

That was why *Finity*, running very little cargo, had made the trip out to this bag-end of all commercial space.

"Alpha's not going to like us much in a few hours," JR said soberly. "Less, when we go ashore."

"Wouldn't expect it," Fletcher said.

"We don't *start* anything," JR said. "If it starts, we just become scarce, get back to the sleepover and don't involve ourselves in any quarrel we don't understand. We're missing two ships we wanted. We work with what we've got."

"These are the tough nuts," Fletcher said. "The ones with damned few options. Alpha's it, for them."

"They're it for Alpha, the same, aren't they? Station's going to be upset with what we have to offer. I really don't want to get afoul of the EC office here. But it's likely we will."

"Afraid that's going to be the case," Fletcher said. "But that's their choice."

Chapter 1   Section iv

Another velocity dump, a vector change . . . Abrezio requested approach data . . . and *Finity*'s path fell, somewhat anticlimactically, within a standard pattern.

Delicate, delicate matter to have a ship like that touch the mast under its own guidance. Abrezio thought of ordering *Finity* to shed all relative motion and leave it to station assistance, which, for one thing, would give them another number of hours; but if *Finity* thought it needed that—and reputation swore they were beyond good—*Finity* could make that request. If he *ordered* it, *Finity* could outright ignore the order, and the EC would be left looking foolish if they made it—while Pell would be the villain if they damaged the mast.

Let an incident happen—God, what were the odds of real damage to the station? To the other ships linked to B-Mast? If he judged wrong . . . loss of his job might be the least of his worries.

Abrezio stayed still. He watched the progress of it, telling himself at any time down to the last few seconds, he could tell that behemoth to brake and abort. But if it didn't listen—what could he do? The entire fleet of runabouts and tenders wouldn't be enough to stop it.

Ops and that ship were in communication. Decisions were being made. When *Rights* had done this maneuver, tugs had pushed her slowly into position.

He watched as that mammoth ship followed the graph without a hitch, velocity curve and position all right on the numbers. They had three, four ships balancing *Rights'* presence on the A-mast. Now they had removed two, and that might not be enough, by the numbers ops was throwing out. They were going to need to use the tanks to even it out, one pumping madly, as was.

Docking proceeded. Once coupling was complete, the data feed would begin—they had no damned choice about that. Station's feed would go to *Finity's* black box, and *Finity's* content would go to station's, no defense, no argument. It was the system Cyteen had designed, and an integral part of the physical hookup for an FLT ship. Of all the data Cyteen had handed out free, the nature of the link between the black box and the FTL engine controls had never been explained . . . or cracked. And Cruz's team had tried, oh, how they'd tried.

They were fools to fight it, in Abrezio's opinion. Information was, and always had been, one of the most valuable commodities a ship carried, though it wasn't until FTL and the black boxes that it actually achieved specific trade value. Just how much of the data coming in on *Finity* would be useful to Alpha was a question. Digital entertainment, published scientific papers, anything copyrighted or trademarked . . . those were the reliable commodities. Not just the new ones, but the statistics on usage of established goods. Vids, books, music: Alpha's creative citizens waited eagerly for usage figures . . . and the station credit that came with those figures.

That feed also contained data on current market prices, prices on goods that flowed freely between Cyteen and Pell, Mariner and Viking. For the most part, those figures were irrelevant to Alpha. *Venture* got only the table leavings of luxuries, and what passed on down the line from Venture got absorbed by Bryant's.

Except for essentials. Those, purchased directly from Pell, did get through to Alpha, and possibly the worst aspect of those painfully transparent trade figures was the fact that he knew damned good and well that what Alpha paid for those essentials in no way reflected what, say, a Viking baker, at a single remove from Pell, paid for them. Konstantin had made Alpha a deal, back when the first shipment designated entirely for *Rights* put them in crisis for simply feeding their citizens. That special pricing continued to this day, for which Abrezio was reluctantly grateful. Reluctantly because the fact was, thanks to *Rights,* Alpha hadn't the return trade to be a truly viable market for Pell at this far remove, but without those foodstuffs from Pell, well, the EC's hand-picked execs would be building their own ship.

Which reality of interstellar economics didn't stop him from feeling like a damned welfare case. Didn't stop him from lying awake at night wondering when Konstantin was going to wake up and realize that long-ago agreement was still on the books and cut them off, or worse, what Konstantin was going to expect in return for *not* cutting off that supply.

It hadn't always been like that. Time was, Alpha had had plenty to offer in return, when the pushers from Sol actually brought Sol exotics. From Sol these days they got precious little to send out along the trade routes, except information, and much of that came in on the Stream: news, political scandals . . . all a minimum of six years out of date, but certain parties up the line paid well to have that data entered into the black box system. Other digital information, things requiring usage tracking, those came in on the pusher ships. Slower still, but more secure. Formulae and processes for products, flavors, pharmaceuticals, books, pictures, vid games, and entertainment vids—of which only those based on Sol's notions of life beyond Sol system sold all that well.

Spacers did like their comedies.

With every Sol shipment going straight to *Rights,* all local interest in the Farther Stars exotics vanished. Alpha simply couldn't afford them. The handful that trickled through, mostly special orders, helped keep their loyal ships operational. Alpha rarely saw the ships that traded directly with the planeted stars.

And now . . . they had four. The dose of fairly current trade stats that had already hit the boards from the first arriving outsiders had sent jitters through the markets . . . mostly from what wasn't there. They'd offered goods, but nothing like the quantity they might carry.

What were they holding back? Alpha was a bare-bones economy. They didn't need it driven home to them.

And then, there was the issue of what Alpha had to send back to Sol system in return for their nonexistent support. Data from the Farther Stars—patents, books, vids . . . the same sort of low to no-mass, security-requiring goods as they received . . . and with a similar, arrogant bias regarding life on the far side of the pusher-ship's route. He'd often wondered how those were received, back on Sol, or if they ever actually got distributed. Black box tech made such things available to everyone. Secure data feeds to the EC back on Sol Station went only as far as the EC wanted them to.

News feeds from Pell and beyond required a vastly different approach. Everything, *everything* had to be vetted. Some things could simply be added to the Stream, to get to Sol in six years, and available for anyone with the right equipment to capture. Some were simply too potentially volatile to send that way. Those they put onto secure chips and sent via the massive pushers to his superiors to decide what could be turned loose to Sol at large, all traveling sub-light, slower than the antiquated Stream.

Fortunately, his predecessors had had the same problem and he'd inherited a system of vetting and a trained team to do all the work along with the office.

Damn the whole breed the Farther Stars were cultivating. Arrogant. Contemptuous of the planet that had birthed the entire human race. And of the stations still owing allegiance to it.

Then he thought of Hewitt and of Cruz, who arrived with their own sort of arrogance. And the people in Sol system making those vids, who damned well hadn't done their homework. And the Company that sent metal for a damned expensive A-mast ornament rather than goods to keep their station's economy alive while they built that monster . . .

And he wondered if arrogance and selective ignorance weren't simply another commodity being traded freely throughout both systems, each rich enough to slander the other with impunity.

Watching the telemetry coming in from *Finity*, he was reminded of the pusher ships coming in: It moved with the same delicate precision, reminder, perhaps, that this crew, at least some of them, had once had a pusher of their own. Oldest in the fleet. Royalty, Cruz had called them, and likely, in their own guts if not their minds, that's exactly what they were.

And wasn't that going to add another twist to the mix of people gathering in his station? Forget the docking, the diplomacy of the next few days was going to be a nightmare. Spacers. He could almost track the thinking of Pell and Sol, but spacers were a whole different breed.

The two remaining pusher ships' crews—Alpha's other contact with Sol-ward humanity—after generations of their own company, weren't arrogant so much as . . . odd, eccentric in the extreme. But they were an understandable breed, still welcomed as heroes at Sol as well as Alpha, treated with the deference they earned in their long, lonely service to the star-stations. Pushers were the link they had with Sol. They brought, besides the goods, a link with the traditions and the past—and their own load of plain-spoken news that would never make it into the Stream. Pusher crews *appreciated* the luxurious facilities the EC provided them as thanks for their extended exiles from the rest of humanity. They were *glad* for what they got.

Pushers, however, were a dying breed, and their culture and traditions were disappearing with them. Pusher crews had had no choice about their difference. Their time-dilated lives and years spent isolated from any other society necessarily set them apart. Friends—and enemies—made during leave were, of necessity, ephemeral. Historically, the pusher crews and station alike had enjoyed those extended leaves free of charge. Historically, a pusher's arrival heralded a grand free-for-all of sex, alcohol, and good times, couples meeting, packing a lifetime of relationship into a handful of nights, as both station and ship injected new DNA into their isolated pools.

These modern spacers, the FTLers, were yet another breed. They *chose* to set themselves apart as something above stationers, worthy of the same entitlements their pusher forebears had won, but with none of the personal sacrifices. They complained mightily about high charges from the station, but they were a profit-making operation. A few months lost each jump transit was nothing against the years of human contact the pushers lost. FTL *should* have helped synchronize the spacers with the rest of the universe and *given* them common interests with the stations, given them ties with the offspring their sleepovers created . . . but it had done the opposite. These modern spacers—these *Families*—arrived with a chronic disregard for stationer rules, diametrically opposed cultural expectations—even languages that only a single ship understood.

These days, rules and security gates separated the spacer Strip—where station just let spacers do much as they pleased, charged them for it, enforced law where public safety was threatened, and generally just tried to keep the lid on—from the rest of the station. Any DNA exchanges in this FTL age happened between ships, not ship and station, with rare exception, mostly in the hospitality industry, and often with unhappy outcome. The gulf of distrust between spacers and stationers had grown wide on Alpha . . . except for the stationers who manned the businesses and bars on the Strip. Some of those had become more spacer than stationer, if loyalties and moral expectations were the determining factors.

It didn't help that commerce, the flow of goods between stations that kept the spacers alive, had changed drastically— heated by a prosperity in the Beyond that the First Stars couldn't match. The market had become far more interactive and volatile. In the pusher years, stations had been economically as independent as the ships carrying goods. Purchase orders had taken years to fill and all of the goods received had been distributed through the station's central purchasing, which calculated the margins and doled out to individuals according to calculated need.

These days, market lag was a matter of months, not years, and while those all-important staples still went through central purchasing, station shops often dealt directly with the market for luxuries. Would the station residents willingly go back to more stable times? Certainly not the ones with a foot in the black market, trading directly with spacers, selling contraband to other stationers.

Spacers, for whom the new system meant economic independence, definitely would not go back.

Was it all Cyteen's fault? If not for that gift of FTL from Cyteen, commerce and colonization would still be running at sublight speeds. If not for that *gift*, Alpha would still be thriving. Maybe. The fact was, progress happened. Those affected just had to find a way to adapt.

Cyteen. Now there was yet another in the disparate grouping of humanity taking shape in the universe. The First Stars tended to hold Cyteen as the evil lurking in the shadows, madly proliferating population, a clone army with which they intended to take over . . . everything. Corrupting the powerful with drugs. Aiming at universal mind control.

Personally, he doubted Cyteen would bother. Cyteeners had always thought in terms of escaping Sol's control. Renegade scientists had hijacked a station core intended for

Viking—or was it Mariner?—and headed for a reachable star with a biologically viable planet. Cyteen's founders had wanted out and away, and ultimately FTL had given them the ability to make that dream an unstoppable reality.

Somehow he doubted Cyteen ever wanted to get cozy with Sol, let alone take it over, complete with all the attached problems.

But FTL wasn't the only game changer Cyteen had bestowed on the rest of humanity; and the last thing Sol needed was the second thing Cyteen had to spread about. FTL had been a gift. This one—cost.

Rejuv. Immortality. *Expensive* immortality.

If FTL was a gift, rejuv provided the funds.

God, what a pain in the ass Cyteen had become with that one. Who needed a drug that allowed a small handful of already too-powerful people to live a double lifespan? And Abrezio *knew* that was happening on Pell. Emilio Konstantin had been an old man when Abrezio had been a junior clerk in the former stationmaster's office. Konstantin had still been an old man when he'd closed Pell's EC offices and dumped the personnel on Alpha.

And that same old man had christened the first megaship.

The same ship, *Finity's End,* that was now in process of docking at *his* station.

Abrezio's nerves vibrated anew to the shock of *seeing* that approach, a juggernaut bursting out of nowhere, not the delicate lance of the smaller FTLs, but a force that made the sun itself react . . .

Damn. He'd worked hard to put that memory to rest.

. . . and his glass was empty.

He left it that way. Having seen *Finity* come in, he needed all his wits about him.

Having seen *Finity* come in . . .

Suddenly, viscerally, he understood why crews from the old pushers, converted as the first FTLers, had thrown up their hands and overturned their seniority, saying helm was no longer an old man's position. That was power incarnate. Adjust the entry vector, aim that shockwave at the station rather than the star . . . *that* was something to fear.

He'd just seen what *The Rights of Man* was supposed to be, but he'd had it insolently handed him by a Pell-based ship, doing things—doing things that the ship his people had labored years on should be capable of . . . but wasn't.

From a few minutes of sheer terror—to helplessness.

Maybe that entry had been intended to push Alpha into deploying *Rights*. Maybe it was just for a look-see.

And maybe . . . maybe it was a warning *against* what they had been building, frantically, for decades.

Showing out, Hewitt had said. He read it another way. Do you really want, *Finity* could be saying, *this* coming in with a rookie crew at the helm, aimed at *your* star?

He was shaken. He didn't know how Cruz and Hewitt had reacted, in their guts. But this scared him.

He wanted to hope his gut was right. He sincerely wanted to hope that the entry was more than arrogant bravado.

Maybe, he told himself, Pell wanted to talk. Maybe that had prompted this sudden visit of three ships—and *that*.

But why now? What fickle god had sent these ships to Alpha, maybe as a long-overdue move toward reason and negotiation, at a time when he already harbored another potential game changer. A guilty secret he'd held for over six months without acting on it. A precious handful of numbers he'd held secret because . . .

Because those numbers—and what they implied for the future of mankind—would create a shockwave as powerful, politically, as the one that ship had created in space. A shockwave with an impact impossible to predict, and the last thing he'd wanted was to put them into the hands of a man like Cruz. He'd been waiting . . . for options, for some clue as to a proper course of action.

Damn it.

Six months ago he'd come in possession of a letter internal to Alpha, a letter from a retired scientist who'd kept working, unfunded, just because it was his lifetime project, which no one else seemed inclined to pick up. For decades, the man had been sifting old pusher data that occupied a massive, seldom-accessed storage in one of the cold sections. Unlike jump transit, in which—by what Abrezio knew—human senses didn't make sense and most of the ship's sensors didn't either, sublighter crews *as well as* the instruments were up and working for the entire trip, recording years and years of data and observations, including curiosities and things off in the deep dark.

Buried in that data, so the old man claimed, was the long-sought key to Sol's FTL future—jump points: sufficiently isolated points of enough mass to haul an FTLer down to normal space and let it refine its path to the next one. What they had was not the single jump point they had hoped to find, but two points that zigzagged their way from Barnard's Star—Alpha—to Sol, a less direct route than they'd hoped, but providing, nonetheless, stepping stones for an FTLer heading from Alpha to Sol and back. The coordinates of the suitable masses—and the paths they followed—nothing in the great dark stayed still—were right now locked in the safe tucked into the floor under Abrezio's feet, a secret not trusted to anyone else, certainly not trusted to station computers and certainly not shared with the black boxes that sucked up everything and took it elsewhere.

The old scientist himself was currently in a very comfortable, closely guarded and monitored confinement, with any luxury he wanted. Fortunately, that wasn't much. A library, a computer, read-access to anything he asked . . . including that wealth of public-information pusher data, which he continued to study, just to see what else he could find. The old man was happy. He knew what he'd found: the discovery of a lifetime that would someday put his name in the history files.

It was sad, in a way. The old man's colleagues and friends were all dead. The only regular outside contact he had was his doctor, the son of the doctor he'd had for years. No one knew why he was sequestered, or even *that* he was sequestered: the man had been, and still was, a hermit. The only real difference in his life pre-discovery and now was his comfort level, and of that, he had never complained. He probably *thought* word had gone to Sol, and had just gone back to his beloved data analysis, trusting he'd done all he needed to do.

Luckily. Had the old man been more set on seeing his name in the history books, he could have made a real problem for a stationmaster trying to do the right thing with the old man's discovery and still struggling with what that *right thing* was.

Abrezio was not accustomed to feeling like a thief hiding stolen goods. But he felt that now, guilty and desperate. The transfer appropriation of the *Rights* plans in the first place hadn't been his choice. The EC rep on Pell had masterminded that matter and passed the plans—along with the responsibility of informing the head offices—on to him, bypassing the Venture office as untrustworthy and the Bryant's office as incapable.

His first year in this office, and the stolen blueprints had landed on his desk. Life had been simpler then, his duty to the Company more obvious. He'd sent those plans, immediately and without a second thought, on to Sol via the Stream, and twelve years later had received his orders to build *Rights* the same way.

And a handful of years after those written orders, Cruz had arrived to take control of the project . . . and look how *that* had panned out.

The EC wanted that ship *built* at Alpha—and he'd done it. He'd found a way to feed his people *and* build it, without a whole lot of help from Sol. With the arrival of Hewitt, he'd begun to get a sick feeling just where EC priorities lay, and it wasn't with the well-being of the faithful at Alpha. It was that ship and the people they sent out to build it.

But while Hewitt and Cruz would get the credit should the project succeed, he and his people, the hard working Alpha citizens who had built it and given up their lives to train on the sims, would be the ones to blame if it didn't.

And that was why, when—with *Rights* just back in dock from a test failure—he'd gotten that letter, he'd kept it completely to himself and that dedicated old scientist. He was not about to give Cruz the chance to pull that place in history away from one of *his* people. He'd been planning to send the coordinates on to Sol via *Atlantis* when it made dock, the safest and securest transmission, along with its notes, cautions, and original data, with a bio of the old man and his dedication to his project.

But *Atlantis* was three years off from Alpha, and would take another decade getting back to Sol.

Not that long, really, in historical data transfer with Sol, and he could shorten it by a bit if he had *Atlantis* transmit it on the Stream, the ancient lightspeed beam to Sol and pushers in transit, once *Atlantis* was well beyond Alpha's system, where no spybot was likely. And once that information was in Sol's grateful hands, Sol authorities could test those numbers, send probes to verify the jump points . . . and have the credit properly established before Cruz ever even knew the data existed.

He *hadn't* planned to trust it to the doubtful security of the Stream from Alpha, a transmission that anyone, theoretically, could intercept, if they lurked and waited. Even if he managed to sneak a top security transmission past Hewitt, there was that other, ever-present fear, that some shadow lurked out there, insystem, something dropped by Pell to tap the Stream for information passing between Alpha and Sol; some robot just mindlessly note-taking and downloading to the occasional visitor that *wasn't* an Alpha regular.

No, he hadn't sent that data on that vulnerable beam, and he began to fear that hesitation had been a mistake. It would have been well on its way by now if he had. But now, with what he had underfoot—and these visitors—he had a new worry.

The old man insisted he'd told no one. Abrezio knew *he* hadn't told anyone, not his secretary, not even his wife, and *definitely* not Cruz or Hewitt. But what if the old scientist *had* acquaintances who'd tried to reach him, people who knew what his work was, and started speculating?

There were, ultimately, no truly secure secrets in a community whose job was creating theories out of isolated facts. And given the gathering of these outsider ships—if *he* could form a worst-case suspicion what might have lured them—

Dammit.

Or—maybe, *maybe* the timing was just a nightmarish coincidence. The letter and the test run had just happened to coincide. Maybe it was just the fact *Rights* had made a test run—maybe Pell just didn't know it had failed.

Six, seven months . . . and here four Pell ships were. Either event could have triggered this visit.

Alpha was such a fragile blip in the dark, right on the edge of trouble. Alpha had for years dreaded the day that some damned committee at Sol decided to go with what they had, build a smaller FTL, and route it through haunted Beta. Wishful theories proliferated: the disappearance of the colony was a combination of circumstances, a mass panic, a wrong decision. It could all be explained. The ship that explored the disaster hadn't looked in the right place. Somewhere, there *were* bodies.

Tell that to *Santa Maria,* which was one of Alpha's two pushers, still making the Sol run. *They* weren't going back there. Nor should anyone else.

The coordinates he had in the safe right under his feet— *were* possibly the answer. Sol to Alpha. Economic salvation, not a death sentence. He'd just needed three more years, for *Atlantis* to arrive, and *take* the burden.

And now . . . he had four Pell ships clogging his B-mast. *Damn* the Konstantins.

No matter what he did now, or didn't do—he risked everything. It was a nightmare.

Confide in Cruz, or Hewitt?

Hell if.

Granted Pell was up to something—his back was against the wall, take it or leave it. His choice right now had to be *his* choice, and to make a right one, he had to know, first of all, what Pell was after.

Rumor didn't just run wild on the Strip: it bounded from bar to bar, gaining embellishment as it went, and while it might be natural that with so many strangers arriving, there was a doubling of uniformed station security presence on the Strip—*rumor* said it was because *Finity* was bringing in Pell security and the EC blue-coats were worried.

Contrary rumor said the issue that brought all these ships was somewhere in the Beyond, that Pell and Cyteen had drifted toward hostilities, and that Pell was out shopping for allies, which *might* mean a trade deal.

Still another rumor said that Pell was joining up with Cyteen and that it was a takeover move, with more ships to follow.

It was certain that *Finity's* crew, the Neiharts, and the rest of these strangers combined would have the weight of numbers on the Strip, and that was not a comfortable feeling. Along with the extra security, there was a growing number of *Rights* crew on the Strip, fancy blue uniforms, conspicuous in the motley flash of spacer crews, whose ship-color jackets might be the same general shade and pattern, but even that wasn't a given.

Rumors aside, there was a current buzz of good times on the Strip. Jobs were on offer, for however long the influx lasted. A few luxuries and some new entertainment had hit the Strip. There was, for stationers, a little stint of better-paying work. Hotels—station officially hated the word *sleepovers*, but the term was catching on—hotels had called up furloughed personnel from such interim jobs as processing and recycling, operations that typically filled the financial gap for stationers running the Strip's hotels and bars and shops, the number of which varied with what ships were in port.

The current bloom of jobs on the Strip had started with the listing of *Firenze* for repair, which meant a hundred-some of the Galli family resident on the Strip indefinitely. With *Little Bear*'s arrival, they'd called up more. When the Patels of *Mumtaz* and the Druvs of *Nomad* had come in, they'd opened every ordinary hotel on the Strip, unbolted the panels that concealed unused frontages and turned on all the colored lights and vid displays in *all* the sections of the Strip.

It was a garish and exciting show. Goods flowed into Alpha from the outsider ships, cheap and flashy things as well as rare tastes and foodstuffs, and the ships' outsider crew spending scrip freely up and down the Strip was enabling workers to feel unnaturally flush, able to buy some of what was passing into Alpha's warehouses, even to speculate on cargo to purchase and warehouse, exotics that might ride *Atlantis* back to Sol, a long-term investment, the sort stationers might make for their kids.

Souvenir and trinket shops were doing a brisk trade—some souvenirs, like ship patches and sparkling pebbles from Sol, had aged into real value, of interest to these wealthy Farther Stars traders.

And perhaps more valuable, these outsiders brought rare metals and minerals to back their scrip. For the first time in thirty years, raw materials had arrived *not* specifically earmarked for *Rights,* and that was the positive side of the matter. Maybe Rosie would finally get his grey-water plumbing fixed.

With *Finity's* arrival, recycling and some maintenance and manufacturing were going on hiatus, absolutely stripped of workers. It was a wonder, some joked, that the station didn't wobble on its axis, with so many stationers called over to the Strip side.

Now the question was, for how long? A typical ship rotation was ten to sixteen days. Travel-worn ships might put in for a bit longer; another might linger for some special problem or wait for a cargo.

But this confluence of strangers from the Farther Stars?

Nobody could predict how long the uncommon traffic would stay at Alpha, or whether—in shopkeepers' wildest dreams—they might portend a lasting increase in traffic, complete with new trade agreements.

Some stationers liked that idea. Local ship crews weren't as happy. As *Finity's End* docked with B-mast, a soft, slow and perfect approach, the scuttlebutt was less optimistic where *Galway*'s crew gathered to watch.

"They're here to put the pressure on," Senior Captain Niall Monahan said, at a back table in Rosie's, Rosie's at its most raucous being the most secure place on Alpha's Strip for ship's personnel to discuss anything they didn't want to reach station admin. *"Somebody's* got an agenda, haven't they?"

A lot of guesses flew about the table, the vast majority involving Pell, and none of the speculation including an offer of softhearted charity from that quarter.

Galway's first shift, Ross Monahan among them, held the whole back of the place. The tables were fixed in clamps, as tables were supposed to be, but Rosie's had this clever arrangement—leaves that locked from table to table to create a meeting spot that let extra chairs jam in tight. *Galway*'s Family, the Monahans collectively, numbered a hundred twenty-four, and fifteen seats to a shift—working posts and backup. Their first and fourth bridge shifts were crowded at several of Rosie's tables, with a few from second and third. They were the largest crew of the largest Alpha ship except repair-bound *Firenze,* whose people held the next-over row of tables.

Ross sat next to Fallan and sipped Rosie's pub-brewed beer, watching the largest ship he'd ever seen move in with pin-point accuracy, and asking himself what it would be like to be aboard—to see what her crew had seen, the massive stations, planets with life, stars that weren't nasty-tempered red. He wondered what the ring-docks were like, that new system of docking that let you walk out a gangway at full G rather than float down the mast; a system designed specifically to keep these so-called longhaulers' mass off a station's delicate masts. It was a system *Galway* had never seen, except under early construction, their last stop at

Venture. He'd seen the vids of docks and ships built to carry cargo in monster containers, some complete with temperature and pressure control, that could carry massive amounts of enviro-sensitive cargo. *Finity* carried those containers in massive braces, loaded by robots. He'd seen the vids, but no vid could capture the sheer size of the ship now coming in to dock.

He couldn't imagine the trade that could support one such leviathan, let alone the number of similar ships rumor said were under construction out at Pell. One thing was obvious: the amount of goods that now flowed *between* stations on the far side of Venture was way beyond Alpha's traffic. Mind-numbingly beyond it. There were two inhabited planets producing goods out in the Beyond, with huge orbiting facilities to process foodstuffs into edibility. Goods *flowed* out there, and now Venture, the one station that made *Galway*'s route viable, was remaking itself to suit that sort of ship. Even *Little Bear* and *Mumtaz*, a third the mass of what was incoming, had that weird bow, a jutting structure on the ship's core stationside of the ship's own ring—conspicuous on those ordinary ships, greatly altering their profile—not so evident on *Finity*.

No matter the size of the ship, the attachment to the ring-docks had to be identical in every way. The same exact structure—with a shape reminiscent of the bow on the ancient sailing ship that was old *Argo's* patch—a ship with an eye to find its way. Ships on Earth's oceans used to have that structure—a ram, meant to kill other ships. Ross had looked that up, back when he was a younger, back when he'd been fascinated with the old pushers and collected all their patches—replicas, except *Santa Maria* and *Atlantis,* which were the real thing. They were his two real treasures, those—which were probably worth a bit of cred out in the Farther Stars, where the real thing had never visited.

Santa Maria's patch was also a sailing ship, but of a later age of Earth. *Atlantis*'s was an early spacecraft—winged, for landing on Earth. He'd once thought—at the time he'd been an obnoxious, rebellious younger—that somewhere, someday, he'd trade those special patches, and have ship-

cred enough to buy most anything on dockside. He'd
wanted a fancier vid player, at the time.

Later, he'd dreamed of shipping out on *Santa Maria* and
making it back again—magically unchanged. The universe
would naturally make an exception in his case, and he
wouldn't get time-lagged from the rest of *Galway* and everyone he knew. He'd just return to *Galway* at Alpha and automatically be senior crew on *Galway* and incredibly swag,
exotic, and cool, and the proud owner of a collection of Sol
exotics he'd cannily traded his patch collection for. He'd
come back to the First Stars with those Sol goods, goods to
bolster *Galway*'s struggling bank account. He'd rejoin his
crew. They'd trade those goods all the way to Pell and be
rich.

His mind had run to stupid things like that. But he'd
resisted the vid player, and now he had a collection he treasured. He'd stayed put, and grown up, and worked his way
to Nav 1.3, which was trainee behind their first shift senior
navigator, Fallan, and their number two, Ashlan, which
meant he actually never knew when his input to the boards
might be what the ship was actually using. But a 1.3 getting
closer to the active nav post meant somebody retiring who
he dreaded losing, dreaded more and more as he worked
beside him, and daily realized just how much he still had to
learn. Ship-clock said he was twenty-four, while more decades than that had passed on Alpha. Nav 1, Fallan—
Fallan was father, grandfather, great-grandfather—in every
sense that mattered. A spacer rarely knew a biological father: it was all on his mother to figure out, from the
sleepovers. No, a spacer picked his own kin, aboard, and
his—the man that he had followed about, tagged after until
people laughed about it, and Fallan had no choice—his was
Fallan. Still was, only now he was half a hand taller than
the old man, and hell and away stronger, and looked out for
him, Fallan never having figured he'd personally passed
biological twenty-one a century and more ago, as stations
reckoned time.

Of course Ross had chosen the Nav track, when he was
only shipboard six.

Of course he studied hard. Fallan wouldn't take on a fool.

He'd grown older. He'd seen the economy getting worse.

And now he sat and watched this foreign giant come into dock at *his* station, crowding other loyal Alpha ships off the mast, taking up space at *his* home station. And he was only twenty-four. He couldn't imagine what Fallan and Niall were feeling. The Farther Stars were changing and moving on, while one after the other the First Star stations shut down, while Sol, the one source of trade that made Alpha . . . *special* . . . remained just—uneconomical to reach.

Youthful dreams never truly died. Riches from a sublight trip to Sol had become the constant hope that jump points would be discovered and all the loyal ships would finally have their day. But this thing moving in now threatened everything that *was* . . . right now. *Galway* was the best ship Alpha had, damned if he'd count the A-mast ornament, but she wasn't—not remotely—*this*.

And he was, he realized, angry about the injustice of it all. They'd worked as hard. *Galway* had her own link to the sublighters—old *Atlas*. Fallan came from there. *Galway* wasn't the first of the Alpha purpose-builts: *Firenze* was that. But they were somebody. They were the best Alpha had. *Galway* just hadn't been as lucky, because *Alpha* hadn't been as lucky. *Alpha* wasn't, and wouldn't be until Sol entered the FTL picture, a part of that massive flow of goods that made Pell produce a ship like *Finity*.

Gaia, on the other hand, was luck incarnate. Oldest of the pushers. First crew to challenge the EC and lay claim to their own ship, and first to lay down the rules as they were. First to carry cargo to Pell. Right place at the right time. Always. Now she had shed her luck on this creature.

Just wasn't fair, that. It was never fair.

"One damn canister," Captain Niall said glumly, "is about a tenth of our hold. And that ship holds two hundred. But she's not hauling cans this trip, that's what I'm hearing."

"Just the fancy stuff," Fallan said. "Warm storage, inside. And who affords that, here?"

"You don't want a taste for it," Pru said, Com 1.2. "You'll remember it forever. Unfortunately, silly stationers will buy. And it makes what we've got not-good."

"That's a gloomy outlook," Ashlan said.

"Had Cyteen wine once. Ever after, I can't drink a red without knowing it's piss-poor. Not a good thing."

"But you had it once," Ashlan said. "Isn't there that?"

"Is," Pru said. "But I can't help it. I don't drink red anymore."

Ross thought, *I'd rather have it once. I'd want to have had it once.* He looked at the vid in the bar, which had gotten uncharacteristically quiet.

Finity's End, the screen sidebar said, *Origin: Pell via Venture via Bryant's. Destination: Pell via Bryant's via Venture.*

Cargo: foodstuffs, dry goods, liquor, works of art, rare earths, metals, pharmaceuticals . . .

Details followed. But they'd seen those long since: flour, sugar, various chemicals useful in synth and printing and fabricating . . . the list was long. The market had already taken the arrival into account. Speculators were definitely at work. *Galway* had already sold their cargo—a good thing, since a supply of metals was going to drive prices down.

There was that one good fortune. For them.

Santiago, still in negotiations, was downright panicking.

Galway ought to be giving the board call: they were loaded and they'd been due to undock and leave for Bryant's in two days, except that station ops had frozen everybody in place, thanks to that monster.

So now they were stuck, bleeding money on dockside, until ops gave the all-clear. They were being careful with the finance. They'd be doubling up in sleepover rooms, and living on bar food to keep the bottom line in the black: that was the order, given the unexpected hold. On the one hand they ached to be underway, and on the other—damned if they didn't want to know what was going on here before they moved out, and what they might run into at Bryant's, which had already had a visitation from these ships, if one could believe the listings. Bryant's was in the same situation as Alpha, resource and manpower poor, while, next station up the chain and also a recipient of a visit, Venture, with unlimited local supply of materials and direct trade with Pell, was soon to have a ring-dock capability, same as Pell, same as Mariner. And Cyteen, and all its stations, presumably.

Ring docks and canisters. A ship that could carry multiple times what *Galway* could stuff in her hold. Four ships that would, eventually, head back to Bryant's and Venture, carrying trade goods from Alpha.

Galway's goods. *Galway*'s trade. *Galway* sat loaded now, so this run was sure; but *Santiago* wasn't. They had to be sweating. And who knew for the run *back* from Bryant's?

Should they undock soonest, once they could undock, and beat these ships getting back to Bryant's, then sell their cargo first of any ship—?

But Bryant's would already *know* these ships had come here and might hold out for a bargain price, leaving them to stack up dock charges far worse there than Alpha's.

Dammit. Just . . . dammit.

Finity's End was firmly in lock, her crew exiting via the personnel lift—three hundred eighty-four of them—all Neiharts, to Ben Abrezio's information, ranging in age down to six months, shiptime, and requiring, *Finity's* com officer said, the *best* single hotel available for all aboard, quiet corridors and 1 g for all.

They had room, *all* of it 1 g, but the logistics would be tricky. Spacers were territorial. They wanted their own space for their own people, and, like a dinner party, if you seated the wrong two people together, it could ruin the whole evening.

Arguments among spacers notoriously could get violent, and tempers were already hot.

The hotels on the Strip were like a layered sandwich set on edge, one behind the other, most-used nearest the strip, second and third level reserved for mechanicals and storage, warehouses and emergency shelter. They had already opened all the regular hotels to accommodate the three visitors. Only one remained. The farthest-back hotel, the Olympian, was space they only used when *Santa Maria* or *Atlantis* was in dock. That hotel had more luxury and it was designed for longer periods of leave, as pushers tended to expect. *Finity* would have no cause for complaint.

The problem was, it shared three exit corridors with the Empyrean, the Fortune, and the Argent. It was against policy to mix crews in the same hotel, but exit corridors were common ground, and not uncommonly, if there *was* trouble, it happened there.

The Olympian had four other exit corridors serving two

other hotels. One was the Opportunity, which served a tag-end of *Firenze* and *Qarib* crew—they did get along, if not sharing-meals along. They already had to share those exit corridors with *Little Bear, Nomad,* and *Mumtaz,* who had damnwell better play politely, in the fairly luxurious Home-port.

Rights personnel held the Empyrean, three hundred fifty-nine persons, including officers. *Galway* had the For-tune, *Santiago* had the Argent. Encounters were inevi-table.

Abrezio didn't *borrow* trouble. But he didn't beg it, either. He ordered onsite monitoring 24/7 in all corridors, with security backup in four offices adjacent.

Bars, too, had been assigned. Housekeeping and hospi-tality, called into service in the Olympian and its two res-taurants, would have polite little printed chits to put in every room *Finity* held, offering two free drinks at a spe-cific bar in close proximity to the hotel's main exit, namely Critical Mass. Those friendly chits were, in post-pusher tradition, a polite indication which of several bars would be considered home turf to a particular ship, and where they had special rights. Critical Mass was waked from three years of slumber, with personnel moved in for however long it took—including a cook. A real chef from the resi-dency sectors.

Finity wanted the best and Alpha wasn't reluctant to charge for it.

Abrezio had had reservations about using the Olym-pian, which necessarily—last available hotel—had put *Fin-ity* and *Rights* sharing one corridor. Hotel corridors could be relatively deserted at certain hours, exactly the right sort of place for trouble to start. Officers *visibly* posted line-of-sight in that corridor were one precaution Abrezio had ordered.

Another was advising Andy Cruz to make a firm pro-nouncement to *Rights of Man* crew and security personnel that they were to duck trouble even if it was offered. Poli-tics, they were told. It was not the sort of rule *Rights* was inclined to expect, and it was a sure bet it would upset Cruz, but there was no other place to lodge the *Finity* crew together . . . and that shared corridor *was* a way to keep an eye on them.

Watch them, the word passed through *Rights'* personnel. Watch them, watch who they talk to and where they contact each other, and look for any clue what they're up to. A good number of *Rights'* crew *were* trained law enforcement. They would understand. One could hope they would explain the facts to their shipmates.

Ships had goods backing their scrip, and this offer of scrip from *Finity* listed things Alpha wanted. Badly. Robotic haggling had fined down what the scrip would represent, and *Finity* scrip was assigned a value that would be clear on the plastic cards and pocket chits that station issued, exchange rate specified. There were a lot of chargeable services, from refueling to hotel and meals, entertainment, souvenirs, name it. And the more *Finity* scrip Alpha could collect, the better.

The ships already in dock had been profitable, so far as that went. The crews of those three ships ate, slept, drank, and minded their own business, excepting the fracas during the shelter-order, for which no citations had been issued—that, in the interests of peace, despite the damage. *Finity's* contribution of goods into the system—not a full load, which might have overloaded the market and driven prices down—was evidently due to be completely minor, enough to cover her station charges and refueling, but damn little else, leaving the crew's scrip the major gain station would have.

Which posed a worrisome question throughout.

Why? Why was *Finity* really here?

He supposed they'd find out, eventually, and meanwhile . . .

Meanwhile—they were getting, among the goods *Finity* was offloading, an influx of luxuries they didn't ordinarily see at Alpha, including hisa artwork and textiles from Pell. . . . *That* capped all, for novelty. It was the sort of lowmass commodity that could see enough profit at Sol to more than justify a shipment taking a decade to get there, not to mention holding it in storage until there was a ship to get it there.

Which opportunity might just come sooner than anyone outside this office could know.

That was the thought dancing seductively in the back of Abrezio's mind, the one bright spot in the problems the visitors posed, that if he spent personal credit to acquire that specific cargo, he could become bulletproof against any change in the economy that Sol-bound FTL might perpetrate on Alpha. Interest in that sort of goods would only rise, if FTL became the rule.

He had a purchase order in the system, one that would put a hold on the goods for twenty-four hours. All it took was a button-push to confirm it. He owned a warehouse. It would lie there virtually forgotten, semi-cold and quite dark, until—until they either proved that jump point and made FTL contact with Sol, or, in the way of things, if they didn't, and trade with Sol continued at sublight speed—it still maintained value. It was a prospect to fund his retirement, in the course of time.

If, however, anything went wrong in this visit and investigators began to look for reasons—a large buy now and goods from Pell in his warehouse could look like a personal interest. It could be turned to look very bad, and he did not trust Andrew Cruz *or* Hewitt not to spin it that way in a serious falling-out. He didn't trust *anybody* Sol sent here not to have ambitions, and a willingness to do anything to look good to those that sent him.

Damned if he did and damned lot of regret if he didn't.

If it ever became an issue, he *could* claim the business deal was to give him reason for personal conferences with *Finity's* captains. A convenient inroad into relations that might yield information.

Which itself could look smart—or very, very wrong—depending on how the visit turned out.

He hesitated over the file, and the button.

He didn't push it. Not this fast. Not before he had some small confidence he knew what *Finity* was up to.

Having done presence-vids and deepstudy on the layout of
the station gave a person a niggling sense of déjà vu on
Alpha's Strip. JR had insisted on it for everybody on the
never-visited stations they'd called at on this run, not for
convenience, but for safety—to be sure everybody knew
where exits and accesses and takeholds were; where police
might be, in case of need—or avoidance. In addition to that
precaution, the senior-juniors, ages eighteen to twenty-
two, were required to go in groups at least of three, and to
keep coms live at all times, with instructions to stay within
200 meters of some sleepover access. That was actually a
fair stretch of liberty on Alpha's Strip. But it was not license to roam.

In general, those under eighteen ship-years would not
be out and about the docks at all. *They* would be in the
sleepover with their assigned minders, midway between accesses, and far out of reach of casual disturbance. Junior-
juniors could go on the Strip only with a senior minder
escort, never solo, and never without a pocket com. Infants
were in one room, toddlers in another, and for the dozen
youngests, classes never let up. Instructors, however, did
get free time, and bar time, as needed.

What *Finity* did not mention in its disclosure list for customs was the force of twenty-odd Neiharts who were staying aboard *Finity* in mast-dock, and the fact that *Finity's*
passive sensors would be active and monitored during
dock. It wasn't that they *expected* intrusion or inquisitive
visitations. It was that they were prepared—in case the
Earth Company at Alpha decided to gather a little information, or do a little first-hand research into the nav systems of a ship very like their own.

It was fairly certain that the station was similarly touchy about *The Rights of Man*, in dock up at the extreme end of A-mast, with no neighbors at all.

Was there a lot of imaging and pinging going on? Oh, yes, on station's side. On *Finity* there was a lot of passive recept going on, and every ping would be noted and logged as to origin, for whatever it was worth.

Finity crew in general was under orders to speak only with other *Finity* personnel in the exit corridors of the sleepover; to smile and nod if smiled at, but not to talk in those corridors; to limit sleepover partners to Little Bears, Mumtazes, or Nomads—more onerously, to limit alcohol, go in pairs or trios, avoid conflict, walk away from fights, and avoid like poison being the reason a *Finity* captain had to go extract them from local courts.

The rule applied to *Finity* captains, too. JR went with Madison, second shift captain, Hayes, the purser, and two of Hayes' junior-senior aides, Parton and Brenda B, to visit station offices and present papers, which was to say, to show up with a copy of the log from last port of call to here, to sign and verify that nobody had tampered with *Finity's* black box—that was the stupidest piece of the stupid red tape, but it had made some Pell legislator happy—and to swear that the crew debarked were all legitimate ship's family, and that *Finity* did not bring passengers, non-irradiated foodstuffs, drugs, weapons, or explosives onto the station.

JR filled out another screen of forms for ship status, and he simply entered NA for *not accessible,* which was the new form, since the ring-docks.

No, *Finity* personnel would not be coming and going aboard the ship while at dock: that was the regulation here, and they could comply with it. Ring-dock was much more forgiving. The airlock corridor they used for ring-dock had a downside ops and executive office, as well as a general takehold, and provided comfortable quarters for everybody who *needed* to stay aboard. But they couldn't use that airlock and corridor at Alpha. They had to exit via a tube—cold as hell's hinges, the thing was; and station's orders were—everybody off. The form noted: *Customs officials may access, y/n* . . . unfunny joke. By EC rules, the ship had no choice.

JR typed N . . . and wondered how long it would be before that "N" was challenged.

Meanwhile the twenty crew staying aboard would be as quiet about it as possible.

It was an interesting visit to station offices, the junior clerks directly dealing with them being unnaturally bubbly and cheerful, darting nervous glances, while EC police and several dour-faced individuals prowled about the peripheries of the office on no particular business.

"Sign, please." It was a tablet, pinned to a stand. The somewhat more senior official spun it about.

JR signed it, spun it back again.

"No abbreviations." The official spun it around. "Legal name's James Robert."

"JR *is* my signature. Always has been." His mother had laid the name on him, the only line of Neiharts that *could* attach that name to an unsuspecting kid. He *wasn't* James Robert Neihart, who'd been *Gaia's* first captain, the first captain to come back and tell the EC hands off their ship, the first star captain to make that claim for all time to come. "Don't argue with a man what his name is." He spun the tablet back. "Tell the stationmaster to ask me personally if he wants it different."

He got back a scowl. And turned his back on the man and the official tablet.

"Bitter beer," was Madison's remark.

"Well, it's not too surprising," JR said. "We're a big pill to swallow. Parton, BB, stay with Hayes. In case he needs a runner."

"We'll do fine," Hayes said. Hayes had the longer meeting there, and they left him to work out the banking and file the IDs for the several accounts, plus pick up personal cards of several classifications, for those who'd be given the use of them.

There was an electronic download, advisable to read: the local list of prohibitions: prostitution and private sale of pharmaceuticals, sale of unlisted goods, hire of local labor, and offering ship-passage.

Pretty well anything likely to involve a personal transaction with a station resident was illegal on Alpha. Anything ship crew wanted to do with crew of other ships was a ship problem and agreed not to lie within the purview of the EC, except prostitution, inciting a riot, action to deface station property, action to compromise station safety, or display or use of a weapon.

Weapon was defined as edged metal or explosive or anti-personnel device of any sort.

Edged or explosive. That was reasonable enough. No station had ever quite dared to ban the length of small gauge roller chain that some merchanters wore for a belt, some as a bracelet that could become a knuckle-guard, and that most ship crew just kept decorously concealed in a jacket side pocket. Having a handle on said chain was, curious regulation on Viking, banned. Not here, apparently. Or the idea of a handle hadn't proliferated this far.

Which *was* their bar? The information said there were three: Saturn, Critical Mass, and Outbound, each of the three shown on the chart as situated beside one of the three sleepover corridors they had at the Olympian. *Please observe this assignment strictly,* the note said, adding, which was ordinary, *except if escorted by another ship's crew.*

Alpha added: *Your presence in an establishment not assigned above will automatically place you in legal jeopardy in the event of a disturbance. Liability will be assigned quickly and fines will be assessed accordingly.*

It *did* provide a list of establishments arranged by ship assignment, with a diagram.

Convenient. The assignment of bars was not a universal matter. Venture, for instance, didn't care where you drank, but they did hang up festive signs saying *Welcome Finity's End,* or whatever ship was in question, over particular bars. There *were* no welcome signs evident on Alpha, and the frontages they had passed on their way here looked alike, which was *not* convenient.

"Xiao's assigned to Jupiter and Lucky Lily," Madison commented, consulting his com. "We're not sure who Lily is, but it says varied cuisines and free dessert with every meal."

"I'd bet on Lily," JR said. Xiao was a man they needed to see. "If the dessert is decent."

Chapter 2   Section iii

Xiao Min was waiting, having a table in the corner of Lucky Lily's, with a cordon of three *Little Bear* tables around him. A fairly young fellow, Min: JR felt something in common with him. They had Mum, the Xiaos had Grandfather Jun, whose advice, like Mum's, would be somewhere important in any transactions. But Grandfather, very elderly, and disliking the noise of the bars, held court in the Homeport sleepover. Grandfather Xiao Jun had forgotten—or disdained to use—anything but *Little Bear* ship-speak.

Min himself was much more flexible—and they were old allies. *Little Bear* had come in all the way from the Beyond, one of the mid-generation haulers, older than *Finity* by a decade, shiptime, as Min had held his post that much longer.

"Ni hao," JR said, and "Ni hao," Min answered him, followed by a hoist of his glass. "Local beer. Actually not bad."

JR sat down. Cousins Madison and Fletcher did, to courteous nods from Min's company, Ma and Shen.

"Good voyage?" JR asked.

"No problems," Min said. "Easy arrival. The Company was very accommodating, but increasingly curious when *Mumtaz* came in. *Nomad* caused *great* concern."

"You didn't mention we were coming."

Min offered a gentle smile. "Given their nervousness about us, we thought it best not. In retrospect . . . perhaps not the wisest choice. You did make a commotion."

"We didn't want to draw out our approach," JR said. "And we're sure they were taking notes. Hope so, actually.

Nasty little system, this, and best they realize that *before* they destroy their own station with that ship. It didn't break dock. We were very happy about that."

"They would not challenge you," Min said. "*Could* not, in truth, and they are not anxious for you, above all, to know their problems. To date—" Min took a sip of beer. "All *Rights* has done is pulse the vanes, which did prove they work. But there was a shutdown. Auto, according to rumor. Definitely unplanned. They sit in an embarrassing position—can, or cannot; *could* perhaps, but won't risk that ship. The Strip is not sure of the details. Sitting as it does—it is impressive for the locals, perhaps, but—" A lift of the mug. "Should *we* be impressed? We think not. So they sit. And they wish us to think they can move."

"Well, at least they didn't," JR said.

"Have you talked to admin?" Min asked.

"Not yet. I just filled out the forms. You?"

"The same." Min said.

"We cleared our manifests," Xiao Ma said. "We offloaded. *Mumtaz* and *Nomad* are waiting. We have declined cargo, as per agreement. Shippers complain. They fear we wish to drive down prices. We have said nothing, and trust they will turn attention back to their own ships. The economy here is beyond delicate. *Finity* has agitated them greatly."

"The other ships. Particularly those moved off to accommodate us . . ."

"We have given gifts to *Firenze,*" Min said. "We have asked for a meeting."

"We'll try to contact *Qarib,*" Madison said. "Are we ready, then?"

"We have the local ships' attention," Min said. "Not to mention the station offices. Where shall we meet?"

"They've assigned us Saturn, Critical Mass, and Outbound.*" JR said, "the latter with a certain hope, perhaps. Do we have room enough in one of those? Or will we need to divide this up?"

Min smiled a second time and traced a symbol in the water on the tabletop, one of his ship's ornate script. "Let's just say—in Critical Mass. That's a big place, from what I can tell. Just reopened with your arrival. It's near here, near Rosie's, which covers the locals, and not too far a hike from Prosperity, where *Mumtaz* has assignment. *Nomad* shares second shift at Red Star. We can reach one another very easily. Critical Mass has room enough, at least for a first-shift meeting."

His finger retraced the symbol, and this time, JR caught it before it faded:

Caution.

"We're on, then," JR said. "1900 hours. Pass the word."

Chapter 2 Section iv

It was standing room only in Critical Mass. The suggestion had been, in a quiet word or two from the newcomers to Alpha, that there should be a few attendees from each crew, to be respectful of all ships' needs. But anxiety being what it was, and nobody having shut the doors, they had a lot more than a few. *Galway*'s senior captain Niall, Helm 1 Aubrey, and Nav 1 Fallan were there. But so was a cluster of more first-shift and a few of second, including Ross, who'd taken his standing orders to watch over Fallan as excuse enough.

"You," Niall said to Ross, drawing him over to a backless seat forced in next to Fallan. Mary T and Ashlan were there, half-sibs, inseparable, now Longscan 1.2 and Nav 1.2. And there was Pardee, Cargomaster, and Aymes, the purser, who navigated an equally vital set of numbers. They jammed in chairs and stools where they needed, never minding the rails and clamps, and a number of other Galways strayed in around the walls. They weren't the only crew doing it. Facts had been scarce. Rumors were getting crazy, and everybody wanted the straight of it.

Most recent rumor held that *Finity* had information on a jump point to Sol, that Sol was opening up at last, and trade routes were about to change—that was the maybe-good, maybe-bad news that was racing up and down the Strip; but some said no, that it was nothing that good. That coming from Pell, it couldn't be. A lot of people were angry, really angry, that any ship from the Beyond was here, rumored to be holding out on cargo—playing games with the markets, some said, because they *hadn't* offloaded but a fraction of what they could carry, and were buying nothing.

Some said—naïve fools—that Pell was going to make amends with Alpha, that *Finity* brought engineers ready to *help* with *Rights,* and maybe work out deals to better the trade they had.

Fat chance, people said to that hope.

A darker rumor said that Cyteen was starting to play rough with Pell, and that Pell was putting out feelers toward Alpha and *Rights* in hope of checking them.

Good luck there. Alpha couldn't stop Cyteen. Alpha couldn't fix the damn plumbing.

So bets—bets such as optimistic people dared make— hoped like hell for the first rumor to be true: Alpha could not only survive if Earth and Sol opened up, it would thrive. And little ships would live. It'd be change, but they could find a way. That was the hope running the length and breadth of Critical Mass.

Maybe James Robert Neihart was here with that news— that was the fingers-crossed hope, as they all waited for him to show. James Robert Neihart, bit of a dark-haired pretty-boy, reports said, who shunned cameras, but who, at twenty-five, had been handed senior command of the newest, fastest, largest purpose-built yet constructed, by vote of the whole ship's family—*Gaia's* family. When others of the old sublighters had been beached and broken, the families had been broken, too—because the first purpose-builts, like *Firenze, Santiago,* and *Qarib,* hadn't been that large—and families had sadly fractured, even taking different names, over time.

Not the Neiharts. *Finity's End* accommodated all of them with room to spare.

A legend. A friggin' legend. Ship and captain.

1900 sharp. A half minute past, a mixed group came in

and spread out along the wall, behind the bar, happening
to block service. Whatever was going to come down, it was
a sure thing that they weren't all rated "local" to the establishment, and if trouble started, being fairly close to a side
exit wasn't a bad idea.

Following them . . . grey jackets, six of them, entourage
for a young man also in grey, with, bet on it, a ship-patch
unique among all colorful patches. *Finity's* patch was just
a solid black and starless disc, the black of space itself,
claimed by the first and oldest of *all* spacefarers, *Gaia*. Not
even a name displayed.

Arrogance. Absolute, chilling arrogance. There had
been a time Ross had dreamed of being James Robert Neihart. Of having that kind of luck. Now, he could only watch
as that still-youngish man made his way steadily to the center of the room, his only badge of office a captain's gold
collar tab. And God, good-looking to boot.

But not that tall. Shortest man in the set. That was a
little surprising.

The stir of conversation died back, thumped to total
death by a bar mug on the counter.

"Thanks for coming," the young man said. "I'm *Finity's*
senior captain. JR Neihart. This is second-senior Madison.
Helm 1 Jim B. Nav 1 Kate. *Finity* deeply apologizes, first
of all, for the inconvenience to *Firenze* and *Qarib*; and secondly for any concern the high-*V* approach caused. It was
necessary and not something we could explain until we got
here."

"Screw that," someone shouted. "Just tell us *why* you're
here."

JR's face didn't even twitch. "We're here because we're
a Family ship—and we don't want to see Family ships run
out of business. *Any* of them."

"Only threat to our business is three ships an' one monster what doesn't belong here," the same voice shot back.

"*We've* no intention of intruding on your routes. We've
minimal cargo, no more. That's not why we're here. We're
here because we recognize the *shape* of that ship up on A-
mast—a certain design team back on Pell is decidedly *not*
happy, but we could care less about that. Not our problem.

We care about what that ship is *for*. What's *its* purpose here?"

"Ballast?" came from Ross's right, and someone gave a snort.

If JR Neihart heard, he didn't show it. "We've got bets on whether we could find our way around those corridors without a map; and odds are on it being more than a little different inside. Won't have a kids' loft, that doesn't even get odds. Won't need one. They've crewed it with hire-ons, not Family. Crew will come and go as the *Company* pleases. The Company expects they'll train station-born crew in one voyage and a few sims."

"Tell us something we *don't* know, ye damned big shot!" That was from somewhere behind, with the thump of a beer mug. The accent was *Santiago*.

JR Neihart's eyes flicked that way, sharp and quick.

"All right. Try this. If that ship *is* planning to trade, no matter who crews her, she's doomed before she starts. First, she *doesn't* have the bow we have that lets us ring-dock, which means the math is against her, regarding cargo. A big hold takes time to load and unload. Canisters make it fast. A lot faster. Only four stations still use mast docking, and you see what extreme measures Alpha— compliments to Alpha's *excellent* chief of ops—had to take to accommodate *Finity*. We also had one of our best people handling docking, a senior-senior in charge who learned on a reconfigured pusher. *Gaia*. I leave it to your seniors to imagine what havoc a novice crew might have caused. And note that most stations will *not* be ready to risk receiving that kind of mass on a mast-end, especially a ship with a bridge full of trainees."

That caused a murmur, and JR Neihart gave it a moment before continuing. "Secondly, *if* they're planning to fill that cargo bay and trade, they're also doomed. Canister racks are the only way to safely stow cans in a cargo space of our size . . . and for canisters, you *need* the ring-dock. *Finity* and her cousin *Dublin* are *why* ring-docking was designed, and why it has become the rule in the Beyond. It's efficient, it's safe . . . and there *are* smaller canisters that a regular cargo hold can accommodate without racks.

There's plenty of cargo that needs pushing or hauling, enough for all the ships in service."

"Doesn't do *us* damn all good if we can't link up to the station." It was no more than a mutter, but this time Neihart's eyes flicked toward the perpetrator.

"Contrary to rumor, a ring-dock *can* accommodate smaller ships with a regular linkup with no problem."

That was a revelation. A really hopeful one, and helluva-alot more interesting than what he'd been saying about *Rights*. With Venture shifting over to the ring-dock, it had been a serious concern.

"It's a matter of an adapting mechanism for all of your ships. The details I'm sure have downloaded in the box-feed. You'll be using it eventually at Venture. But installing the canister adaptation on that ship out on A-mast would require an overhaul, a complete change in cargo config— assuming it has such. The larger canisters can't be loaded manually, and require mechanisms inside the hold. *You* don't need the loading machinery for smaller ships. Just the smaller canisters."

"*How* small?" somebody called out and someone else: "That's his bad back askin'."

"Controlled-environment cans that stand no taller than that doorway, and fit a regular hold."

Another great bit of news. Controlled-environment cargo . . . inside the regular cargo hold?

Damn.

"As for your back . . ." A hint of a smile broke through Neihart's somber expression. "A ship at Mariner rigged a cradle out of chain and lock-plates. Seems to work on half-and quarter-cans. A manufacturer at Pell is planning reusable cans that'll fit a five-by-five cargo lock."

There was a general buzz at that and again, Neihart gave it time to sink in. The rumors had them facing obsolescence and ruin. But some little ship out there had bodged a fix—just . . . figured a solution to slinging those canisters about using stuff every ship carried. They'd bodged it, the way ships bodged regular things, the way people just coped with a problem when they had to with whatever they had lying around. It was in the best tradition.

And if stations upstream were actively accommodating little ships, actually seeking ways to bridge the gap between big and small rather than catering entirely to the *Finitys* of the universe . . . God, it was an escape hatch in what they'd thought an absolute wall.

If *Galway* could get that adapter, if a makeshift rig was *that* easy done, Ross thought, and then: God, *was* it that easy? What *wasn't* this fancy captain telling them? This man whose ship-cred could buy every Alpha ship in dock and still take his crew out for dinner without feeling a moment's pain—what did *he* gain?

Damn, he'd come in here resolved not to buy what JR Neihart was selling. His attack on *Rights* had been pretty much as expected, but now . . . damn. His stomach was upset. And Neihart, damn him, had seen that attack wasn't working. He'd shifted his sales pitch over to the canisters, to the concerns he knew damn good and well they all had. Con job, maybe . . . telling them they had a future

"But there's a serious problem in that idea," Neihart said. "And that problem's sitting up there on A-mast. Look at our ship's outline, the size of our hold. That ship's hold space is way under what it could be. Its personnel ring is way over. That's a ship that's not designed for cargo. A ship that's drained Alpha of resources. A ship that's *owned* by the Company. And some think cargo-handling isn't its objective."

There was utter, cold silence. You didn't say bad things about the EC. It wasn't against the law, but it just wasn't smart. The blue-coats monitored the Strip for trouble, and you didn't want to sound like trouble.

There were a lot of people here. Station didn't like overflow crowds in places even when everybody was in a good mood. Any minute, the blue-coats would be showing up.

And station would be noting which crews were in the forefront.

"So what are you sayin', Finity?" A shout from the table ahead, from Julio Rodriguez, who rose halfway out of his seat. "You came all this way . . . four of you . . . to reassure your shit-poor cousins? Is it *Pell* talkin'? They tryin' to get us to desert Alpha and go kiss Konstantin ass? Well, screw you!"

"No, sir! Not Pell. We don't endorse *any* station—or the EC—controlling any ship. We contend that the EC shouldn't *own* a merchant ship. It hasn't been so from the beginning—that was the whole point behind *Gaia's* refusal to stand down after the first voyage—and it shouldn't be so now. Trade is our realm now. It's your realm . . . not the EC's. The EC hasn't given a damn about the stations out here. They haven't sent resources to maintain Glory or Alpha or Venture. They could have. Pusher loads could have handled it. But instead, they've built that ship. They could have helped you maintain your ships. But they haven't. They've built that ship, and built it with limited capacity for trade. So what is it for? And how does it serve you?"

"Bullshit, Finity. What's it to you?"

A single dark brow lifted. "You're Family. Family ships matter. The trust and the trade our ships have built up with the stations are both at issue. The EC intends to go into competition with Family ships? We say no."

There was another buzz, longer this time, and again JR Neihart let it run its course.

Rodriguez straightened. "You said 'we.' So who are you speaking for?"

"For *Finity's End*."

"For *Little Bear*," a dark-haired man said. And: "For *Mumtaz*," a hawk-faced man said. And a dark-skinned woman, "For *Nomad*."

"You're outsiders!"

"Are we?" Neihart asked. *"Captain* Rodriguez, do I have the honor?"

"You do, sir. And it's a question we want answered. *Need* answered, before this goes any further. If not outsiders, you who trade in volumes we can't even imagine . . . even the smallest of you . . . what are you? What do you *remotely* have in common with us?"

"Fair question." Neihart gave a deep nod, and Julio Rodriguez raised his chin, mouth hard. "Not as much as we once did and not nearly as much as we hope to have in the future."

Rodriguez opened his mouth, and Neihart raised a hand. "Bear with me, just for now. 'We' is *not* Pell, or Cyteen or any other station. 'We' are—as of now—some forty-six of sixty-three families like your own, hoping to make that sixty-three of sixty-three, including the ones operating past Pell, where we also have Families out getting signatures. Old Families. Ship Families. Families that may have sub-divided and spread out through space, but who remain part of the original twelve Families that have served the star stations through all the shifts and changes, and who have been *loyal* to a set of principles that have served all inter-ests out here for generation after generation. One of those principles, the absolute most basic, is *ownership.*"

Julio Rodriguez's head tipped, his eyes narrowed.

"From the beginning, we've served all interests," Nei-hart said, "but these days the only ones looking out for *our* interests . . . is ourselves. The stations can't do it. The EC *certainly* won't do it. Thus far, those of us serving beyond Pell have maintained our rights to independent ownership against two very powerful interests."

"Easy to say when your ship isn't mortgaged to the hilt."

"And why is that?"

"You know damn good and well why."

"Lack of cargo from Sol is only part of the problem. Time was, no ship ever went into debt. Time was ships hauled necessities between stations and in return the sta-tions took care of them, kept the systems and equipment up to date and *gave* the crew a place to stay when they were in port . . . but we no longer deal in that simple economy. Now there's credit. Now ships have books to balance, and they pay stations for services. Alpha still covers your re-pairs, as they did in the past, but those repairs happen at the station's priority, not yours, and they charge you dock-ing fees and for food and bed when you're forced to layover for mechanicals. In the Beyond, we pay not only for lay-over, but for the repairs themselves. Our cargo comes out of station-credit at one end and goes into it at the other. We are completely independent. That's the reality of modern economics. We forty-six *respect* your efforts to maintain your pride and independence in a difficult situation, but we fear for your future—and our own, thanks to that A-mast ship and what it implies about the EC's view of the future."

Another muttering interruption. Dangerously close to opinions you just *didn't* have, not on Alpha.

And this time, Neihart didn't wait for it to die down.

"We have indeed had the advantage in this new economy. More, perhaps, than you realize. Beyond the fact that we have two bio-rich planets in our FTL routes, beyond the fact we have several mineral-rich systems with thriving stations, beyond the fact that the tech keeps evolving and Alpha has never brought your ships into compliance with the new standards . . . beyond those obvious advantages, there's the fact that *we* deal directly with the decision-makers of the stations we serve. Thanks to that ongoing dialogue, they understand that their prosperity is directly linked to ours. The better our ships, the faster our turnaround, the more trade they have with the other stations and the more money they make. *You* have not had that ability. Your stationmaster does what he has resources to do. But the decision-makers that affect your livelihood, who decree the fate of the stations you keep alive, have sat at Sol, untouchable, out of reach, issuing out-of-date orders that make no more sense now than they ever have. They don't care about keeping your ships current, they don't care about sending enough product to keep trade with the other First Stars healthy and your books in the black. They only care, as they always have, about their *projects.* Their current *project* has shut down Galileo Station, shut down Thule—thereby cutting your routes in half—and brought extreme hardship on the rest of the First Stars, which were never gifted with the resources this construction has demanded, and who have depended on shipments from Sol for simple survival . . . shipments which have now given way to the demands of that ship. And without cargo to carry, without the tech upgrades the old agreements once promised you, your ships are doomed."

"Dammit," Rodriguez said, turning to go, "this is bullshit. I'm out of—"

"*Unless* you get help."

Rodriguez froze. Turned. "Help! From *where?*"

"Not from Alpha. Unlike Pell and all the other stations in the Beyond, stations that were built without EC endorsement and who have long since denied the EC any say over their operations, the First Stations have no choice but to follow EC directives and accept EC personnel. Your station here can't help you, because the EC tells your station director how to spend his resources, and the EC has other priorities."

Chilling statement. Dangerous. And true. Julio Rodriguez sank slowly back into his chair beside his brother.

"And you'd get no more help out of Pell or Cyteen, either," Neihart said. "Not unless, yes, you defected to their routes, and then you'd be competing with each other for their attention *and* still having to pay the bills. Even if they did agree to a refit, you'd be generations paying off the debt. They simply don't care. Out there, stations think of other stations as potential markets—numbers, not people. And our ships are simply a means to transport product to those markets. All they get from Alpha is luxury goods passed on from Earth, which they can easily live without. And in recent years, with even those luxury goods cut off, they rarely think of Alpha at all, let alone Glory or Bryant's. They *do* worry about Sol. They worry about the EC trying to come in and take over administration once Sol finds a route. And that ship up there looks to them like there might be a plan to make that takeover happen with or without that route. They *really* worry about Sol *or* Alpha getting desperate enough to make a run through Proxima, risking all the bad luck that star harbors just to get an FTL link to *their* stations. The bitter reality is, all the stations in the Beyond would just as soon all the stations this side of Venture would fail, leaving Sol, when it does break out, whether through Proxima or some as yet unmapped jump point to Alpha, a scarcity of bases to bridge the gap to the farther stations."

Which meant their dream, the future every Alpha spacer had invested their lives in . . . was the nightmare of all those stations beyond Venture. It was a pretty good summation of bleak reality.

Nobody raised an argument.

"That's what the *stations* out there think about your stations. For you and your ships . . . If asked, they'd probably

like to entice you into trade with *them,* but the motivation
would be to leave the First Stars to rot. And as I've already
mentioned, to get remotely competitive out there, where
the stars are farther apart, the jumps longer . . . you'd have
no choice but to get a complete overhaul . . . which for some
of you still wouldn't be enough. Without a modern purpose-
built ship, you'd go bankrupt, and the stations wouldn't
even notice. You ask if we speak *for* Pell. No. But we've
spoken *to* Pell, to Cyteen, to Mariner and Viking and Venture, with one conclusion: we all have a problem and that
the problem lies up there on A-mast: a massive ship that's
taking hire-on crew. The stations' position is that that ship
may be designed *not* to carry cargo, but EC enforcement
personnel. That's where their concern lies. The forty-six
Families' position is that, if it's trading, if it's hauling cargo,
a Family, maybe a consortium of Families, should get it."

"The hell," someone said—a Firenze. "*I* don't want it!
Built by Alpha repair shops from a stolen blueprint? She
can't even get out of system!"

"Who do you think *should* run it?" someone else
shouted. "You already said our routes are only good for
scrubs like us. You got another big Family out there itching
for an upgrade, to take what this station has gone bust tryin' to build?"

Neihart lifted a calm hand. "You're Alpha merchanters.
You should have *Rights*. In every sense. *You* should own
her. . . . If it's a merchant ship."

The whole room fell silent. Ross propped his chin on his
hand, trying not to make a fist. The Neihart captain's proposition was an event horizon. Believe it even a little, and
you slipped right over the edge into a whole lot of trouble.

"They won't do that." That was *Firenze*'s captain,
Giovanna Galli. "Ever."

"You deserve a lot better than you're getting," Neihart
said.

"You can tell Pell and your friends not to worry. That
ship won't survive jump," *Qarib* helm called out. "We let
those sim-trained fools shadow our boards on a milk-run.
They're hopeless. They parked the ship in the core of

Bryant's Star—thanks be to God that that was *not* the board that brought us in."

Neihart said quietly, "The first FTL crew was sim-trained."

"Scary damned business, too," Fallan muttered, in Ross's hearing. "But yeah, they sure were."

"Aurora," JR Neihart said. "First FTL. Following the robot probe. Cloned-men running her, monofocused, cold as machines themselves. But give 'em credit, Cyteen did it. Right down the path the probe pioneered. And if they'd popped into Mariner's sun on that first run, I'm sure Cyteen had backups ready. They'd have tried again, until they got it right. For all anyone knows, the ship that made it *wasn't* the first to try."

Cloned-men. Infallible procedure. Infallible memory. Azi.

"But I'll tell you something," Neihart said then. "With all their money, with all their resources, Cyteen *didn't* go on to create a merchant fleet of their own, never even thought of competing with us. Cyteen decided it was smarter, politically and economically, to convert the pushers and let the Families do what they've done for centuries now, sim-training for the FTLs during the stand-down for build, but *with* the background of generations of experience, and *trading* with every station regardless of politics. *Even Cyteen* respects the Families. *Even Cyteen* understands the economy of doing that. The purpose-builts at Cyteen, at Pell, at Venture have *all* been handed over to the Families, asking only a certain loyalty—but not exclusivity. *Exactly* the contract between the first pushers and their star-stations and Sol. The stations maintain, the stations supply, the *ships* carry goods. Alpha used to *honor* her ships and take pride in their upkeep . . . but what's Alpha done for you lately?"

"Don't blame Abrezio!" someone said. *"He* didn't decide on that ship up there."

Damn, Ross thought. Don't say it. Don't blame the EC and bring the blue-coats in.

"No . . . he didn't," Neihart said. "As always, Alpha's fate was in the hands of whatever committee on Earth thought it made sense to build *Rights*. Some committee decided to build a ship that *could* have given you one long-hauler and made trade with the Beyond viable, that *could* have made one or more ship Families wealthy ... then they gave it a minimum of cargo room, turned it over to a bunch of sim-trained stationers? Take a look at our ship, which *is* a merchanter. Take a look at *Rights'* design. I'm telling you, *Rights* was never meant for cargo, never meant for a Family. Never meant for commerce."

Someone from the door shouted: "That what your crystal ball says?"

Julio Hernandez lifted a silencing hand. "Known fact, Finity? Or speculation?"

"Have I been inside her? Have I seen orders? No. But history and what we do know are more than enough for concern. Fact: the First Stars have an economic problem that reflects clear back to Sol. Fact: the EC has been bleeding funds into the First Stars for centuries. They can't be happy about that."

"The First Stars," Galli said. "That's not what you call us. That's not what the Farther Stars call us. They call us the Hinder Stars. They call themselves the Beyond. Beyond *us*. Beyond any care of us."

"You're *right,*" Neihart said, again not what anybody expected. "You're absolutely right. They don't care. But fact is, you *and* the Beyond have a joint problem. You think your problems will be solved when Sol breaks out. That you'll have direct access to the Sol market. Become the ships that ply the Sol-Alpha route, bringing Sol goods back into the market with a vengeance. But that's not likely, is it? Not with what's building up there on A-mast. Not with the precedent it sets and with Sol sitting on who knows how many more, some of which likely *are* designed for cargo."

There was quiet, deathly quiet.

"The EC really only has two—peaceful—choices at this point," Neihart said. "And you tell me which is likely. If they're going to maintain the control they've always claimed was theirs by right of original construction—they can break out in force, with station-born crews, to reach the profitable stars, to bypass their loyal ships and hand those lucrative routes over to hired crew, with the vast bulk of profit going straight into the EC coffers . . . or they can cut the cord, relinquish all control, and let Alpha link up to Pell. I *wonder* which one they have in mind."

It was a cold, cold picture *Finity's* captain painted. There was a thin murmur of comment throughout the bar, crew talking among themselves.

"If the EC finds the jump points, if they manage to sim-train crews . . . what are the odds they're going to give a damn then about the futures of all of you? The question, of course, is who *does* own the ships and stations? And more to the point . . . *who* has the right to ply the trade routes?"

Damn, Ross thought. There was no question of a station having its own ships, let alone using the power of a planet to back some esoteric interest. He'd never personally thought too much into *Galway's* future. It had never looked that good, where things were going, unless Sol *did* break through and make Alpha the gateway Alpha had been, back in the pusher days. They had a lot to gain from that—he'd always thought.

Things would be good when that happened, he'd always thought. He believed it, at his most optimistic. If not for him, then for his children. Or grandchildren.

But what if Neihart was right? What if, back at Sol, the EC was building a whole fleet of these mega-ships designed to enter the market and out-compete smaller ships, the moment that FTL future arrived?

"You think they'd do that?" he said quietly to Fallan. "You think they'd pay us off like that?"

"Ross, lad, the man's sayin' somethin' true."

Ross turned back to Neihart just as Neihart's gaze passed over him. He'd swear it paused for an instant on Fallan—maybe knowing what Fallan was, or who he was.

"There's a memory on *Finity*," Neihart said, just before his gaze moved on, "passed down from *Gaia's* first run, a story you probably know. *Gaia's* crew had just made the first-ever manned mission to another star, pushing the core of what would become Alpha Station, a core built at Sol to be ready to go into operation the instant it was put into orbit around the star. *Gaia's* first crew *founded* this station.

They coined the term pusher-ship. And when they got back to Sol, there was a crew trained and waiting to take over *Gaia*. It wasn't a surprise. They knew Sol intended to hand *Gaia* to another crew, and have that first *Gaia* crew live out their lives on Earth, as heroes, of course, supported by all of Earth. Earth and Sol Station thought that was a fine and proper thing to do. But by the time they got back, the crew had different notions. The crew had gotten out of sync with Earth-time. They'd spent all those years as alone as crew could be, connected to Sol by the Stream, communications always years out of date, but connected to each other aboard in a closeness that had become family. There'd been no way to anticipate how the trip would change them. So *Gaia*'s first crew said no. There'd be no change of crew. They wouldn't even open the hatch until there was an agreement that *Gaia* belonged to her crew forever. She swore she'd go where Sol needed, haul whatever cargo Sol gave them, but she'd make her own law and solve her own problems. And when Sol tried to talk them out of that ownership clause, when Sol talked about money, and rewards, *Gaia*'s crew insisted that all they wanted was provision and maintenance for *their* ship, to be kept up to whatever the technical standard would become, and to set out again. And Sol *agreed*. *That* was the compact Sol made with the first deep spacers.

"The pushers that followed all asked no more, no less— because they all discovered the same truth: our ships are home. And by the time those first few trips are made we're fundamentally different, differences that grow with each passing generation—time lag fits us into our own universe, our own sense of what's important. Not as fast now as in the days of the pushers, but we're still fundamentally *different* from stationers. And . . . something those of us who serve the Beyond have realized . . . we're *valuable*. Ship-born Families know things. We know how to trade with stations that aren't like each other, and that, plainly, *don't* like each other much. How do we do that? We do that by being—best case scenario—sixty-three Families that trade honestly and don't give a damn whether our next port of call likes our last one. We've had to make a forceful point of it now and again, but we maintain that principle, and so do you. We don't give a damn about stationer quarrels—and stations' accepting that fact has created peaceful commerce. It means you don't have a Cyteen mega-ship pushing in at, say, Venture, using the power of a planet to play havoc with the market there. We don't have some fuss between Cyteen crew and Mariner crew touching off some corporation on Pell. *Peace* exists because stations can't touch each other, except through us, and *we* don't take sides.

"Stationers can be as weird and as different as they like. They can have their quarrels. The Families have very simple interests: the safety of our ships, *ownership* of our ships, our freedom to go where and when we decide to go—and the *peace* we enforce simply by the exercise of our freedom."

Peace—existing *because* of the ships. That was a strange way of looking at a ship's function. Peace wasn't an issue, here in the First Stars . . .

He thought of that ship on A-mast.

Yet.

"The EC," Neihart said, "has *never* grasped the situation out here. The EC hasn't figured out that you here today, the very Families that have kept their stations alive, are on the verge of economic ruin. They don't see that their program has worked incredible hardship on this station—but more to the point, they're not set up to care. They answer to their member corporations. They promise things they can't deliver, but they can pass the blame out here and nobody back on Earth can check the facts. If they had good sense, if they gave a *damn* about the people living on the stations they *claim* they own, they'd have built more pushers. They'd have sent out probes seeking jump points. They'd have poured all their resources into repairing and modernizing *your* ships, to expand Alpha's commerce, to compete in the Beyond, to *join* the trade rather than try to dictate its future. They could have done all that. But they haven't. Why? Because they're obsessed with control. Never mind the fact they don't own Pell or any of the stations beyond, not even by their own definitions. The last core built at Sol was Venture's. They actually don't own

Venture anymore, but they haven't figured that out yet. For reasons which are frankly beyond my personal ability to understand, they evidently can't comprehend that they could have a profitable trade with Pell and the Beyond— once they get there—if only they'd give up this notion that everything in space *belongs* to them. Even now there's no damn reason that four more pushers, even before they find a viable FTL route, couldn't bring Sol peaceably and profitably into commerce for which Alpha could be the gateway. A constant stream of Sol exotics could revitalize these oldest stations."

God, Ross thought, how many times had *that* come up during his lifetime? Two ships. Two shipments. Ten damn years apart. Even without the diversion of those shipments to *Rights*, what they'd carried historically to Venture didn't *begin* to compete in the market *Finity* implied was arising out beyond Venture. With four more pushers . . . ten, twenty, coming in a year apart . . .

"They can't seem to grasp why, if Alpha merchanters *had* a longhauler that worked, they'd be welcome at Pell, welcome at Cyteen, that they'd be *welcome* in the trade. The obvious answer to the problem, if somehow the EC could be made to understand it, is to hand *Rights* over to the Rodriguezes, or the Monahans, or the Gallis or the Rahmans, who could actually run her—once they put a meaningful cargo hold on her. *If* we were able to make that clear, *if* we were able to make them understand—but they've never listened, never truly tried to understand."

The bar had gotten quiet, and into that silence, James Robert said quietly:

"We need the power to make them listen."

Now a solid murmur broke out at every table, and Ross, with Fallan and Niall near him—tried to keep silent. To listen. To not get caught up in the rampant speculation, the growing lists of pros and cons and what-the-hell's-Finity-saying?

He was bridge crew, youngest, not quite seated, but bridge crew. He was supposed to maintain a steady calm— but he didn't feel calm. He looked at JR Neihart with no less envy—but now with questions roiling in him that were answerless, because no matter the answers station could offer, so long as that ship was being built as she was, there were just—no choices. No other place to be. No other rules available. No other future.

Alpha spacers had been hanging on for years, taking what they could get, and knowing that the whole system of trade was changing, and knowing, *knowing* that station couldn't bring them into that new era with *Rights* sucking up every resource. Year after year, from when he'd been a junior-junior, they'd been building that ship. All the funds, all the materials pushed out from Sol or brought in from Bryant's went to *Rights*. Alpha crews had muttered at it, sworn at *Rights* from time to time, laughed at *Rights* when it made its aborted run. They'd had dark thoughts that Abrezio must be lining his pockets in the process—but where could he go to spend it all? There was certainly no visible evidence of luxury living. They passed from anger at Abrezio to anger at the managers Sol sent them.

That *Rights* and her hire-on crew would perform as advertised to do—nobody believed that any longer. They'd *seen* how well sim-training worked. They'd heard how her crew had failed on *Qarib*.

And yet, JR reminded them, the first FTL crews had *all* been sim-trained, human beings, even if they were azi. The real breakthrough was the tech itself. Using that tech . . . If you were willing to lose multiple ships and lose multiple crews, you could figure it out. Eventually.

Expendable people. Limitless resources. The only place other than Cyteen that had truly unlimited resources— including people—was Sol system.

JR was right: it was crazy that *Rights* should be this kind of priority at Alpha . . . unless there was some plan the EC wasn't talking about, like Sol being close to *making* the breakout people had been speculating on forever. Maybe it *was* trying. Maybe they were desperate enough they could send an endless stream of ships until one got through . . .

And there was that other point he'd made, the same observation Fallon had made only hours ago: blue-coats *were* in greater and greater evidence on the Strip, markedly so in the last few sleepovers. How many? How many had been hired and trained to fill a ship not designed for cargo? They had no idea. But if *Rights* did get to Bryant's, if it moved to try to lay down EC law in some station Pell-ward of here, there was sure to be trouble.

Peace, JR had said, existed *because* the Families were the buffer.

Peace . . . existed *because* . . .

Red flashers started rotating in the ceiling.

Somebody banged a mug on the bar hard, repeatedly, and a Santiago jumped up atop the bar, scrambling to her feet, shouting, "EC's shutting us down! Blue-coats! They're shutting the doors!"

"The hell!" somebody up front shouted. "They got *no* right!"

"Stow the chains!"

"Run for it!" It was a *Galway* voice, Pardee's, and nerves reacted—Ross found himself moving. Niall and Fallan and the rest moved—*no* blue-coat was going to lay hands on critical crew of *any* ship. Niall led the way to the fire door.

Santiago crew came over the row of tables from the front, eight of them, cutting them off, and then jammed up in the aisle as others did the same. Ross left Mary T and Ashlan, went over the next table, knocking two beer mugs to the floor as he went, but a press of bodies blocked that row, too, half the red-dyed, overcrowded room all trying for the side exit, and by now the klaxon sounded: doors were closing, mechanical, unstoppable.

"Well, this is a mess." Ross turned to Mary T and Ashlan, on the other side of the table. Mary T was holding her arm, looking pained. "You all right, Mary?"

"I'll live."

The doors had all shut, trapping a good many people in the bar. Niall and Fallan and Pardee had got out.

Some, however, hadn't even tried for the doors. JR Neihart was up at the bar with a number of *Finity* crew. The two bartenders and the wait staff were there. So were a number of other outsiders, one with a captain's gold tabs, another with the compass rose and 1 of a first-seat navigator. Then there was a straggle of Santiagos, several Qaribs, and a handful of Firenzes, people Ross knew at least by sight.

The frenzy was over. Everyone stranded inside was calm, quiet. Usually the doors would have re-opened by now, at least one door would, and the blue-coats would be taking names. The doors stayed shut.

Which made him wonder what was happening on the far side of the doors.

"Kettle of fish he's raised," Ashlan said. "Station's upset."

And Station had been listening to it all, Every word. Of course it had.

The shouting had died down to angry cursing. He looked to where *Galway* crew had been seated.

"Niall and Fallan got out," Ross said, looking around. "So did Pardee and Aymes and Aubrey, looks like. God, what a mess."

"It wasn't illegal," Ashlan said. "It wasn't illegal, our being here."

It was a question: What could station make of it? Fomenting a riot, if station really wanted to make an issue.

But putting them in one bucket with the outsiders?

Could get damned ugly on the Strip, if they lumped Alpha crews into the Neiharts' actions.

"They're sure taking their time," Mary T said.

Wasn't the first bar raid for any of them. It happened. Station could be touchy. Usually there was a write-up, sometimes a fine. Usually bystanders got out of it.

Laying a hefty fine on the outsiders alone, however, might not be what station wanted to do.

Several minutes went by and still there was no move to open the doors.

"We could have more than the usual trouble, here," Ashlan said.

"Well, hell with it," Ross said. There was one group intact, over by the bar.

Finity hadn't run. *Finity's* two senior-most captains and several of her seated crew were calmly ordering drinks, as the red lights kept flashing, which meant it was clearly against the law to serve alcohol. But the bartenders of Critical Mass were quietly drawing beers, and food was arriving from the back. A woman who'd sat on the bar, perhaps for refuge, slid down behind, and got a bottle of wine out of cold storage.

Well, that was a few more regulations the meeting was breaking

"What are we going to do?" Ashlan asked. "Ross?"

Ross shrugged. "Don't know where's more interesting now, out on the Strip or in here. Looks like the bar's still functional. And they're serving. Hell, if they arrest us, at least the company will be interesting. Wait it out. See what happens. All we can do."

Mumtaz and *Little Bear* captains joined *Finity's*. *Nomad's* captain had made it out the fire door. So had all the Galways present, except the three of them. There were maybe fifteen, twenty of the Mumtazes, five or so of the Little Bears, and a few of the Nomads. The talk was all casual, nothing of outrage, nothing against the administration.

Took a while for the lights to go back to normal, and a few minutes more for the main door to open, letting in a good seven or eight blue-coats with tasers at the ready.

But by that time everybody was seated, with drinks, a few of the *Finity* crew peacefully playing cards, while the officers stood and chatted.

Chapter 3   Section i

If *ever* there'd been a wrong man for a job . . .

Ben Abrezio resisted the temptation to call civil security and remove Enzio Hewitt from *any* authority involving the Strip, for actions contributory to a riot. A demotion, however, would break the Cruz-Hewitt problem wide open, would be a decade-long issue thrashed out in communication with Sol, and, Hewitt being the later appointee, Hewitt was the one who *might* still have his backers in office.

It would be stupid to do it—but, *damn*, it would feel good.

There were cameras in the Strip's bars, shops, and hotel hallways that automatically cut on—for safety and legal purposes—in event of an emergency, such as a takehold order . . . or a mandatory securing of an area. The cameras and microphones in Critical Mass had recorded everything, and what that footage told anyone, *anyone* with the slightest understanding of the situation, was that the police raid on the meeting in Critical Mass had been a questionable call. *Highly* questionable. Not so much as a hint of violence had come from the assembly. No advocacy of violence.

Now, thanks to Hewitt's order, they had twenty-four individuals detained as participatory in or inciting a riot, and numbers still accumulating for the injured. Unfortunately, as that vid clearly showed, the meeting had been, if not exactly quiet, orderly and *completely* legal until security, Bellamy Jameson, formerly head of all Alpha security and now under Hewitt's command on the Strip—had flashed the emergency warning and decided to move in, at which time spacers, already on edge, already distrustful of station security under Hewitt's rules . . . reacted.

Two agents had been shoved to the ground and trampled in the side-exit, one with a concussion, and then, masterpiece of planning, Jameson had locked the bar down entirely for three-quarters of an hour, causing even more trouble dockside, as irate Alpha spacers argued with the police and tried to rescue their fellows trapped inside.

Maybe, *maybe* Jameson had been smart to focus outrage on those locked doors rather than have a traveling disturbance hit the Strip and gather force as it moved from bar to bar, but if security hadn't raided the meeting in the first place it wouldn't have been an issue. He suspected, knowing Jameson, that he'd had a choice in one but not the other. Hewitt had ordered him to move in and he'd done what he could to save a damned mess. Fortunately— thanks, perhaps, to Jameson—they had *not* had a spacer riot on their hands. Inside, as the footage showed, *Finity's* crew had set the tone. Those locked in had relaxed, quieted down, and by the time the doors opened, the people in Crit Mass had been surprisingly cooperative.

Abrezio didn't trust the calm that currently lay over the Strip. Not in the least. Hewitt had started something that could flare up again without warning, and he, Ben Abrezio, had to make certain it didn't.

Damn Hewitt, who was currently, conveniently, *unavailable.* They had Captain James Robert Neihart and crew, backed by Xiao Min, Asha Druv and Sanjay Patel, all madder than hell, *with* an issue, and they had local ships with personnel in lockup that didn't damned well belong there. Adding to the debacle—that firedoor net had caught local captains Giovanna Galli, Diego Rodriguez, and Niall Monahan, also madder than hell, and worst of all, unjustified use of force had injured no few spacers, one of them elderly, as some fool had tased Galli's fourth-shift helmsman and caused a pile up right in the doorway.

Hewitt and his high-handed security rules *needed* to be put on the next pusher back to his beloved, oh-so-superior Sol-station. God . . . didn't he wish?

Was there *any* justification? *Could* the meeting have

broken up in riot? That hadn't been *anywhere* suggested in anything JR Neihart had said, never mind he'd implied a hell of a lot more that wasn't to Abrezio's personal liking. But there'd been nothing—absolutely nothing—actionable, however uncomplimentary to the Company . . . which did *not* administer Pell, which was *Finity's* port of registry, and by tradition, *Finity's* rules applied inside that bar—so long as there was no abuse of person or bar property.

Fact was, these ships were outsiders, allowed to dock here, as of course they had to be: a station had never refused docking. Fact also was, Critical Mass was under *Finity's* rules. Fact might be that *Finity* had abused traditional courtesy, that *Finity* had assembled allies and made fairly inflammatory statements to Alpha's local haulers, but it wasn't illegal unless it caused illegal action—which it had not . . . yet.

Did it warrant careful monitoring? Yes. Did it warrant lockdown? No, dammit. And now *he* was in the position of having to explain the mess to their elite visitors.

Annoying truth: the calmest, most dignified of the lot had been *Finity's* crew. Untouchable, at least in their own minds. Hewitt's office had objected to his order to Jameson to stand down, to release the locks and just get names and statements, and *not* to arrest anybody in the bar. Offenses, Hewitt's office insisted, had been committed, laws had been broken. And Hewitt's policy trumped *Finity's* rules.

According to Hewitt's office, Hewitt himself being . . . unavailable.

Arguable, to say the least, but more to the point . . . did you charge spacers who'd sat fairly quietly through a now-notorious and inflammatory speech, a bar raid, and the tasing of seated crew—with quietly sitting and drinking alcohol under a lockdown? They hadn't been drunk. And while it was illegal to *serve* alcohol under those conditions, it was not chargeable against the spacers; it was against the bar owner, who also had a legal responsibility to judge a situation and apply prudent measures.

Spacers had a keen sense of the ridiculous. And this was way over their tolerance. If he'd allowed Jameson to do as Hewitt had ordered, had he had Jameson issue those cita-

tions against the spacers who were remaining calm inside
a bar under siege . . . he'd have a real uprising on his hands.

So what did he do? Fire Jameson? *Jameson's* emergency
text had been his only warning about Hewitt's order to
move in and arrest those remaining in the bar. Jameson
had practically begged him to countermand that order.
Jameson was his own appointee. Jameson had been, pre-
Hewitt, a decent and compassionate officer. And when the
time came to challenge Hewitt, *if* it came, he'd need a lot
more reason than a hazy call on a bar fight, and Jameson
was his best bet as an inside witness who might be on *his*
side.

So . . . what? Apologize to *Finity* and their allies? That
might quiet the noise on the Strip, but locally, among Alpha's permanent residents, Jameson's hard line with the
supposed threat of riot was already playing well. Somehow,
though stationers had no access to the security files, *somebody* had released vid to the news, vid showing the chaos
outside Crit Mass, vid focused on the injured security officers and entirely missing the grey-haired, frail old man
now being treated in the infirmary. Thanks to that vid, station sentiment would call Jameson a hero, and Hewitt
would take full advantage of it.

Not exactly a stretch to figure who'd sent that carefully
edited vid.

But the impression had been made and strong police
action made citizens feel safe. It advised drunken spacers
that rules were rules, and kept problems on the Strip from
exiting the Strip.

Regardless, the Stationmaster's job was to smooth out
the messes others dropped in his lap.

Apologizing to *Finity* and their lot might read as good
politics on the Strip *if* he stood Bellamy Jameson down at
least long enough to get the problem visitors on their way
and clear of Alpha, but that didn't put the blame where it
was due. Explain the situation privately to the outsiders?
Hell if he wanted to admit the massive problems lurking
beneath the surface in Alpha station admin. Whatever he
did now, Hewitt would make the most of it. Lose, lose. For
the sake of the permanent citizens' peace of mind, he had

no choice but to back Jameson. Didn't mean he couldn't let Jameson know, privately, that he was not happy and that *he* wanted a call involving any unrest on the Strip, no matter the hour and no matter what Hewitt ordered.

Before any action was taken.

Most frustrating of all, after all was said and done, that speech of Neihart's *still* didn't answer what in hell *Finity* was really up to. It wasn't casual blather about spacer rights that had *Finity* calling a formal meeting with other crews, talking about ownership of ships, and stations' obligations to repair whatever broke down.

And—*dammit*—where in *hell* did *Finity's End* come off saying Alpha should do more than any station of its size and resources did nowadays? Sure, he could have tried to redirect some of those resources from Sol, but that would have gotten him kicked out of office and someone else . . . like Cruz . . . put in, which would have meant *no* resources going to fix the Family ships *or* the station residencies. As it was, he'd gotten what he could from Venture and fought a running battle with Cruz for allocation of those resources as well. He was *not* a bad administrator.

At least one of Alpha's ships had stood up for him. There was that.

Dammit, Neihart *insisted* Pell wasn't behind his visit, but it increasingly felt like a Konstantin action, right down to the splashy system entry and the subversive, silver-tongued speech in the bar. Emilio Konstantin himself loved a camera. Slick, smooth, never a stumble, never a search for words . . . and this JR Neihart was every bit as good, possibly better. Certainly better looking, if nothing else. It was even possible Konstantin had provided the language. Hell . . . hearing it, he'd almost found *himself* agreeing with *Finity's* captain and feeling he wasn't remotely the administrator he tried to be.

But what could Pell gain by agitating Alpha spacers to make a claim the EC would never grant?

Discontent?

Disorder?

Force *him* into defying the EC?

Was this the beginning of the end? The someday-payback he'd feared for years? Trade *Rights* for food to feed his people? For the continued loyalty of Alpha's spacers?

Dammit.

One thing was for damn sure: There was nothing innocuous in the proposals *Finity* was trying to float out on the Strip. And, God help him, what if the implication were true? What if the EC was building more of these megaships in anticipation of a breakout, and training crews to put *his* spacers out of business?

Damn. And it all played against those numbers that rested in that floor safe under his desk—it all played against the possibility that *that* was the real issue . . . that Sol *was* that close to arriving on the scene.

Was it possible Hewitt had actually called it correctly? *Was* a riot against the station and the project Konstantin's goal in coming here? Local captains demanding *Rights* in return for perceived neglect?

Problem was, there wasn't damn-all he could do to shut *Finity* up, other than declare martial law and line the Strip with blue-coats. . . . And wouldn't *that* win hearts and minds on the Strip?

Besides, the words had already been said, the ideas planted.

Maybe he was overreacting. Maybe Pell simply wanted to know whether *Rights* could be brought into play, and to know what Andy Cruz was able to do. *Finity* had certainly shown *Rights* what an experienced crew could do . . . in spectacular and public fashion. That entrance had scared hell out of him and most everybody else on the station. *Rights'* morale and the Company's prestige were affected.

And wounded pride, especially in a man like Cruz, could result in very stupid actions.

Was that it? Had Neihart been sent to push his administration to risk that expensive mass of metal in an act of political bravado? Solve the problem in one spectacular demonstration of hubris?

If only . . . *if only* . . . security had stayed out of the picture. Let the meeting reach its conclusion. Maybe he'd have a clue what *Finity* was really up to. He damn sure wouldn't be facing a meeting with angry ship captains.

At this point, whatever he did or didn't do, he looked bad, Cruz looked bad, the EC looked bad, and spacers as a class *liked* the EC to look bad. Any misstep was an incident to be told and retold as fast and far as FTL ships could travel.

He'd known, *known*, dammit, that the decision to build an indisputably company-controlled ship of *Finity's* class would cause trouble on a scale impossible to predict. He'd tried to advise against it, when Cruz first arrived, and gotten . . . Hewitt. Earth had *never* understood why the first pusher crew . . . ancestors of these Neiharts in more ways than blood . . . had refused, after that first voyage, to hand over their ship to a new crew. *He* knew the passion behind that refusal, having spent his life on a star-station, having dealt directly with spacer crews for over two decades. Cut one and another bled. And the third would come at you bent on mayhem, even if the whole lot had been at loggerheads a minute before.

The EC had never understood that out here, beyond the reach of anything but pusher-ships, there was Station culture . . . with its own set of ties . . . and there were spacers, with theirs. And if one wanted to refine the issue— there were the First Star stations and there were the Farther Stars, including humanity's offshoot, Cyteen, and its wild growth. They were all human, but in spite of the DNA . . . the differences became profound. Their respective worlds were contained and isolated from one another. The physical and psychological requirements of their separate worlds, their separate lives, were just . . . different. You had to accept that. Deal with it. Because out here, there *was* no escape. Stations needed spacers and spacers needed stations.

In that, he and James Robert Neihart were in complete agreement. And Neihart's notion that the Family ships provided a buffer between stations was dead on. But all that stood between Alpha and Earth Company headquarters on Earth and on Sol Station were the pusher ships. And he doubted the EC admin had the remotest idea how the pusher crews thought—they'd been caught by total surprise when old *Gaia* had told them they weren't giving up their ship to another crew, and the pushers had only gotten stranger over time. Sol Admin found it puzzling enough that they were dealing with two different histories in the two pushers that still served them. *Santa Maria* had been the ship to discover the terrifying mystery at Beta, and yes, that ship kept extremely close tabs on their people at all times. They believed Cyteen was heading for an alien apocalypse—it was not a topic you ever wanted to mention with them; and during their Alpha layover they usually held at least one lengthy religious service with live candles, which made safety officers nervous. *Atlantis,* when that pusher was in port, was just, well, there for a party, and breakage happened. Fact was, the two pusher crews lived in utter isolation for a decade at a time, inward-folded, time-dilated, and *different.*

Company headquarters didn't understand such mindsets, and probably wouldn't give a damn if they did. Not because they were inherently cruel—historically, the EC was a generous employer—but because they were a company. As long as the pushers did their job, just like any of their employees, any idiosyncrasies of behavior during their station time were just something they let Station management handle as delicately as possible—ignoring a few broken rules in the interests of keeping the system going.

It wasn't that the EC didn't understand different cultures and world views. Sol had Earth, historically a mass of conflicting cultures. Sol had Mars colony, mostly research, and the Belters, insystem miners, and Lunabase . . . all . . . *all* . . . extensions of the Earth Company, the most remote only a few light-hours apart. There were, one understood intellectually, many differing mindsets to be considered, but all interconnected, not just historically but, in the case of the space-based units, by the company itself.

For the EC, that second connection was the only one that mattered. The workers at the facilities were employees, and the only rules that mattered were those the company set. Cultural differences were on their own time.

The whole attitude was fundamentally different. Earth's

culture didn't embrace multi-generational groups isolated for years at a time, groups whose only *constant* reality was what had become the Family, or the Station, and, in the case of the spacers, groups who *could* if they cared to, tell a station to go to hell, and just leave.

Forever.

That was what the EC truly didn't understand, had never come face to face with. Independence. *Real* self-reliance. Spacers no longer needed the EC for survival. That had been true from the time the Pell station core had left Venture, bound for a star with a living world.

Neihart had made a lot of good points in what he'd said. He'd brought clarity to a problem Abrezio had been dealing with for years. The EC at Sol had no concept of what it took to make the star stations run smoothly . . . in that, he agreed with Neihart. And one day, perhaps soon, FTL was going to replace the pusher-traffic to Sol; and Sol was going to be plunged into a new reality, one in which decisions had to be much faster, decisions whose consequences were months, rather than years, away.

At which point, which had been *his* thought while listening to Neihart's speech, Ben Abrezio could play a key role in making that transition run smoothly.

It was a safe bet that the first FTL ship *out* of Sol would bring EC reps with notions that wouldn't make much sense in the First Stars, let alone as far out as Venture.

But the EC's *goal* would be profit—the same as everyone else's.

He understood the situation. *He* had psychologically bridged that gap for years. *He* could direct Sol's first steps with experience and common sense, and *make* the EC that profit . . . only grant they sent him somebody willing to stand still, watch, listen and learn.

Unlike, God help him, Cruz and Hewitt.

Cruz was too mono-focused on the *Rights of Man* project, and not even twenty years at Alpha had given him the knack of getting cooperation on the Strip . . . a useful art, while running a project indefinitely sidelining local shippers' needs. Cruz wasn't the man to be setting general station policy or negotiating with spacer crews. His interests weren't the EC's, either. His interests were accomplishment. Recognition. And his social skills were mildly wanting.

Hewitt . . . God help him double . . . had only one response to a challenge. Force. He'd almost bet that raid on Neihart's meeting was *meant* to rough up the visitors, and that the firedoor corridor being put in the hands of six-month recruits to Enforcement was a setup designed to draw blood, no matter whose. Hewitt wasn't socially skilled either—but Hewitt knew how to touch off tempers and take advantage of the emotional reaction. And while Bellamy Jameson had brought the force, he'd bet Hewitt had sent Jameson the personnel, then sat back, listened, and waited. Hewitt had let Neihart lay it out and work the pitch up and up, and *then,* right before Neihart's denouement, he'd slammed the hammer down, intending to make the most of whatever fell out.

Bet on it, Hewitt had also taken notes on who was there, so he had his little list of locals he could pressure, including, possibly, the bar owner. Cruz managed to offend people because he had his notions of entitlement, but he wanted to be liked, and he wanted to be important. Hewitt didn't give a damn about being *liked*. He just wanted to be in charge. Wanted power. The two of them together—Cruz and Hewitt—God knew, regular people who came off a pusher-ship passage were just a little odd. The voyage did that. But whatever demons personally drove them, whatever ambitions had driven these two, with their aides, to become the men the Company chose to send out here— and whatever the voyage itself had made them, ripped loose from family, friends, nation and personal ties—

Neither of them was what the Company needed in control here, working with spacers, or with the Farther Stars and whatever deal *Finity* had brought in with them. Not now, and *especially* not once Sol joined the FTL routes.

The EC needed a guiding beacon, not a supernova.

Ben Abrezio hoped to be that guiding light. He hoped to matter hugely to the human future, and thought that might actually be possible, depending on how he handled this situation. He hadn't anticipated it, but it presented an opportunity. If *he* could negotiate with these ships, right here, right now, if he could possibly secure some agreements with Pell, agreements even leading to increased supply and ring-docking in Alpha's future, he might be able to set up a system so healthy and potentially profitable that any EC representative arriving after the fact would be forced to think twice before undermining it. He couldn't do it within the transit-time of a message to Sol, but Sol's entry would be more symbolic than substantial at first. The Sol-based EC would be feeling its way.

At first.

If those coordinates he had in the safe panned out, *if* goods started flowing from Sol, more diverse and more exotic than Pell, the introduction of those goods from Sol into the interstellar market would have to be finessed.

That was the rough spot. Konstantin would *not* be happy with the competition: Pell's economy would take an initial hit, with Earth's biological riches fully in the game. But things would level out. Pell had its value, as Alpha would, a bridge between the Cyteen and Sol markets and a necessary buffer between two very different mindsets.

Damn. It was a scary place to stand, but the potential . . .

Sol was the one power that could challenge Cyteen, if Cyteen, with its engineered populations and reckless expansionist notions, became a problem, and Pell was, whatever else, still linked to Earth in history, in ethics, in law, in traditions . . .

Damn . . . Definitely scary, but if the Konstantins played *their* cards right, Pell could become a *new* Sol, a bright new future for mankind.

If he could start those negotiations with Pell here at Alpha, during this visit . . . he could become the central point of exchange, in touch with both Pell *and* Sol, able to *be* the bridge.

What hadn't *Finity* had time to say in that meeting? Anything new? Or critical? Damn Hewitt for the timing.

Was *Rights* becoming a Family ship an idea the Neiharts had come up with on their own? Or was it Konstantin's power play, to push the EC into a corner?

Did it really matter? Regardless who was pushing the buttons, he was damned sure *not* going to hand over his largest card as the opening bid in a game he wasn't even sure was the right game to play. He'd believed for years that the Konstantins wanted to force the First Stars' stations into mothballs and leave Sol sealed in the past as long as they could—it had surprised him to hear Neihart so openly admit to that. It was unthinkable that Sol would *never* find an FTL route, but every year that arrival was delayed gave Pell that much more time to strengthen its position. He had absolutely no doubt that the Konstantins carefully controlled Pell's export, and that the biostuffs that made it past Venture and Bryant's were barely enough to fill Alpha's standing purchase orders was no accident. Supply trickled. It did not flow. And that was policy. Pell wanted them not to die—but not to live that well, either.

When Sol broke out, Pell wanted Sol occupied with reviving its own, determinedly loyal, stations.

It had been a long, long time since Alpha had gotten all its biostuffs from Sol. Pell was far faster in trade. His predecessor, with Pell to fill the gaps, had depleted the reserve that Alpha had traditionally maintained when shipments were years rather than months or even weeks apart, a reserve against the possibility of pusher-ships lost in transit. One of his own first decisions, coming into office, was to build that reserve back up . . . only to have Pell cut them off entirely, following the infamous theft of the *Finity's End* blueprints. Relations had thawed, trade had resumed, but then Sol's pusher shipments shifted completely over to materials for *Rights,* which threw Alpha and all the other First Stars into *complete* reliance on Pell.

Pell knew the situation, had actually increased the export of food along with the price break, but they were still sending just enough to keep the station alive. Uncanny, Konstantin's ability to judge that margin. But it was the ships that carried those supplies that were hurting the most, if he was honest with himself. Without the exotics from Sol for those ships to carry out of Alpha, their ability to cover dock charges grew increasingly problematic. Pell had to know that if Alpha lost its ships to other stations—

Alpha would have to shut down. And if that happened by the *choice* of Alpha's regular ships, Emilio Konstantin avoided public censure, never mind he'd have choreographed the whole thing.

If Konstantin's policy succeeded, Sol's ships would arrive to find a deserted station—maybe to a string of deserted stations. Potentially stranded. With only a light-bound message taking years to ask for help. Gruesome scenario.

Damn the Konstantins! He hadn't signed up for this kind of problem when he'd accepted his promotion twenty-plus years ago. First damn thing he'd gotten had been the plans for that monster. He'd gotten those, done what had to be done . . . and now—he could almost believe Konstantin had planned the whole damned course of events *including* the theft of the plans. Smug bastard had probably unlocked the door to his office and left the damned computer on.

And waved a cheerful farewell to the EC agent as he left.

Well, he had beaten Konstantin at his own game. Despite Cruz, despite Hewitt, *he'd* done his best for Alpha's loyal ships. He'd met with the captains, forgiven a few charges he could control, helped them through hard times. He couldn't think that Neihart's rhetoric could peel them away—he couldn't think that spacers so long loyal could leave Alpha in the lurch. The Strip was a home to them, unique in the places they visited.

But he also needed to give them something, *something* to offset the lure Neihart was dangling in front of their noses. They needed some hope that the situation here on Alpha now was not going to be the situation tomorrow, that trade was *going* to get better. The small ships could *not* compete at Pell. Neihart himself had said that.

Ten years—one pusher-run. He needed to keep them loyal for that ten years. If he transmitted those coordinates today, along with his fears regarding Pell's plans, Sol would have them in six years. He had no doubt Sol was equipped to test that information and get some results within a year. If the points were viable, Sol could have ships here within a decade—sooner, if they were already building and training in anticipation of the discovery of jump points. He could bring the local ships' captains in on the secret, give them hope, ask them to wait that ten years. . . .

If he dared transmit. Dammit.

Or, he could sit on those coordinates, could cast his lot with Pell, could *enlist* the help of these visitors, and they *might* save his station; but at what price? Without Sol's imports to sell, Alpha would remain a poor cousin surviving on Pell's charity—unless the ever worrisome Pell-Cyteen business headed for a trade war, and Pell decided it *needed* Sol's backing, at which point he could pull those coordinates out of mothballs and hand them over.

That Pell-Cyteen business was hardly a certainty. Everyone feared what Cyteen planned with its potential armies of clones, but all Cyteen had ever done was milk a bunch of rich fools and hand out FTL for free and build stations out where no one else had ventured. He hated to depend on some undefined hazard for Alpha to become a major player in this interstellar chess game.

Inside a decade, if he transmitted that data, reckless of eavesdropping bots, he could put FTL in Sol's hands. Time would lurch into rapid motion when that happened. Everything would happen faster and faster.

And spiral out of control if he wasn't careful.

He had to keep Cruz in check—keep *Rights* and its force under his control, not Cruz's or Hewitt's, and keep Alpha's loyal ships focused on reality, not promises. That speech of JR Neihart's was *not* innocent. Riots were not the only threat to station security. Neihart was here to recruit the Families to some nebulous idea, promise them whatever he had to promise and recruit them—

To what end was something he *had* to find out about before he made a choice regarding those coordinates.

He needed someone on the inside.

Following the board-shadowing run to Bryant's and back, *Qarib* had set itself at odds with Hewitt and Cruz and the whole *Rights* project, and by extension, Sol authority itself, calling Hewitt an agent of Satan, or the like. *Santiago* was a possibility, and Julio and Diego Rodriguez were good people, but whether they could keep anything from their crew was a question. With Giovanna Galli and *Firenze,* he had extreme financial leverage, but subtlety of approach and Galli were not even acquaintances.

Which left *Galway.* She was Venture-built, but with no ties there in the last few decades, station-time. And she was the largest, most modern of all the ships that supplied Alpha. The Monahans could have opted, when they'd gotten that ship, to head out to Pell and take their chances there, as other ships had done. But they hadn't. They'd remained loyal to Alpha. Old favors, old history. Niall Monahan had a head on his shoulders. And did understand discretion.

Abrezio looked at the screen, at the names listed on Bellamy Jameson's report. Ship personnel who'd been at that meeting. Those who'd gotten out before the lock down, those who'd remained inside. *Galway* names on both. First shift who hadn't escaped. First shift, including Niall Monahan, in the lot who'd been intercepted and roughed up at the door. Their Nav 1 was the old man in the infirmary.

Oh. My. God.

Damn Enzio Hewitt. Damn him. Damn him. Damn him. Human history could turn on one fool's heavy-handed order.

He tapped a button. His secretary, Ames, answered.

"Contact Captain Niall Monahan. Request his presence here at his earliest convenience. And make certain that man of theirs in Mercy Infirmary is getting the *best* care."

Apologies were in order. Diplomacy was in order. *Galway* had every right to be upset with station management.

But if any ship was likely to feel unease in *Finity's* arrival here—in a change in the trade routes—

Galway, as Alpha's best and newest ship, definitely had reason to ask—what was in it for *them.*

"That the one?" Jen Neihart leaned past JR to tap the portable screen. The image paused. Another tap and it zoomed in on a young man sitting down the table from *Galway*'s Niall Monahan, smooth morph between images: *Finity* security had spaced their wearable cameras out at the fringes of the meeting, to cover the room—the way they had spread out a web of anti-spook devices to assure nothing sneaked into or out of their equipment in this stretch of very comfortable sleepover rooms.

JR nodded, not at all surprised that Jen had spotted the target on her own, no matter that there were two other people in that shot who were fairly close to her age group.

"Easy on the eyes," Jen said. "That one has his choice of sleepover invites, I'm betting."

"You mean—*he's* good-looking enough *not* to be suspicious of *your* interest."

Jen threw him a coy over-the-shoulder. "Why, Uncle James, sir, is that a back-handed compliment?"

"Don't give me that face. And a little respect, there."

Jen laughed and tapped the screen to unpause the image, leaned an elbow on the little wall-fixed desk to support her chin, intent now on young Ross Monahan.

Uncle James, sir, indeed. She was, in fact, JR's niece by blood, her mother having been his late half-sister. And she'd taken ruthless advantage of that association among her peers from the moment he'd been voted senior captain.

Jen had been a scamp from earliest days, but from the cradle she'd read people the way nav read star charts, and she'd been a thorough pain in the ass as a junior-junior—*way* too clever, way too few principles and way too quick with the excuses. She'd been an angry, orphaned kid for a few significant years, a kid far too smart for the rules, always asking why, constantly at war with authority and, on one occasion, stripped of all privileges for three shipboard months. Her aunt Frances, who'd assumed parental authority, hadn't known what to do with her—until hormones had finished their run and Jen's brain had settled down to . . . well, *finally* a real interest. And in what?

She'd focused, to shipwide amusement, on the one institution with which she'd become so frequently and intimately acquainted.

Security.

It proved a perfect fit, particularly for undercover. She'd become smooth enough to leave most of her targets thinking they'd almost gotten what they wanted . . . a talent which had found a natural career on docksides from Mariner to Venture—but not as the lightweight people thought she was. The smooth-as-silk wiles she'd polished, getting away with mayhem on board, had found whole new uses on this run.

You wanted information station didn't want to give you? Put Jen on it.

You wanted to know what another ship was up to? Give Jen a couple of days.

Right now the question was how the situation in Critical Mass had shaken out, locally—and what the local sentiment was about that faulty copy of *Finity* sitting up there.

A night on the Strip, a few key hookups, and some serious talk with some young man—Jen thought she could do it, easy as on Pell dockside.

But . . .

"A word of caution," JR said. "Look at me, Jen. *Look* at me."

"Listening." Watching the replay. Without the slightest flick of an eye in his direction.

"This is Alpha, Jen. Let that soak in. This isn't even Venture. You *don't* know it the way you know Pell or Viking. Local terms are different. It's the Strip, not dockside. They're starting to call themselves merchanters—but the station calls them spacers, as opposed to stationers, and never call them shorthaulers. They won't like that word, anyway. Their loyalties may be like ours, to their ships and

family, but their *pride* . . ." He paused, trying to think how
to make the point. "What we call the Hinder Stars . . . *they*
call the *First* Stars, and with good reason. For a long, *long*
time, the Hinder Stars were all there was. These Families
have never been beyond Venture. There've been *several*
ships in their backgrounds, but only a small handful of stations. You've seen the Strip. This place is old and showing
its age, but it has a long, long history, not all of it sweetness
and light."

"Beta," Jen said, with all the callous assurance of the
young.

"You book-know it. But you don't life-know it, niece.
It's important here. Things flowed *from* that incident."

Jen shrugged. "Beta Station went silent. Next ship in
found it deserted, everything left in place, just no people.
The ship spooked out of there, reported it. Nobody's been
back—not being *stupid*."

"Alpha and Glory sit right near it. And ever since, this
station has been Sol's only link to the star-stations. Still is.
But the pushers are down to only two. And one of those
two is . . ."

"*Santa Maria*—who was the one that carried the news
about Beta. I *know* that."

"*Santa Maria* cycles between this station and Sol, keeping that history vivid, every couple of decades. It *owns*
this sleepover that nobody uses *except* them and *Atlantis,*
when they come in. And now they've had to open it up for
us. Biggest and best to give the pusher crews a special
welcome—an exotic, all-out luxury break from ten years of
isolation. A special honor for the crews who've sacrificed
the most to keep Sol connected to what Sol made possible.
Touchy point, that. Tread lightly and respect the favor
they've done us. Pushers aren't ancient history here. *Sol*
isn't ancient history here. Us being here, in *this* sleepover,
which is theirs when they're in dock . . . that's going to ran-
kle with some."

"Noted."

"Don't just note it, *respect* it. Got it?"

She blinked. Her lips pressed tight. But she dipped her
chin, once. He rarely had to take the tone with her, but it

was important. And she would remember, he had every confidence. She was just tight-focused on the image of young Monahan, getting only-she-knew-what from every twitch he made.

"The *possibility* exists that, if Sol *is* building a long-hauler like ours . . ."

"It could decide to use Beta as a jump point," Jen said in clipped tones. "I'm up on all that. But nobody's that stupid. Whatever happened at Beta wasn't natural causes and nobody in their right mind would risk spreading whatever happened there."

"Nobody on this side of the pusher route, but Sol doesn't have the perspective. For Sol, the 'Beta incident,' as they call it, is going to be, at best, ancient history, at worst, a bogie tale from a ship in a hurry to get out of there. What Sol *might* do, in their frustration to escape the bottle they're in, is something this young man has every reason to fear."

"Idiots," Jen said.

"Idiots who might draw whatever took out Beta to take out the station this young man's ship depends on. *That's* what he lives with. Sink into that mindset. Fear's real here."

She tapped to pause the vid, and twisted her head to look at him, a slight, worried frown line between her brows. "Some folk back on Mariner say that would be a good thing. That we ought to just close Alpha and Glory down, leave a nice big buffer around Beta, and just go on developing in other directions. That if Sol wants to get out, they should be looking for a route direct to Pell and leave the Centauris alone."

Problem was, between Sol and Pell was a very nasty little flare star, UV Ceti. It was a damned inconvenient place Sol occupied.

"This is an EC station," JR said. "And yes, you'll hear Mariner natives say, forget Sol. But Sol won't let that happen. And in real life, people *know* Sol won't let that happen. And Alpha and Glory, sitting out here, closest to Beta and all that went wrong there, depend on Sol. Emotionally, that's their lifeline—because they *know* the deep Beyond would cut them off in a heartbeat. Only thing *they* know about Mariner is that the EC never authorized its construction, and that Pell and all the stations that came after destroyed their way of life."

"Well, they'd be all right if dealing with Sol didn't mean dealing with the EC. That lot's rich, they're crazy, and they want to run things. Look at that ship up there—when this whole place is run down and falling apart."

"A ship that's a threat, niece. A threat in more than one way. You've seen it: closer to Alpha we've gotten, the more blue-coats we see, and this is the mother lode. Young, mostly male, and trained to fight, make no doubt. Bet on it: that ship is no merchanter and it never intended to be. It's designed to move enforcement to Bryant's, to Glory, to Venture—wherever the EC wants them."

"If it could move."

"Possibly. But even if it shut down on that trial . . . that ship *will* move someday. And when it does, when Sol breaks out—we don't know that that's the *only* longhauler Sol's building, do we? They have resources. Once they know how, they could send ship after ship filled with blue-coats. Earth's had wars from way back, people taking what they want by force—because their mindset's all about shortage, in spite of all those resources. It's something we've left behind. You can't draw borders in space. Freight has to move. We know it. We need the stations, they need us, and if we don't agree we settle it with a barroom brawl and shake hands after in the infirmary. But that's not the thinking the EC will bring. I don't think all these centuries have told them you don't own a moving rock. They're going to bring their rules, they're going to bring more people than we've ever seen, and they think they own all the rocks they can find. Territorial notions spreading at FTL speeds. We can't let that happen."

"They say that's why Cyteen is manufacturing people as fast as their machines will make them."

"Which—listen to me, Jen—is *why* we're doing what we're doing, trying to make certain it doesn't end up with station-folk and planet-folk deciding all the questions.

Which is why *you,* if you do this, have to use your head, and remember that this *isn't* Pell, this *isn't* Mariner, and you *can't take chances."*

"I get it that Alpha's different. And I have to adapt. And that you really don't want to have to get me out of lockup."

"Get it that, if you let something slip, it could be expensive. *Real and lastingly* expensive."

She turned at that, head tilting on its palm-prop to corner-eye him. And shrug. "Expensive enough you wouldn't bail me out?"

"Expensive enough you'd be famous for it forever. And so would I, for sending you. Not in a good way."

"I'll be careful." Soberest look he'd ever seen on Jen's face, even sidelong. "I really will. I do get what you're saying. I don't figure what these people think, staying in this place. I don't get what they want to fight over. I'm a little scared."

From Jen, that was major.

"Stay that way. Shorthauler, Jen. Alpha hauler. Not a trace of the Beyond in their thinking. Half the time they and the stations out here think in *pusher* time. Major, *major* factor in their thinking. They're in a very little bubble where time moves very, very slowly and things don't change much. Supplies, orders, trade choices . . . all need a built-in two-decade lag."

She turned completely from the screen, squatted, leaning against the desk support, to look up at him. "Why? Why *do* they stay here? I mean, I get that the small ships couldn't be competitive in the Beyond, but they could get in queue for new ones at Venture."

"It's a long queue. A real long queue. These ships weren't lucky, Jen. They were in the wrong place when the purpose-builts began to be handed out. Venture doesn't just give the ships away out of the goodness of their hearts but on the reasonable expectation that they're going to get a return on the investment, with the ships they build carrying trade to and from lucrative markets."

"And the Hinder Stars . . . aren't lucrative."

"Not any more. These ships were operating here on a small, low-mass trade in luxuries. You're too young to remember when exotics came on a regular basis from Sol. One shipment could provide enough to keep these local ships in the black and Alpha in good supply. But FTL just slowly changed things. And then those stolen plans made their way to Sol and it was all material for *Rights,* from then on, no concern for the local ships, *except* from Alpha and the stations they keep alive."

She glanced up at the screen, frozen on the moment where he'd said *Rights* should be given to one of the Alpha Families, and on the hungry look on young Ross Monahan's face.

"Earth's still *real* to this lot, Jen. Real—in the perpetual hope that they'll *find* that route and have all the luck Pell had. There's a mother lode of trade, just waiting, on the far side, if Sol finds a jump point that leads to Alpha and not to Pell."

"What are the chances?"

"Astronomers think decent, at least. But it's not a certainty."

"They could shift base to Venture, get real ships. And still reach Alpha."

"No point, really. It's only for these older ships that the Hinder Stars make sense. This lot . . . for them, everything, every hope, every reward comes from the EC. And *only* from the EC. They're stuck. So don't speak too hatefully of the Company. They may hate it more than you, but they'll resent your saying it."

She grunted. "They're still Family ships. Can't tell me they aren't just a tad bit jealous of *Finity.* Can't tell me they don't want out of here."

She reached up, zoomed in again on that one face that did, indeed, stand out from the rest. The old man next to him—that look was unfathomable. Those eyes had seen things a lot older than his current ship. But the young one was wide open. No way that young man didn't dream of having a longhauler's capabilities at his fingertips. The sleeve patch, below the tangled knot of *Galway,* was the compass rose: Nav-track. A tighter zoom brought up the 1.3—which on a two-by ship wasn't seated crew, just trainee, but—

Bright young man. To be first-shift nav trainee at his

age—even on a ship *Galway*'s size—meant a quick mind and a spookily good memory. But that young man would know only a narrow set of routes to and from Alpha. Calc that changed, but not that much. Not that demanding. The fire, however, the interest—

Galway would have seen *Rights* growing year by year on A-mast, fast forwarded in time-dilated leaps of assembly, from girders to a massive new reality.

Salt in a small ship's wounds, that would be. JR felt sorry for all of them.

Pell was worried—slightly—about this reported megaship.

To his observation, Pell didn't yet grasp the half of it. The ship itself wasn't what they should be looking at.

Run-down also didn't describe that situation on Alpha. By the look of things, the bar menu, and the response of the market to their cargo—Alpha's ship-building thus far had gained Alpha nothing other than a lot of EC enforcers. Police. No station-folk idly passing an evening on Alpha's Strip—an iron separation of stationers from merchanter areas, fines and arrest threatened. A dearth of shops and trinkets. Entertainment offered here might have value as antiques, but some of it wasn't working.

Galway's captain, not that old himself, had just shaken his head and glowered—no such wild thoughts in that one. The old one, Nav 1 by his sleeve, was impossible to read.

But the young man, one life away from a seat at *Galway*'s boards, might dream, if only for a moment.

"*Galway*'s Venture-built," he said to Jen. "Modern, compared to the other ships based here: the best they've got as a regular. I've tried to get history on her—why she ended up Alpha-based; but I think it was favor-trading, EC at Venture helping out the EC at Alpha. The old man beside him—I'm pretty sure that's Fallan Monahan, one of the real old-timers, off the pusher *Atlas*. And that, mind you, is another very different attitude. Different. Just different mindset."

"Like Mum."

"Mum actually knows this man."

"Really?" Jen rolled the scene back, focused in a bit closer on the old man. "Not like Mum. He looks ancient."

"Mum minus a lifetime serving Alpha. A long time ago. Real long time."

"Before us."

"Definitely before us."

"Could *Mum* talk to him?"

"Maybe. But right now—you picked out the one who's talked to us. This young man . . . Ross Monahan: He talked to Fletch after the lockdown. He's curious. He's the kind of ambitious individual that could get tracked into *Rights,* if they could ever wash the Family loyalty out of him. Nav 1.3, trainee in a two-by, four-shift ship. Came over for a near-beer, introduced himself politely, talked to Fletch, who told him there'd be more at another meeting, at which point young Ross shut up and sensibly sat with two of his cousins until the place opened up again, listening far more than he talked. Which is saying don't sell him short. He may be looking at *us.*"

"How's his dockside record?"

"Next to yours, immaculate."

Jen mock-scowled at him.

"Clean," JR amended. "One disorderly connected with a birthday party. The lad's a saint. That's it."

"Preferences? Pairings?"

"No record. This crowded a dockside . . . that's unusual here. Three ships overlapping is rare. It's a real small inbred circle, Alpha, so inbred you'd better exchange genealogies with your potential partners. And you don't find stationers mixing here. So it's possible there's nobody he's tied to."

"Mmm." She tapped the screen off and stood up, putting on her jacket. "You want him, Uncle, sir . . . you've got him."

"Don't get cocky, young lady. Remember what I said. Watch yourself. Keep us posted where you are. Don't assume *anything.* Don't assume *he's* not looking for information. Don't assume *station* isn't."

She turned and her face now was anything but coy or

smug. "I absolutely know what's at stake. I *do* know. And this is absolutely *not* the place I want to get stranded."

Chapter 3   Section iii

Rosie's traffic was low for the hours between dinner and sleepover, those hours when crew on liberty either had hooking up or serious gaming to do. There was a fivesome in a dice game in one corner and a couple of determined drinkers with *Firenze* patches—things hadn't gone well for that ship today: test power-up of the cranky nav system had completely failed. Two crew had gone out to *Firenze* today to try a programming fix. Two had come back in deep disappointment.

Ross . . . was just sitting. Waiting.

Things weren't going outstandingly well for *Galway,* either, or for any of the regulars up and down the Strip. The blue-coats had made no friends tonight. Sullen groups gathered . . . in various places a little less monitored . . . grumbling among themselves, waiting—as the captains sorted out what they *did* know.

Galway hadn't called a crew meeting yet, for one very major thing: because senior captain Niall had gotten a see-me from station admin. Whether other captains had gotten the same, Ross was hesitant to ask, figuring the less ships looked askance at each other or passed fragments of information, the better for junior officers who should not be letting confidential bits of business slip into the rumor stream.

He wished Fallan would contact him. He'd heard nothing since he'd been released from Critical Mass's front door. But there was nothing, and so he sat with Mary T and Ashlan, nursing one of Rosie's specials, waiting for news, radiating a warn-off to cargo-ops cousins who drifted in, seeking answers he didn't, at the moment, have.

Yes, he'd been *at* the meeting. Yes, he'd stayed *inside* Critical Mass after the blue-coats locked the doors. Yes, he'd heard what the Neihart captain had to say, and no, he left opinions about that and about the blue-coats to the senior officers for right now. Fallan had gotten roughed up, had gotten slammed around in the melee, it wasn't clear whether it had been the blue-coats doing the shoving, but yes, he was damned mad about that. How was he not? How was any *Galway* crew not mad about it? You didn't shove an old man into a wall, whoever you were, but until he heard from Fallan what had happened he wasn't expressing an opinion to anybody.

Didn't mean he didn't have one. The blue-coats had gotten too damned excited about shutting them in, and the crowd had gotten way too excited about getting out before they got written up and before ships got fines. But fact was, station authority had gone way over the edge, and if the blue-coats were going to shut the doors, they should have shut them fast, not waited till there was a jam in the outlet.

Sure, there was a lot for station to quarrel with in what JR Neihart had said, but that didn't make it illegal. The station could *claim* Neihart was creating unrest. But if the station tried to make it illegal to say that sort of thing, if it was illegal even to say that maybe Alpha ought to do what Pell and Cyteen had done, and *give* the ship Alpha had built into Family hands—that was just an opinion, wasn't it? Opinions weren't illegal.

And it wasn't threatening riot. Was it? Certainly there'd *been* no riot . . . not even raised voices . . . until the red lights had begun to flash.

Give *Rights* to the Alpha Families, JR Neihart had said, and then, as if those words had been a trigger, blue-coats had swarmed the meeting, and as everybody jumped for the exits, they'd shut the doors, trying to trap those present.

It had gone absolutely crazy from there.

It was only natural. Escape was what people did when there'd been a bar fight and there'd be charges to settle.

But it hadn't *been* that. They weren't, damn it, guilty of anything. There'd *been* no fight. *Nobody* was guilty of anything, and the Neiharts, who'd had the most to fear, had just sat there, calmly ordering drinks.

That . . . had stopped him. He'd jumped for the doors along with Niall and Fallan, but while they'd run for it, he'd delayed to ask himself what *Finity* was doing. How *they* were reacting. He'd thought—*This is stupid. Station's being the fool. Station's in the wrong, not us. And the Neiharts aren't budging.*

And just that quick, it had been too late: the Santiagos cut him off, trapped him and Mary T and Ashlan, because of his delay. The side door had sealed and the front door sealed, and he and two of his cousins had been standing there behind the tail end of the Santiagos, who also hadn't got out.

He wasn't wholly proud that he'd stayed that moment to look back, that he hadn't kept with his captain and crew, but he had, and there he'd been, trapped in the bar, while chaos went on outside.

So he'd gone up, ordered a beer, and paid his respects to JR Neihart.

And stared, because the man unexpectedly looked him right in the eyes—no smile there, no matter what the rest of the face was doing. It wasn't threat. It was just presence, a powerful man wondering, he'd thought, just what this *Galway* navigator thought he was, or whether he was making a statement, still being there, a wet-behind-the-ears jumped-up trainee, *nobody* to another ship's senior captain—cheeky even to *approach* another ship's senior captain or make his presence evident.

And he hadn't had an answer.

He still didn't. Didn't know to this hour what he'd felt, beyond stunned and upset.

Damn the Neiharts, if they'd gotten *Galway* into trouble. Niall still wasn't back. There might be several captains called on the carpet.

Would he like to sit nav aboard a ship like *Rights*? Like *Finity*? In a heartbeat. But trade *Galway* for it? There were upgrades and then there were quantum leaps.

Scared hell out of him, it did. Just because the EC

thought sim-training that crew should be doable, didn't mean it was.

That *The Rights of Man* should become a Family ship—that *Rights* should go to *them*, Alpha's ship-Families—maybe to a merger of more than one. . . . Ross personally didn't know how that would or could work out. He'd seen *Finity* come in. JR Neihart had said that hot entry was *necessary*. JR Neihart himself had been mid-list when the whole senior crew of *Gaia* had stepped aside to put their young people in charge of *Finity's End*. JR Neihart had been promoted up to senior at one go, and the same story with a lot of the crew, because the big ships were a whole new universe—and older crew just stepped down to advisory. That was what Fallan said.

God. Scary prospect. And the *Finity* crew was all one family, knowing each other. What would it be like to merge with *Firenze* or *Santiago,* whose ship-speak wasn't *Galway*'s, who didn't read each other like a book? *He* couldn't sit a mega-ship's boards with the team he knew. He wasn't sure *Fallan* could, the best they had. And trust their lives to some other team?

Hell, no. But then—any of them would be a damned sight better than any stationer in the same post, wouldn't they?

"Would you take it?" he asked his cousins, out of long mutual silence. They'd talked out their reactions to the blue-coats' raid in the first five minutes. "That ship. If they gave it to us . . . if they had us go in with *Firenze,* say . . ."

"Rights?" Mary T asked. "Hell, no. A monster ship designed from smuggled blueprints? Put together by engees who can't get *Firenze*'s problem fixed in three tries?"

"They did get it out of dock," Ashlan said, in irony.

"Nah," Mary T said: "Too frickin' big. Merge with the Gallis? We're different. We're not them. They're not us."

"We wouldn't be blood-related to everybody," Ashlan said suggestively.

"Yeah, well, related often enough," Mary T said. "What I hear."

"Am not," Ashlan said, old argument. "Me pa's on *Santa Maria*. Headed for Sol."

"More than *we'll* ever do," Ross said.

"Unless they find the jump points," Ashlan said. "And then, hell, *Rights* won't matter. We'll go there, and they'll have shiny new ships just waiting for us. Won't have to share with anybody. That's the promise, right?"

"Believe that when the codes are in my hand," Ross said, drily. For as long as there'd been FTL, the EC had promised that when Sol finally found that jump point, they'd reward the First Star stations and the ships that had kept the stations going. It was even possible there *were* ships like *Finity* just waiting for them, when they could jump to Sol to claim them.

Sol was doing its best in its isolation, to keep up with the technology that came to it down the Stream. They—the ships that served Alpha—believed in Sol and believed that when Sol finally found the route to the Hinder Stars, it would continue to make Alpha its base.

But damn if it wasn't getting just a little difficult to keep the faith.

Maybe . . . maybe those points *had* been found. Maybe *Rights* was just waiting for them to be proved and that someday payoff was just around the corner. Maybe *Rights* had been given to hire-ons to protect the essential Alpha crews against the dangers of a ship built from blueprints and theory. It was even possible that that ship and the blue-coats were here to defend Alpha's loyal ships from money-grubbing visitors. To protect their interests in that lucrative trade.

Somehow . . . he didn't think that was why *Finity* was here. He wished the blue-coats hadn't intervened. He wanted to know what JR Neihart *would* have said.

"So what's your bet?" he asked his cousins. "What *are* these outsider ships here for?"

"Making trouble," Mary T said flatly.

"Wasn't a thing wrong with what the man said. It's *right*, what he said."

"It's *Rights*, isn't it?" Ashlan muttered. *"Rights of Man* . . . the way Alpha admin defines them. Maybe it means all those blue-coats to uphold those rights according to the EC. Blue-coats get all the rights and the ships that serve here don't get any."

Mary T frowned, rolled her eyes toward the overhead and surrounds. "You don't know who's listening."

That was the way it was. It hadn't, Ross thought, been that way when the day started. But that was the way it was now—that they had to think about what they said and worry that somebody was listening. They always used a *little* discretion on the Strip. And Ashlan had said it in ship-speak, which somebody might translate if they wanted to, but . . .

"Listen to us," he said. "Listen to us running scared, who did nothing wrong. *Nothing.* Why in hell did the blue-coats pick on Niall? Why's *he* been called in?"

"Because they didn't dare lay hands on a Neihart?" Ashlan said. "Those four ships just about outnumber the blue-coats, all told. Station's the one running scared."

"Fuist anois," Mary T said. Hush.

Ross shoved his chair back on its slide. Got up from the table.

"Where are you going?" Ashlan said.

"Nowhere," Ross said, then caught himself. A surly tone wouldn't help matters. "I'm fine." He lifted a hand. "Back in a bit."

He had no such intention, point of fact. He wanted to find a cousin who *hadn't* been locked down. His com wasn't telling him a thing. He wanted to know if Niall was back.

He wanted to walk. To shake off the thoughts.

He got as far as two frontages down when com did beep.

It was Niall's message. *Check on Fallan ASAP. Mercy Infirmary, 210 green. Says he's ok. Be sure. I'll be there when I can.*

Infirmary? His heart sped. And guilt settled in it. Of all people—Fallan.

He began to walk much faster.

Niall Monahan.

One of the good ones. The dependables.

And not real damn happy with Alpha at the moment.

"Come in," Ben Abrezio said, and watched a sixty-year-old who looked thirty walk in—*Galway* patch on a plain grey jacket, red and green and black Celtic knot-figure on the patch: Abrezio had asked once, during a more pleasant meeting. It meant something about unity, or some such.

And unity was the item in question at the moment. Monahan's face was grim, brows knit.

"Sit down, captain, please."

Monahan didn't move.

"It was *not* an order from this office," Abrezio said. "I understand a senior member of your crew was injured in the commotion. How is he?"

"Haven't been allowed to see him," Monahan said. "Security has a *guard* on him. They *say* well enough. He's an old man, damn it!"

"A mistake," Abrezio said. "I'll have the guards removed immediately." He tapped the intercom and gave the order, got a slight nod from Monahan: acknowledgment. Nothing more. "Let me assure you, captain, that it was not my order that put them there, as the lockdown was not my order, but I take responsibility for station security actions, and the matter is being looked into even as we speak. Station extends profound apologies . . . to all ships involved. And to the establishment. And reluctantly, to our uninvited guests. Alpha appreciates its loyal ships, captain. We know you could be elsewhere. We are *sorry* for what happened."

Monahan just stared, waiting, maybe, for a dismissal, apology delivered.

"Sit down, captain. Sit down, please."

Monahan moved the chair and sat down, no happier.

Abrezio pushed the stop button on the session recording; Monahan's brow twitched.

"There are things I'd like to say, off the record," Abrezio explained, trying to keep his voice from betraying his nerves. "We have a problem, here, which was not helped by a security officer's rash decision, and I hope to prevent it from becoming much worse."

Nerves, yes, worse than he'd ever suffered. So damn much depended on the next few minutes. He got up and went to the sideboard to pour from a carefully preserved bottle. The best he had. Scotch, real Scotch that had come in by pusher, tended to lose its color over time, but it preserved the essence of its unique flavor. He gave both glasses a generous pour. "The real stuff, this."

Monahan took the glass. Waited. Abrezio sat down, took a sip and Monahan did.

"Cards on the table," Abrezio said. "I'm worried about those ships and why they're here. Cyteen . . . is not the EC's friend, and half that lot who've come in here proposing changes is actively trading with Cyteen. Which is Pell's policy, and a deal they've worked out. That worries me. These outsiders come in here, saying they want benefit for you . . . but it's a question—why should they come all this way? Purely out of the goodness of their hearts? I personally find that difficult to believe. I have my suspicions Pell is deeply involved, but I admit to a certain bias in that and I'd value your opinion on their intentions. I'd very much value that. If you've heard anything we haven't. What's this talk about turning *Rights* over to you? Is that the first you'd heard of it?"

Monahan held the glass on his knee. Said nothing for a moment, then: "You recorded the meeting."

"I did." No reason to deny it.

"Then you know everything I know. My *opinion* is that they're here because *Rights* crew reached Bryant's, and because *Rights* has tested her engines, and that some plan has been triggered by those events. I'm not sure what they're offering. Right now it's pie by-and-by, and a lot of talk about Alpha Family crews taking over *Rights*, which I strongly doubt is going to happen."

A little edge to that statement. No surprise. "It's not in the plan. But—not to the disadvantage of Alpha's loyal merchant trade, and not to Alpha's disadvantage, that much I can say. The Company appreciates loyalty—and it reserves privilege for its loyal ships. You had a choice of stations and you chose Alpha, even after Venture gave you *Galway*."

"No one *gave* us anything, sir. We earned that ship. We sat on that list for thirty years, station time."

"With Alpha's backing. With Alpha's release of *Atlas* to their breakers. We are interconnected, Captain, and we take deep *pride* in *Galway*. You're our finest, our best . . ."

Monahan just looked at him.

"The point is, yes, you've earned every benefit you've had. Absolutely. You *are* valued. I am personally sorry—and, yes, embarrassed—about the unfortunate incident, and I *don't* want a repetition. In order to prevent it happening, I'm afraid I have to impose on that treasured loyalty a little more right now. Please listen to what I have to say."

A sip of the Scotch, a sideways glance at the still mostly full glass. "I'm listening."

"Thank you. We are, not surprisingly, concerned over this sudden, unannounced influx of Pell-based ships. We suspect a more serious threat than a look-see at *Rights*. Pell's close relationship with Cyteen concerns us. Venture's growing . . . its Pell-ification, if you will . . . concerns us. We should ordinarily and in all common sense be *allied* with Pell. But we cannot, *will* not, be taken over by them. We have our responsibilities. We *are* EC. And how we deal with this situation could impact the future of far more than Alpha. *Finity's* captain persistently said *we* . . . and no matter how many times I review it, that *we* remains ambiguous. *We* can do something about it, was his point, just before security interrupted the meeting, and I mortally wish Neihart had been able to finish that point and tell us who that *we* of his really is."

He paused, giving Monahan a chance to fill in that information. He didn't.

"He talked a great deal about ships with combined interests, but what I very much fear is that *Pell* is trying to get a presence here, to undermine EC tradition and impose Pell's interests on us, much as they have on Venture, whether in collaboration with Cyteen, or in a precautionary move against Cyteen. They've grown increasingly self-important, since the introduction of FTL into the system. They would put themselves up as the new Sol, with the power to dictate how *this* station runs. You must understand I *can't* allow that to happen. We *are* the EC's voice, the only real connection they have this side of the pusher divide. We must keep their base, the one they created and have maintained for centuries, ready to welcome them. I fear Pell means to challenge that loyalty, to take over control of the station, using our vulnerabilities to force the EC out. I also fear they want to control the Sol trade, when it joins the FTL circuit, cutting out our loyal ships. I fear they plan to take control of the *Rights* build—promising whatever it takes to get the local ships on their side, promises that *they'll* not be bound to deliver on."

Another pause. Monahan drew a breath. Shrugged. "Possible. Keep going."

"It's easy for the Neiharts to say what *Alpha* should do, whether or not it's possible. No matter they have *no idea* of our circumstances, *we're* the ones that came out looking bad. Pell sent that ship, a ship that has a *specific* grievance against us on the *Rights* matter. That's pretty clear. A ship that's dedicated to Pell's interests above all others. I have to ask myself . . . *why else would it come?* That system entry of his was designed to put the fear in us. The sudden pile-up of additional bodies on the docks, the presence of numbers that test our facilities, and without *any* warning. They created the crowd pressure, then called a meeting to throw around accusations of misbehavior on the part of station. They're entitled to speak. And unfortunately security overreacted."

"I have a man in infirmary, sir."

"I am keenly aware of that. And very sorry. Security overreacted and a reprimand has been given. But there's a nervousness up and down the Strip right now, not unrelated to the push these outsiders have put on us. Everybody's worried. Everybody's asking what this visit means. Which I suspect is very much the desired effect. Speculation breeds fear . . . and anger. And the most available scapegoat is station authority. It's possible that, had we not reacted, Neihart would have kept pushing until we *did* react. Still, it's unfortunate it happened. Period. People were hurt. And now, people are worried. *Security* is worried, and no good can come of trigger-happy authority."

"Point." Monahan's scowl didn't lessen.

"Captain, I *need* your assistance. Badly. And favors now *will* be remembered. I promise you."

Another sip, a moment to think. Niall Monahan was not a reckless man, but not reluctant to express an opinion, either.

"How *big* a favor do you need?"

"Not that big. I need someone on the inside. I'd like you to appear interested in Neihart's proposals, and keep *us* abreast of what's in the works. Satisfy our mutual curiosity—while being quite sure that, henceforward, station security will definitely step very gently in your presence. The Company remembers extraordinary service. It *will* reward it."

"In specific?"

"Say that depends on the quality and usefulness of the information. But say that this office already considers *Galway* uniquely valuable, and *Galway* will be a priority with us for a long time to come. In informing us, *Galway* will be protecting *all* trade that comes through here. Protecting *Galway*'s own economic future."

"And all you want is information?"

"Yes."

"What *kind* of information? Specifically."

"Information the visitors might hand other merchant ships, but not want this office to hear. We want to know what they offer under the table, and what they want. We want to know what they promise and what they allege about us in places not so well monitored. Be friendly, encourage confidences, and tell us what you know. That simple."

Silence. A fairly lengthy one. Then: "Keep the blue-coats off us. Pick up my man's infirmary tab. And I get *your* personal call number, sir. I'm not putting my people out on a tether with no quick-call to protect us."

Abrezio hoped . . . God, he hoped . . . his relief didn't show on his face.

"No question. Absolutely. I'll give you my direct contact, my secretary's direct contact, and my home contact. If you can't reach me by the first two, tell my wife—her name's Callie—that it's an emergency, and *she'll* find me. You know the Strip. You do what you need to do, your way. For contact, yes. I'll also give you the personal number of Bellemy Jameson, head of security. Mr. Jameson *will* be cooperative if you call him." If he wanted to keep his job, Jameson would, and *damned* if he would go through Hewitt to issue the order to station security. "I assure you of that." He jotted multiple numbers and names onto a notepad and handed them across the desk. "In general, you won't need an appointment: just walk right on through the back offices corridor directly to this one. If it's off-shift, the personal number will still reach me. I'm never far from my com."

"I'll find what I can," Monahan said. "Good or bad."

Somehow, Abrezio thought, as Monahan left his office and he reached for the phone to call Jameson—somehow he doubted there'd be anything *good* about it.

Chapter 3   Section v

Mercy Infirmary #210 Green sat in a better area of the Strip, sandwiched between a clothing shop and a fast food restaurant: a plain pressure door with *Mercy Infirmary* stenciled in large letters, and a long corridor behind it—with, once you walked in, a *you-are-here* and an arrowed direction for Emergencies/Outpatient Services one way, and Admissions/Visitor Services the other, at a T intersection. Ross stopped and looked either direction.

Visitor Services seemed the best bet, in a hallway made cheerful by warnings about venereal disease and the risk of jump drug addiction, with call numbers for various services. A single anomalous vase of aged imitation flowers sat at the intersection, and down a stub of a hallway, there was the further choice of Vending and Admissions.

Opposite that, an information desk manned by a fresh-faced teenager otherwise occupied by a game unit.

Attentive, however. The kid looked up, focused, said, "Yes, sir?"

"Looking for Fallan Monahan."

"Fallan Monahan," the kid said into a mike, and got a tinny robotic answer. "B five." The kid pointed to the obvious B at the next side hall and looked at his display. "Room five." And returned to his handheld video game.

No information to be had there. Ross took the directions to B, walked down a short hall provided with several hard chairs. The door of room 5 was open, and Fallan was lying in bed, looking asleep and not too bad—except the screens beeping and blipping around him, with sensor patches stuck on his temple, his hand, his arm, God knew where else, and a huge machine arm arched over him.

Ross gave a gentle rap on the door frame. Fallan opened his eyes, saw him, shifted an arm under his pillow. That movement stopped with a grimace and a shake of a patched-up arm. "Damn sticky-patches. They call all hell down on you if you mess with them. How're you doing, kid? Those idiots arrest you?"

"We're fine. We're all fine. Mary T, Ashlan, and me." Ross came to the bedside, helped Fallan adjust the pillow, moved a chair close. Fallan was paler than he'd ever seen. Maybe it was the unforgiving lights, but Fallan looked like hell, his grey hair spiked and tangled, his paper-thin skin, telltale of years and years on the pushers and now on *Galway*, white and transparent, looking too fragile for the adhesive patches stuck at every pulse-point. "How about you, sir?"

"Doing all right." Fallan waved a sensor-patched hand at the adjacent table, where a bin sat with a small bottle and several packages with a blue "charitable gift" stamp. "Collected me a few consolations. Bottle's local vodka, from *Nomad,* Pell tea from *Mumtaz,* and some kind of fruit sweets from *Little Bear* . . . I mean, I got a *thing* going here."

"Looks like," Ross said, pulled up the sole chair, unpadded and a bit tippy, and sat down.

"You?"

"Not a scratch. Completely out of the action.—Fallan, I'm *sorry.* I should have kept with you!"

"Hell if. *I* should've sat still. Old instincts. Got excited, ran for the door like a fool teenager and shouldna done it. Were you in the hall? That mess outside?"

"Not so quick as you. Gotta work on my reflexes. Stuck inside in a jam-up of Santiagos. Just too slow on the jump. I looked around, and you were off and so was Niall, and then the damn Santiagos came over the tables between us and you. We thought, all of us, me, Mary, and Ashlan, we thought you were away safe. We had no idea the blue-coats had done more than lock the doors and take names. Barkeeper decided to keep pouring drinks, so we had us a beer. So did the *Finity* lot, and we just all waited for things to sort out and the doors to open. Barkeep backed us when the blue boys finally came through and started taking names. We went on to Rosie's. We'd heard Niall had got a see-me from Abrezio. So we waited where we thought everybody would come. Then I got a message from Niall that you were in here and *he* wants to know you're all right. Damn, Fal, I'm *sorry.*"

"Oh, it was stupid, but not you. Hell, you got yourself another beer, didn't you? Not your fault I ran, not your fault the blue-coats started swinging sticks. Then somebody's down and it was merry hell. Fools. They had no legal call even to lock the damn doors. Way over-excited. One of the blue-boys tased a Santiago right at the door as he was trying just to clear the way, and then everybody was pushing and shoving and falling all over each other. I hear there's a Santiago down the hall, don't know if it's the same guy or not. Don't know how he is. That's pretty well all I remember." Fallan drew a deep breath, and one of the machines beeped. "Damn that thing. I'm clear-headed enough now, I think. Do I sound clear?"

"Clear as ever."

"They say I hit my head. That I probably won't ever remember that bit. Ever. I don't like that. Never have lost a piece of my memory before."

Nav, for God's sake. It was no minor thing.

"Well, ever's a long time for you, old man. You can spare an hour and not miss it."

"Ha. Don't you pull any games on me. The old man knows it was three minutes twelve seconds he was out."

"Trust you to track it."

Glum expression. "I cheated. They *told* me. They didn't want to, but they told me. I'm still going out from time to time, just phase out and wake up. Not liking that, Ross. *Really* not liking that."

"Y'know, it's called *sleep,* Fallan."

"I *do* know, an' that's not any kind of real sleep. They better not give me drugs. I'm not having any stand-down. We make our run out of here and I'm going to be at my post, dammit. Not stayin' here, no matter what any doc says. They say I'm in here for twenty-four hours, f' God's sake. Observation. They *do* know not to give me drugs. They got to know that."

"Who's your doctor? You've got one, right?"

"Dr. Bocali. E. Bocali. Wet behind the ears. Jack came in." Jack was *Galway*'s own number one medic. "Told me be patient with 'em. Patient. Nanos. Hell and damnation. Station medics are all right for a cut finger, but they got no concept. No concept."

No concept of the physiology and training that brought a navigator up out of jump aware and *remembering* his place, his next moves when a ship dropped into realspace. You didn't just *take* a post on a ship, you trained for it life-long and only a few, five percent if that, actually qualified at Nav or Helm. Seated as Nav 1.1? Come up out of jump-haze that aware, with infallible memory and a plan?

Station medics couldn't comprehend just how important that three minutes and twelve seconds was to a mind like Fallan's, that could account for every waking moment of his life, that knew, absolutely, the difference between reality and not-reality. Had to. Lives depended on it. And not just the Family. These medics' own lives could be at risk if something went wrong. Nav could never hesitate, never question what was real.

What he heard from Fallan tasted bad. The whole thing tasted bad. Idiot station medics messing with Nav 1's head. Wasn't right.

"You'll be fine," Ross said. And God, he hoped that was true. Hell. It was Fallan who'd got him interested in nav, and if Ross had one mission on the Strip, ever since he'd been free of the minders, it was staying close and taking care of Fallan. The first time he didn't . . . look what had happened. "When are they letting you out of here? You want me to sit with you?"

"Hell, no. Get out there. Help find out what's goin' on with the blue-boys an' bring me news."

"I'll do that. But I want to know when they're letting you out. I'll pick you up."

"Hey, I don't need a minder."

"I owe you, Fal."

"The hell."

"Do. I screwed up. I got my head wrapped tight in what they were saying up there and I didn't move fast enough."

"What you talkin' about?"

"I froze, Fallan. I got distracted and I friggin' froze. Which is how those fool Santiagos got between us. They came over the tables, they jammed up in the doorway, and the doors shut."

"Well, Critical Mass ain't the boards, is it? Two beers down and we ain't any of us all that smart."

"I froze."

"An' I was bein' a fool. If I'd remembered I wasn't eighteen, I'd have sat still like a sane person and not scampered for the door with the youngers. Stuck around for a beer and charged it to Neihart, wouldn't I? Not feeling my age at the

time. Dunno why I did it." A pause. A frown, like looking
into the dark, trying to see. "Or . . . I do. I was seeing *Gaia*
crew up there."

"*Finity,* Fallan," Ross said, suddenly scared. "It was
Finity's End crew."

"*Gaia,*" Fallan said firmly. "They *were*. They *are*. There's
a ship with the luck." Deep breath, which set the monitor
lines to rippling. "And drop that look, kid. I'm tracking true.
Ships change. Crews don't. Family's family. Luck's luck.
And when that fight broke out . . ." Fallan stared off into
years and decades before the likes of Ross Monahan had
ever been born. Before *Galway* herself was born. "I knew
me a girl once. I saw old *Gaia* after her convert to FTL, and
I knew me a girl. It was Venture dock. And I was *Atlas* crew.
There was a mixup in a bar. *Gaia* and *Atlas* against old *Boreale*. She shouldn't have looked at me. But she did. After."
Deep, deep breath. "After was *quite* a time."

"Nothing wrong with *your* memory, old man."

A lopsided grin, as a little color touched Fallan's skin,
and his look returned to the present. "Nothing wrong with
that sleepover either, Ross-me-lad. I swear to you, never a
touch of better-than-you from that girl. We just hit it off.
We did. We spent a two-week layover, and we went our
ways. Don't know if she's still alive. Name was Lisa. Never
forgot her."

He'd never heard Fallan talk much about the old days,
except in terms of ports visited and trips made. Fallan remembered things—lost things, forgotten things, but Fallan
always said the next station was the important thing. Fallan
would talk about the days when Thule was up and going at
its treacherous star, the precautions they had had to take,
and the devastation that star had worked when it cut loose.
He'd talk about Glory back just after the discovery of FTL,
when Glory had some of the gloss still on it. Now it was a
sad, forlorn place, that smelled, even—smelled of age and
chronic neglect. Nobody went to Glory now without special effort. It wasn't on the path to anywhere anybody
wanted to go. They just kept it alive—EC orders—a resource, they said. But for what, nobody was sure, even the
people who lived there.

And those people, even if they wanted to, couldn't leave. There was nowhere for them to go. Even if some station, Venture or beyond, would take them in, they'd have no meaningful station credit to transfer, and there'd be no jobs available for people trained in technologies decades behind every other station.

It was . . . scary. He'd never had thoughts like this before, like what would happen if the stations they serviced just . . . ceased to exist. They'd carried supply to Glory, because Glory needed it. It was . . . what they did. There was no profit in it for them, but by ancient agreement, there was a place to sleep when they got there, and fuel for the next leg of their route.

And if Pell cut off Alpha . . . if those jump points to Sol never were found . . . Alpha itself could become like that. Pell could write off all the First Stars. Even Venture was eventually disposable, if Pell began to define itself as the origin-point for humankind. Or if Cyteen did. Everything back here, within ten lights from Sol, could just be written off as ghosts of the past, irrelevant, and best forgotten.

Dammit. That was poison-thinking. They *would* find that jump point, and Alpha would become the thriving station it once had been. Better than it had been, because Sol goods would flow freely to markets hungry for the new and different.

He looked at Fallan and thought, *If it weren't for* Finity *coming in here, if it weren't for these outsiders, you wouldn't be lying in a hospital bed.* The visitors from the *Beyond,* as they called it, were all talk, and the talk, all of it, was only stirring up trouble that would benefit no one except those that sent them. That was all it amounted to. There was no way some amalgam of Alpha Families was going to lay hands on *Rights,* just no way. And if by some miracle they did, they damned sure wouldn't defect to Pell. The EC might not be powerful where these outsider ships came from, but it controlled Alpha, had it locked down tight. The blue-coats numbered about one for every three spacers, in normal times. And Sol itself wouldn't give them up. Its orders were continually, so Alpha said, Be ready. We're coming.

All these visitors had altered the normal balance of Alpha residents versus spacer crews on the Strip and made the stationers nervous. The trade these people brought had lowered the price of flour and wine, hurt *Santiago's* bottom line, crowded the Strip, and caused, now, *two* riot calls.

Damned straight they owe you an apology, Fallan Monahan. *Finity and* the blue-coats.

"Wot'cha starin' at, boy? I got me a wart or somethin'?"

He shook his head to clear it. "Yeah," he said, finishing their old joke. "Right about . . ." He tapped his right temple. "Here."

Fallan chuckled, winced, and shut up.

"Much pain?"

"Just shaken up. Mortal headache. And that memory gap. *They* aren't so worried about that. They claim it's kind of natural when you get hit on the head." Fallan's look said it was not natural, that it wasn't the first knock to the head he'd taken, and that, between them, he was a little scared. That he'd *be* scared until that missing time came back. Nav didn't drop stitches. If anything, they were hyper-aware, picking up things most people didn't, multiple things at once, so if Nav was staring off into space, Nav was doing multiple things regular minds didn't lay hands on—and you didn't ever talk to them, not even on social occasions, if you saw them timed-out.

Like now. And from the look, those thoughts included *Gaia* and a girl named Lisa.

Ancient memories surfacing. Time-jumps. He didn't like that.

Damn the fool blue-coats. Damn the Santiagos while he was at it. So a fight broke out. You didn't shove anybody senior, you didn't shove a junior-junior, and you damned well didn't shove Fallan Monahan, even if you were the law.

Ross wanted, sincerely, to hit somebody—but that wouldn't help the situation. So he just clenched his hands and watched as Fallan's eyes drifted shut again.

The monitors stayed steady. Everything seemed all right. Still, Ross sat there a moment longer, reluctant to leave.

Fallan's eyes slitted open. "Trying to read me, are you?"

"Trying to be sure you're all right."

"I'm fine."

"Fallan, if you want—"

"What I want is out of here. Which won't happen for twenty two hours, seventeen minutes and a parcel of seconds, station time, so I'm stuck."

"I'll stay."

"No, you won't. I don't want anybody sitting and staring at me like some spook."

"Niall said . . ."

"Yeah, well. Niall's not here. Tell Niall I said no. Go. Get. Don't be a pain."

"Niall said take care of you."

"And you tell Niall I didn't need a minder when I was a junior-junior, and I still don't need one. Tell me. How do you solve for the El Dorado drift?"

A chilly sort of question; navigational problem from the far-out dark. "Don't need to because we don't go there. Which you *do* remember, don't you?"

"Uppity kid. I'll give you that one to solve, next shift we sit."

"FTLs've never been there. You *couldn't* remember it."

"Makes no nevermind, Ross-me-lad. I know all the old places. Know their quirks and their works, and I can *feel* a star about to flare."

"You can't. You watch the readouts like everybody else, you faker."

Fallan gave an eyes-shut grin. "Niall's never sure on that. I've had him on for years. Continue the tradition."

"Don't talk to me about tradition, you old faker. I'm not doing your work for you. Get well and get back to work."

"I'm never wrong, howsomever. You should remember that."

"You probably aren't," Ross said. The readouts were ticking up. "But you better make those machines happy or there'll be some medic in here."

"Some damn bot, more like. Blinky eyes. Looks like a trash can. I'd like to re-label the creature. Been thinking about that as a parting gift."

"You're doing better."

"Filch me one of those medical waste labels?"

"Go on. You know I can't."

"Useless kid. Learn yourself some slight-of-hand. Useful, that is. Your stayin' here . . . that's not useful. Go. Get."

"Yes, sir," Ross said, and sat.

"So?"

"So you going to show me the approach on El Dorado? Or is that a fake?"

"Not a chance til I shed this headache. Go. Now." Fallan reached a finger for the buzzer.

"Going," Ross said, and got up and left, staying for a backward look from the door.

"Get!"

"I told him it wasn't smart," was Bellamy Jameson's word on the whole affair, after Abrezio had explained the situation on com. *"But he said the moment they said anything about* Rights *and what it was for, they needed to be shut down. I tried to wait, got pinged from Hewitt's office to stop stalling. The doors . . . that was just plain stupid. I called it wrong, boss. I knew better and I called it wrong."*

Long time since Bellamy had called him that. "At least you had the sense to contact me before going back in."

A wry chuckle. *"I can only hope Hewitt doesn't check my private texts. He's not happy about how that went down."*

"Well, you can help make it right now, Bellamy. Just do as I say, and don't bother telling Hewitt. Don't lie if he asks directly, and if that happens, just send him to me and I'll deal with it. We need the Monahans to trust us. They're our best hope to keep this under control . . . whatever *this* is."

"No problem. Hewitt's all right, I guess, but between you and me, I wish you still controlled Strip security. He just . . . doesn't do it. He gets it, he just doesn't give a damn if he upsets the crews."

They should have had this conversation a long time ago. Bellamy, once head of all station security, had had no choice when Hewitt used his EC orders to take over Strip security. By those orders, situations that directly affected *Rights* and her crew were, theoretically, under Hewitt's jurisdiction. Yet another example of dictates coming from people who had no idea what the reality was out here, what kind of contingencies needed to go into orders like Hewitt's. But those orders did *not* exempt Hewitt from answering to station management, if station management was ready to take the heat, and if Bellamy was disgruntled . . .

That was actually helpful.

"Help me get through the next couple of weeks, and I'll treat you to dinner."

Old, old code between them. Dinner . . . and a chance for completely off the record discussion.

"Never turned down a free meal, boss."

Chapter 4   Section ii

A dark-haired girl was sitting in one of the hard chairs in the infirmary corridor, spacer type, plain grey jacket. She stood up, oblong package in hand, and Ross spotted the sleeve patch, the arrogant, featureless black patch that was *Finity's End*. No patch but that, no patch for trade or seating. Junior crew.

He stopped, stared with no good feeling. *"Finity,"* he said.

"Galway," she said.

"Ross Monahan, Nav 3, first shift. What do *you* want?"

"How is he?"

"What's it to you?"

"Concern. On the part of my ship. On the part of everybody. Honestly."

He'd walked out mad at the whole situation, wanting someone or something to direct that mad toward. The girl with the package and the jacket patch didn't look directly responsible. That didn't help much.

He scowled.

"Fourth captain knows him. Knew him. Long time back. You were in the bar earlier, weren't you?"

"I was there."

"Senior captain mentioned you. Didn't expect you here."

James Robert mentioned him? To *her*?

He tipped his head back. "Yeah? So what'd he say?"

"Ross Monahan. Third nav, first shift."

"Which I just said."

"And that you stayed after the doors shut, and had drinks with us. Seemed sensible enough."

Us. Meaning members of the Family. Not her. He'd have remembered.

"I stayed. Not my choice. Had a drink; that was all. Meanwhile my captain's now on an admin call and our Nav 1 got hit on the head and knocked out for three plus minutes." He jerked his head toward the door. "Should be *me* in there, not him. Should've been me between him and whatever got him. Instead, I got cut off and caught inside, no thanks to your captain and his talk of who's owed what. Any fool should've known that would trigger the bluecoats." That . . . felt a little good. A little release of the pent up anger that had had nowhere to go.

She bit her lip, said in a low tone, "I'm so sorry."

It was a sincere tone. An earnest, pretty face and sorrowful stare that met his without a flicker. It left him nowhere dignified to go from there. But it in no wise moved him to let *Finity* crew into the room with Fallan asleep.

"That for him?" Meaning the red-wrapped package pressed to her chest. She blinked and held it out to him.

"Pell whiskey."

Pricey stuff. Not true Scotch, which Alpha sometimes shipped outward, but almost as pricey this far from Pell. He'd seen it on offer, never spent for it, not even a single drink.

He took the package. Heavy. Full-sized bottle.

Well, *Finity* should throw a bit of scrip around, after a mess-up like that. "You sending one to my captain?"

"Dunno. Could well. I'm sure senior captain would like to talk with him. Apologize in person. But this bottle is for your Nav 1, from fourth captain. She remembers him."

She remembers him. *She.* Instincts twitched.

"What's her name?"

"Lisa Marie. We all call her Mum. She remembers him. From way back."

Fourth captain. Damn. Captains didn't talk to seated

officers of other ships. But—somebody from a long time ago. *Lisa.* Was there *any* chance?

"Chance he might like to talk with her," he said.

"Might could do that. I'll carry word."

"Appreciate it."

"How is he? Can I tell her that?"

"Knocked out for some three minutes. Concussed. Pretty weak. *Nav.* You understand me."

"Absolutely. I'm so sorry. He's to get the best. *Finity* says. We'll cover it."

"Why?" He was a little surprised, a little offended, not sure what else. "Fourth captain's say? Or Senior Captain's conscience?"

"Either way you take it. If your captain gets any chaff about this from admin, if station isn't taking care of you ... tell any of us. Senior Captain wants to know. He doesn't want people taking damage from our being here."

"Bit late for that, isn' it?"

That got him a quick look. An emphatic: "Nothing illegal, Galway. Not now, not ever."

"Not talking law. Talking delays and sudden influx of lux-goods driving the prices down.—Why *are* you here? Why are *all* these ships here?"

"That's for the captains to talk about. But say we're not here to hurt any local's trade or routes or business. That much I do know. That's not what we're about."

"Yeah. Well, it's hurt already."

"Enough to cover station charges, no more. And first captain's trying to make it right. There'll be another meeting."

"When?"

"After the captains talk." She looked down to her hands, fingers interlaced. Her thumbs tapped silently. Nervous tick, maybe. "Buy you a drink, Ross Monahan?" she asked, polite-sounding. And the eyes that came up held nothing but kindness. A hint of hope, maybe. "I'd *like* to. No strings, no business. Your choice."

... Never a touch of better-than-you ...

Easy to expect otherwise, considering the ship, considering the history.

He'd been, maybe, a little rude, counting it was a *Finity* captain who'd sent the package, and counting Fallan had had a hookup with *Gaia,* once upon a station call. Maybe with this same fourth captain, though she'd for certain not been a captain then.

And now this *Finity* girl was offering him a drink, maybe hoping for information. And maybe she knew more than she said. If there were things to learn from her, maybe he *should* try to find out.

If there was another meeting coming, maybe *Galway* should know whether to attend, or what was on offer. He hadn't heard the result of admin's talk with Niall, and he hadn't had any order yet telling him *not* to talk to a nice *Finity* girl who'd shown up with a 300-cred bottle of whiskey, instead of the anything-fermentable vodka most stations produced.

Hell. He might get in trouble. But he wouldn't get Fallan in trouble. Fallan was the offended and innocent party and there was that bottle of whiskey at issue, which Fallan certainly wouldn't turn down.

He wouldn't get Niall in trouble, either, considering his only orders from Niall since the dust-up had been to check on Fallan. He couldn't see how a drink with a *Finity* girl could cause trouble . . . and it *might* explain things.

"Ross?"

He met her eyes, then slowly shook his head. "Sorry. Can't."

Her eyes clouded.

"Not without a name, Finity."

She grinned, and the whole room seemed suddenly brighter. "Jen, Ross. My name's Jen Neihart."

"Well . . . I guess it's all right then." He shook off the effect of that smile. Couldn't let such things distract him. "There's some kind of little bar next to the eatery," he said. "Next door. I don't want to go off too far. And . . . well, I don't want to be seen around with you. With any *Finity* crew. Nothing personal, but we got *enough* going on with admin right now, thanks to you."

"Understood," she said.

He raised the wrapped bottle. "I'll take it in to him. I'll tell him about it, if he's awake."

Fallan wasn't. Or he was deep in calc, which Fallan sometimes did, just to occupy his mind. The screens were all ticking away, steady, reassuring.

He added the package to the bin with the other gifts, and quietly left.

Chapter 4   Section iii

It was a hole-in-the-wall place that served as drink source for the eatery and indirectly served the infirmary, as a place where people on an infirmary vigil could catch a snack or a drink. They ordered drinks and chips to cushion the alcohol, and faced each other across a small, scarred table, under a changing neon that went from red to blue to purple.

They sat in lengthy silence until the drinks came, and then just eyed one another until a sip had had time to hit bottom.

She had dark eyes, Jen did, and she was a little on the skinny side, but fit-skinny, by how she moved. Not tall. The wiry sort who, as a youngster, frequently got sucked into maintenance, because they'd fit the narrow spots.

Or served as runners, in their early years. A little old, maybe, to be a runner. But who knew? On a *big* ship, maybe—

The sleeve didn't give a clue. Just that one patch, saying *Finity* owned deep space, though they were newer than *Galway*.

Gaia hadn't been new, though. That was what that patch claimed. First and oldest of all ships. Shiver, you new-comers to space. We were *here*.

Yeah, well, he said to himself. We have our history, too, off old *Atlas* and older *Argo*. We were sub-lighters, too, least Fallan was, in the pre-convert days. We just weren't as lucky as you. Didn't happen to be where you could get the big help. We threw in our lot with Alpha, when everyone else left her to starve.

Still here. Got a *right* to be here. Who're *you?*

He didn't say any of that. Just . . .

"So what *can* you tell me? Alpha's not your route, not even near. You come in empty. So your manifest says. Hard to make a profit that way. Plan to undercut us on your way out, maybe, with that big hold? Hate to tell you, Sol stuff is long gone, til *Atlantis* gets in. Bit of a wait, that."

He didn't expect her to tell the truth, either, maybe not to answer at all, because he couldn't, right now, muster a nicer tone. The magic of that grin had vanished, leaving him with just that patch, and what she and her ship had brought in. All the questions. All the distrust. It was as if, sitting down in this meeting, the situation just came down on him.

She took a moment, rotating her drink on the tabletop, while moisture crawled down the side.

"Answered that already, Galway. We're here to help, not hurt."

"So you say. Doesn't make sense. Ships don't run this far just to lose money."

"Here's definitely a little out of the way for us," she admitted, drawing shapes out of the puddles on the tabletop, loops and lines. "Alpha's been out of the way for a long time." And glanced up. "But maybe not forever."

"You *know* something?"

A little shake of the head. She had a quirky sort of smile that he somehow trusted more than that grin. "No. I don't. But not forever, still. What I think, not what I know. Alpha's part, you know, part of the whole web. Merchanters can't make profit without ports. Last thing we want is to see any ports shut down."

Last thing we want . . . *Did* she know something? It was a weird topic to start with, but it was a weird circumstance that brought four outsiders into Alpha, too.

"So?" he said. "Keep going. I'm listening."

"I can't say because I don't know. I truly don't know and

if I did I couldn't say. I just know we've been meeting with various ships and crews at other stations. But it's captains' talk, not crew's. It's all about that."

"Meetings at other stations. What stations?"

"All the way from Mariner."

"So what do they say, your captains, when they meet? What do all these ships say?"

A shrug. "Not for me to report. Likely you know more than me on this one. You heard what my captain said in there. I wasn't at the meeting."

"Lots of words is what I heard. Lots of stuff about *Rights of Man,* with no fix for it. He talked about ownership. And Families. We already *own* our ships. That's not an issue at Alpha. Getting *finance* for our ships, getting cargoes, getting services, that's an issue."

"Captains will say, when it comes down to it. I can't speak for them."

"Your JR said *we* could do something. Made it sound like we could demand *Rights* for some Family. How likely is *that?* Not a chance in hell, is what any Alpha ship knows. And what's up with the other ships? Who's *we* in the first place?"

She shrugged, meaning even if she knew, she wasn't saying. Couldn't, any more than he could give away *Galway*'s secrets . . . if *Galway* had any.

It was just . . . weird. If FTL with Sol were imminent, he could imagine outsider ships maybe coming in to beat other ships, to be first in line to lock into the routes, to mess with local trade and maybe throw some foreign goods into the system to sweeten the interface. But if that was the case . . . wouldn't the locals be the first to know?

If it was all about *The Rights of Man* . . . why the talk of giving it to a local Family? That Pell and places beyond were upset about the EC running a merchant ship—one that carried a lot of additional personnel along with it— seemed pretty obvious. Question was . . . what did they think they could do about it? Were they here to stir up trouble between the station and the locals, and while everyone was distracted, were they going to try to do something with *Rights*—like maybe take it by stealth and force, put a crew from *Finity* on her . . .

But imagination stumbled there. Take her and do . . . what? There was no proof *Rights* herself could even make one run, let alone be pirated clear to Pell. Destroy her, maybe. That would set whatever the EC planned back more than just the materials and time. Alpha couldn't take another twenty years of neglect. Destroy *Rights,* refuse to trade with Alpha . . . and Pell would have a ruined station as a buffer between them and Sol.

If Pell were truly that ruthless.

Maybe Pell was out to take over Alpha. If they backed *Rights* out, isolated the blue-coats on the station . . . But that didn't work. The four ships together *couldn't* try to take Alpha itself. They were *way* too few for that, even if stationers weren't fighters. They'd *become* fighters if they had to.

So that was all just crazy.

Unless they used control of *Rights* as leverage.

Cyteen outright hated the EC. That was a given. Pell had pitched the EC entirely off their deck when *Finity* was starting its actual build. That was fairly famous. It had finally let the EC come back, but rumor said it was a very small office and had to rely on Pell's security.

Everybody knew that Sol was eventually going to have its own opinions about Pell and Cyteen, but as things stood, Sol could talk all they wanted, and even Alpha didn't have to listen. Orders from Sol, orders that could kick up a fuss with Pell, all came on the Stream, a couple of decades behind-times, and with no manpower to back them.

Did Sol figure as a problem that would bring Pell rushing in?

Not yet. But as JR Neihart had pointed out: that could change overnight—everything could change overnight, if Sol found the necessary jump point.

Could it possibly be that close? Could Sol just—turn up, faster than the Stream could tell them it would happen? If they found the jump point . . . hell, yes. And the thought of a first-time crew coming insystem at who knew what vector . . . in a ship the size of *Rights*? That carried a whole lot of scary.

Jen was looking at him, wondering, he supposed, what he was thinking, in the growing silence, knowing, probably, that if she asked, he'd tell her as much as she'd told him . . . which was nothing. It was beyond awkward, and the worst was, if it weren't for the mystery surrounding her presence, he thought, maybe, there'd be no awkward, only possibilities. That her silence was loyalty to her ship and captain, nothing more.

"I've got a question for you," Jen said, finally, breaking that silence.

He shrugged. "Go."

"You said any fool should have known. Call me a fool, but why *did* the EC jump on the meeting in the first place? We weren't doing anything illegal, were we?"

"Not exactly."

"Even by a stretch?"

"Not exactly."

"What do you think they thought was going on?"

He shouldn't have said that. She wasn't a fool. He was getting that much. Her captain definitely wasn't. And if the point hadn't been to set the blue-coats off, could the situation really be *that* different . . . out in the Farther Stars? Did they really think they could swagger in, start bad-mouthing the EC . . . and *not* set the blue-coats off?

"They're blue-coats. They're suspicious anyway. And there's a lot of strangers on the Strip. It's more people on the Strip than I've ever seen. So they're jumpy. Everyone is, case you haven't noticed. You came in like the devil was tailing you. You scared hell out of people. Figuring is, now, you *meant* to scare hell out of us."

"We had a choice, come in slow, way out, and keep people in suspense for days, or come in fast, and not. And this being a touchy star, yeah, fast, if we were coming in close. By what you say, either way people would be upset."

"Upset doesn't cover it. This is *Alpha*, f' God's sake. A short hop from Beta. Bogies coming out of the dark *upset* people here."

She tipped her head. "What do you mean?"

"You could have talked! Three hours, the boards had just the *incoming* message. No ID. No origin. Nothing. And the telemetry, when we saw it . . . God!"

"I don't know what you're talking about. I'm sure we sent the ID. First pulse. Always. I wasn't on the bridge, so can't say I saw the button pushed, but I'm sure we did."

"After."

"Soon as we could. Standard procedure."

"You saying station's to blame? You saying *station* kept it from us?"

"I'm saying I'm sure bridge sent the ID. Didn't want to scare anyone. We're not like that. Captain knows about Beta. We all do. He reminded us, last thing before jump."

"So you say."

"No reason, Ross. No reason not to tell."

Even if she was telling the truth, something about that mysterious entry still rankled.

"You and these other ships. You're all together. Same reason."

"Definitely."

"They knew you were coming."

"Definitely."

"So why didn't *they* say who it was?"

She blinked. "I . . . don't know." She stared into her drink a moment, then pressed her lips against . . . dammit . . . it was that quirky smile.

"What?"

"Well . . . it's Min. Xiao Min. *Little Bear*'s senior captain. It wasn't *our* Senior Captain's orders, that silence, I can tell you that much. But Xiao Min. . . . he likes *moments* . . . if you know what I mean. He . . . reads people, situations, by how they react to *moments*."

And *Finity*'s arrival had definitely been that. And if she was right, if *Finity* had sent that ID on schedule and it was Abrezio who kept it quiet . . . well, this *Min* might read something into that, for sure. Ross was trying real hard not to read too much into it himself.

"You're here. Together. You and these ships. Why?"

"To talk to Alpha merchanters. We want it clear it's not just *Finity* on her own. We rep a lot of others, that's what, and they're here so it's not just our word on it."

"But you won't say who you rep, and what you're here to talk *about.*"

"I can't say when my captain hasn't, not even if you were Nav 1. And I won't. Captains need to hear from captains first. Sorry for that. But I can't. Your captain will get a call. Likely would have already, if the EC hadn't interfered."

That was definite. And he couldn't work past it. He had to respect her loyalty. Situation reversed, he'd do the same.

"So my captain's gotten called in by admin. Nav chief's in infirmary with a head injury. We're loaded up to go, but we can't go because Alpha's not clearing any ship to go, which means our schedule's *screwed* and we're losing income *and* reputation. It's kind of a hard day, Jen Neihart. All thanks to your ship."

"We are so sorry. All I can say. None of us did the shoving. None of us closed those doors. And that's the truth, too. There was no call for that. There was none of us called for anything that threatened harm."

"Except saying we should take that ship."

"Didn't say you should *take* it. Said the station should *give* it to somebody who can handle it."

"I was there," he pointed out defensively, but thinking back, he realized she was right.

"And *I* know the Senior Captain wouldn't say go take it. That'd be against the law." Her eyes narrowed ever so slightly and she leaned forward, crossed arms on the table. "Listen, Galway. Something maybe you haven't thought about. You thought our entry was scary-fast. You say station had three hours of wondering what was coming at them and that made tempers hot. You think about what every other station is thinking and wondering right now, knowing that ship out on A-mast exists, wondering if that ship out on A-mast actually has the same engines as brought *Finity* in, wondering when that ship might actually make a jump and come into *their* system with a bunch of novices at the boards trying to remember which way's up, and maybe not finding it before they blow the station to smithereens. Dunno if that was on my captain's mind, or Min's, but it's something to think about."

Echo of his own worries, and with fewer unknowns. Those stations further on *knew* that *Rights* existed, had seen *Finity* in action. For nearly twenty years they'd known *Rights* was coming . . . and then they'd have gotten news of that first trial run and its sudden shut-down, aborting the jump. Bryant's Station, as their destination, had to be wondering . . . what if that first run *hadn't* aborted?

He'd be wondering, too. He'd be worried, if he was stuck on one of those stations, sitting target for a badly aimed bow wave.

"I don't know, Ross," she said, face earnest as hell. "I'm not the captain. Not certain why he chose to come in close. I do know we could have come in far and spent days and days meandering in while rumors flew, or we could come in the way we did, and by the way, *maybe* put the fear of God into some people who had better know what they're putting into the hands of novices. You're Nav. You know it. If stationers trained on sims ever take that ship out and don't plot a careful entry, they're going to kill themselves, and probably a whole lot of others. If Alpha's *really* unlucky, they're going to survive the trip out and then cash it all in on the way *back*."

Was that the real reason they'd come? A dramatic wakeup call to the station? Could it really be no more . . . and no less . . . than that? For years the grim humor on the Strip had centered around the ways in which that sim-trained crew could foul up. That humor had turned black and lost the laughter, thanks to *Finity's* entry. That much couldn't be denied.

She'd relaxed, her point made, and sat, head propped on one hand, the other tracing patterns on the table.

"Alpha is the world of not-going-to-happen," Ross said, to himself as well as her. "Things hang forever. This is a pusher-world: nothing happens fast. An EC world: everything operates on *rules*. The blue-coats . . . they got scared. They didn't have a rule. That's what happened. Somebody tried to make a fast decision about that meeting and nobody had a rule. So it went every which way." And with a sense of betrayal in the realization, recalling his own thoughts—that Alpha was the best the First Stars had to offer—and realizing how little that meant, in the world she came from: "There's only one place more backward than here and that's Glory, which is down to a few hundred people keeping the lights on. You ever been there?"

"Never, well, not since we were *Gaia*. Then, yes. Me personally, no. Never. You?"

"Regular. Part of our run. Where's yours go? Pell?"

"Pell, Viking, Mariner, yeah, definitely. Pell's our home station."

Exotic places. Places at the edge of the rest of the universe. The Beyond. Rich places. "Different than here, I'll imagine."

She didn't answer right away, just looked at him. Something in his voice he maybe wished wasn't. Then: "Every station's different."

"What are they like, those places?"

"Viking's plain, all utilitarian. Lot of bare metal. Noisy. Clangs and thuds and echoes. Mariner's bright. Lot of color, little shops. Lot of Cyteen stuff coming in there. Pell's got a lot of color, too. Vid displays everywhere you look. And you got Downers moving about: I've seen a couple."

Downers. the indigenous intelligent species of the planet Pell circled. God.

"I've just seen pics," he admitted, trying to sound casual

"Well, it was off at a distance. Not much more than dots, but they were little. Like youngers. But then Pell's docks— they're huge. Makes everybody look tiny."

Ring-docking. Again. He'd seen pictures, sure. But the sparkle in her eyes, the tone of her voice when she said it—was the awe of someone who'd just impressed hell out of the world *he* knew. Someone who resonated to those faraway things in a way that told him there were wonders out there *she* knew, and he had never seen.

I knew me a girl once, Fallan had said, in that same tone. *I knew me a girl once. I saw old* Gaia *after her convert, and I knew me a girl . . .*

As the pushers faded, and *Gaia* changed, and everything changed. And Lisa still remembered him, and he remembered her.

She shouldn't have looked at me. But she did.

The way, he thought, maybe, he was looking at this girl, off *Finity's End*.

And she didn't turn away.

Their hands rested naturally close to each other on the little table-top. He moved his, stopped, because *shouldn't have* was the truth. But dark eyes gazed back, eyes that had seen all those sights, and he stared back, thinking, *If—*

Her fingers touched his. He felt it. He moved his hand forward, fingers to fingers.

And stopped, thinking: *We're not their match.* More than the difference in the ships, what she'd seen, who she'd been with . . . they were biologically close to the same age, but in experience . . .

"I know you're sitting with your friend," she said, "and hanging close here. But if you'd like company in the watch, I'd be happy to stay. I've got nowhere I really have to be."

Fingers touching fingers. Fingers curled in fingers, and doubts faded.

"The on-call hospice is two doors over. I'm going to check in there for the night. My com's tagged to Fallan's room. I don't expect a call. They're just observing, and he doesn't want me hanging about. But the on-call's where I'll be. Company for supper, maybe, if you don't mind this place, which is what we've got." He gathered nerve to say, "Sleepover, if you like."

"I don't know," she said, and it was a reasonable caution on both sides. Their ships didn't know each other.

He could be a problem. She could.

But Fallan and a *Gaia* girl had known each other, in the day.

"Let's just go where it takes us," he said. "Supper. I'm buying."

"Fine with me." She added, not an objection, "Shares."

She paid for the drinks. They were hand in hand when they left.

And it was more than supper, after.

Wasn't her first time, wasn't his. And between strangers,

in a first sleepover and under the circumstances, manners
were in order, definitely.

Peacemaking, of a sort. She'd have no bad report of
Galway when she met up with her cousins; and he couldn't
say his impression of arrogance in *Finity* held out in Jen
Neihart. She was just, well, sweet, somebody he didn't
know if he'd meet ever again after their respective ships
left Alpha, and he damned sure didn't want her ship traf-
ficking in *Galway*'s territory—but damn, *she* was nice, no
politicking, no fuss, no complaining, no tale-bearing about
some other crew. Just happy. Just—

Damn, he wished she *were* a Galli or a Rodriguez. He'd
be glad to go on seeing her from time to time.

Real glad.

He'd checked in with *Galway*'s autocall. She'd done the
same with *Finity*'s. Their ships *had* to know where they
were, not necessarily that they were together. He'd also
checked in with the infirmary, but the report was "doing
fine"; and no call came.

Until morning, when the call sounded loud and clear,
and he waked to remember he was in bed with someone.
She waked and sat up, sheet fallen to her waist.

"That's the infirmary," she said, a fact clear enough on
the wall-screen. "God, it's 0900."

He reached to the nightstand and punched the button.
"This is Ross Monahan. Infirmary?"

An actual human voice said, *"Mr. Monahan, your party
is ready to check out."*

That was good news. It was real good news.

"I'll be right there," he said. "Don't let him leave. I'm
coming."

"Do I get to meet him?" Jen asked.

"Dress," he said, and looked for his clothes, which were
not neatly bestowed in the only chair, but mixed with hers,
on the floor. He didn't order room lights, just started gathering up his—morning shyness, it was, light only from the
bathroom. She hugged the sheet to her and asked, "Can
you pass my shirt?"

"Sure." He did that, snagged his own, sitting on the edge
of the bed. He tossed clothes over, and they dressed,

quickly, took advantage of the complimentary toiletries, put on boots and jackets, his with the triple knot of *Galway* on the sleeve, hers with the dark of deep space.

And faced each other.

"Do again?" she asked. "I would."

"Sure," he said.

"Tonight?"

"If Fallan doesn't need me." He opened the door, hand-printing the lock, which sent the tab to *Galway*'s account. "Let's help him carry the swag home, get him set up in the sleepover. Maybe we can set up a meeting, him with your Fourth. He might like that."

"Matchmakers," Jen said. Her slight smile made a set of mischievous dimples. "I love it. Let's."

Chapter 4   Section iv

"I'm fine," was Fallan's word. He had a gel-patch on his forehead, the dissolving sort, the card said. He was *not* supposed to take long walks, exercise, or carry heavy loads for a few days. He was *not* cleared for duty as yet, and he was damned mad about it.

But: "Who's this?" Fallan asked when Jen came through the door, and he pushed himself up out of the chair. "Don't tell me I'd forget *this* girl."

"You've never met her," Ross said. "Jen Neihart, Fallan Monahan. Fallan, somebody on *Finity* says they know you. Old *Gaia* crew. Name of Lisa."

Fallan sank back down into the chair. "Don't kid me, boy. You're saying Lisa? *Lisa Marie?*"

"Fourth captain on *Finity's End,*" Jen said from the doorway. "Lisa Marie."

"Good lovin' God."

"Your Lisa Marie is evidently who sent you a real expensive bottle of whiskey," Ross said, while Jen stood in

the doorway. "She evidently remembers you, too, she's real
sorry you got knocked down, and I'll suspect she's apt to
have dinner with you when you can walk without wobbling.
Doc says no sex for five days, however."

"Hell," Fallan said, pushing himself up again, not quite
as easily as he might have. "I'm feelin' better already. God.
Alive and well, and Fourth on *Finity's End*, no less."

"Used to be Senior on *Gaia*," Jen said. "Fourth on *Finity,* yes, sir, absolutely. We call her Mum. Most times we
call her Mum."

"Feeling a *lot* better," Fallan said, and grabbed his jacket
off the bed. "Dinner, you say. I'll buy. You tell her so."

"Later," Ross said firmly. "Day, maybe two. Right now,
you're going right back to the sleepover. And no fuss, Fallan Monahan. You're going to do what you're told at least
for tonight. Niall's going to be all over me if his nav chief
dies of pure stupidity. Just take it easy. I'm sure Jen here
will relay a message to your friend."

"No respect. No respect," Fallan said, beginning to fuss
his way into his jacket. "Your generation, no respect."

Then he stood still, frowning. "Damn. Niall. Abrezio.
How'd that summons come out?"

"No idea," Ross said. "Sorry to say—I was on-call for
some old guy in sickbay. *And* busy."

"That what you call it?"

"Come on. Jen, you carry his loot. I'll see he doesn't
take a dive."

"Walking just fine, thank you." Fallan held up his hand,
with the blue medical stamp on it. "Got my official release
from this damn lockup. Stop for breakfast? Stuff here is
crap."

Breakfasts and suppers were how the Family got together, operationally speaking and socially speaking. It was the hour between maindawn and maindark, when all four shifts met, shared meals, talked, and caught up on goings-on during the off hours.

The Zenith restaurant served the Olympian Hotel sleepover, and it truly wasn't bad, in JR's estimation. Not so fancy as some, and the offerings on the menu were limited, but they did well with what they had, and the menu had some things *Finity's* galley didn't. The fruit juice was heavily processed, but the local Earth-seed non-processed greens were very good. The pancakes were downright special, and made their way onto plates with steak and salad— first and fourth shifts were having breakfast and second and third were having supper, that being their o' clock, and, the Zenith being an obliging restaurant, there was no snobbery, no division of menus, no "this is the breakfast chef, this is the supper." Just mix and match as you liked.

"Better than Bryant's, by a far distance," was Fletcher's judgement, with a lot of agreement.

"No plastic eggs," Madison said. "How do they make those things? That's what I want to know."

"You don't ask," Fletcher said, "if you don't want the answer."

"Seen a food lab once," Boz said, down the table. "Put me off my food for days."

"Don't tell me," Madison said.

"It's—" Boz began, and voices from all the tables in range shut him down.

"Boz never missed a meal in his life," Kate said, and Mum:

"The pancakes are *lovely,* aren't they?"

Com unit gave a distinct quiver in JR's pocket. He put down his fork and took a look.

W, it said. *42.* And: *80 of 100.* The first letter identified the source: Walt, aboard *Finity,* at dock.

The second message meant, *Pretty well what we expected.* And the last was, *Customs attempting access.*

"Well," JR said. "Customs inspectors have shown up at the lock. I may need to cut breakfast short."

"Oh, finish your tea," Madison said. "They'll be arguing back and forth for an hour at least."

"Probably I should call Abrezio's office."

They weren't *supposed* to have crew left aboard. Alpha rules did advise that station customs *might* pull a random inspection. Given that Alpha had its own version of *Finity* at dock on A-mast, it was a fair guess certain people were dying to have a look inside the original, and *random* had nothing to do with it.

The on-board crew was using their own communications to reach them at the moment, a convenience that could be shut down once station figured out there was someone aboard. Station might notice that little blip of contact—if they were monitoring just about everything going on with *Finity,* which was highly likely.

Alpha wasn't supposed to be bugging the sleepovers, either, but they'd found and disabled a few fairly old-fashioned units. They'd warned the minders not to let the children mention certain topics, and the minders understood the seriousness of it all. They'd also doubled up on minders to keep the junior-juniors in line, a much harder proposition: they were keeping the kids confined, which they didn't like, but so busy with games and new distractions their heads must spin, and *Little Bear, Mumtaz,* and *Nomad* were doing much the same. It wasn't saying somebody might not slip, in one of four ship crews, but not spreading information to all ages and levels in the first place was the best security.

"Bet's on," Fletcher said, "that station admin calls before mainday lunch."

"Well," JR said, and topped off his cup, "I may start my

watch with station offices. Or not. I think I'll give them just a while to figure it out."

Fletcher said: "You're not going anywhere solo, Senior Captain, sir."

"We'll see how it goes," JR said, "but then I've been surprised before. Same for all of you—nobody goes anywhere alone." Sip of tea. "Abrezio's coming on watch. Give him at least time to have his morning tea. And we have a meeting I don't want to postpone."

That reaction last night had been . . . unexpected. They'd known the EC was strong here, stronger even than it had been on Bryant's, possibly as strong, if the blue-coat numbers were any indication, as it was reported to be on Glory, which was really nothing but an EC outpost now, maintained only at direct EC orders. Venture maintained an uneasy supremacy of its station administration over the EC offices, while Pell had outright put its EC office on notice that another incident, no matter how minor, would see the EC not only kicked off Pell, but very likely off Venture as well.

Getting rid of them here . . . would be a much harder effort.

But that wasn't their concern. Stations would do as they pleased.

As long as that pleasure didn't include invading a Family ship.

Chapter 5   Section ii

The message had gone out. *Finity's End* was standing off the customs people. But that was not what brought in, at a casual stroll, Xiao Min of *Little Bear,* who, passed at the door of the Zenith, settled at the same back table as *Finity* personnel, and ordered tea on his own tab.

Asha Druv of *Nomad* followed, a woman of middle

years, who wore fairly conspicuous flash—a purple jacket that sparkled, Mariner-style. Min, by contrast, was all black satin.

Then there was Sanjay Patel, who had a taste for gaudy electronics; and the *Mumtaz* crew jackets were embroidered in floral magnificence.

Not the least conspicuous company ever to assemble.

And Sanjay brought with him a stout, grey-haired woman in silver studs and black denim, red ship patch with a white fleur-de-lys: Giovanna Galli, she was. Of *Firenze*. Madison and Boz cleared chairs for Sanjay and the *Firenze* captain. JR rose from the table. So did other Finitys, a courtesy to a newcomer, who bobbed a responding courtesy.

"Finity," Galli said. "You're JR."

"I am, ma'am. You're Giovanna."

"Yes, sir, that I am. My ship's been screwed up, down, and sideways by Alpha admin, and I'm taking a raw edge of a chance coming here. I had to get five of mine out of detention yesterday. But I don't see the situation for us can get much worse."

"If all goes as we hope, it will get much better.—Please, have a seat."

"Yeah, well. We'll see." But she did sit, accepted the tea someone passed her, as everybody sat back down.

"You can talk here in relative safety," JR said. "The local coverage has been . . . temporarily disrupted . . . and I'm fairly certain the blue-coats will be busy elsewhere."

"The 42," Min said from down the table, meaning the coded alert from Walt aboard *Finity*. Warning about the attempted boarding.

"Yes," JR said. "It's not critical yet. Won't be unless they bring a cutter. Give the waiter a moment." A young man was bringing a rolling tray with refills, and he stayed to clear breakfast dishes. "Second and fourth shift can go off if they want."

"Hell, no," Mum said, clearly set to stay. She snatched her cup out of the waiter's reach and held up the empty tea caddy. "Fill, please."

"Yes, ma'am," the answer was, and the waiter took it, replacing it with a full one from an adjacent empty table.

Mugs followed. The tea caddy went the round, a new full water-pot chased after it, and, for Giovanna and Madison, the sweetener.

The waiter left.

"Customs just made a try," JR said. "We got the signal via the bundle, no problem. We're just waiting for the complaint."

"No movement against our ships," Min said.

"Us either," Asha said. "But they're dying to get a look inside *Finity*."

"Well and good, but they may try you next," JR said. "Just to see if they can, if nothing else."

"We are ready," Min said. "We anticipate it."

"You locked out customs?" Giovanna asked.

"We have our protocols. Their form had a polite yes/no about access. I checked no. I believe we all did."

Nods up and down the table.

"So we did tell them," JR said quietly, "and one hopes they'll enter quiet discussion about it."

"Ha," Min said.

JR shrugged, and addressed himself to Giovanna. "We don't allow inspections at any other station, either. Customs is welcome—if they observe restricted areas, only goods destined for offload. No wandering at will, and they go accompanied by a crew member who's empowered to say no."

"I hate to say," Giovanna said, "but access is not exactly an issue for us, since some very large ship moved in and bumped us off the mast."

"We do apologize for that. We hope to make it up to you."

A bitter laugh. "We have to get a special pass and hire a runabout to get aboard our own ship right now, and scheduled work's stopped. Last try was a bust, and nobody knows what the schedule will be. Listen, this isn't Pell. It's not even Bryant's. Things wait. If you're not in their face complaining, you get nowhere, and now that we're out there under bot control, we'll wait. We got a free push out. Bastards will probably charge us for pushing us in when you leave. You take up a lot of room, Finity. In all senses."

"We're aware of that."

"And you being what you are, the law doesn't apply, does it?"

"Customs has no need to wander through your ship. What comes off your ship, yes, but not what's staying on it."

"Like I said—you being what you are, Captain. And ring-docking's not happening here. Hell, we can't even repair what we've got. We got that black hole on A-mast. Until that ship goes jump, and probably after, good luck to us: Glory's the bag end of the universe, and we're the next stop up from them."

"Stations have obligations to us," JR said, "Conditions they have to maintain. Among other things."

"Good luck with that here." Giovanna drained her tea. "If that's all you wanted—"

"It's not. One understands you've had an ongoing nav problem."

"*One* would be correct," Giovanna said, scowling. "One would be damned correct. For the last five years, our ship has been in Alpha's hands more than ours. Perpetual repair job, which they keep patching. And we're delayed again."

"You need," JR said, "a repair they haven't been willing to give you."

"Repair, hell, I need a whole damn system. First engee's told them time and again, and instead of listening to him, they just keep patching it. And patching it. And patching it."

"If it's ghosty on entry, it's probably physical in origin, probably happening on a quantum level and likely involving the sensors," Boz said from down the table. "Programming's not the fix. Your engineer's right."

"So he's right. But we got no choice. Yeah, sure, we need a new system. It's damned scary making jump when the damn unit may or may not drop you out where it's supposed to. Last breakdown, it took us eight months—eight friggin' *months* to limp back in. Who wanted to trade with us, then? Who'll trust us for the next run, when we know damn well we can't guarantee anything *like* a delivery date? We *have* to set it wide and hope it doesn't get generous and drop us into the star."

"Terrifying," JR said, and meant it.

"Tell me so. I got a hundred forty-seven crew and two kids, who put their lives in my hands every time we leave port. I don't get a helluva lot of sleep on that thought. I don't want to take those mamas and kids out again." She shoved her chair back. "Excuse me."

Next to her, Madison put a hand on her arm. "We do have an answer, Captain."

"*Answer*? What friggin' answer?"

"A fix," JR said. "I'm not leading you on. Listen to me. Alpha hasn't the capability of fixing *Firenze*. That's why I wanted to talk to you ahead of all others—and ahead of Abrezio. Hold here for a fix. *Stay* at Alpha until the ship is safe." Giovanna started to protest the obvious and JR lifted a hand. "You can't go out again the way you are."

"So what *can* we do? What can anybody do?" The stress showed, long-held and desperate. "Where's a fix? Where's a new system going to come from?"

"We'll get it."

"Like it magically appears."

"*We* can get it. Yes."

Her eyes narrowed. "We. We . . . who?"

"Merchanters. There are sixty-three Families, of which you're one, and four more sit at this table. Station provides for its two pusher-ships. Free board, free room, free stay, free fuel, and free service. But we're FTL. We haul for ourselves. We make profit. And we take losses."

"Tell me about it," Giovanna said between her teeth.

"Any of us can have a run of bad luck. Alpha itself has had no favors, in that ship build up on A-mast. But cargo has to move, and stations can't wait a decade on a pusher arrival. The old *Gaia* Agreement applies to the pushers, not to us. But it *can* be adapted to us. There are sixty-three Families, and we're obviously faster. We meet needs, and it takes all of us, of whatever size, to keep modern stations going. Healthy stations mean healthy trade and healthy industry, which means prosperity for all of us, merchanters and stationers alike."

"Yeah. So. We're little ships. We're an *old* ship, broke down at a station that can't help us. One of your precious sixty-three Families is going to end up doing bit-work and scrub on Alpha if Alpha can't get us running. And if we break down again, *maybe* we can limp into Bryant's, who can't fix us, either."

"Venture could. There is a way the sixty-three can get you running. Will you hear me out?"

She shrugged, mostly looking at the table. "As long as you're paying for the tea. I can't afford this place."

"It's our tab, Captain. Please. Just hear me out."

Giovanna still wasn't looking at him, hadn't for the last while. She took a clean cup, dropped in a tea packet, poured hot water from the pitcher, and added a packet of sweetener.

"I'm listening," she said, still not looking at them. "Surprise me."

"It's like this. A few pushers are still working. But in the spirit of the old agreement, stations have built us ships—at their own expense—and with very few strings attached."

"Yeah, well, and first you have to get approved, and the waiting list at Venture is five decades long, station time. We age fast, ashore."

"A fix is shorter."

"But they don't hand *that* out for free."

"Hear me out. The old compact still does have a moral force. In your case, Alpha's failed you. They're pouring everything into this Company ship that sits useless at dock, while you build up station charges and risk your lives every time you leave dock, bringing them goods and keeping them alive. Yours isn't the only ship in difficulty, but yours is the most egregious case we've run into."

"Yeah, well. Small consolation."

"Our interest is in *not* losing one of the sixty-three. And if stations can't do it—if a ship is needed for a Family to expand, or an existing ship needs repair . . . *we're* the bank. We can make a loan—and you're running again."

"There's got to be a stinger."

"Payback, as you can."

"We are so deep in debt as is. Station can't carry us."

"And won't defy the EC to deal with Venture for the parts you need. The group I'm with doesn't intend to have the system go down to sixty-two Families. So some of us have gotten together with the intent of taking care of our own."

She frowned into her tea. He gave her time to parse that. Finally:

"Bloody hell. *How?* And what's in it for you?"

"How? Sixty-three Families helping each other. A mutual fund into which everyone pays . . . when they're able. What's in it for us? We help you now. We pay for the repairs *and* for the station charges, get *Firenze* running. Once your ship's healthy, and you're running in the black, *then* you pay in."

A short look up. And at the teacup again. "That's too good to be true. What's the hook?"

"Sixty-three of us paying in, sixty-three of us negotiating prices, and leaning, however gently, on a capable station to perform in a timely manner regarding one of our members. That keeps everyone's equipment in top shape, modernized as needed, and stations learn they *have* to prioritize *our* needs, no matter what idiot orders come out of Sol—or Pell, or even Cyteen. Just the cost of doing business. It means no more bottom of the priorities. No more eight months out in the range, limping in and lucky to have made it *that* close. We can help you. Not charity. Mutual support. Interest-free. We're not making a profit off each other's bad luck."

"You're serious."

"Dead serious."

Giovanna took a sip of tea and her hands shook. "Is that what you come here selling?"

"That's *exactly* what we're here to sell."

"Even interest-free, we couldn't pay it back. You've seen Bryant's. You've seen here. The trade's too small."

"More ways than credit to pay back. Helping you, frankly, who are in *deep* as you can get, makes a statement, not just to the ships who haven't yet signed on, but to the stations as well. There will be standards of maintenance. You can call on other ships if you're in trouble, and if a station messes with one of us, things will not go smoothly. Let me add the other things we're asking. Sovereignty. No inspections. What comes *off* the ship is all customs gets to see. What's on the ships, or who's on the ships, is that ship's business. No law on our decks but the law we make. A ship's reputation is our consideration. A ship's viability is our consideration. In the long run, if all goes as planned, the First Stars will become far better off than they've been in generations. And if a Sol trade develops, and you need longhaulers here—those ships should be yours. Not the EC's."

"Not for me. I saw you lot come in." The voice was shaky, between laughter and emotion. "But—bucking the EC—"

"The EC bucking *all* the merchanters, everywhere, wouldn't be the best idea they ever had."

"You made the point yourself. There's some thought they're building their own ships at Sol. That they'll come in and we'll be—" A shrug. "–done."

"If our agreement stands, no hired crew will be welcome beyond Venture, especially if half their cargo is blue-coats and their crew is sim-trained stationers. Pell's not fond of the EC. They haven't got a good name at Mariner, Viking, or points beyond. Cyteen certainly won't deal with them. And it's worth noting, even Cyteen, with all its other notions of upending nature, and with all its resources, works with Family ships as a matter of policy. They don't compete with us. They have a deal with Pell: trade works, they get what they need, when they need it. They're happy. We're happy. We're pleased to oblige, but we're not obliged to please. We do *not* run scared of them."

"How do you arrive at that? Power, we haven't got."

"Bottom line, we serve all stations without criticizing their politics, so long as their politics keep hands off our ships. The EC's a weak threat outside the Alpha-Glory-Bryant's triangle. Here, thanks to all those blue-coats, maybe the EC rules prevail, but at Venture and beyond . . . they're pretty well ignored. Sure, some FTL could show up from Sol, any day, any hour. We take that as a given. But before that happens, before the EC shows up and tries to give orders, we want a fundamental principle established, in writing, with all the sixty-three Families—we want our system working, and our sovereignty established. That's what we're here to get—a signature from every Family here. Simply put, any station that won't deal fairly with one of us will be cutting itself off from the rest of us, and good luck moving cargo or information without us."

Giovanna's eyes darted from one to the other of them. "The EC is *not* going to like it."

"All they have to do is conduct business as usual, and we assure supply gets to them. We'll be talking about rates and fairness. But it's in nobody's interest to harm a station—or to lose a ship. We need the ports. Stations need the ships."

"It's a risk."

"How many times are you willing to order your helm to push that button, knowing previous fixes on that unit have failed? *That's* a risk, Captain. We'd like to say we helped, we'd like to cite *Firenze* as one of ours, and prove the point—that we aren't First Star ships or Farther Star ships. We're merchanters and we're taking care of each other, and together we can handle a big bill. Once you're up and running, you'll pay in when you can. And go on paying in. In the long run, we'll have funds to keep any given ship in repair—we keep the station shipyards in good operation, and we keep cargo moving where it needs to go."

"And you've got signatures. How many here?"

"If you agree, you're the first at Alpha. Of the sixty-three Families, we have twenty-four signatory and a handful still considering, this side of Pell, twenty-two beyond. And we have the Quens' *Estelle* over at Viking and Mariner, doing exactly what we're doing here in the First Stars, gathering signatures, with *Dublin* and *Fame* working over in the far Beyond. We have the finance, with the ships who've already signed, to help you. We *can* do it. We *will* do it, if you say the word."

A long silence. Giovanna's face was white. "Say I agree . . . What happens then?"

"To start with, a consult on your ship's problem. I'd be happy to send over several of my techs and engineers—I think other ships might, as well, to put hands on the system on *Firenze* and estimate what's needed. We'll talk Venture into expediting a system. The system will need to be ported

in, then installed, which means a long stand-down, and
your nav team will need to be familiar with a new board
before you move again."

"We can't survive the stand-down. We are *flat,* sir. We
are beyond flat, we are deep in."

"Part of the loan, if you're willing. You'll repay at zero
interest any layover charges above the basics we negotiate
for you with station, plus your dues, proportional to ship
size and class, over whatever time it takes."

A long, dubious stare. "Dues. Who's the banker?"

Smart woman. Key question.

"None of us and all of us. The dues are setasides in each
ship's reckoning, ten percent of profit, ship's honor to keep
that sum ready to be used on projects voted on by four or
more Families in the area—so we can make fast, necessary
moves. Four signatory Families are here, at this table. You
have to join our number, agree to pay in your ten percent
once you're running, and we'll negotiate with station to
provide you a reasonable living until your ship is operable.
What your job costs, plus living expenses, is an interest-
free loan repayable in addition to the dues, at additional
five percent of profits. There will be *no* claim or lien against
your ship. It's on the honor system. We'll negotiate the re-
sumption of your routes or see that *Firenze* finds another
berth—we have every interest in having you paying in right
along with us, and we'll be watching over the case to be
sure things happen as they should. What it costs is never
more than fifteen percent, and if we can build the fund up,
we may be able to lower that a bit."

Giovanna was a tough woman. She lifted a knuckle to
take away just a little moisture from one eyelid. The jaw
was set. Hard.

"I'll take it. *Dio mio,* I'll take it, damn sure. Abrezio
may lock us out for agreeing to this, but if we can move, it's
his loss. You want access out there, well, she's open, if you
can get to her. How much can I tell my crew?"

"Keep it strictly to yourself for, oh, until maindark. I
want Abrezio to hear it from me first. I'm going to talk to
him after we're done here, on excuse of the knock they just
gave on *Finity's* locked hatch. I'll talk about that and get

around to the other thing—one leads logically to the next. But after maindark, share it with your people, and then whoever you wish. I intend to tell Mr. Abrezio everything in a fairly friendly way. If we can get enough local ships signatory to what we're doing, we're going to negotiate with Alpha about rates and standards. The station has its own problems, and I'm not sure the EC is *their* best solution, either. But that's Abrezio's call. If he decides to challenge the EC, one solution that would serve both merchanters and station is to turn *Rights of Man* over to a combination of Families, including yours, and operate her as a merchanter, which would give Alpha and its merchanters range enough to go most anywhere, but, as someone said—do you really *want* to take on a ship built by the people that can't fix yours?"

Giovanna gave a derisive snort.

"Still," JR said, "that's something the station has to decide for itself, with its own alliances. *Our* business is protecting merchanter interests."

Giovanna's lips went to a thin line, then she laughed and laughed, and went red in the face. "God, oh, God, Finity, yes, you got us. I got to call Family council, but you, Captain Neihart, you got *five* ships with you at the moment." She offered a broad, strong hand across the table, a handshake jarring the teacups. "And if you need us, we got a hundred forty-seven of us on the Strip—with friends up and down. We're at the Fairwinds Hotel. Bar's crap, but you're welcome."

"Same to Firenzes at the Olympian. Saturn, Critical Mass and Outbound are the bars." JR stood up and shook Giovanna's hand. Min and Sanjay and Asha added welcome-ins to their own assigned facilities.

Likely by tomorrow maindark there'd be some romances and sleepovers, doors opened, drinks poured, probably way too many of them. Captains had their ship's dignity to uphold, but it was a very emotional, very tightly lidded excitement behind that reserve. The relief of a woman who no longer had to risk a hundred forty-nine lives on a nav system that—he could guess—was suffering from a sensor problem, a processing problem, and outright physical deterioration. Whatever it was wasn't going to get better in successive jumps. *Firenze* was one of the earliest purpose-builts, and God only knew what else would need an update. Easier, likely, to replace the system entirely, from sensor arrays that told the ship where it was to nav computer that told the ship where it was going.

That meant transferring funds from Alpha to Venture, for a system that, if replacing sensors and system *and* boards, could come in together and be installed a lot faster than piecemealing it and trying to get it to talk. It was the smart answer, but an expensive one. Alpha's engineers had ducked that choice. Alpha's engineers wanted to keep station admin happy, and admin, who had been spending all its credit on *Rights,* was not wanting a large expense.

Admin might look quite favorably on an option that took that problem off its books. Particularly since *Rights*, that extremely expensive mast ornament, had some ghosty issue of its own.

Dare one figure that Alpha's engees were no better at assembling FTL systems than they were at analyzing a nav system, and that all their assurances weren't making *Right's* exotic systems talk to each other any better than *Firenze*'s antique ones were doing?

He shook hands with Min and the others, said, "I'm going to be visiting admin. My crew will track me. But stay alert."

"Absolutely," Min said. Oldest ally, Min, among the purpose-builts. *Little Bear* was a generation younger than *Firenze,* but she'd had two centuries of upgrades. *Mumtaz* was all new, and *Nomad* was middling-so.

What they also were was *steady.* There were two stations the plan had looked for local resistance. One was Cyteen, with an admin they weren't approaching yet; and the other was here, in the still-beating heart of EC authority.

Which was easier to deal with? He wasn't sure. Benjamin Abrezio was reported as a decent administrator. But he'd also been the recipient of gifts from Sol, and still received his orders—dated as they might be—on the ancient Stream.

It was certain that when their merchanters' alliance did

make clear what they'd come to say, the six-year Stream would be reporting it to Sol and Earth.

Not a happy reception there, he was well sure.

But come mainday turnover, when the bars were again at their maximum breakfast-supper load, Giovanna Galli was free to drop information that would get attention from admin, and raise expectations among the merchanters—who weren't called that name, here on Alpha, but merchanters they were, all the same.

It was time.

Chapter 5   Section iii

A message from Niall was waiting for Ross when he arrived back at his assigned room. Jen had had breakfast with them, helped get Fallan to his room, then headed off with a wink.

Matchmaking.

Ross grinned to himself as he pushed the button, then froze.

Niall wanted to see him. Just him. The guy who'd just spent the night with a *Finity* girl.

Immediately. Room B-257.

"How's Fallan?" was Niall's opening remark, as he waved a hand at a chair. Ross sat.

"Not bad. Not good, either. He lost a few minutes. Worries him."

"It would. I'll talk to him."

Silence, while Niall stared at him. Then: "Ask it, Ross."

His heart bumped up a notch—not guilt. But not guilt-free either, and he wanted to know the depth of the problems they had. "So what happened with Abrezio? Are we in trouble?" It could involve fines. Big ones. "I don't see as we were doing anything."

Niall shook his head. "He apologized to *us*."

"Apologized." Station authorities didn't call you in to apologize.

"Took responsibility, but said it was the blue-coats acting solo. Unauthorized."

"Well, *that's* crazy."

"I suspect there's more to it. Chief Jameson's not a bad sort. Wouldn't expect it of him. Which means it was likely an order from Hewitt. But that's station's problem. Not our business. Abrezio said it won't happen again."

"I'll believe that when I see it."

Niall shrugged. "I got the feeling he wasn't pleased. And ultimately, he is in charge."

Ross said, wryly. "Thank you, sir. I'm sure the entire Strip will be relieved."

"He asked about the meeting."

Abrupt vector shift. This . . . *this* was why he'd been called down.

"So. What did you say?"

"The truth. What he said. They'll know. They'll be cross-checking every record their cameras made, comparing every angle, looking for the smallest suspicious twitch. You were in there, after. You actually talked to JR Neihart."

Did I say that? Ross wondered on the instant. But didn't ask, before Niall asked: "What did he say? Assume everything matters."

Ross shook his head. "Nothing. Just talked with his people. Had a beer, with the rest of us. Said we should just relax and wait for the blue-coats to sort it out. Kind of kept the lid on. A lot of Santiagos got caught there, too. They were at a back table, all worried. He told the bartender serve them drinks, on him, and the bar did. Not everybody was happy, but most were. A couple came up to the bar."

"Mad?"

"Curious. Ashlan and Mary T and I, we just kept quiet and listened."

"Did he say, about Fallan?"

"He didn't know, then."

"You think?"

"I didn't hear anybody say it. I didn't find out until I got *your* call. We'd gone back to Rosie's to listen for the gossip, but it was just buzz about the blue-coats and them shutting the doors, and about what the *Finity* captain said, what he didn't say, and what he might have said, if the blue-coats hadn't shut us down. Same as everywhere. About JR, a little. Questions what he's up to."

"You visited Fallan."

"Straightaway, yes, sir, I did. Have you seen him?"

"Not yet."

"He was looking better this morning."

"You didn't stay with him. *You* were with a girl last night."

He felt his face a little hot. "He said go. And she was waiting outside. *Finity* captain had sent her . . . fourth captain, not senior. She knew about Fallan. Her Fourth knew him from pusher days. And you'd said—you'd said find out things. So—I did." He refused to be embarrassed. He had left Fallan only when Fallan told him to. "I put myself on call. Any alarm on those sensors and I'd have gotten the call. I was right friggin' next door. Sir. I was doing what you ordered."

"Not exactly."

"In principle, sir. I'd have gotten a message. I'd have been over there lightspeed. He said go. You know how he is. I can't argue with him. He was threatening to stick labels on the medbot. That's Fallan. He wanted me to get out, so I got."

"Girl's name's Jennifer Neihart."

"Yessir. Jen."

"Senior captain's *niece*. Daughter of his sister."

"She didn't say that."

"Chance meeting?"

"She was sitting outside. Waiting. She had a gift for Fallan, from Fourth Captain. Big bottle. Pell whisky."

"Spendy. What did Fallan say?"

"This morning? He was happy. Real happy. He'd hit it off with the woman, long time back."

"Fourth on *Finity*. And the Senior's niece. That's heavy attention, that."

"Fallan's attention. We all know what he is. Everybody on Alpha knows he's special."

"Except some damn blue-coat."

"Except that. And it was a damn disgrace he got knocked down. All up and down the Strip, people say so."

"You were all up and down the Strip?"

"Jen said. Jen said her Fourth was real mad, that word's passed, and there's a petition going up and down the Strip, stating it was the blue-coats' fault, and it was *pusher* crew got tagged. Don't know if it was *Finity* that started it."

Niall sat there, frowning. "We should have. The admin call—I guess I made it pretty clear what happened. And we did get an apology from admin. And an offer."

"Offer."

"From the station."

Dammit, he didn't want to have messed up Niall's situation with Abrezio. That was their livelihood and their future. But he didn't like the notion that what he'd seen and hoped for a moment—was just because he'd been a fool. A fool pulled completely off course by a pretty face and a bottle from the richest ship going.

Fallan *had* told him to go. He had already *been* going, on his own judgment, when he'd run into Jen.

Am I that great a fool? He had to wonder.

"So," he asked Niall, "what does station say?"

"Just—what I told you beforehand. *Finity's* upsetting admin, no stretch of the imagination. And they're hinting a whole lot that's not going to happen, you know it's not, Ross."

"Rights."

"Isn't going to happen. So Fallan's been approached and you have. You—maybe coincidentally with Fallan, but it's also possible *you* were the first objective, since you were so friendly with them in the bar. And since you're young and . . ."

"I wasn't *friendly* with them . . ."

"Well, you certainly were in the sleepover."

He couldn't dispute that.

"Finity's proposing what's not going to happen, Ross. They know it. We'd like to get past that. Find out what's really on their minds, not just their propaganda."

"We. We, as in *Galway?* Alpha? Or the EC?"

"A little of everybody. Abrezio's not the villain in this. He's had to deal with Sol's priorities for a long time: he needs to keep his reserves for maintenance, he wants to keep both interests happy—yes, he'd like to have the ship upgrades, the ring-dock . . . the works. But our situation's different. We don't have the volume the Farther Stars are moving. It's not economical for us."

"We could run to Pell and back—if *Rights* could run at all."

"And where from here? Beta? That's out. The old stations? They're chancy places leading nowhere useful, at the range we have to use. We sit at the head of a highway that leads pretty well to Sol, and Pell had just as soon Sol never travels it faster than sublight. Pell won't help us. Pell has no percentage in improving Sol's port of entry into everything it's got. Pell's allied to Venture—Venture's colluded with them from the beginning. But the rest of the First Stars—Pell had just as soon see lifeless. Deserted. A problem for Sol to resurrect step by step. That's *not* in our interest."

"What Jen said—yeah, sure, we talked about it—was that the last thing *Finity* wants is any port shut down. That merchanters can't make profit without ports."

"I'd like to think that. But truth is, profit comes with growth and while the *other* end of space is growing, this one isn't. There was a whole lot of suggestion and damned little substance in that speech of Neihart's."

"Which was sort of interrupted. Maybe it was going to what Jen said. Maybe he's got a proposal from Pell, something Abrezio should hear."

"Maybe. But why didn't he just go to Abrezio and lay it out? What else did this Jen say?"

"That she didn't know and couldn't say if she did. That it was for her senior captain to say."

"Oh, that's helpful."

"If she asks me what *you* said or Abrezio said, all I can say is: I don't know and couldn't say if I did. Which would also be the truth."

"So maybe she's dropping just the points she wants you to follow. You going to see her again?"

Anger had no place between him and Niall. But it was real close. "No, sir, not if you say not."

"Good time?"

"No one's business, Niall, sir, but . . . yeah. It was."

"No reason to stop. Just be cautious."

"And you'll ask me what she said?"

"What do you think?"

"You want me to spy. *Abrezio* wants a spy. Does *he* know I spent last night with a Neihart, too?"

"For *all* of us, Ross. For the Family. For the ship. We need to know what we're in the middle of, and who's lying to us."

"Maybe nobody is."

Niall put a hand on his shoulder. "Ross. Little cousin. Don't try to make everybody right. Won't happen. Good spies get *accurate* information, even if it's upsetting."

Little cousin, *hell!* He wanted to shrug off his captain's hand . . . but he didn't. Because Niall was right.

Damn it. Just . . . *damn it*.

"You said there was an offer from Abrezio. Is it good?"

"It's good. In the short run . . . preference on cargo. No dock charges on this stay. And right now—it's helpful. Our own cargoes have taken two hits on the market, and these people have just been through the whole string of stations with their offloads, no way they're not. We're not going to shine real bright at Bryant's, not after these ships have spread the wealth—so, yeah, we're officially a little worried."

It made uncomfortable sense. He'd seen the market here bounce like mad, seen speculation so hot it had triggered a four hour cool-down on trading—ending in a serious depression in the cost of flour and Pell wine. Wasn't all bad. It meant lower prices. It was good for stationers, excepting those making money on the market. Ships like this, moving through little stations—destabilized things.

"So we get our pick," Ross said.

"The way things are, it's a good thing. And more than that. Good of the ship, Ross. Good of the ship."

"God." Good of the ship . . . yes . . . but at whose expense? *Galway* wasn't the only Alpha ship hurting. *We need all the ports . . .* Jen's voice whispering in his head. *All part of the web.* All the ports . . . and all the ships.

Damn. He'd never thought this way. Loyalty to the ship . . . yes . . . but there was a bigger picture. One he was just beginning to see.

"Just go enjoy the girl's company. But take notes. It's well possible *she* is."

"To learn *what,* f' God's sake? What should I keep close?"

"Not a thing. Tell them anything you know. Listen hard. Read between the lines. Chance meeting or not, you've gotten attention and so has Fallan."

That stopped him cold.

"Don't spoil it, Niall."

"Spoil what?"

"Their Fourth, and Fallan. Don't get in the middle of that. God, you know how many years back that is, how long he's remembered her? And vice versa?"

"Ross, lad, you *are* a romantic."

"I happen to remember—"

"Och. Yeah, I have a heart. I appreciate the situation. But if you think *Finity's* Fourth, in that great ship with four full shifts to run her, is a lissome lass with nary a thought in her head—"

"If you think *Fallan's* a fool—"

"We're *all* fools, men and women. Or capable of being. You don't get more callous with the years and the ports: the anger and angst go, but the feelings come on, with all the experiences heaped high. Good thing for us all that wisdom generally comes with them, and you can lead our Fallan just so far, but he's the prankster and hard to catch. If she impressed him that much—and if, whatever she was then, she saw him for what he is, maybe he'll get a good slice of the truth from her. And if he does or doesn't, he'll be sure it doesn't hurt us. I have no doubt of that. *You,* being a young fool, are another question at all times, Ross Healle Monahan. But I have to turn you loose. You'll be believin' things Fallan wouldn't, but there's no way to stop you."

That stung. "You could just say don't."

"I could. Should I? And would it do any good?"

"Captain, sir, I'm not a fool."

"We're all fools. You didn't hear what I said."

"I heard. I don't *intend* to be a fool."

"Best a young man can do. Sleep with her but don't get drunk with her. And don't set your drink down."

"It's not my first sleepover."

"The ship's relying on you, Ross. On your good sense. Find some currency we can spend in Abrezio's office, and keep your wits about you."

He didn't like it, he *really* didn't like it. He felt a little dirty agreeing to the idea. But if *Finity* was intending harm to *Galway* . . . however it came . . .

He took a breath. "Yes, sir. I'm in."

So JR Neihart wanted to talk.

Ben Abrezio wasn't sure *he* wanted to talk to JR Neihart—not yet, and not on the likely issue. Ships were supposed to be left accessible. *Finity's End* had been left locked.

That had just become clear, though it hadn't been *his* choice to send customs up there to try. He had, in actual fact, given orders that the visitor ships were to be left alone, ever since the first one in had put "N" in the "customs may access" blank, a response that had triggered an immediate notification to his office. He hadn't specifically targeted the customs office in that order, but, dammitall, it was implicit and someone had ignored that directive.

Generally inspections were hit and miss, done occasionally, very occasionally, most not going further than seeing the condition of the cargo hold and checking the manifest for goods *not* offloaded as well as goods delivered. The procedure *wasn't* going to catch the bottles of expensive liquor or the luxury goods up in crew quarters, destined for private sale at the next station and not on the manifest. It wasn't going to catch a pocket-sized packet of drugs or hand-weapons in a cabin locker. If contraband wasn't taken down onto the Strip, its existence wasn't station's concern, unless there was evidence of a significant shipment that was going to cause problems for the next station.

Not that customs ever found anything. Their local ships didn't cause problems. They hadn't caught anything but a mistaken offload on two or three crates reaching the cargo area in the last two years, and catching that was actually to the ships' advantage, as they'd have had to account for its absence at the next station and hadn't received credit on Alpha.

Illicit passage—people-smuggling—wasn't at issue with their own ships. And the number checked off at the lift on all these ships equaled the number in sleepover rooms.

And yet customs, even knowing the delicacy of the situation, had taken it on themselves to inspect *that* particular ship, never mind he'd told them—explicitly—to hold off on confrontation with the three previous outsiders?

He knew damned good and well *why* customs had made that decision, and he had a strong suspicion that the stern reprimand he'd just sent down to customs would ricochet into another office and cause a retaliation. But it was a damned high and wide action, and a breach of order he didn't intend to let slide.

Question was: which office?

He had a short list of possibles. Hewitt had high notions of his own EC-granted authority. That authority did not, however, extend to the customs office.

But Cruz—

Cruz *could* have ordered that inspection, though it should have come to the stationmaster's office for approval before being implemented, particularly as it directly countermanded Abrezio's previous instructions. And Cruz, who had near-unlimited authority where it came to anything affecting *Rights of Man,* would, more than anyone, want a good long look at *Finity's* boards.

Cruz might well have had the same thought that had come to *him* in the night, and that idea entirely upset his stomach . . .

It was a serious question, whether there was cargo undeclared in *Finity's* hold, or whether she now stood empty—a massive ship that moved at massive energy cost, transporting *nothing* material. It didn't make economic sense. But Alpha had to be her turn-around point—didn't it?

Had to be—unless *Pell* had what he had in that floorsafe, and meant to test it with one of these four, maybe *had* tested it, long ago, and meant to send the lot of them through, get the jump on the Sol markets and the all-important connections . . .

Damn.

So now, thanks to Cruz, *Finity* was proved to have left her airlock unaccessable, contrary to regulations, and within a very short time of that attempt to board her, there'd been a meeting of the outsider captains at one of *Finity's* restaurants. An Alpha ship captain, Giovanna Galli, had participated in that meeting. Cause and effect? Or coincidence? A smart man assumed a connection.

But he didn't know. Couldn't. Station surveillance of that meeting had been thwarted by equipment *Finity* had deployed.

Interference with station systems in any way, shape, or form was against the law.

Violation.

Locking a ship's access while at dock was a violation.

Meeting with a local captain was not a violation, but secret meetings and talk that led to violations . . . was a violation.

He had ample excuse to call in Giovanna Galli, for starters, at least to ask what the outsiders had said.

But while he was meditating that move, it was JR Neihart at his door, wanting to talk to *him*.

Finity had not played by the rules about access, and he was relatively sure now that none of the other outsiders had either. Likely *all* the ships were locked. He was *not* sure now that they were vacated, as ships were supposed to be while at dock.

Damn Cruz, for forcing this into the open, for pushing an already delicate situation to the brink of . . . what? The last thing they needed now was a *Finity*-led riot on the Strip, with damage resulting. Or a direct confrontation with station police or *Rights* personnel.

He wished he could believe it was all coincidence, the outsiders coming in, Cruz pressing his authority. He wished he could convince himself that no one knew about those coordinates in his safe, but he'd be a fool not to consider that potential goldmine a possible factor. Maybe *Finity's* arrival, maybe everything Cruz was pulling was designed to trigger a takeover of *his* office . . . and those all-important numbers it harbored.

Transmitting them on the Stream remained a risk. More so if either of those factions knew about them. There was simply no knowing whether one of those ships—or Cruz himself—had deployed something in the path of the Stream—or whether something had long since been set there to tap into everything.

Time, of which he'd thought he had plenty, had suddenly become precious. Waiting for the next pusher to Sol seemed increasingly questionable. If he sent the data today, it would make him potentially the savior of the EC's authority—but even at light speed, it would be six years for the information to get to Sol, an unknown time to test the *validity* of the numbers, and even if the numbers checked out . . . the situation here could well change before Sol could take action. They had no defense if Pell learned about those coordinates, less than none if Pell learned that he'd sent them to Sol. Pell could demand he give the coordinates to these four Pell ships . . . in which case, Pell got the jump points and, with these larger ships, an instant stranglehold on the Sol trade. Or if Pell decided on a more radical course, like taking over Alpha . . .

These ships didn't bring force enough to do that, physically, against all the station inhabitants, but Pell *could* get an economic chokehold on Alpha . . . by simply refusing to sell them the biostuffs the residents of the station needed in order to survive, until there were agreements set into place. Agreements that would make Alpha an adjunct to Pell, not Sol.

Either way . . . it was *all* a question of time.

The situation needed finesse, not confrontation.

Finesse . . . when Sol had given him Andy Cruz—and Enzio Hewitt. *Not* ideal, given the situation.

They had worked together, he and Cruz. At times, especially before Hewitt arrived, they had worked together quite well. Cruz understood that his one and only function was to get and keep *Rights of Man* fit and ready, and keep Sol's most critical entry-point, Alpha, ready for Sol's FTL breakout. Cruz himself admitted, after his first decade on Alpha, that Sol's first move out here would bring in a batch of ideas that wouldn't work and that *both* of them were essential to Sol's making a smooth transition.

Since Hewitt's arrival, however, all that had changed. Hewitt had no patience with spacer politics, didn't deal well with the social aspect of Family officers. *Bloody feudal system,* Hewitt called it. And increasingly, since Hewitt's arrival, Cruz appeared to share that opinion.

Well, good thing for everyone involved that neither of them would be involved in this upcoming meeting. Respect and tradition was the way spacers worked. And the social niceties were the oil that made the machinery function. A little whiskey, a little polite talk, a few suggestions—granted they had a conflict of expectations, they'd work it out. *He* was experienced in dealing with the type. Sol's golden boys refused to learn. So . . .

"Send him in," he said to the intercom, and waited.

Chapter 6   Section ii

Benjamin Abrezio, Director of the EC office on Alpha, stationmaster, as stations outward called the post, a title Abrezio himself allegedly preferred. By whatever name, Benjamin Abrezio *was* the executive authority, here on Alpha.

An authority not, from what JR had been told, without its challengers.

Little Bear, Mumtaz, and *Nomad* had done a good job of reconnoitering and socializing since the meeting, exchange of jacket patches, buying of drinks back and forth—trading woes and wishes, and keeping it all sorted, tabbed, and shared about. In fact, they'd scouted out information wherever they'd been, from Mariner to Alpha, and the official word was—Benjamin Abrezio was a reasonable man, and Cruz and Hewitt were Sol-based EC to the hilt, imports who'd spent a significant number of years arriving here by pusher-ship, in two widely separated phases of the build.

Abrezio was the man who'd received the stolen documents at the beginning of his career. Station-born, a man who'd served fairly well in office since, fairly well liked by local spacers. That was Abrezio's reputation, that of a reasonable administrator effectively hamstrung by orders from Sol and by the presence of two officials sent from Sol.

The reputation of Andy Cruz, the next highest ranking EC man on the station, the titular executive officer over *Rights of Man*, was not so encouraging. Cruz had a lot of authority on Alpha . . . anything he considered affected *Rights* he could at least petition to get control of. And yet Cruz . . . was not a concern, as JR saw it. Cruz had overseen the building project. It was this new man, Hewitt, the most recent import from Sol, who had marked an ominous change: more personnel in uniform, more enforcement presence on the Strip. The relationship between Abrezio and Cruz was rumored as not always harmonious, and that between Abrezio and Hewitt—was somewhat pressured.

JR hoped so. Hoped that pressure would work in his favor.

"Mr. Director." JR gave Abrezio his EC title, kept the tone pleasant. "Thank you for the time."

Abrezio stood up, offered his hand. JR took it. "Scotch, Captain?"

"I'd be pleased, sir. Thank you." He waited while Abrezio went to the plexi buffet and set out two glasses.

"Ice? Water."

"Neat, sir. No ice."

"I'd have been appalled," Abrezio said, and poured two, neat, both generous.

JR accepted one without comment, took the chair Abrezio indicated, in front of his desk. Abrezio settled, and had a sip. JR did—act of good faith returned.

"So, Captain, to what do I owe the pleasure?"

Not a mention of customs' attempt, or the action at Critical Mass. He doubted Abrezio really wanted to discuss either matter.

"I must say, Mr. Director, on behalf of all of us, that we've been given extraordinary consideration in our arrival. We know we've represented an unprecedented pressure on facilities."

"Unprecedented, to say the least. But we have tried to be hospitable. We naturally wonder *why* four ships we've never seen before show up here all at once."

"We *are* traveling together."

"To Glory, as well? They can't accommodate you in anything like our facilities. Their last pusher call was a hundred years ago, areas are shut down, and the pusher housing is allotted out to residents."

"Perhaps we'll have to stand off under power, there," JR said. "We appreciate the advisement."

Abrezio took a sip of the Scotch, quick and definite. "So—your business. What sort of cargo still in reserve, do you mind?"

"Some foodstuffs. Not enough to hammer the market, only enough to offer a little choice. A few staples to reinforce reserves. A few trinkets. A few luxuries. The last thing we want to do is work a hardship for your local ships."

"So. And your purpose, Captain? I'd appreciate bluntness at this point. We've been stressed. We are stretched to the limit. We assume this visit is not happenstance or without purpose."

"It is not, sir. And we do owe you honesty, which I'm prepared to deliver." A sip of Scotch. "Let me first define *we*. *We* are an organization of merchanters with merchanter interests. We are numerous, and growing with each port of call. We are establishing agreements with various ships, to support those mutual interests, and this is our position. Centuries ago, on the first return of *Gaia* to Sol, the EC and the pusher ships established an agreement, as to the ownership of *Gaia* and the responsibility of stations to her and to her pusher cousins."

"And we do maintain that bargain—with our pusher ships. FTL merchant traders are another sort of creature."

"We agree. Absolutely. *Gaia* delivered EC cargoes to Alpha for no charge, and Alpha sent them on to other places, maintaining, fueling, supporting and supplying the pusher crews. You still have that relationship with *Atlantis* and *Santa Maria* for supply of all sorts of goods—not unique in this day, but certainly of longest standing. The advent of FTL, the proliferation of ships, the development of companies not within the EC, plus the ability of ships to purchase their own cargoes, in part—all this has complicated the situation for both stations *and* ships."

"And makes impossible the relationship merchant ships used to have with the station. A station has its own needs."

"I agree, sir, Perfectly well understood. In the days of pushers, maintenance and updating was relatively straightforward. For the First Star ships, much of the refurbishing could be done at Sol and for the rest, those who no longer made the Sol run, the necessary equipment could be brought from Sol. But when an FTL ship needs extensive repair—or specialized updates—who does it? Who pays? The ship? Her station of registry? The stations she serves? Stations are no longer all things to all comers. Stations specialize. And it's not extraordinary that a ship has a problem its primary station can't solve."

"You're referring to the Galli ship."

"It's an example, yes, but by no means unique. The Gallis get the dregs of cargo because their timely arrival—in fact their arrival at all—is by no means guaranteed. At this rate, the ship and its Family are destined for bankruptcy, or worse, if that nav unit finally fails completely. What they likely need is a completely new nav system out of Venture, who built her in the first place. A system it would take a year to manufacture, customize and calibrate, and another half year to ship. Cost would, of necessity, include the travel, lodging, and return of personnel expert in its installation. The ship in question can't afford it. Few ships could. But can *you* afford the loss of one of your two large ships, sir? Not to mention the human life if the old system fails?"

"We have had the ship under repair. We will redo the work."

"You *have* done. Several times. It's obvious there is an ongoing problem that may lose Alpha a ship."

"Is that the reason for your visit here, Captain? The reason for *four ships* arriving here at the edge of everything?

To force Alpha into covering this economically ruinous overhaul?"

"In some degree, sir, though we had only caught the rumor of the Gallis' situation as we passed Venture."

A decided frown. "And how is it Venture's concern?"

"We heard of it there. Scuttlebutt on the docks. If it's not an official concern for Venture, it may become one—for merchanters as a group."

"Is this a threat, Captain?"

"Not at all. As a group, sir, as an organization, we're offering to support *Firenze* on station hold, and to put several engineers on the problem to analyze it. If it's what they think, our first question is—can Alpha replace the nav unit and sensor array?"

"No. We can't."

"Can you build a new ship for them?"

Lengthy silence. Obvious evidence was riding atop A-mast. But so was the fact the resources were unavailable. And so was the fact that the only FTL ship Alpha had ever built was the monster on A-mast. And it had failed its first attempt at jump.

"No."

"I will point out, sir, there *is* a large ship available."

"I will point out, Captain, that *that* ship will not come under discussion."

"Understood. Entirely understood. So, with that option officially off the table, the alternative is to seek resources available at Venture, a new nav unit and array to be shipped here, along with personnel to install and test the system."

"And you're prepared to engage those resources. You. Personally."

"Not me, personally. We, collectively."

"Meaning?"

"Merchanters, Mr. Abrezio. Merchanters."

"Merchant spacers. Backed by Pell? Or what?"

"Backed by no one but ourselves. Collectively, the sixty-three Families who move goods between stations. *All* stations."

He left a silence. He let Abrezio think, and think twice.

"All stations."

"All stations. Venture. Pell. Viking. Mariner. Cyteen. And farther on. Sixty-three Families who don't want to see it reduced to sixty-two. We will pay all charges for *Firenze* crew to layover here at Alpha, as long as it takes for an order to get to Venture, for Venture to manufacture the components; as long as it takes to bring technicians to Alpha to install the system, and to get *Firenze* back in ordinary operation—at which point *Firenze* will likely convey the technicians back to Venture, and begin paying back an interest-free loan of whatever magnitude it has to be. We expect to agree on a set price for their sleepover costs per seven maindays, and we expect basic services and meals on a per diem rate. And likewise for the technicians when they arrive, which we expect would be in a bit over a year. When *Firenze* goes back on the schedule, her first run will involve cargo for Venture, to provide transport for the techs. Once we know the extent of the problem—and our engineers are going out today to make that inspection— we'll negotiate a settlement of past and future charges with you, figure the design specs, and send out an order to Venture."

A moment more of silence.

"And the funds?"

"Will materialize in the form of credits at Venture, which I think you would prefer to Pell, and shipping and labor at the market rate current at time of purchase. It's good business for everybody."

"Including merchant spacers?"

"It prevents any of us from getting into the Gallis' situation. Ever."

Abrezio frowned. "It requires a dent in your profits."

"What did *Gaia* ask, in lieu of everything Earth offered? Maintenance of the ship, and comfort of its crew. Our ship is everything. Money is nothing—unless we can't obtain enough of it to solve a problem. That's the way it's always been."

"You—who have no want of luxuries."

"We transport them. We enjoy a few. But we don't always have them. There's always next run."

"This organization of yours. It stretches—how far?"

"Wherever merchanters go, sir."

"Including Cyteen's territory."

"There, too."

"Have you ever been there?"

JR shrugged. "Not yet. Our turnaround is Mariner. But we never say never."

"There's political power—where there's money."

"There's not a lot of liquidity—so to speak—in our funds. And we're not interested in controlling anything other than our own ships. We have our principles, same as before. Maintenance of our ships. Freedom of movement. Regarding which, sir, we don't admit customs to our deck."

"Our regulations demand inspection. You chose to dock here. No one forced you."

"There is a regulation dating from the establishment of Bryant's Star Station—which requires that no ship may be denied service, supply, fuel, or station access, whether by direct link or transport."

"I am perfectly aware. However, no station is obliged to provide these gratis, and no station is obliged to admit persons to freedom of the docks if they are disruptive, violent, or threatening same. Station integrity is the paramount rule."

"As is ship integrity."

"You are, at this moment, Captain, on Alpha's deck."

"And we are enjoying your hospitality, sir, under the Bryant's Star Accord. While here, we observe your rules. *Our* rules begin at our hatch. We have offloaded certain goods, which passed customs inspection on arrival on your deck. We have received credit, which we have spent in your facilities. You do not have the right to inspect what is *not* arriving on your deck. If you have particular concerns, we will be happy to admit customs to our hold, under the watch of our own people, but *not* to our ship's ring and not to our downside deck. That is *our* regulation. And it will apply to *every* merchanter in our organization."

"That will pose a problem, Captain."

"I understand your concern. But we are not an EC entity. *Atlantis* and *Santa Maria* are EC built, and your rules may apply. Where the EC maintains its own ships—it may ask access to them. Where merchanters maintain their own ships—the EC has no right of access. By freeing stations of their ancient obligation to maintain our ships, we are declaring ourselves independent sovereign states. Each ship. Each Family. But we are signatory to a common agreement of principle, and *that* is one of them. Our decks—our rules."

The frown never ceased—a perplexed frown and a troubled one. "I am not prepared to agree."

"You are, however, hospitable and reasonable." JR lifted the half-empty glass. "And we respect your rights on your own deck. If you wish us to withdraw and stand off, we shall, but I hope we can simply ignore the issue—as you have with three of us you have not apparently tested."

"I'd like to know how you *know* we tried entry, Captain."

"I'd rather not explain that. It would be inconvenient to have an argument."

"Then I do know."

"We still needn't have an argument. We'd much rather extend some help here, which would include getting one of your ships back in good running order, which could bring you more frequent calls at Venture—and better supply."

Abrezio wasn't entirely happy. That was a given. "Sixty-three sovereign states, is it? Chaos."

"'Our decks, our rules' binds all. Even us. We want to fix *Firenze*. She's too new to go to the breakers. You'd benefit from her repair, her custom, her service. On the other hand, we *can* transport the Gallis out of the Alpha Reach, and you'd be a ship short. So will you be if they fail a jump, which is a real and present danger until that system is replaced. So it's much the same for you—give or take the matter of conscience. I'm asking—*asking* for your help, Stationmaster. You have a good reputation. I hope you'll give that help."

"A good reputation, give or take the presence on A-mast."

"I'm not mentioning that."

"Except to a bar full of Alpha merchanters."

"As a principle, Stationmaster, nothing more. That ship is part of the agreement you have with Sol EC. It's nothing to us, other than a real and present safety concern. I don't know why that ship aborted its run. If it was unexpected, I'd suggest you get another batch of techs to go over systems, concentrating on the vane alignment. That's my opinion."

Very guarded expression, that. "Concern for our welfare, Captain?"

"Concern for human life, sir. If it wasn't a planned shutdown. Safety systems could be suspect. But I'd look at the vanes first, then the nav sensors."

"I'll relay your concerns. Remembering how you came in here."

And there it was. He drew a long, slow breath and let it go. Reports had said that entry had set a few alarms off. "A safety measure, among other things." *Well that someone here,* he thought, *see a longhauler in operation.* But he didn't say it. Abrezio had his limits. A proud man in a bad position, who'd been handed a number of unpleasant things to swallow. "I think we've expressed our concerns, each." He finished the glass. "I do mean my observation on the shutdown, sir. I know the type, to say the least. But I won't stress the situation further. I'm *not* going to agitate against station authority. The EC isn't my target. In point of fact, I'm not for shutting down any station: they're our livelihood, too, and your health is our health. You have your agreement with the EC. I'm asking you to consider another with us, to the benefit of all parties involved."

He stood up and set the glass on the metal strip at the edge of the desk, offered his hand. Abrezio considered a split second. And took it.

"I'll appreciate your cooperation, Captain, and your discretion. I *don't* want a repeat of the incident at Critical Mass."

"Nor do we, sir. We'll do our best."

He took his leave, exited the office, and gathered up Fletcher, who was waiting in the outer office. He kept a pleasant expression.

He didn't change that until they were well out of the executive offices, and through the section door that led onto the Strip and its gaudy neon.

"We talked," he said to Fletcher. "Fairly frankly. He reacted moderately—not happy. I didn't expect that, considering *he* has to explain to Sol. But he discussed. We discussed. He didn't like us dealing with the Gallis. He certainly didn't like the independent states concept. The organizational concept has him just as worried . . . justifiably, in all logic. If we meant harm, we could do it. Believing we won't— is a bit of a stretch for him."

"You think he's giving *all* the orders?"

"I don't think so. I don't think he'd have tried the hatch entry, among other things. He's got a lot of other points of trouble to worry about. As I read him, *Rights* is an albatross hanging about his neck and likely has been ever since his first days in office."

Since those early *Finity* plans had landed on Abrezio's desk, the man really had had no choice in the matter, not on this station. Billingsly, the man who had stolen the plans, had been vocal enough about what he'd done, long before he hit Alpha's dock, and he'd left on the next pusher back to Sol, where he was reportedly some kind of hero. Abrezio had had no choice but to transmit those plans on to Sol.

"If Abrezio didn't order the inspection," JR said, "it had to be Vice Admiral Andy Cruz."

Fletcher gave a derisive snort. "What's there to be admiral of, I'd like to know."

"Precious little—at the moment. Buzz on the Strip says he's ultimately in charge of the station police." It was a question: Fletcher's crew had been busy checking the local security.

"Not the civilian side," Fletcher said. "Civilian side is a Bellamy Jameson. Cruz's authority is anything to do with that ship. It's that other Earth-born import: Hewitt. He's Cruz's chief of project security. Came in on the last pusher. Hewitt runs project security, and he's coopted control of security on the Strip and A-mast. Cruz is in over-all control up there. Something like the action at Crit Mass could have gone from Cruz to Hewitt without going through Abrezio's office."

"The outcome of which seems more than a potential problem, I think. And Cruz's *ship* isn't working."

"Not a happy man, that."

"Definitely. Abrezio seems to have a problem—and we don't want to make it worse."

Chapter 6   Section iii

A new rumor ran the Strip full-force. Rosie's was full of it.

Fixing *Firenze* was the heart of it.

And *Firenze*'s signing with the visitors . . . in return for it . . . was a subject of intense debate, not greatly helped by a handful of Firenzes drunk an hour and a half after maindark. "We're alive," was one recurrent theme; and a staggery *thank you* was scrawled in maintenance marker paint on the decking outside the Olympian and the Prosperity, the Red Star, and the Homeport, across from each other, which housed the visitors.

Station maintenance was busy scrubbing the illicit marker paint, but the word was out, the outsiders were going to *pay* for *Firenze*'s repairs, and *Firenze* was going to stay parked until they rebuilt the whole sensor array, inside and out, and completely replaced the nav system.

"God, who'd they sleep with?" was one comment.

"Is station going with it?" was another.

Galways gathered in some numbers, not in the restaurant attached to the sleepover, but in the back corner of Rosie's, which they held as *Galway* territory. Ross was there, having a sworn promise from a junior runner to notify him if Fallan stirred out of his room.

"So what's this story?" Ross wanted to know, and Ashlan elaborated, much as they had, which was that the outsiders were here to pay *Firenze*'s bills and see her fixed.

It was good news—sort of.

"What are they asking?" was the logical question. Jen hadn't said anything about it, but then Jen would say it wasn't her business to talk for her captain.

Fair enough. But—that question was major.

"Rodriguez senior is talking to them now," the word came back. "He's a harder sell."

Definitely that. *Santiago* would be asking how *Firenze* got an assist and how *Santiago,* which ran in the black most times, now had to compete against a ship with newer systems . . . it wasn't all that charitable, but it was a question, and Diego Rodriguez was the hard-nosed type to ask it. It underlay, certainly, the thoughts in Ross's head. Do we now have to contend with a Pell-funded competitor? Is it a move to divide us?

Niall didn't look that happy today. He sat with Owen O, second-shift captain, and the two of them had their heads together, nobody questioning them, since there seemed to be no answers.

Then Niall tapped his mug with a spoon, getting attention, and said, "Station's likely to have a word about this. Somebody go feed the music box."

The harmonium was cheap—took chits you bought at the bar, and sometimes got for free with a big bill. The chits were the way it worked, mostly, Ross had always thought, to prevent bar fights: if your chit was in first, you got your selection, and most of them were loud for a reason, guaranteed privacy at every table near a speaker if you kept your heads down and didn't encourage lip-readers.

Aubrey fed it, came back as a loud synthesizer number wailed from the speakers, and dropped into his chair next to Owen. Helm 1, Aubrey, usually sat right next to Fallan. Not this morning. Nav 2.2 was in that spot: Celine, and since the ruckus yesterday, and since there was no imminent prospect of getting a board-call, second-shift was determined to back first-shift in whatever action broke out next. The whole Family was on premises: Fallan getting knocked about had everyone up in arms, determined on asserting the ship's honor.

"So, now," Niall said. "I'll say this quiet, and in pieces, so you can say it down the table. Just be accurate, cousins.

First: Fallan's back in his sleepover and doing well. He'd be here, if Jack weren't sitting on him." A pause as that worked its way down the table. "Second: I've talked with Abrezio. His opinion: it's Pell behind this. His theory is, it's not going to be an armed incident, but economic pressure aimed at the First Stars, namely us." Another pause. "Third: He offers us the station's gratitude and, more to the point, favorable treatment if we will, first, stay loyal to Alpha, and second, keep him informed. Four: My understanding with Abrezio is that we're an Alpha ship and we'll tell him what we learn. Five: *Finity* has invited us to talk, to which we've not responded, and won't until we've had time to speak with *Firenze*. I've had a taste of James Robert's gift of the gab and don't intend to let it sway common sense. Keep your ears open. We need to know what the outsiders represent and where this money's coming from. Anything you learn, bring to me ASAP. Change seats."

That meant everybody in direct earshot should move, possibly go up and order a refill, and sit down again in a different order.

The harmonium was blaring, other tables in the place—and there was a fair crowd—were talking twice as loud to be heard. They all got up who'd sat near Niall, went up to the bar and got a refill on tea, then came back to different seats, at other tables, while other people got up to go sit near Niall. It was a family shuffle. It was quiet, it passed information in two directions, and it was fairly discreet, give or take everyone in Rosie's knew a conference was going on.

Ross passed the word, and got back, from Dubya Ashlan, the news that *Firenze* crew had been talking to *Qarib* and *Santiago,* and that *Qarib* was talking to *Nomad,* which was the Druvs, in a restaurant over in the outsider-occupied part of the Strip.

Word was spreading fast, that was sure. "Go tell Niall," Ross said, and Ashlan went. Ross stayed where he was, answering questions, listening to talk, gathering rumors of talks, and crew hookups that involved every Alpha ship but *Galway.*

"Everybody but us," was the judgment at the table

where he was. "What they got? A stand-off til Niall signs on the line?"

"Not exactly," he said. He wasn't supposed to inject new information: it was supposed to come from Niall, to keep straight what was official and what wasn't. "Can't say more than that. But we had a contact. Ask Niall."

"Come on," Connor Dhu said.

He shook his head. "Not minor. They've asked for a meeting; Niall hasn't answered. Yet. Niall's taken it into account. I can't say more than that."

"Is it," Connor asked—Engee's mate, second shift. "Is it that lot you talked to in Crit Mass?"

"Uncle Connor, I can't and you know it."

"Bet you," Connor said to Netha, beside him. "You and Mary T and Ashlan, hooked up with the Neiharts and the Xiaos."

"Yeah, well," he said, "I'm not the destination of any message, am I? Ask Niall, you."

"She pretty?" Netha asked.

"Damn all," he said. "Can't a man have a drink?" He didn't know who'd talked, or for that matter, who'd witnessed, but somebody had. "I was reconnoitering."

"Is *that* what we're calling it these days?" Said with a big grin.

The second he'd said it, Ross knew *that* was going to become famous on second shift.

"'Scuse me." He got up, and Netha reached up and pulled his sleeve.

"Sit down, sit down, Ross. What's the truth of this *Finity* girl?"

Nothing for it. He sat. "She brought Fallan a bottle. From a woman on *Finity* that Fallan knows. Or knew some God-many years ago, in convert-days. They were in a bar-fight together. On Venture."

"And she sends him a bottle," Netha said, and exchanged a glance with Connor. "Good stuff, I bet."

Fallan . . . was going to kill him.

"I've got to go," he said, rising a second time, as there was a second general shift, a significant stirring in the *Galway* tables.

God, that was not particularly discreet. But Fallan had likely been inquiring after him, and that kid at the infirmary desk had probably had interesting gossip to pass on, not least of which would be a *Finity* patch inquiring after a Galway.

And a Galway leaving with a Finity, plain as plain could be.

He went back to Niall, bent close to Niall's ear and said, "Second shift engees know I met up with a Finity."

"What did you say?"

"I said—" Maybe he had said too much. "I said about the bottle, about a woman on *Finity* Fallan knew, a long time ago. Didn't name names. They knew about me drinking with the girl."

Niall nodded. "We're nothing if not a sharin' lot. I'm not surprised. You're marked, Ross-lad, marked. But *don't* be telling them your own ideas. Refer 'em to me."

"Yes, sir. I did, sir."

"Sit."

There was a vacant chair at the moment, in the general shifting about. He sat down in Helm 1's place.

"You'll be seeing this girl as you can. Keep us aware where you are."

"She says she doesn't speak for her captain. That's her standard answer."

"Well, you don't speak for yours, *do* you? That'll be your standard answer. But you'll be meeting this girl often as you like—I take it that's not an upsetting idea."

"No, sir." His face felt hot. Probably he should say he didn't like the situation. In part he didn't. On another level he wanted to know. And on another, still, he *wanted* Jen Neihart to be a sweet, innocent girl, and her ship to be a ship they'd meet again, in better times.

Better times was *not* a thought he'd ever had, where it came to the progress of things on Alpha or anywhere else *Galway* touched.

Repairing *Firenze*. God. It was an air castle, the notion. But seductive.

"Is *Firenze* believing the offer, sir?" he asked.

"Can they say no?" Niall shot back.

Aubrey was back, expecting his seat.

"Move Celine down one," was Niall's word, aside to Aubrey. "I want to talk to this lad."

The table was reassembling. He didn't have Fallan to buffer Celine, who was going to look at him and ask questions of her own. Dark, quick eyes, those, herself no youngster, and another nav, second shift. He slipped into the chair next to Niall and looked concentratedly at the table top.

"Understand this," Niall said. "We're committed to Alpha. Are you understanding that?"

"Yes, sir."

"You're careful what you say to this girl?"

"Yes, sir. I am. I'm way conscious what I say, and I'm not getting drunk and I'm watching my glass, the way you said."

"What's your sense of her? I'm giving you credit for having some."

"She's careful, too. Doesn't say a thing I haven't told you."

"Which isn't much."

"There isn't much, sir."

"You like her? Personally, how do you like her? I'm not talking about in the sheets."

"I like her. It's a short impression. I think she's good and I think she's honest. But I think she's honest for her ship, not *Galway*, and always will be. Not being a total fool, sir."

"You'd be about right. If you start thinking any differently—come tell me."

"She wants to set up a meeting. Fallan with this captain. I think—I think I got swept up in the moment."

"Fallan wants to."

That was a question. "I think he does."

"Our Nav 1 and their Fourth, when he feels up to it. I'm not inspired to have that unchaperoned. I'd say you make it two tables, and you keep an eye on the both of them."

He had to say it. "Medics say no sex."

"Well, I rely on you to remind him of that, don't I?" Niall was quiet a moment. "It's important we find out what the game is with these people. If *Finity's* come here to bring Pell into the economics of the First Stars, that's going nowhere good. What cargo has Alpha got that Pell wants, outside of Earth goods every ten years? What are we for a market, going back to Sol at pusher speeds? Bad news for us, is what. And if *Firenze* is the wedge they're choosing, and we've got *no* word what they've promised elsewhere, what are they going to do? Move *Firenze* up to Venture, and then maybe *Santiago*, maybe even *Qarib*? And with the ring-dock they're building and all, what will we be *there?*"

"What will *here* be by then?" Aubrey asked. His was one of those voices that could rattle china. He kept it way low. "If big forces are moving, Niall, how the hell do we resist?"

"I don't know," Niall said. "Honest to God, I don't know. But Alpha's offering, for what it's worth. We hold out, we figure loyalty's worth something. I don't know what. Yet."

Niall never kept things back—his hopes or his misgivings. He let crew know, when they were shut away safe inside *Galway's* hull. If there were surprises, they shared them, but mostly Niall said what was on his mind. And honestly given, nobody trusted any stationer that much.

But Niall said it: Alpha was where they had piled up favor-points, that currency without which there *was* no trust. The one balance that could never be transferred elsewhere.

There was quiet on the Strip—at least to outward appearances. Quiet everywhere, relatively speaking. It didn't mean peace, in JR's estimation. It meant people drawing back to think, to plan, and to talk—doubtless Julio and Diego Rodriguez of *Santiago* were doing some consulting. Certainly Abrezio was consulting. And various other levels of his administration were.

JR and his fellow captains had their own consultation, again in the restaurant, with the same anti-eavesdropping precaution. *Nomad* and *Little Bear* had presented their case to *Qarib,* smallest of the Alpha ships, and, along with *Firenze*, chosen to be moved off the mast.

"They're a little Family," Asha Druv said, "but they've got fifteen kids under ten years old, five of them of Galli descent, they think. Longtime connection, that, the largest Alpha ship with the smallest. Giovanna had a close talk with the Rahmans before we did. And Nomads have a long-ago tie to *Mercury*. As does *Firenze*. Way back."

Mercury was a ship of legend—not the first pusher-ship to defy Company orders, but one that had defied Company directives in spectacular fashion, moving upset stationers out of Glory and on to Bryant's—not utterly stripping Glory, but beginning the slow decline of the whole Glory Reach.

"What's the consensus from *Qarib?*" JR asked.

"They're a little ship, specialty cargo. Worried about competition, as they should be, but there's room for their kind of operation. They're not pleased with their situation at Alpha. They were picked to let twenty-two personnel from *The Rights of Man* shadow their boards, a delegation headed by Hewitt, and, the senior captain's words, they *argued* with seated crew on procedure and readings before jump, were hopelessly, dangerously disoriented on system entry, made technical errors, interfered with active crew, and during system run-in, they refused all offers of a social nature. They stayed to themselves, complained about the food, and attempted to deny they had brought alcohol aboard as well as pharmaceuticals that they refused to disclose, both contrary to *Qarib*'s rules. They refused inspection of their quarters and were prepared to use force in the matter. That was on the *way* to Bryant's. On the return trip, Hewitt assigned another set of personnel to shadow the boards, who fared no better, and then he tried to insist the senior captain sign a document stating their performance had been satisfactory on a trainee level. Aki Rahman refused to sign, so Hewitt proceeded to the alterday captain, trying the same, with the same result. After *Qarib* docked at Alpha and saw the backs of these trainees, there was a call from the *Rights* watch officer again asking for the document. They refused it. The next shift *also* called, wanting the document signed, and tried to claim the signature was a condition of their payment for having these trainees aboard. Rahman again refused. It went all the way to higher offices before somebody finally gave up and paid. Word is, it was Abrezio's sig on the credit, not Cruz's."

"One supposes they wanted it for EC official consumption. One also supposes Andrew J. Cruz was deeply upset."

"I'd say," Asha said.

"Did it dispose *Qarib* against other proposals? Or dispose them toward us?"

"They view Abrezio somewhat favorably, but they are not fond of *Rights* or its command, and least of all its personnel. They're wary of our offer, but their word regarding *Rights* undergoing more training at their boards was definite."

Xiao Min had listened intently, a slight smile on his face. "I believe his expression was 'rot in the deepest pit of hell.'"

"Aki Rahman says he *is* interested to hear us," Asha said. "He also asks, 'Need we serve the godless Cyteeners?'"

We answered that no ship will be forced to serve any port, but as a group we would wish members to make special consideration in humanitarian interests, and to support fellow members no matter what their origin. They say they will hold a family meeting, but Aki himself is disposed to sign, provided we place no personnel aboard their ship."

"That's two, then," JR said. "*Santiago* is also meeting, and the senior captain wants to know that others are signing, and that they will not be left to defend the document alone, once we have left Alpha. I have assured him that should a station withhold services or charge inappropriately for them—they will have assistance from the organization as a whole, and it will not be assistance directed by or funded by Pell. He's wary, appropriately so. He fears the inconvenience of upholding Alpha merchanters would leave them on their own to face the EC's wrath. We have promised this will not happen. Those who sign, until they have signed, have to take that on faith."

"As agreed." Asha nodded. "These ships expect intervention from Sol. They hope it comes soon and they hope it *never* comes. They see the Sol route as the big prize, but they're convinced Sol's been building ships—and that those ships, with non-family crews, will be awarded the Sol-Alpha route."

"What does *Qarib* expect Sol will do?" JR asked, that having been *Nomad's* contact.

"I hear the same sentiment we heard at Bryant's, only more specific." Asha began to tick off the points on her fingers. "When Sol does get here, there's a suspicion they'll immediately replace Abrezio, which won't be good. He'll be a resource, but Cruz will likely be in the ascendant, and bets are they won't even listen to Abrezio, if history is a guide. Alpha will be important immediately, and they'll be waking up the mothballed stations, which will be good for merchanters, but which makes absolutely no sense in terms of usefulness to science, and some, well, pose a risk to life. But they are territory, and Sol thinks in those terms: they own it, they should have it, it should function and provide revenue. The bet is that Sol won't be smarter than it was in the first push outward, and constantly referring back to its home office, which will still be half a year lagged, at best. What worries *Qarib* is the thought that Pell may snuggle up to Cyteen. According to their sources, Bryant's Star thinks Venture's going to peel off and join Pell, and that *that's* going to be a flashpoint, once Sol gets here, and if they sign with us, they'll be on the wrong side of the blast."

"*Santiago* has the same view," JR said.

"What we offer scares *Qarib*," Asha said. "They're small, they've been marginal for so long they don't see any other way to live; but our proposal of converting to courier service, running parts, criticals, and a modified heated storage—they do want to hear more about. They're fairly emphatic they will not deal with Cyteen, and they will not deal with Pell if Pell allies with Cyteen."

"We can still work with them," Xiao Min said.

"Definitely," JR said.

They had built their own collective idea of the routes Sol could best use, that would bring the Hinder Star ships the greatest profit . . . once Sol broke out . . . granted the route Sol found led to Alpha.

If the route from Sol lay via El Dorado, as some theorized, that would bring them straight to Pell—but the flare star at El Dorado was not a comfortable waystop. Thule, also mothballed, leading to Bryant's, was possible, but involving a lot of construction, and pusher-loads.

And if Sol ever grew desperate enough to take the extant path via Beta to Glory—the whole of the Beyond was going to be upset. If Sol ships came via Beta . . . it was very possible every station beyond Alpha and Glory would break tradition and close their docks. *No one* wanted to risk whatever lurked at Beta getting into their station.

The route to Alpha was the optimum—in so many ways. It would support the Hinder Star stations' entire string, maintain their way of life, and *not* bring Sol into direct contact with Pell. Even if they had to three-hop it, an Alpha-Sol route was still better than any other option.

"Timetable," JR said, "is still guesswork. What I'm

hearing of Glory, we *could* bypass it. Glory's used to being bypassed. It has no merchanters of its own. But the people there deserve consideration, even so."

"The ship out there at the moment is still reckoned to be *Bluebell.* And only *Bluebell.*"

"She has to come back to Bryant's, so we may meet her on the way out. Them and the Browns' *Pixy. Miriam B* and *Come Lately* are still to find. And locally, we still need *Galway.*"

"Monahan's still not meeting?"

"We've got a contact with them, but the captains are ducking us. Senior captain got swept up in the Critical Mass fracas, and got a see-me from Abrezio, who very probably wasn't happy. Foodstuffs are high on the list of what they carry, and, yes, we sent a ripple through their local market, but they'd already offloaded and sold, and only had a small ship-owned offering even so, so they have no real complaint. It's my guess Abrezio put the pressure on, and I haven't pushed, but I have other routes to reach the senior captain informally, and I'm pretty sure they'll have heard talk on the Strip by now."

"No reaction from admin."

"Nothing," JR said. "Third day quiet and not a thing. Word's settled, now. We've gotten a few additional questions. We've tendered the agreement to *Firenze,* and we have it signed. *Santiago* is looking it over and talking to *Firenze.*"

"Should we give it to *Qarib?*"

"I'd say go ahead," JR said. "If admin wants to transmit it all over the station, fine. There's nothing in it to hide."

There *was* an ongoing merchanter action that wasn't set forward in the contract, except in the clause that agreed not to visit a station under sanction. That was the tough one.

But it was also, as he had explained to the Gallis and the Rodriguezes, the teeth in the organization, the ability to require compliance. First part was getting every single Family ship to agree—no one would have believed two decades ago that it could happen. The sixty-three Families were independent in culture, in many cases using a ship-speak almost incomprehensible to outsiders, except for ops, and maintaining their own customs and rules.

Cohesion? Cooperation?

There were very few points on which they could all agree, but those few were the essentials: ship sovereignty and Family sanctity. Those were in the document, and there was virtual ink on the virtual lines, spreading in all directions.

Would Cyteen someday decide the Families were no longer useful, and begin building competition, and excluding them in some future dispute with Pell? It could happen.

But not if merchanters could slam a no-go down on every single cargo that moved, while carrying them for Pell.

Or vice versa, unlikely as it seemed now. Any station or association that wanted to rough-handle one isolated merchanter was going to find life and supply very—very— difficult.

Chapter 7   Section ii

Third day and Fallan was not only on his feet, he had a rendezvous in the European, best clothes, no visible gelpatch—he'd combed his grey locks sideways—and his best jacket, with a spare *Galway* patch in the pocket, for a little gift.

Lisa Marie was coming. Jen assured Ross of that, by com: she had left the sleepover and was on her way, not alone. Jen was with her.

Fallan was not on his own, either. Ross was with him.

"Wonder if she's still pretty," Fallan said.

"Pretty as you, I reckon, give or take the patch job."

"Wicked, Ross, wicked. Whatever we are, honest years have made us. That was a time, that *Boreale* scrap. We laughed, God, we laughed." A pause. "I am so nervous."

Their Nav 1 was nervous. Man habitually threw a huge

mass of metal from one star to another, played causality catch with gravity wells, and *he* was nervous.

"Kinda hoped a body grew out of it," Ross said.

"Nope. Gets worse with age."

"Look, if you spook out I'll have to catch you."

"No, I'll go, I'll go. I just hope I don't offput her."

There was, in the distance, in the gentle curve of the Strip, a dark-haired girl Ross was fairly sure was Jen, and another figure beside her.

"I think I see them."

"God." Fallan fidgeted his jacket straight, checked his pocket, made a pass at his hair.

"You're fine," Ross said.

"Can't match that whiskey. But I got her a thing she can't get anywhere else."

"The *Galway* patch?"

"Oh, we got to trade patches. But a thing I got on Glory."

"What would *that* be?"

"Chunk of rock."

"Well, what kind of rock?"

Fallan took a wrapped object out of his pocket and unfolded the cloth as they walked. It was actually a shimmery, shiny, polished piece of metal and glass, about the size of a bar chit, the surface all marbled and colored, with iridescence in it.

"That there, Ross-me-lad, is a piece of Galileo Station's shields after EV Lacertae blasted her to hell. Cranky bastard, that star, but producing one pretty piece of glass. There's still salvage to be had there, but nobody that keen on becoming part of it. You won't find *this* on offer at the tourist shop. Guy who collected it in the first place probably risked his life and the guy who traded it to me was probably a thief. They were evacuating the station. Didn't even bother to mothball her. Wasn't that much left *to* mothball. We took fifty-six people out of there."

"God, you were *there?*"

"Oh, no, we came in fourteen days after the big blow, and they were damn glad to see us. We didn't try to handle cargo, Just packed people on and got 'em back to Glory."

Fallan wrapped the piece again and tucked it back in his pocket. "It's not radioactive, or anything. Had it checked."

"That's a long time ago."

"A real long time ago."

They were within hail of the Finitys now. Jen gave a little wave. Ross waved back.

Captain Lisa Marie was trim, grey hair short and straight—a grey satin jacket and nothing about her to say she was one of the captains who had scared hell out of Alpha. Her smile, which was all for Fallan as they met, was impish and sweet, both, arms open—no standing on ceremony or rank.

"Fal," she said, while Ross stood by watching. "Well, look at you. Nav 1. I'm not surprised. I knew you were here. I *didn't* look for you to get in a bar fight first off."

Fallan laughed, she laughed. They hugged each other like long-lost friends.

Ross looked at Jen and offered his hand. "Got a rez for four, separate tables, respectable distance from each other. Dinner?"

She took his hand. "Sure. *She* gives the orders, but I'm sort of to stay in the neighborhood in case she needs anything." She grinned. "Look at 'em."

Chapter 7   Section iii

They had a table a quarter of the restaurant apart from Fallan and Lisa Marie. They splurged a bit on the dinner, the both of them staying off alcohol, being, by that token, both of them on duty.

Niall had said—find out what he could. And, Ross was fairly sure JR Neihart had said the same to Jen. It was only natural.

Meanwhile if there was finding out going on over at that

other table, it was a good bet it was more about where have you been and how's your life and do you remember when?

If, however, they got around to, so what brings you here? they were stepping off the edge into something a little less old friends and right straight on to what are you up to?

"You told your Fourth, I hope, about the doctor's orders. Two more days."

"I told her, and she said she got it," Jen said, and took a bite of her entree, pasta with white sauce and meat and veg. She swallowed, and seemed pleased.

"He's tough as they come, but some things, dunno, your body just has its limits." He took a bite of his own. A meat pie. Meat from Sol. Nothing more informative on the menu about it and a lab was undoubtedly involved, but, damn, it was tasty. "I got assigned to him the last two runs, you know, working my way up, shadowing him, before, someday, I get a number. And I swear, he's been so many places, he just never stops surprising me. Stuff that's way before *Galway*. And, I mean, my great-gran's out of *Atlas,* but I never heard those things from her."

"Your grans and mum still with you?"

"Sure are. My mum's a fitter, third shift."

"You're a four-shift operation."

"We are." He was glad to say that. Four shifts, when some ships were three or two. They weren't near in *Finity's* class, but they had no shortage of high-level crew, no layabouts, except the youngest and a couple of seniors gone frail and no longer able. He didn't say that. You couldn't brag to *Finity's End* that you were that good. But they were. When *Galway* moved, what time you weren't asleep or on some post or other, you scrubbed, you studied, you stayed with everything going on. Point of pride. And Nav 1.3 trainee wasn't shabby for a young man. Not at all.

"Lot of sibs?"

"Sister," he said. "Also a fitter. Works with Mum."

"I'm an only. One of a kind." A smile, between bites. It was talk they hadn't gotten around to on that sleepover night.

"You're the senior captain's niece."

"I am."

"How is he?"

"Honestly? Kind of sweet. But don't spread that around. He'd kill me."

"I got to ask again. *What* in hell are you up to?"

Eyebrows lifted. "It's pretty well all over the docks."

"Well, yes, a story is. That's what they're saying. That you're signing on *our* ships to some sort of agreement with somebody, that you're paying repair charges—that you're charging a fee."

"Sort of. And not quite. The agreement is among ourselves. All merchanters. We organize a repair fund, available to any ship in need, as an interest-free loan. You have to pay back sooner or later, and the dues we pay is what creates the repair fund. We help each other when we're in trouble. That's the deal. Because stations can't. That's not the economy anymore."

"Where do *we* get the money?"

"Sixty-three families each committing a portion of profit which *we* don't bank: everybody just reserves it— we're not giving stations any funds they can manipulate or hold. Ship gets into trouble the way *Firenze* has, we get it fixed right. New system seems to be what they need. And they'll be able to get financially healthy again and pay it back. If they never can—well, we'll all survive it."

"That's crazy."

Jen shrugged. "Together, all of us everywhere, with our assets, we're pretty potent. We stay autonomous, we just support the whole system."

He forgot what he was eating. Swallowed. "I guess it could work. So it's all true, everything they're saying."

"I have no idea what 'they' might be saying, really. But that's the deal. And here's the further deal. Someday we're going to have Sol come in here and shake everything up. And the EC'll try to dictate things. You know they will."

"They still do," he said solemnly, and gave his entree a poke. "Every decade or so they send somebody to mess things up."

"That'll speed up, won't it? You know it will. And Sol will give orders. It always has."

It had gotten serious very suddenly. He looked up into dark eyes. Foreign eyes.

"All right," Ross said, "plain talk. Question. How do four ships *afford* to come out here empty?"

"Not empty. We've done a little commerce along the way. Enough. It's not about making money on this trip."

"So what is it about?"

"Doing while we *can* do. Before Pell and Cyteen have another spat. Before Sol arrives, having built God knows how many ships and declaring we don't matter."

"I don't think they'll think *that*."

"We're a way of life, Ross Monahan. And we're not them. *Rights* seems to be their design, their notion of interstellar trade. Will they listen to us? They never have."

He rested his fork beside his plate, stomach just a little upset, conscious of Fallan and *Finity's* Fourth over at the distant table, one hand in another, beside the wineglasses. "Will *you* listen to us, Finity? Seems a good question."

"We *are* you."

"Not so much. Who's given us a damned thing, while Pell gets rich?"

"That's the point. We're proposing to do exactly that, to even out the luck. *Who's given us a damned thing?* Who will do it, when Sol shows up?"

"Here, we kind of look forward to that. We *don't* look forward to outsider ships showing up to take the routes out from under us."

"That's not part of it. Never has been. We've *got* our routes, same as every other ship. We're all part of a network. Sol breaks out, we'll want what you bring us, same as now, just a whole lot more. Good for everyone. We hope to make it so Sol's got no choice but to deal with you and the other Alpha ships."

"Sol *will* need us." He wished that didn't sound as if he was trying to convince himself. "That ship up on A-mast— it's to show they're serious and they're not out of the picture."

"Why ever would they spend that much building a ship that doesn't move?"

"Because they didn't *intend* for it not to move. They'll get it working. Someday."

"It's pretty huge, isn't it? Not the ship. The problem."

"God." He picked up his fork. "It's a good dinner. Let's enjoy it."

"Sure." She picked up hers. "Not here to fight. Really not here to fight. It's their evening. And Senior Captain told me not to get into business."

"Business is what you call it."

"Business is what it *is*. *We* have to make ends meet, while stations and planets work it all out. And if Sol brings ships in that want to replace us, we have an issue."

"Isn't going to happen."

"They built *Rights* here at Alpha. A demonstration of power. You said it."

"Jen." He was out of arguments. He was supposed to get information. *Niall* said it. But she was proposing things that made the evening uncomfortable; and it was Fallan's evening with Lisa Marie.

Granted Lisa Marie wasn't arguing the same over there at the other table. Judging by the occasional hand-holding, it didn't look as if that was the case, but he'd lay odds those two could argue and flirt at the same time.

"Sorry," Jen said. "Really. Just . . . No, I'm not going to say it. Enough politics."

Maddening. He wasn't going to ask. He truly wasn't going to ask. He finished the entrée, and cast another look at Fallan and Lisa Marie.

Those two were talking to the waiter, signing out on it, by the look of things.

He'd wanted dessert. He'd *wanted* a better dinner conversation out of Jen. He was not in the best mood—all of which was way under the scale of things wrong in the situation.

Make it so Sol's got no choice . . . God. What if they'd been bugged? The blue-coats did that sort of thing. Niall's talk with Abrezio could fix any charges, but not before he and Jen got hauled in for questions. If they dared touch *Finity*'s crew. Not to mention a *Finity* captain at the table over there.

The blue-coats hadn't made any move against *Finity's End*, or any of the other three. They wouldn't. *That* was power—that size, that number of people physically out on the Strip. Abrezio had to think—that it wouldn't be a good move, to haul in *Finity* personnel.

Ross wasn't sure Niall's agreement with Abrezio was that much protection to him or Jen.

The protection it afforded couldn't outlast the hour if Sol did by some miracle drop a ship into Alpha system without warning. That was the cold, small thought—that if that was imminent and Pell somehow knew it and *that* was why *Finity* and the others had *really* come here—

And if those jump-points were found . . . the great some-day hope of everybody at Alpha . . . it was all too possible that no agreements would stand, because Abrezio might no longer be in power, leaving the question: would some Sol-born stationmaster do right by the ships who'd remained loyal despite the hardship, or would Sol-built ships replace them before they knew what happened?

All that flashed through his mind in seconds. One card stacked on another. Who he was with, who was with Fallan, what Niall had asked, what Jen was saying, what had happened with the blue-coats. Abrezio calling Niall in to talk deal.

Scared man, Mr. Abrezio. Scared not only of the four visitors, but of blue-coats who had overstepped their bounds and locked down a meeting involving *Finity*'s Senior Captain.

And that—*that* just stuck sideways in his mind and jammed up everything else: the realization that once the four strangers left, things weren't going to be the same as the day before Abrezio's authority was challenged, and Abrezio and those allied with Abrezio might not be any safer. Abrezio wasn't the only one running things right now. *Rights* command, Cruz, and project security, Hewitt, and some of the officers under them had been sent all the way from Sol.

"We'd better pay out," he said.

"Got it," Jen said.

"Finity's not paying our tab."

"Already done. Fourth Captain has to have an escort. It's the rules."

"Hell."

"Got to go with them," she said. *"Finity"*'s sleepover. She has to. The—"

"Rules. I get it." Fallan and Lisa Marie were on their feet, headed down the middle of the restaurant. Ross managed to intercept them, gave a respectful little nod. "Don't know if this fellow's told you, Captain . . ."

Fallan caught his arm and pulled him aside. "Two days. I got it. Go on with you."

"Two days," he said. "God, do I have to call Niall?"

"Off with you," Fallan said, let him go, and hitched onto Lisa Marie on his way out.

Jen's hand slipped onto Ross's arm. "We'll tag 'em. Captain knows about the two days. We won't let any harm happen."

"How precisely are we going to prevent that?"

"Mum's got her ways, and she's on his case. Come on. My room this time. We're right down the hall. Sort of."

For a half-cred bet he'd tell her off and leave. But one part of him wanted to stay tagged to Fallan, in case; one part wanted to know what the inside of the Olympian looked like; and there was Jen holding his arm in case he'd forgotten the night he'd spent with her in a cheap one-night room near the clinic—Jen, who'd just said things that, if station police had been listening, and well they might, might just slip it into a file and wait.

God. Stay with him, Niall had said. That was *his* rule.

Find out what *Finity's* up to. If he believed Jen, Jen had laid it out for him. However it added, Abrezio wasn't going to like it, among others.

He went, passed the door, Jen's hand linked comfortably with his arm, two spacers headed for a night of doing what spacers did, behind two others.

Probably the police *were* listening. And watching. And he hadn't been thinking about that when they'd sat down to dinner.

Chapter 8   Section i

Buzzer went. JR reached for it, remembered where he was, where the bed was. "Lights," he said, one of the Olympian's useful amenities, and lights came up to dim, medium, and full as he found his wristband and punched in.

W42, it read. 4/13. And 90/90/5. Then: 1.

Damn. Damn. And damn.

JR hoisted himself upright against the headboard, keyed 222, and 9090.

Damned right, 9090. Standing orders. Nobody who got into *Finity* got out with anything they had brought in.

Customs agents had got in, this time. At least they had gotten as far as the number 1 e-hatch, in hardsuits. He had no idea what the full story was. But the security team had them, wouldn't be letting them go without a search, and it was very likely he'd be hearing from somebody on this one.

Rapid knock and the door opened. Fletcher was there in a bathrobe, and Madison was right behind him.

JR didn't bother to key out. If there were more messages, he wanted them. And it was very likely not going to stay as quiet as the last attempt.

"We're secure," he said to his brother captains. "Tell Mum stay with her guest; it's all right."

"They're persistent," Fletcher said.

"Give them that," JR said wryly. He slid on the wrist unit, sent his own advisement to Mum. "Fletch, Madison, you can probably go back to sleep."

"Hell, no," Fletcher said. "not til we hear the rest of it."

"I'm hoping there won't be a rest of it," JR said. "And I'm somewhat betting Abrezio's sound asleep and actually innocent. If you want a job, send runners over to Min, Sanjay, and Asha, and tell them we have an ongoing situation." The time was 0418. "I'll meet you in the breakfast room. Let's not wake the whole hall. We have to trust Walt to handle this." That was their senior security aboard. "He'll use his ingenuity. We'll just cope with it. The only thing I told him was not to hold them longterm: we don't want any side negotiations with admin."

"Walt was saying he wanted a souvenir from Alpha. Worrying about being away from the action."

"He's got his wish," JR said, reaching for his shirt. "Bring the gear: we're going to set up for a command conference. Our allies need to be realtime with this."

"We'll be there," Fletcher said. "Does Mum know?"

"She's not in need-to-know this watch; she's got a guest. I'm sending her a stand-down, along with everybody else." He was keying as he talked. "We've got two *Galway* crew here tonight and if there's trouble, I don't want it to land on them."

"This is likely to get noisy before it gets better. Inside, were they?"

"No question. Walt's got 'em, checking them for implants and pocket coms." Those were the standing orders for intruders. "Station is not going to be too happy right now. Account for all crew, no exceptions."

Chapter 8   Section ii

Jen had sat up, Ross realized: he propped himself on an elbow and watched Jen watching something handheld. Pocket com, likely. And in the waking muddle of sleep, he knew he was *not* in his own room, nor close to it: that he was in the heart of *Finity* territory, and so was Fallan some ten doors down. Meanwhile something was going on that had Jen sitting on the side of the bed consulting the com.

"Something wrong?" he said quietly.

"Not that bothers us," Jen said.

"Fallan's all right."

"I'm sure he's all right. Order is to stay put."

The hell, he thought. He swung his feet over his side of the bed and started feeling after clothes.

Jen leaned across the mattress and put an arm on his shoulder. "Ross, it's *Finity* business. If we'd been ordered out, we'd all go, but they won't want a guest wandering around out there."

"Something to do with station?"

"Something *Galway* may not want to be tagged with."

"You know more than you're saying."

She was a shadow in the dark. A breathing presence. "I'll tell you the truth I think I know."

"What?"

"Customs tried earlier. They didn't get in. I think they're back. Trying to get aboard our ship."

"It's the rules. You leave the mast-access accessible."

"For a visit on alterday shift?"

It was odd. So was anybody locking customs out. "Rules say—you leave the ship open. No layovers aboard. It's that way. It's that way everywhere."

"Our deck, our rules." Her arms came about him. "Last thing we want is *Galway* getting into whatever trouble happens out there. But *our* rules say: customs—or *Rights* personnel or whoever—is not going to get access to *Finity*. No way."

"They'll raise a fuss."

"Probably." Jen's arms came about him. "It's cold. Come on, Ross. Back to bed. They won't tell us a thing. But it's pretty sure there's going to be a lot of people yelling at each other come mainday. We'll just go to breakfast and ignore it. Not your fault. Not Fallan's. Senior Captain will sort it out. And I assure you we won't do anything to harm the station. Not our purpose here. Asserting ships' rights—is."

Ships' rights. Damn. What did that even mean?

It *was* cold, outside the covers. He pulled the blanket up and settled down, chafing Jen's chilled arm, his imagination going out to the mast, to the dark and the cold out there, where you went up to your ship via a lift. Cargo, excepting delicates, moved by utility pusher, out in the uncompromising cold and dark. *Finity* and two of the outsiders were set up to receive cargo differently, by a process he'd seen only in diagrams. *Finity* could kick cargo out a hatch, for the little bots to grab and move, and apparently had done, but there was a whole corridor designed for ring-dock operations that by all he could figure wasn't even hooked up to the station. Ops supposedly went on there while the ship was docked. Executive offices were there.

"You've got people aboard?" he asked.

"Might have."

"What are they going to do if customs forces that lock? And which lock?"

"The tube-exit we used for egress to the mast, likely. We really hope they won't do that. Or try any of the e-hatches. That's all I can say."

"You think somebody could get hurt in this?"

"Possibly." She rested a hand on his shoulder. "Breakfast with me is optional. If it goes badly—you may want to slip out of here before maindawn, in case station sends in the bluecoats to arrest the lot of us."

Slipping out was not his notion of how to handle whatever trouble he'd gotten himself into. Pride was in it. And a lifelong reluctance to run scared of stationers with notions of importance. Jen, while being the trouble he'd gotten himself into, was properly warning him, and it might be smart to get Fallan and get out. She *was* the assignment Niall had set him, but so was, above all, Fallan's safety. If it came to a push-shove between *Finity* and EC Customs, he had choices to make, and priorities to sort, and getting Fallan hurt in a literal push-shove between the outsiders and the station bluecoats was not an option.

"I might do that. Leave near maindawn. Take Fallan with me. I won't go without him. And he's apt to tell me sit

down and have breakfast like a proper fool." He turned
over and stared at the invisible ceiling, sprinkled with
faintly glowing stars. The Olympian *was* something. Bed
that could sleep six, destined for one. Bath that spent water
like it was nothing. Comfortable chairs in two rooms, a
computer desk, and a separate room for the bed and lockers. It was truly, truly something. Breakfast probably
would be, too, and he was almost resolved to stay and wait
for the explosion.

And for that push-shove . . . EC Customs was no spacer's friend. If they did decide to give your stuff a going-
over, they were guaranteed to leave it a mess. Sometimes
they'd hold you up at the lift, accuse you of bringing stuff
in to sell, and they might just confiscate personal stuff that
might get administratively "lost" when you were headed
for boarding on a tight schedule and applied to reclaim
your item.

No, if *Finity* really was going to take *them* on, *Finity*
could sell tickets for that match.

Fallan would buy, he was fairly well sure.

He heaved a deep sigh.

"You upset?" Jen asked.

"No. Just thinking about breakfast, and what would be
smart."

"Just ride it out here. *Finity's* not going to buckle, I'll
guarantee you that."

He wished he could be as confident about *Galway's*
situation. Ships were signing with *Finity. Galway* was the
only one that hadn't. And now what?

JR Neihart had opened with a pitch for *Rights* to go to
local spacers. And now he was butting heads with the most
disliked of EC institutions. Which was all well and good
until somebody went a step too far and the chains and the
tasers came out. They had one hell of a big ship *and its allies* hard-docked on B-mast, *Rights* on the A-mast, and if,
God forbid, one of the two mega-ships decided to assert
itself . . .

Forced boarding . . .

Finity had tube-docked here, she'd said. Flimsy old-
fashioned tube-dock to a small forward airlock, the way

they still docked at Glory. Scary place for Customs to use cutters, if they thought they'd get access the hard way. And if not through the hatch . . . how?

There were other ports on a ship. There sometimes needed to be. And the cargo portal. Ships were vulnerable that way. No emergency hatch was ever locked. So if customs wanted in really badly—there was actually nothing stopping them, on any ship he knew.

He'd never seen a ring-dock. Or the apparatus that linked to it. He wanted to ask Jen how *Finity* actually *did* dock at such places. A technical question. But under the circumstances, it was probably too sensitive a question.

It might not be just a customs inspection at issue. Given the design of *Rights* and the nature of *Finity,* more than customs undoubtedly wanted inside. That was not a thought that led back to a quiet sleep.

Their deck, they said. Their ways. Their rules. And he had no doubt now that there were *Finity* personnel still aboard who weren't going to let customs—or anyone else— in. So he and Fallan could be sitting here with some sort of messages getting *to* the crew here in the Olympian, all waiting for an EC try at *taking* the ship.

And what did he do and what did Fallan do, being where they were, with what was going on?

If he and Fallan headed for Niall now—from here—they carried the problem with them.

Stay put, he thought, and recalling the *Finity* crew quietly playing cards in Crit Mass while the world outside rumbled—Stay put, stay quiet, and if somebody official noticed, well, they'd try to be dignified, business as usual . . . at least until all hell broke loose.

"I think we'll stay for breakfast," he said.

"Good," Jen said, and hugged him tight, head under his chin. "That's probably smart. Get some sleep. You and me, Fallan and Mum, nobody heard a thing."

Calls at 0430 hours were *never* good news. Abrezio felt after the com on the nightstand.

"Ben?" Callie asked.

He found the unit, pushed the buttons in succession and got, in text, *"Customs entered ship* Finity's End *at 0349. Violations found. Communications out, agents' situation unknown. Situation ongoing."*

"Ben?"

"I don't know," Abrezio said. "I don't damned well know. Customs! Damned idiots! Lights!"

"Ben—"

Abrezio threw himself out of bed, grabbed his robe. "I'm going to the office. Go back to sleep, if you can, Callie. It's nothing you can do."

He headed for the bathroom and the closet, in that order, com in his pocket, dreading another beep. He didn't shave. He had a razor in the office. He flung on clothes, proper suit: if he had to knock heads, he couldn't do it in casuals.

"Should I worry?" Callie called forlornly.

"Honey, I don't know." He came back to the bedroom, shrugging his jacket into order. "I told Cruz to hold off. Diplomacy's in serious jeopardy right now, and I need to talk to the Neiharts. There *is* something you can do. Call Ames and tell him get to the office. I need him."

"I'll do it," Callie said, and emphatically, as he turned for the door: "Call me if there's anything else I can do. Promise. I'm up."

He lifted a hand, silent thank you, and left. No breakfast, no tea, no waiting for information to get to his private com. He flipped to his office mode and the stack of messages arriving was scrolling off the screen as he hurried out the door, and down the corridor, headed to the office, trying to control his breathing, not to arrive in evident distress.

Ames wasn't there. Security was. The officer scrambled to his feet.

"Sir. There's something going on in B-mast."

"I believe there is," he said calmly, then palm-printed the lock on the executive section. "My secretary will be coming. Advise me of anybody else who shows up."

He kept walking. Lights came on, presence-activated. He opened his office, shivered in the slight chill the place acquired in alterday, and sat down at his desk. The computer came on automatically, showing 122 in the message-waiting overlay in the corner.

He didn't want to wade through them. No way. "Computer. Christophe Mabele," he said to the system. That was the alterday B-mast security head, and presumably in charge. "Location. Status."

"Christophe Mabele. B-Mast office."

"Contact Christophe Mabele. Visual up."

Stupid machine. Stupid system. It couldn't tell him Mabele's situation. He had a vid image of a desk, police moving about, a computer voice calling on Mabele. Mabele's face appeared, unhappy man, with the ceiling lights in the background and a number of people shouting in the vicinity.

"Mr. Mabele," Abrezio said. "What in hell's going on?"

"Sir." Long pause. Mabele was unshaven. And sweating. *"We have lost contact with the team. We're trying to learn their status."*

"Start at the top, Mr. Mabele."

"I'm trying to get the facts myself, sir. Finity's End *has a locked hatch. They've refused access."*

Finity's End was not a name he wanted to hear in a crisis. "I'm aware. What team and why are they missing?"

"Customs team went out the B-mast main lock, sir. Toward Finity's End. *With a utility pusher."*

Ship's emergency accesses were the *only* logical objective. "Who authorized that?"

"Director Maclean, sir."

Maclean was alterday Customs Director. "Put him on."

"He's out of contact, sir. I think he's suiting up to go out there."

"Nobody's suiting up until I get an explanation. Tell whoever's with him stand down, stand off, and tell me who in *hell* suggested they should use an emergency hatch?"

"I'm trying to find out myself, sir."

"Get to it. Stop Maclean. Get me an answer. And *nobody* goes outside until I clear it."

"Yes, sir."

He clicked out. Saw, by the green telltale on his desk, that Ames was at his console, outside.

"Ames!"

"Sir?" Ames appeared in the open doorway.

"If I have a call from JR Neihart I want to take it. Has he called?"

"No, sir."

"Put him through if he does. I'll take calls from *anybody* that's got information on *Finity's End* and the Customs Office."

Ames stared a moment as if he had a question, then, as if he decided against asking, left the doorway.

The multiple messages backed up in the phone queue were from Maclean, Mabele, and the alterday Cargo Office, probably regarding a utility pusher, whose proper job was snagging zero-cold cargo and shifting it to a mast portal. It was *not* a transport device for customs agents deciding to violate the emergency hatches of a politically sensitive visitor. And who had roused out a customs team at this hour, with no new ship in?

He wanted a drink. It wasn't the hour or the situation that made it any sort of good idea. His gut hurt, and that was unmitigated tension.

He decided on strong, sugared tea. He made it for himself, letting Ames stay at his post, fending off what needed diversion, monitoring the security sifter channel for any surge in any topic in the regular areas of the station as well as the Strip. *"Finity"* was a word bound to surge once information got out.

He waited. He had word from Mabele that Maclean was

coming to the offices, back into the station ring. He had word that there was still no communication with the team, but that the utility pusher was still grappled to the safety bars beside *Finity's* personnel emergency hatch.

Cargo hatch he might find some way to excuse, with some delicate maneuvering. But *emergency* hatch? That was into sensitive territory. There were bound to be cameras. And video of customs agents prowling restricted-access areas of *that ship* was bound to get to Pell. Charges of all sorts could be leveled; espionage, sabotage, data-theft, petty pilferage of crew items—God knew what. All that, they could deny, match vid record with vid record, all manner of claims and counter-claims—but with this damned *organization* that the Neiharts and company were selling . . .

Or claiming to sell. Damn. Wasn't *that* a question?

Finity still had personnel aboard. Or had automations talking to personnel on the Strip outside Alpha's regular communications. They had picked up numeric output they could intercept, but not crack—so sparse, they were likely pre-arranged signals. The first customs attempt, the one defeated by the locked access, had generated those from within the ship, and one response from the Strip.

He'd bet it was going on now. He hoped it was. And that whatever had cut the agents off from communication was an electronic problem, not a matter of four dead agents. They'd never had such an incident. He didn't want it now. He hadn't found the right time and the right issue to open extensive talks with the Neiharts, but before they left, before any of this company left, he intended to have a detailed discussion, and he'd hoped to manage some sort of leverage in negotiations. Now—Customs had changed the tone of the discussion entirely.

It was 0520 hours.

"Ames," he said to the intercom.

"Sir."

"Call *Finity's* senior captain. He can't be sleeping through this. If he seems unwilling, tell him I want an amicable solution to this situation."

"Yes, sir."

Time ran. 0525. 0526.

The com beeped. *"Sorry, sir."* Ames' voice. *"They say they're dealing with a situation, and they'll discuss it later."*

"Call them back. Tell them we are urgently concerned about the safety of four of our personnel."

"Yes, sir," Ames said, and the clock ran. 0548 hours. *"Sir. Second captain says they are safe and the senior captain will call you after he's reviewed the situation. I asked when. Second captain said about 0700."*

"God." One fear allayed, but nothing pleasant in the prospect. Persisting in contacting *Finity* could be the thing to do, to show some strength of position. Or it might complicate the situation. *Finity* was going to want to know where the agents had been going and what they had been doing. "Orders stand. Just keep me informed of developments."

Tell the visitors that he hadn't authorized the intrusion? That was giving away his arguments piecemeal. And damned if he wanted to admit his growing lack of control over his own subordinates. If the agents were safe, then he could use the time himself to get his facts—and his personnel—in order.

Maclean. In principal, Maclean. He didn't want to go to the offices himself. He didn't want to call Maclean away from an active situation in which Maclean knew the details. But—

"Sir. Finity says they're releasing the agents. They want our personnel out of the vicinity of their airlock, and they'll put them outside at 0600."

"Tell Maclean get his people out of the lift system. No interference, nobody waving guns around."

"There's also, sir,—"

"Yes?"

"There's a rumor starting to circulate. That there's been an incident, sir. There's a little aggregation of spacers in the mast offices area."

"Ours or theirs?"

"Uncertain. Some are Firenze. *Some are* Nomad. *And* Little Bear. *Those are the patches spotted. They're not do-*

ing *anything. Just—they're right by the lifts. Something's going on."*

"Give me Maclean. No, give me Mabele." He didn't want to give Maclean any possible way to redeem himself.

"Mabele's on, sir."

"Mr. Mabele. What's the situation? Have we confirmed *Finity* is *not* vacated?"

"We have, sir. We don't know how many are aboard or where located, but we have had contact with Finity's *third captain, John Neihart, who requested free communication with their own security personnel left aboard. We registered a complaint and reminded the captain that ships are to be unoccupied during station-stays, and that the airlock is to be left unlocked. Third captain says he defers that issue to the senior captain and says that they are sending our personnel to the office area. The lift is operating right now. We're trying to clear the immediate area, but there are a number of people—including Captain Giovanna Galli and Captain Xiao Min—who are present and resisting requests to stand back. We've tried to handle them with respect, sir, bearing in mind the Neiharts are lodging complaints about their e-hatch situation, but all of a sudden everybody out there's doing ship-speak and not understanding a word of Standard."*

Spacer tactics. Galli spoke perfect Standard. With a drawl. "Just don't let it slip out of control. Take charge now, my order. Get the agents into the offices and debrief."

"The lift's here, sir." A pause. *"Sir. We've got a situation. Excuse me. Get those men under cover. Get them coats. Get them into offices. Now!"*

"What's going on?" Abrezio asked. "Mr. Mabele?"

Mabele had put down the com, or at least quit talking. Confusion came over it. Shouting. Hooting and *laughter.*

It wasn't reassuring.

"Mr. Mabele?"

More shouting and hooting.

He made out *EC pigs,* and *Got served what they deserved.* The tones were not encouraging. He'd known there was resentment, but this . . .

"Mr. Mabele, what's going on?"

No response. No response. And no response, just a great deal of yelling, ending in: *"Clear the area. This office is closed!"*

Voices. Scattered laughter. Voices using ship-speak, and not a familiar one.

Then Mabele. Finally.

"We have them, sir. They're here. They're inside. I'll de-brief them and report. I have a call from Finity's *second captain reporting the unattended pusher attached at their lock. They say they will let it maintain there for six hours. They want it removed within that time frame. I can't autho-rize that."*

Damn Maclean. Let him retrieve it—was the thought in Abrezio's mind. But he said patiently, "I'll put a request through to Cargo. I'm sure they'll want it back. The agents are safe?"

"No injury, sir." A pause. *"No uniforms. Strip-searched. Cold as hell and barefoot. Medics are checking them over now. They . . . don't appear to be customs officers, sir. They're saying they're enforcement."*

Enforcement. Abrezio drew a deep, difficult breath. "Go see to it, Mr. Mabele. I'll want a full report."

Call Legal? They had a monster ship attached to the mast with crew aboard, a very powerful spacer Family looking for an issue to use, and it was, at the moment, a situation no longer limited to a misplaced cargo pusher needing retrieval, and an alterday Customs manager that deserved a career *running* a utility pusher for letting some-body make a move on that ship. God only knew whether any of the enforcement agents handling that craft had ex-perience with it, and they'd run it up against that same ship's hull. If *they* protested the rough handling of the agents, *Finity* could come back with the risk of damage to their hull and the illicit use of an emergency hatch for po-lice entry . . .

And that was just for starters.

He needed Hewitt. *Now.*

"Sir!" Ames' voice, in outer office. A door had just opened, a chill draft arriving. "Let me advise—"

"The *hell!*" Cruz arrived in his doorway, in high temper, shaven—neat, uniformed. Annoying but hardly surprising since Cruz had announced himself as on alterday shift, ever since . . . no surprise there . . . the arrival of *Finity's End*.

Abrezio, unshaven, straight from bed, in a shirt grabbed in the dark, glared back. "I haven't had breakfast, I'm not in a good mood, and I've got a hell of a situation over in B-mast, where some damned *fool* from enforcement attached an unauthorized pusher to the ship we most don't want to piss off right now, *and* made an illegal entry—so give me good news, sir, or it can wait!"

"That *ship* is in violation up and down the list, and they've assaulted investigating agents!"

"Agents caught illegally entering private property! Or did *you* issue a search warrant? I certainly didn't. Perhaps Mr. Hewitt made out his own?"

"Justifiable precaution. *Necessary* precaution. We don't know who's aboard, what they're carrying, or what they're doing with unauthorized communication equipment that's transmitting signals *we can't read!"*

"So *you* sent in security *disguised* as customs men, without a warrant, via the singlemost sacred entry port a ship has? Brilliant move—if it didn't violate every understanding we have with the ships that *keep us alive!"*

Cruz's face was red. "Damn you, Abrezio. If you had the balls to stand up to these people, to keep *me* informed, this would never have happened. I want to know what this Pell ship is proposing to those ships that 'keep us alive.' I want to know what they brought into this system, what they're planning, what deals they're cutting and why in hell *Firenze*'s debt is being paid in *Finity's* scrip!"

"Why? *Why?* Because, *Mr. Vice Admiral* Cruz, that friggin' great construction project that's bled us dry for more than twenty years and bids to do it indefinitely, is sopping up resources that could've had *Firenze* in safe running order years ago. We're lucky not to have lost her, and our only choice now is, paid or unpaid, to freight in a fix for her from Venture—a fix which *Finity* apparently can and will arrange and pay for. Damn straight I'll let them, because *Alpha* can't! And because if the system *isn't* replaced, we're going to lose a ship that *brings* us the supply we don't get from you! *I* want to know who the hell authorized this beyond-stupid move? *You?*"

"That ship is in clear violation of EC regulations, sir. You are glossing that point."

And you, you arrogant bastard, are glossing a far larger one. Abrezio thought, then drew a breath. "Mr. Vice Admiral, do not confuse *law* with EC rules. *Finity's End* is *not* an EC ship. None of them are EC ships. They choose not to abide by EC rules on their own decks, and we're in *no* position to argue, because, like it or not, we rely, ultimately, on Pell's good will for biostuffs, and will for the foreseeable future."

"It's *Alpha's* choice to rely on outside supply!"

"Choice? *Choice?* Since before you arrived, it's been the EC's damn order to *me* to *find* supply so that *Rights* materials can occupy the whole damn pusher load! Don't tell *me* the problems of finance and supply, sir. The Company should be damned grateful we'll have *Firenze's* crew staying here piling up debt somebody else agrees to pay in scrip *and* in rare earths, grateful that someday in a conceivably achievable future one of our two largest haulers is going to be back in full function so that supply *does* come to us from points farther in. I'm *tired* of trying to explain to our *citizens* about repairs that can't be made, and lights that can't be replaced. I'll be damned if I let your stupidity extend those hardships to failing scrubbers and lack of flour! Right now I have a utility pusher that was taken out by a damned rock eighteen days ago, which also needs to be fixed and for which I have *no spare parts.* Thanks to you, Mr. Cruz, and your refusal to release supply to the station, I'm up to my ears in problems, and at the top of the list is one of our three remaining pushers, which is currently grappled to the hull of *Finity's End,* and which I would like to see removed under its own power, rather than cast adrift to go banging into us or something *else* we don't want it to hit. Because *you* refuse to take responsibility for that illegal search, *I* have *that* little detail to attend to before I get breakfast, Mr. Cruz, and I'm getting damned hungry, so I'd appreciate you getting the hell out of my office and letting me take care of the mess *you* created."

"I have been charged with the responsibility for the protection and operation of *The Rights of Man*, . . . sir. *You* may be running scared of her prototype, but I will take every opportunity to get information on it, its operations, and its activities on this station. You also have a duty, sir, as an EC officer, to protect the EC's reputation *and* its resources, and not to cozy up to spies and intruders, whose purpose here is quite clear. Information. Intimidation. Humiliation. *Anything* to undermine the successful completion of *The Rights of Man*. They work for Pell, and they're here to be sure we don't make that link to Sol, ever. They want to see the majority of humanity isolated. Permanently. They want to relegate the EC to an historical footnote."

"In your opinion."

"My *opinion*? *Pell* calls us the Hinder Stars. The stars left behind. From their view, we are *nothing* but metal-poor resource-sinks of absolutely no use to their expansion. They don't want to link up with Sol and Earth and find themselves outnumbered and out-resourced. They don't *want* civilization to link up with the motherworld. No, sir! *Pell* is cozying up to Cyteen—how not? They've *disconnected* from us. They graciously allow a powerless EC presence, but they have far more in common with Cyteen and its *reckless* colonization of systems—that might provoke God knows what out there."

"The way Sol did at Beta?" He couldn't believe he was actually defending Cyteen. "Fact is, they're expanding more slowly than Sol did, in the beginning, give or take the FTL factor. Leave Cyteen and every other cliché space bogie out of this, *Mr.* Cruz. In fact, just get the hell out of my office."

Cruz drew himself up, looked down his nose at him. "*Finity* is in violation of the docking rules, they're communicating back and forth with crew left aboard that ship with equipment they're not supposed to have, for what operations we still don't know, and if all that activity is all right with you, *Director*, then you and I have a strong difference of purpose and plan. *I* am loyal to the EC. I serve its interests, and I have a strong sense of outrage, sir, in the humiliation we've been served. Spacers come and go. The maintenance of law and order on Alpha is for the protection of its citizens. And you seem bent on making excuses!"

"*Finity* is not the one I'm being forced to explain to the citizens. I'm not the one that sent four agents out there to make an illegal entry into a Pell-registry ship. If there's a risk to citizens, it's in the over-eager use of EC *rules* to breach *laws*, Mr. Cruz, a distinction on which a great deal rests. The same laws that protect the privacy of a civilian's home cover non-EC ships. Those *laws* guarantee ships safety at dock and guarantee peaceful conduct of business in a regulated zone, where we give and take in a civilized way with ships that are not otherwise under *our* rules and regulations. We cannot *appropriate* them, we cannot act in ways which suggest *piracy* and espionage, with which we are—now—unhappily and forever tainted. It is a distinction *Finity* has challenged, and which we are in no position to defy. Thanks to *Rights* and its *needs,* the First Stars are no longer supported by *Santa Maria* and *Atlantis.* Thanks to *Rights* and its *needs,* we rely on a biostuffs supply chain which emanates from Pell. Thanks to *Rights* and its *needs,* we depend on Pell for the means to sustain our internal food production, we get the elements for our printers from Pell and Venture, and we get pharmaceuticals from Cyteen labs. We *are* interconnected, Mr. Cruz, and *not with Sol . . .* largely *thanks* to *Rights of Man* and its needs—so do not lecture *me* on the function of a system to which you arrived as a complete outsider, and have *refused* to understand."

He'd said enough. More than enough. He, in fact, *hated* Cruz, he *hated* Hewitt, and he was relatively sure it was becoming mutual.

But they still had to work together.

He took a breath. "I'm out of sorts and I need my breakfast, sir. Doubtless you're on the end of a trying number of hours, yourself. Neither of us has gotten satisfaction. Nor will we, until we come to some sort of agreement. I would offer to share a breakfast, but I have elements of this business to mop up, before I dare take the time. In lieu of breakfast, I would offer you a session this afternoon, a relaxation, if you will. We may strongly disagree, but we are required to work together. I would prefer to do so amicably."

"I will have to decline. I am on alterday schedule at the moment." Cold. Deadpan cold. "It will be the middle of my night."

"And I will have to insist, sir," Abrezio said, in a tone that left no room for discussion. "We cannot delay or avoid this."

Cruz frowned, dipped his head, and strode out.

Chapter 8   Section iv

An image was making an appearance, passed from com to com—before some prankster managed to get it up on one of the scheduling displays—four unidentified men wearing only towels, arriving on what looked like the lifts in the B-mast offices lobby, where a crowd had gathered.

"What in hell?" was Ross's reaction, when he saw it, at breakfast with Jen, in a restaurant populated by Finitys, at a table a row apart from Fallan and Mum. People turned and looked from one screen to another, and yes, it was on all the number two screens.

Quiet surprise rippled through the room.

B-mast. The problem with Customs.

2.35 minutes later, the image vanished, returning the screen to the schedule board.

"What's going on?" Ross asked directly, and Jen drew a deep breath.

"Customs guys. Security did what they had to do—tossed them out, confiscated whatever they came in with. We *wouldn't* have hijacked the schedule feed. I don't think Senior Captain will be happy with *that*." Jen gave an impish shrug. "But security *did* give them towels."

"God." He didn't want to be amused. It was damned

serious. But no spacer was that fond of EC Customs, and it *was* damned funny, given nobody got hurt. He looked at Fallan and Mum, who had their heads together over breakfast. Fallan had probably been better informed, start to finish of the incident. "Customs and the blue-coats get orders to push now and again, and, yeah, they get no sympathy from us whose heads get cracked. There's going to be a big push when you pull out. *Galway's* ready to move. We'd be a lot happier to make our run *before* you go, because admin is going to be frothing mad to reassert the rules. And there's *going* to be cracked heads before all's said and done. No question."

"Abrezio?" she asked. "I heard he has a pretty good reputation."

"Abrezio's the reason there's running water on this station. The problems came in with—you know—"

She tipped her head, looked puzzled. "I don't know."

He found himself doing what everybody did on Alpha when the topic of *Rights* came up in places that might be bugged: ducking his head to make lip-reading harder; lowering his voice, speaking in generalities, while the girl opposite him—probably read the body language and was embarrassed for him, dammit. But if he got himself in trouble, he let Fallan down, let Niall down, let the Family down. "Look, you know what arrived here, with all its problems. Whole damn Pell office got shipped back here, took over the project—started it, really. Word is, they'd had standing orders, once they could get those plans, to hightail back here. Pell threw them out, but at least some would've come anyway. Began organizing and confiscating mats long before the word of the theft could get to Sol and back. Cruz . . . he came in on the next pusher, along with a hold full of dedicated supply for . . . it." Maybe she wasn't that well informed by her own higher-ups—and she was probably primed to ask questions and find out things. Likely Lisa Marie had her own agenda. Everybody walked nervous circles around the same truth, and the only people who didn't know what was going on were young, or feckless, or strangers to the station.

"Cruz is the darling boy of the EC hardnoses," he said,

and darted a glance up, eye to eye. Hers were brown, dark-lashed, prettiest eyes he'd ever seen. Which might figure in the urge to make her really understand Alpha, even beyond what she might well be assigned to find out. "Every scrap Abrezio gets for regular operations he pulls out of Cruz's hands with Cruz objecting all the way. What we need done—we can't get here even if we had the finance, because it's all dedicated to that ship up there. We keep hearing it'll be better. But it's been going on long as I've been out of the junior-juniors. And I'll bet you, I'll bet you anything that Cruz is why Customs did whatever they've done. No accident it came down on alterday, while Abrezio was offshift. It's no secret Cruz wants more than anything to have an up close and personal look at *Finity*, and now he's had a serious, public comeuppance. If you see people going a little over the edge laughing about this—*that's* the subtext. I wouldn't say we're always happy with Abrezio, but Cruz has changed things, that's what I hear the seniors even of Niall's generation saying. Cruz is a son-of-a-bitch who thinks when Sol does get in here, that he'll step ahead of Abrezio and be the darlin' boy of the whole EC back at Sol. *If* his ship ever runs. That's the embarrassing fact. He's planning for a coup, and you set him down. Hard. With the help of whoever got that picture. That's prime, that. That gladdens the hearts of everybody who's ever had to deal with that bastard." Something struck him, in memory of the image that had flashed up, a face, not one he knew well. He reached for his own pocket com and thumbed through recent transmissions. "If those men even were Customs. God. That first one—I think that's Hewitt. EC enforcement, *Rights* project. I've only seen him on vid. But if that really is Hewitt, *Cruz* is really going to be spitting."

"Abrezio authorized it?"

"No. No way. I don't think so. But Cruz could. Hewitt might, either one. You reporting to JR?"

Hesitation. A nod. "Yes." Deep breath. Her hand closed on his, on the table. "Ross. I have to be honest. It's my job. I'm ship's security."

He moved his hand back. "You never said."

"You never asked."

"I think I'd deserve to know!"

Her hand advanced again. Fingers over fingers. "I'm telling you now. Do you think they'd let Mum walk around the Strip *without* security? I had to be there. But I'm telling you now. I'm telling you because it's fair, and I don't sleep with people I don't like. I've only ever slept with one guy, on Mariner, and he wasn't an assignment."

"So you *were* assigned to watch me."

She dipped her chin. "But that's *not* why . . . the rest. I didn't need to sleep with you. That was my choice. *Mine.* I *like* you. I like Fallan. I like you both, and Mum likes you, and I don't think I'd get anything but the truth out of you in any case, which is partly why I'm telling you now. So tell me—did your ship send *you* to learn about us?"

"To find out what you're up to, and to keep an eye on Fallan, just because, well, he's ours. And he's in love. And capable of being stupid, even if he *is* the smartest man I know."

"Good reason. He's got Mum's attention." Fingers moved on his. "Ross, I seriously like you. I can't say love because I don't know you, but if you're ever in any port I'm in I want to find you. You *are* special. You've got special friends. And I don't think Mum will lie to Fallan. I get the feeling she's that way with him. She'd steal him if she could. But he won't. I get that, too. So does she."

Twists and turns. Jen was like that, truth and words shifting about like smoke, hiding and showing what was a structure of forces. Nav was like that, things you couldn't see pushing and pulling, and when, on some drunken off-shift, you ever described what it was to helm, they put up a hand and said, just give me a point, nav, and don't make me crazy.

Find us information, Niall had said, and, God help them, sent two *navigators* into the heart of *Finity's End*, to try to make sense of it all. What did he expect from this outsider ship, but smoke and mirrors?

"What in hell are you, the ship, really up to, Jen?" He curled his fingers around hers. "What are you doing here?"

"What I said, Ross. I didn't lie. Our deck, our rules, for every merchanter out there, and all of us have to stand firm, help each other and keep the stations from fighting each other. We keep Cyteen and Pell apart, and we keep them connected. We keep the Hinder Stars going. All that. We want to make sure every Family ship that needs help gets it and that no monstrosity with hired crew is going to move cargo. You want a problem, Ross—that's when Cyteen decides it can spare the effort to replace us with cloned-man crews. They've *got* the tech—damn sure *their* first FTL didn't abort the run. Fortunately, they gave their first long-hauler to the Rileys, not some azi crew. But they've got tapes, now, that can create perfect crew, if they so decide. Right now—we work; and so long as they can see we're a good thing, we go on working. We're creating an organization, a structure that's an advantage to everyone involved. We declare independence, financial and legal, from all stations, we deal with everyone and they don't have to deal with each other. It's a good plan. A solid one, but we *have* to get it in place before Sol gets in here and provides a third pushy side to the whole Pell-Cyteen question, with *their* resources, and their notions of hired crew . . . and their notions of who *owns* everything out here."

He listened. She made sense. A very scary kind of sense . . . given that, if Cruz's security chief had breached *Finity* and gotten tossed, there was going to be serious push-back. No way not.

"I think," he said, with a side glance over to Fallan, then back to her. "I think maybe I should get ourselves back to *Galway* territory. It could get tense on the Strip. And if we have escaped station's notice in being here, we'll be lucky. We need to talk to Niall."

"Understood. Go. We're covering the bill. Drink up and go."

He swallowed down his juice—too rare to leave that; and a decent cup of tea—got up and went over to talk to Fallan and Mum. Fallan was reluctant to go. Mum—Mum understood all that was going on, no way that *she* hadn't been informed of everything, and probably had Fallan's own interpretation of the incident as well. Mum understood and she shoved Fallan out the door—with promises.

They took the long way back to *Galway*'s territory,

wending their way past another breakfast spot, pausing to have a cup of tea, then meandering on through a shop display or two.

There was an undercurrent on the Strip, amusement, yes, but a curious expression on certain faces, a mix of a little worry, a little satisfaction. Blue-coats were out in number, and the Strip was quiet.

For now.

Chapter 8   Section v

Rumors.

Abrezio had heard them here and there, caught them in tones and looks and subtle wording, rumors adding up to one thing: the schism between himself and Cruz had ceased to be an internal matter.

The names of the agents were not being released—on his orders—but that did very little good. That picture had gotten out and the fact that one of the four was the project security chief—was a flaming disaster. Talk was that it was Hewitt's operation, that Hewitt had gone off on his own and done it without Cruz knowing—that wasn't so, but it provided a useful buffer. Abrezio only hoped his own name stayed out of the talk—and that Cruz's name stayed out of it as much as possible. Hewitt—was unfortunately indelibly tainted, and *that* wasn't going to go away easily.

Rights, not station security. And now the rumor was asking, even in resident hallways—why during alterday?

It was a perfectly logical question, with an obvious answer: to do it when principal authority was in bed asleep—either innocent of the move, or trying to look innocent.

A stationwide schism soon became apparent—some saying *any* action was appropriate since *Finity* had scared them all and these four stranger ships lingered without any reason ordinary citizens understood; others saying to hell with that: they didn't want a Sol-born EC brown-noser running *their* station and sneaking around in the dead of mainnight. Let them get away with a breach of a visiting ship, and what was to stop them from inviting themselves unannounced into private apartments?

Maddeningly, what happened had also splashed discredit on the Customs Service, and on its manager, for allowing *Rights* security to go out dressed as Customs. *Damnable* man. Maclean had no business taking orders from Hewitt *or* Cruz, not without sending a query up to him, no matter the hour . . . and now he'd apparently done it . . . twice. Abrezio was not a vengeful man. He didn't see any benefit in carrying grudges. But he did in taking notes. And Maclean's finances deserved investigation—just to see if there had been under-the-table motivation.

He doubted, though, that the motivation had come from Hewitt, as he doubted that Cruz had resorted to bribes. Likely he'd offered something less tangible—like an exchange of favors, present or future.

Cruz, independently ordering Customs to make the initial move without consulting admin—and Maclean complying without checking? That was bad form. If, on the other hand, EC Enforcement, by whatever means, had had officers *pose* as customs, and Maclean had gone along with it—*that* was an outrage.

He couldn't reprimand Cruz or Hewitt. He didn't want the action laid at his door, but even more, he didn't want to advertise a schism in the upper management of the station. Not now. Not when he had *Finity* and its partners organizing some sort of move that was going to recruit Alpha's ships—with the likelihood that whoever or whatever was behind *Firenze*'s ungodly expensive repair was going to make demands, ultimately, and become a power player for somebody.

On the one hand—he had a station to keep viable, a trust handed down to him, Sol's gateway to the colonies it had set up.

On the other—if Sol found its own way here, as could happen any day, with no warning, Sol would find everything in shambles. An outlandishly expensive ship that couldn't jump. A station falling into disrepair, no matter it was Sol's own orders that had pushed it into that state. Maybe neither he *nor* Cruz would survive the arrival of Sol authority, politically speaking—but right now, he couldn't abdicate. *Wouldn't* give up. Not yet. Right now—*damned* if he let Cruz pull another such stunt as he had.

The question was—how he could stop the man? If he made an issue of this incident to try to get Cruz under control, the move might not be understood by stationers as a whole. Alpha citizens saw *Rights* Enforcement personnel as their own sons and daughters, their cousins and their protectors. Seven years ago, Hewitt had shown up and begun recruiting, eliminating station unemployment virtually overnight.

And after two decades, Alpha citizens had become psychologically dependent on *Rights*, no matter the thing was an expensive doorstop. Alpha citizens had been told *Rights* was an asset, ultimately, their way out of a downward slide, worth every sacrifice. *Rights* was going to save them, economically, and *Rights* was their way out, their escape if the unthinkable happened and the station came under threat.

There was one possible way around Cruz, one possible way to protect himself and to protect Callie's future. A way that didn't entail caving in to the visitors. If Cruz was going to blame every problem on him—it also headed that off. If these Pell ships had arrived here suspecting he had a route to Sol, if Pell was bent on finding it out—there was a way he could at least establish a date on which he had taken definitive action on Sol's side.

Even if *Finity* had set some receiver out there tapping into the Stream . . . even if they had cracked Sol's code—it wasn't going to stop the message. And the date—the *date* of transmission—

God, he wished he didn't have a disaster on deck on the day he did it. The timing was bound, eventually, to come out. But today was what he had. The longer he *didn't* do something—

He *could* maintain he hadn't wanted to do it with the visitors here. But—the pressure they put on *was* a reason. He had the excuse for silence—in being sure—and the excuse for going ahead: a threat to the project, but not of his creation.

He tapped the call button on the com, and moments later:

"Sir?" Ames said, from the doorway.

"Go out and keep that door shut. I'm not here. I don't care who shows up asking entry."

Ames, wide-eyed, stepped back and shut the door.

There was a covered pad in a pullout on his desk. It had a thumbprint lock, and he opened it, sliding his chair back as the entire desk lifted clear of the carpet and powered itself forward.

Ames had no clue. One well-kept retired scientist knew. The people who kept him knew that he knew *something,* and might suspect, but they had jobs guaranteed so long as that seclusion lasted, which paid them very well. And they knew that.

There were others—in communications—who might guess, before the day was out. Speculation might also run to the fiasco Hewitt was involved in. Let them theorize. It took a computer to breach the code, and those on Alpha that might do it were harming themselves if they tried and talked. Whether *Finity* could crack it—was a question.

But once that data became part of the Stream, it was unstoppable, and secrecy and timing and motives—all that was for somebody later to figure out.

The drop-safe had a palmprint lock. Abrezio got down on one knee—that was a bit more difficult than in his youth—and opened it.

The chip was in a typical wrapper, fifteenth pocket in a set of chips that had key data and hard resets for various station systems . . . hiding in what was not exactly plain sight: only four people could open the safe and only two of those could move the desk without major damage. Ames was not one of them.

Neither was Cruz. Or Hewitt.

He pocketed the chip, closed the pocket securely, not that he intended to be running—then closed the safe and put the desk back in proper position, snug down against the carpet as if it had no possibility of moving.

Then he exited the office. "I'm in, but not receiving," he told Ames. "I'm going up to ops. Is Friemann on duty?"

"Yes, sir," Ames said. "Has been since the early wake-up, sir."

"Call him, tell him meet me at the end of the hall." Friemann was his personal security, and came with Turman, Challas and Godfrey, not the youngest and fittest of security teams—Challas in particular was broad of girth and Godfrey was expanding with age; but they were his ordinary accompaniment, had been for a decade and a half, and he felt safer when he reached the lift and saw them hurrying up from the side hall, a little out of breath and in other than good order—Challas was still working on his coat. They were a comfort and company, in what was a lift-ride up to a place familiar but ominous in its potential—the nerve center of Alpha Station.

It sprawled on for a fair space. Techs were used to seeing him. Supervisors wished him good morning, and told him their concerns, in a few cases, nominally what they were to do about recovering four hardsuits and a utility pusher from *Finity's End*. "I'll contact the senior captain and request it," he said. "And I want it clear Customs had no clearance to access outside equipment. I want the request examined, records preserved as evidence, and reprimands issued, all the way up."

"Yes, sir," was the response.

Damned sure the suits would come back stripped of recording capsules, including their activity log. Which made proving anything harder. But that became trivial, after today.

The office farthest from the entry was the oldest on the station, dating all the way back to the first century of Alpha's existence. Everything here was antique, deliberately maintained much as it had been, the bare metal, the tarnish of occupancy. Plastics had been replaced with ceramics that preserved the look. But otherwise—it was historic, this area. And he hadn't been here in years. Usually the feed to the Stream came through regular station communications.

"Sir," a tech said, astonished—caught unwarned, with breakfast on the console.

"I have a transmission," Abrezio said. "It's interrupt-worthy. Just insert it. I'll give you a palmprint on the send."

"Yes, sir." A cheerful shrug. The Stream had, in its day, carried technical queries, scientific discoveries, pictures of newborn babies—chess matches and idle lovelorn chatter for lonely pusher-ships years out from station. Stream-techs handled autofeed, mostly, things prepared to be sent by various departments. He'd rarely been up here. The man minding the Stream-feed was, however, one of the old faces.

He handed over the chip. It went into the slot and entered the Stream within a second or two.

"Want a confirmation of send, sir?" As the tech handed the chip back.

"Sure. Yes," Abrezio said as casually as he could manage.

And that was that. A lightspeed transmission would reach *Atlantis, Santa Maria,* and Sol in due course. Abrezio hoped, but could not verify, that it didn't hit any other receiver out there in the dark, but if it did, if Pell had a receiver transmitter in place out there, it would still be too late. The button was pushed. The jump point coordinates, the supporting data—everything he had on the topic—was on its way to Sol at the speed of light, nothing slower; unfortunately no faster.

A ship could outrace it. But had no way to get there.

Unless—it had the coordinates.

The Strip was uncommonly quiet, just a feeling of tension running up and down. A lot of blue-coats. A lot of wolf-whistles, in a particular significance of mischief aimed at uniforms in general.

Rosie's was *Galway* turf, right near the Fortune, which was the sleepover *Galway* held. There were cousins, oh, ten or twelve of them, the *only* customers at this hour.

"How was it?" Ashlan called out, Nav 2 on Fallan's shift. "Hey, Fallan! You, on the medical restriction! Were you good or were you bad?"

"I was," Fallan said archly, "very, *very* good."

Laughter attended. "Come drink some breakfast! It's one of those days! Rosie's oven's on the blink again and he's serving toast and cold beer!"

"Gotta stay sober," Ross said. "We got a report to give."

"Damn straight you do!" another cousin said. "You were right in the middle of it."

"Not the ones that got the exposure," Ashlan said impishly. "God, I'd have given money to be there."

"Not a single Galway in the crowd?" Fallan asked.

"We didn't hear about it until it was all over. We want first-run details!"

"Well, I had my breakfast, but I'll take a near-beer. Some guy who got sleep last night can get it." Fallan dropped into a chair and Ross sat down by him.

"You didn't," Ross said under his breath. "You swore you wouldn't."

"Not so much," Fallan said, likewise under his breath. "Mostly we talked. We filled in the gaps, hers and mine—

some of the gaps. Interesting stuff. Want to sit for a bit. Tell you later."

"You know anything I don't?"

"Maybe."

The near-beer arrived. So did the dozen cousins and Rosie *and* the wait-staff, standing close.

"Well, it's pretty simple," Fallan said. "The outsiders all lock up tight, and they *don't* vacate, and they take the position customs can be escorted through the hold regarding goods proposed to be offloaded, but they don't set foot elsewhere."

"So," Mary T asked, "who's going to say what-all is elsewhere?"

"Long as it doesn't exit the ship, is it Customs' business? That's the outsiders' say on the matter."

"Does Pell go with that? Does the Beyond?"

"Not sure they have a choice," Fallan said. "And sounds like they don't much give a damn, so long as their cargo moves. That's the thing in contention. Even Alpha Customs skips inspections more often than not. They haven't tried a one of these newcomers, until they decided to make a case of *Finity,* which just happens to be a working ship, as *Rights* isn't, so—and they didn't go to the hold. They hard-suited and grappled to a hatch up in the ring, of which *Finity* had certain suspicions."

"So the e-hatch story," a cousin said, "is true."

"That's exactly true. They got inside, but they were carryin' cutters, cameras, and such, which *Finity* security didn't highly appreciate. *Finity* security shut a section of corridor, told them if they used those cutters they were going to be highly unappreciated, and told them they could stay in that corridor until those suits became real uncomfortable, or until *Finity* left port, if they wanted to be permanent guests. Or they could shed the hardsuits and get searched, and then they could go out the nice, mostly warm tube access to the personnel lifts and go free. The so-called 'Customs' boys decided they wanted out, so *Finity* let them shed the suits and come out and cooperate. And the howlin' part is—one was Hewitt himself, as turns out, not that he was admittin' who he was. But the cutters, the cameras, the data sticks, all that, *with* the hardsuits, *Finity's* got. Hewitt and his boys was given souvenir towels, with *Finity's* own logo, and they was let go to the lift, not a scratch on 'em. That's *Finity's* account of it, which I had direct, with pictures. They weren't the ones who put them exiting the lift up on the schedule boards. I know that on a *Finity* captain's word, which I believe. And *Finity* didn't gather that crowd down at the terminal to embarrass the administration, either."

"Word is, that was purely local," a cousin said.

"Much as we love Customs, we so love Hewitt more." That, from another cousin, with a mutter of laughter quickly dying as Niall and his brother captain, Owen, came in.

"So what's this?" Niall asked.

Chapter 9   Section ii

Fallan had to tell it over again, with Niall and Owen in the party, and Ross had a cup of strong tea and dry toast. His stomach was upset all the while, and finally, as he had a chance to catch Niall isolated at the door, he said, in shipspeak, "Jen, the girl I was with, Jen's *Finity* Security. So you know."

"Did *you* know?"

"She told me last night. Says Fallan's Lisa Marie wouldn't be walking around without security, and she's it, at least the part I know about."

Niall leaned against the door frame, still inside, arms folded, "Well, makes sense. I'm not worried about it. Fallan and this woman, well, good for them, I think. He'll say what he wants, but he'll be listening, too. You get a good sense of this girl?"

"She told me on her own. For what reason I don't know. I like her. I think she likes me."

"Well, that's the way of it, isn't it, as should be. A tie with *Finity's* no bad thing. They're wanting to talk to me and Owen. And I know pretty well what the deal is—same as the Gallis and the Rodriguezes. And there's a percentage in not signing, actually. I can talk to you. And you can talk to this girl."

"Yes, sir."

"So pass this word. I'm *thinking* about it. We're doing all right as we are. There's no percentage for us in changing that. I need more understanding how this actually works, how widespread it is—damned sure I don't want to be signing onto something that's going to leave us worse off than we were if it turns out, say, that they have a handful signed up and it turns out then to be something illegal or just politically upsetting to the wrong people."

"I know what you're saying. Fal doesn't think so."

"Get him. I want to talk to you two for a bit. My room."

"*Finity* would say, sir, don't talk in rooms. They're using equipment to tell when they're being listened to, and to screen their whole area. Jen says they've got bugs in the bars, just about everywhere. Jen says if you want to talk, safest place is somewhere on the open Strip, face the wall and be sure they aren't lipreading you."

Niall just looked at him. "That a fact?"

"I know Jen's said shush a couple of times, and we've moved. She's got some way to know. I think it's something she carries."

"Some girl you've got."

"Why does admin need to bug the damn lavatories, is what I want to know. If it's so. And Jen says it is. Back of bars, lavatories, restaurants, entertainment parlors. She says they don't work all the time, but they can decide they want to listen to you. And the damn cameras are everywhere."

That was a longtime given, the cameras. And the occasional snoopery.

"Go get Fal. See if we can find us a spot to talk."

"Yessir."

The place impenetrable to bugs—they hoped—turned out to be the very tight confines of Rosie's employee lavatory—theoretically immune to bugs mostly because unless the typical user talked to himself, there was little point in bugging a space barely big enough for one. Fallan was no heavyweight, neither was Niall, and Ross the same—the Monahan genes didn't run to large people. So Ross squeezed in between the metal sink and the wall, Fallan sat, by the light of an overhead LED that barely lit the place. Niall's back was to the door, and by the directional glow of the unmirrored LED, his face was all shadow, only his red hair catching the light.

"So," Niall said in *Galway*'s shipspeak, looking at Fallan and with a nod toward Ross, "his girl is what she is, yours is, well, what she is, and he thinks you're all right being headlong trusting in the situation."

"Straight answer, I judge yes, if you mean what happened. They're in the right."

"Side of the angels, eh?"

"Swearing to it, cuz. Nobody got hurt. Nobody."

"General honesty?"

"Stake my life on it."

"Stats. Have you heard them?"

Fal nodded, and fished a data stick out of his pocket. "This."

That was the first Ross had heard of a stick being passed. It was the sort you could slip into a com and read, or listen to. Niall took it as if it were apt to catch fire, then took out his com and pushed it in.

The com screen lit up. And it said—Niall held it, twisted round so they all could see the text.

We ask the Monahans to join us in organizing a mer-

chant alliance for mutual support and protection. We have signatures from a majority of ships operating between here and Mariner, a total of forty-nine of the sixty-three Families, since three more have signed here at Alpha. Meanwhile Estelle *and* Dublin *are seeking signatures of the Families within their range of operations, including Cyteen and its colonies. We have four other ships we hope to contact between here and Pell. Our alliance is founded on ownership, sovereignty, and mutual financial support, effectively an insurance system. We will, by negotiation with the stations we serve, maintain the following principles: stations will trade and move commerce only by our ships. Every Family will govern what happens on its deck, and no station and no other Family will intrude onto the deck of a Family ship, nor withhold services to try to coerce a Family ship to surrender personnel or cargo. If a station operates in violation of the agreement, there will be no trade with that station, except in humanitarian emergency, until the infraction is resolved.

Can we enforce this? We are preparing to do so, in the expectation that sooner or later, Sol will arrive with its own orders; or Pell will fall out with Cyteen; or vice versa. We are not willing to see stations make decisions that endanger our livelihoods and risk our lives.

No ship of our alliance will go it alone. In principle, we also protect the stations: if a station has a viable population, it should be served. This is the responsibility that goes with the privilege we are demanding. We profit by having ports to serve.

We are available for further discussion of the proposal. We will continue contact as we are doing and will accept messages by that means, but we also extend an invitation to the Monahans to visit any of our premises on Alpha, and to satisfy themselves as to the terms and applicability of the organization we represent. Signatory to this agreement:

JR Neihart
Xiao Min
Sanjay Patel
Asha Druv
Giovanni Galli

Diego Rodriguez
Rahman Aki . . .

The list went on to Families operating at Bryant's, and Venture, to Pell, Viking, Mariner, and beyond.

Niall drew a long, long breath, and Ross found a chill spreading through him, contact with the unheated wall and sink on either side of him, maybe, but the message was far wider than anything he had expected from the rumors floating the strip. The list of names included the Reillys and the Quens; it involved the Fasads, the Romneys, the Dales, Kriegers, Lukowskis, Joneses, Coskis, Olvigs, Gweris, Krejas and Beaumonts . . . names he'd heard in spacer tales, and seen written in the history of Glory and Alpha, but, God, it truly was a roll call of Families spread out as far as Cyteen.

Niall popped the stick out and palmed it, passing it back to Fallan with the kill-it sign.

Then nodded, solemnly, which said everything.

Niall opened the door, and they extricated themselves into Rosie's back kitchen storage, which had one dying LED that came on with movement. They went on through the kitchen, no different than many a longtime patron who knew the facilities in back were closer than the public lavatories six doors down.

Never had used it for a critical conference, not in Ross's memory, but that wasn't saying it had never happened, in a station over-supplied with cameras and bugs. That all had come on when the actual *Rights* build had started up, when the first big pusher-load had arrived—

When they'd gotten security-obsessed, and when the blue-coats had gone from a few grey-haired guards who'd tell you move along, the senior-seniors said, to young hard-noses armed with tasers, young toughs told it was their job to prevent angry talk. He hadn't seen the change, but he began to think, with the incident that had knocked Fallan down, that it was worse than he remembered, all the way over to scary, counting where they'd been last night, and the disrespect of the blue-coats on the Strip since yesterday, blue-coats and Customs and pushy *Rights* crew all finding disfavor up and down, in subtle catcalls and whistles from people who didn't seem to be looking.

Admin hadn't shut down the bars and shops. That was a step they could take. But fact was, the catcalls weren't coming from the visitors, who weren't highly visible on the Strip today—staying likely to their own bars and restaurants and such—but from isolated local crew, few in number. Workmen were out, with a ladder, or possibly they were plainclothes blue-coats: workmen were always suspect. Supposedly they were replacing a light.

It was not a nice mood on the Strip today. Admin certainly wasn't happy.

They made a brief foray back to the hotel to change clothes and let the Monahan presence on the Strip fade a bit. It seemed a good idea. The more time that passed with nothing to attract particular notice, the better.

Chapter 9   Section iv

Tea with Andy Cruz, an executive meeting, Cruz with his subdirector, Black, and with Enzio Hewitt, Hewitt showing up in spit and polish, a uniform with too many unnecessary buttons, in Abrezio's jaundiced estimation. Project Security, part of Earth Company Enforcement, the ECE, was supposedly subordinate to the ECSD, the Station Directorate, which was Abrezio's office. Abrezio's official appearance this afternoon was a business suit and a small collar pin, which damned well outranked the gold braid and the buttons.

But then, they weren't discussing fashion this afternoon. Wouldn't even mention Hewitt's lack thereof, in his appearance on every number two screen on the Strip, and the public appearance of three of his special operatives, whose appearance was now and forever known to every spacer on the Strip. They carefully weren't mentioning state of dress this afternoon.

Ames was there, carrying a computer linked to everything useful. Adima was there, head of Records. So was Systems Director Stacy Oldfield, a formidable woman with thirty years' service in Ops, and no great fondness for *Rights'* intrusion into her list of priorities. She was politically canny. She didn't express her distaste. She smiled winsomely, beaming like somebody's grandmother, and managed to say to Hewitt, ever so innocently, "We have been asked to make arrangements to recover four hard-suits and a pusher. Do I understand correctly Enforcement would like *Ops* to handle that operation?"

"We have other problems." Hewitt turned sharply and walked off to join Cruz on the other side of the large table.

Oldfield smiled benignly, and Abrezio thought to himself that it would be a cold day in hell when an alterday department head honored another unusual request from *any* arm of the ECE. The one that *had* complied—Maclean claimed a subordinate had supplied uniforms supposedly for an undercover operation on the Strip; and a construction foreman had given way to Hewitt's rank. It had gone as it had because the request had come on alterday, when higher supervisors had been offshift, an oversight that wouldn't happen again, not in any branch of Ops, including construction: Abrezio had ordered reference to mainday authority—his office—for *anything* involving operations on B-mast.

The easy, forgiving way stationers had gotten along for hundreds of years was not going to survive Cruz and his programs, Abrezio had realized that long since, and this current situation had brought those differences into full, unforgiving light. In the early days of the *Rights* project, they'd made rules, they'd tried to foresee problems, and the increase in enforcement for the security of the project *had* employed a goodly number of young people—which had been a good thing . . .

In the eyes of the citizens, *Rights* gave them good jobs and put them back on the map, so to speak. It was proof that the EC still had plans for them. There was hardship, but there was hope.

The Strip was a dicier piece of politics, but he'd managed over the years to keep peace with the Strip and its shifting denizens, even if alcohol and anger got out of hand now and again. But the Strip had its own rough humor, which had come, last night, at direct odds with both Customs and project Enforcement. Well that the result *was* humor, and that it had found an outlet, no matter that his administration had suffered embarrassment, no matter that the ECE's morale had taken a serious hit. Worse could have ensued.

Worse might still ensue, if humor turned; and bet on it, the story would break out repeatedly through the years, particularly since Hewitt was probably destined for office once Sol did get here—now a likelihood with a date attached—and there was no way he could ever get rid of the man unless Sol itself shipped him on.

The man had taken unforgivable advantage of a convention old as human presence in space—e-hatches just were not locked. Why should they ever need to be? By definition they were for emergencies, and a suit with a hole in it didn't allow time for hi-how-are-you's.

Well, after this—maybe they would be, and the why of it would always cite Alpha Station, under Ben Abrezio as the highest authority, no matter he'd been asleep and off-shift.

Damn Cruz *and* Hewitt.

Abrezio imitated Oldfield's nice smile and sat down at the head of the table. It was war. Oldfield was on his right, Ames next to her, Ops and Admin respectively; Black, the *Rights'* project deputy-director, under Cruz, was on his left, with Hewitt on Black's right; and at the other end of the table—Cruz.

Oldfield kept smiling pleasantly at Hewitt, with a subtle hint about the eyes that said she was visualizing the man that lay underneath all those buttons . . . and finding him lacking.

Servers moved about, pouring tea, providing wafers.

They were themselves ECE, under a supervisor who saw them out the door once the service was done.

"We have a problem," Cruz said brusquely.

"We have several," Abrezio shot back, "and a hell of a lot more serious than the potential loss of equipment or the current attitude on the Strip. I'm speaking of the disaffection of our local ships, on which this station depends for its existence. We have a merchant ship we can't fix. That ship is now offered alternatives it would be a fool not to accept."

"And because of this blatant attempt to win ships away from this station, to control our supply of life-essentials and be *sure* the Company has no secure path back to its stations," Cruz said, "we attempted, in vain, to find out what's inside the ship that's leading the attack. Expecting your *support,* my people were reprimanded . . ."

"The Strip is *laughing,* sir. You may be very glad that *that* is the reaction."

"Are we to understand," Hewitt asked, "that this is the response our administration will make? We were attacked, carrying out a lawful function under EC rules."

"After an unlawful entry, sir, *nothing you did* could be lawful. Do I have to get Legal in here to explain that, or do you grasp the situation?"

"I will not sit here to be insulted."

"Mr. Director," Cruz interposed. "I have to take Mr. Hewitt's side. Your office has had ample opportunity to take a harder line with these people."

"My office does not *choose* to take a harder line with ships perfectly able to take their trade elsewhere. My office is trying to keep this station and its ships running, which depends on *supply* from places other than Earth. If that cuts off, we are in deep trouble, sir, and telling Sol about our impending starvation would surely stir them to action— in something a little under six years, oh, and immediate response if they happen to have a pusher-ship available. Which would get here in—"

"We do not *need* a primer on the matter, sir. We need leverage, of which we have none."

"Leverage. I have to ask what orders sent Mr. Hewitt

into *Finity's* e-hatch, given that word *leverage*. You surely weren't intending to hold that ship hostage."

Silence, narrowed-eyed and tight-mouthed.

"I also have wondered . . . where did they catch you? Where were you headed? To the hold . . . or to the bridge? Were you, perhaps, hoping to invade files? To download data that might help *Rights'* vanes do more than . . . hiccup? If so, I think you're very lucky to have been given a towel."

"This is no laughing matter, sir," Cruz snapped, and Abrezio met his hard gaze, frown for frown. That . . . had hit a nerve.

"And I'm not laughing, Mr. Cruz. Fortunately, *Finity* is."

"We were unarmed," Hewitt said. "We were threatened with lethal force."

"Unarmed. You carried tasers and cutters into a supposedly empty ship. The legitimate owners of that ship might well be forgiven for taking exception. Laughter and a cold ride in the lift is relatively benign. I am *glad* the Strip is taking it all as a joke, because what could have resulted was an all-out clash between spacers and enforcement, which would fix your name in history in a far worse light, I assure you. Rescue yourself with a sense of humor."

"Humor, sir!"

"Yes, *humor*. You are alive and back on the station instead of chucked out *Finity's* lock without a suit. I recommend you locate a *generous* sense of humor and promote it within your own command as well."

"Sir!" Cruz said.

"Mr. Vice Admiral, *sir*. I suggest you look beyond your own balance sheets, and consider the ramifications of setting these people off. We're struggling to repair rather than replace, all over the station. We're not up to handling the kind of damage outright sabotage could inflict. Unless, of course, you're willing to release your stranglehold on the materials storehouse. Since I sincerely doubt that will happen, I suggest, Mr. Hewitt, that enforcement take the incident as a case of high spirits and view it as a relatively good-natured response. I suggest that pronouncements from your office should defuse, rather than inflame, any sense of outrage. *Smile,* Mr. Hewitt, because a population out there, straining at the seams of our facilities, is stirred up by *Finity's* proposals and outraged that the ECE, masquerading as customs, took a route off-limits to station use."

"We are *not* smiling, . . . sir," Hewitt said darkly. "And if you choose to fold all objection to an attack on us . . ."

"I say again, Mr. Hewitt, *smile.* I am choosing to regard the incident as settled. *I* am not going to fault *Finity* for being on guard . . . especially since *you* proved their suspicions correct. We will negotiate *politely* for the return of the hardsuits and pusher craft we have scant resources to replace, should *Finity* decide to keep them."

"Whose side are you on, Mr. Director? Pell's?"

And there they had it: the direct challenge to his loyalty. Cruz had been prepping for years to step into station office the moment the Sol gap was bridged. Tell Cruz it was now out of his hands, that the clock was running, and that Sol authority was very possibly—assuming Sol had their own FTL ships and crews just waiting for the critical coordinates—going to arrive here *before* Cruz had gotten *Rights* into working order? With Abrezio, the source of those precious numbers, as the hero of the moment?

Knowledge might be power, but knowledge unshared was greater power.

"I am on the side of our survival, Mr. Cruz." By now the lightspeed message was headed out of Alpha system, a few hours out on a nearly six-year journey to Sol. It was beyond recall, what he had done. *He* knew that should worse come to worst, Alpha *could* survive, by the skin of their teeth. They had water, the recycling functioned, and they had supplies enough to sustain basic food production for six or seven years, granted all estimates were true and Sol had probes ready to test those coordinates and get back with an answer. That was the margin he had. When it ran on to eight, nine, ten years, only the charity of spacers and nearby stations could keep them functioning. And even then, only if all their ships didn't desert them. Stations had bled to death before. Ships that did call had relieved the pressure on supplies by taking away some of the population, all non-essential personnel, splitting up families, shutting down whole sections, reducing consumption to a minimum, until there was no margin left. Then a station died. Galileo and Thule had gone that route, hastened by the violence of their stars—not the only cause, but a major part of it.

"Survival," Hewitt echoed. "By conspiring with Pell?"

Definitely a challenge.

By the terms of Alpha's Charter, the ECD, the Earth Company Directorate, dictated policy and the ECE, Enforcement, carried out that policy . . . which put the ECE, in this case, Hewitt, *under* the ECD . . . Abrezio himself. Which meant, bottom line, *Abrezio* was in charge. The *Rights* project had blurred that line, sending first a Sol-office appointee, Cruz, to control the project, and then complicating the issue with a Sol-born ECE director, Hewitt, with his own mandate: protect the project. Cruz and Hewitt, Sol-born and EC to their core, had no loyalty to Alpha. They'd given lip service to that hierarchy for years, but respect it? Respect *him?* They never had.

And right now he had Cruz sitting at the end of the table, obdurate, angry, and immoveable—*Cruz*, who had been given, in the form of Hewitt, implied control of anything he deemed necessary to protect *Rights*. That control should, at most, be confined to station security, but while customs might get its policy from *his* ECD office, customs' security operations often involved the ECE, which Cruz *could* order—should he deem the project threatened.

And all it took to make ECE actions at least borderline legal was for Cruz to *say* he felt the project was threatened.

It was *not* an optimum situation. But when had Sol taken particular thought for the citizen component of Alpha? Abrezio had suspected for some time that Cruz was prepared to override the Directorate's control of policy, should he decide it was in his interest. Hewitt, he was virtually certain, had come with his own particular empowerment. Once Hewitt had arrived from Sol to take over security in A-mast, Cruz had used Sol's directive to leverage

Hewitt from project security to a direct interest in Strip security, with Bellamy Jameson increasingly uncertain of his authority outside citizen areas.

Black, who had arrived with Hewitt, appeared simply to work for Cruz—sub-director, under Cruz's authority. Basically, he filled out forms and reports and gave Cruz deniability, in this instance. Black sat there looking at no one, smug, taking occasional notes.

Smug . . . the lot of them . . . not knowing what was speeding its way to Sol.

"I want to make it clear," he said. "You *will* vet any change in policy with this office, and you will not undertake general police operations on the Strip or any operation involving the ships in our space without also clearing it with me personally. If I am blindsided once more by some midnight operation, if I am kept out of information, if I am in any way surprised by some dealing with ships and crews, I will invoke provisions of the Charter to declare a state of stationwide emergency, in which police power rests entirely in *my* hands, and civil law is suspended. I am not bluffing. I can do it, and I will."

"Do it, and the home office will hear about it."

"I'm sure they will, but be aware that Sol in its wisdom left *one* power in the hands of station administration alone. That power has been entrusted to me, and I stand by the decision to use it if the safety of this station is at stake. One more thing: we will *not* discuss the balance of powers outside this room, but rest assured, I can and I will take that measure."

Cruz closed his notebook. Loudly.

"The home office will hear."

"Be my guest, Admiral. I've already made *my* report."

The log would show a transmission on the Stream. But the content from the stationmaster's hand—took his signature and thumbprint to unlock. For a system several centuries old, it still defended itself adequately.

There followed a significant moment of silence in the meeting. "Move the meeting adjourn," Adima said.

"I don't think we ever actually called the meeting to order," Oldfield said. "But for neatness' sake, I second."

"Antiquated rules. Antiquated thinking. Power vacuum," Cruz said, and stood up. His allies stood up.

Oldfield sat quietly tapping her stylus on the table surface, tap, tap, tap.

"Moved and seconded," Abrezio said. "We stand adjourned."

Jen was standing quietly at a shop display, grey jacket, black patch, dark hair, seeming quite engrossed in a try-it display that marched miniature models across a black field. Every junior-junior on ships that called at Alpha had probably run the lingerie displays, about which some ships cared and *Galway* never had.

Jen was, however, looking at jackets.

"Nice one," he said.

"Waiting for you," she said, hooked his arm and walked him away toward nowhere in particular. Could bugs pick them up? Easily. Was somebody interested? It was a good bet.

"How'd it go?"

"I'd say favorable."

Station, if it was eavesdropping, probably could put that together. But at a certain point it wasn't that important what station thought. If they all signed . . . if that list on the stick was accurate, and all those ships were signed up . . . then they could stand in the middle of the Strip and shout out that they were likely going to sign with *Finity*.

"Quiet all along," he commented. "Except the blue-coats." Those were standing, not walking, and standing in pairs or clusters, just watching. Taking notes of who was together, maybe.

"Senior captains laid down the law," Jen said. "No hijacking of the vid. No rowdiness. No drunk and disorderly nor even disrespectful. Senior captain says if he has to liberate one of us from lockup it'll be serious. I imagine various captains have said a lot the same. Not saying there's probably not shopkeepers who've had run-ins with Customs themselves."

"And had more luck getting stuff through by talking to other crew," Ross said. "Always has been the situation. Crews here get along. We're polite to our merchants. We're not used to having assigned turf, and there was a little fuss when they assigned *us* to particular bars, but they gave us Rosie's and the Fortune, so we weren't upset. You can *be* anywhere else—we could go to Critical Mass, no problem, and the bar wouldn't complain about a flood of customers. But if a fight happened, presumption of innocence goes to the assigneds."

"Funny they didn't presume *us* innocent," Jen said. "That Hewitt guy sent a real angry note to the captains."

"Well, strangers are never innocent." He gave her arm a hug. "Station can't pick a fight with us locals, that's how it works. That's the thing we have to assure them if we do join up, you know, that Alpha's going to get cargo. And they will. People like Rosie and his staff, Farah and her kids at the Fortune, we wouldn't run out on them."

"That's the way with us," Jen said. "We've got people on Pell that we always see. People on Venture and Mariner we care about. That's the thing. We're *not* going to leave the stations worse off than before. Better, is our hope—ships that can keep schedules. Cargoes that arrive. Maybe more cargo, at least nothing worse. And if a ship is out for repair, maybe we can work with the stations—divert for a run or two. I dunno. I dunno that end of it. But we're not selling doom for the stations, far from it."

"It sounds good. I just don't see how it works out."

"The more ports the better. More for us. More for you."

"I don't see how it's more. We're not one of the newest ships. And other stations have their regulars."

"There's Venture. We call at Venture sometimes. We might run into each other there."

"The chance of being there at the same time . . ."

"Fallan and our Fourth, all those years," Jen said, pressing his hand. "Neither of them ever forgot. That's special." A pause. Her fingers were gentle on his. "I hope we do meet after this. I don't think I'll forget you."

He was sure he wouldn't forget her, for a variety of reasons, not least of which was she confused hell out of him. She could be all business and then shift into friend, and to this hour he didn't know which one really *was* business, that was the hell of it. Thoughts of her were all tangled up in threats to life and livelihood, a major shift in his whole world. And she'd been, well—

She'd occupied his thinking uncommonly often since they'd met—for various reasons, including an occasional suspicion of betrayal. There were two girls he knew who were on station at the moment, and he hadn't, in the craziness, had time to message either of them, just to wave once, in passing. And *she* probably thought he was with the other one. But Jen had a way of both fascinating and worrying him, all at the same time.

She'd lived in his mind a few short and worried days, and he could honestly see himself down the years, maybe as long-lived as Fallan, thinking of her, wishing he could tell her some fool thing, because, well, Jen had a universe-view that in a lot of ways made sense to him. She wasn't full of herself, she'd told him the truth—all the truth, he hoped—about as soon as she could have gotten a decent reading on him: he didn't really begrudge that. He hadn't told her every family secret either.

Fact was, in not very long at all Jen had posed a serious disturbance in his way of life. He did like her. If she said sleepover he'd be right there. He'd never understood what people said about chemistry until it hit him like an oncoming rock.

And yes, he could find himself in years to come wondering where she was. Which was fairly useless, with *Finity* coming from a whole other set of runs. He could find himself from now on measuring the local girls against Jen, and thinking—it wasn't the same.

Bad case of it, he said to himself. Stupid case of it. And he felt her warm hand on his and her arm wrapped around his and thought he wanted that to last, to remember, as long as possible.

God, he had it bad. He wished she'd start a fight so they could just break up and be over it.

He wanted her. Really badly.

Hell. "Nothing doing at the moment. What do you say we go back to your sleepover."

Squeeze of his arm. Fingers tangled with his. "Sure."

Chapter 10   Section ii

Jen was back. JR noted that. Back from a short trip out of *Finity*'s close territory, near to *Galway*'s, and now bringing *Galway*'s Nav 1.3 back with her, straight to her room.

That wasn't part of any plan. Mum and Fallan Monahan were the main channel of communication, *Galway*'s senior captain having ducked invitations to talk, for whatever reason, and if Jen had new information, if she thought she was in pursuit of something critical, she could signal. Right now Jen seemed to be engaged in something not so critical, and what shook out of that, well, Jen was due some private time, and the message to Niall Monahan had now gone out by different means. Mum had said she expected Fallan to come back, and Mum, while not delivering details to the curious, had had, she said, a very nice visit, and yes, Fallan Monahan was very special. She'd returned with a rare little treasure, a unique gift—it had passed scan this morning— that summed up a relationship that was what it was: old, not blind, and very special.

It was Fallan who carried the message to his senior captain. And by now, all those blue-coats posted about had probably reported contact at crew level between *Finity* and *Galway* and put two and two together. Presumably admin was watching, trying to figure whether *Finity* was on the level and trying to decide whether to try to enforce its rules.

JR didn't think they would. There'd been no message from admin, no see-me, and no protest at any high level. Investigation hadn't figured out who'd posted the notorious picture onto the schedule board, and it hadn't stopped it circulating on com, which was reportedly creating a little stir now in residential sections.

Rumor from the shops and bars said that residents were a little upset that Customs had provoked an incident with their visitors, that the general feeling was that it had been a stupid move, that *their* big ship couldn't move and *Finity* could, and that *Finity* was signing up *their* ships to some sort of organization and they were, yes, generally worried.

Here at Alpha, the wall between the ships and the station residents was fairly impenetrable *except* through the residents in direct contact with the Strip, the waiters and shopkeepers and bartenders who dealt with them directly, and the order of the hour was to talk freely, answer questions, deliver reassurances, and above all indicate that *Finity* wasn't planning any action against the station, not in the deal with the ships and not in response to the boarding attempt. That it was ready and willing to return the hardsuits and the pusher if some agency would just step up and find a way to collect them.

Apparently Customs didn't want to do it, because they were officially disengaged from the problem and no official wanted to go on record to reclaim the items. And Maintenance and Safety didn't want to go ask for them because they weren't the ones who'd left them up there. That left Enforcement, apparently, who didn't have orders to do it, because, well, they had no orders.

The denial of responsibility was interesting. Nobody had done it. Nobody had ordered it. Nobody was responsible at any lower level, and they weren't touching it even with gloves on. Sooner or later somebody would have to own up and do it, or *Finity* was going to have to cast the pusher loose with all the gear aboard it, and let Maintenance and Safety chase it down before it hit something.

JR hadn't ordered that, no matter he'd given station a deadline for the removal. So far as he was concerned, he was prepared to wait until undock—or for an official appeal from some agency. As yet they didn't have it.

Station residents did seem to be confused. Some were

upset about the picture. Others were apparently trading it about on their personal coms and laughing about it.

The situation didn't seem to be leading to another try by Customs. And one person was said to be particularly upset—Vice-Adm. Andrew J. Cruz. No one had directly said that Cruz was behind the move to get aboard *Finity,* but his chief of security being one of the boarding crew left little room for deniability. Never mind the objects being held for return included high-level credentials, tools, weapons, data sticks, and enforcement badges, all official.

JR wondered if they thought they'd have just proceeded to push buttons and throw switches as they pleased and that a watch on duty in the lower corridor wouldn't have noticed.

Trying to download or upload to the systems would have certainly led nowhere good—just wandering about would have led nowhere good in fairly short order. It was not a pushbutton start on *Finity's* systems. The immediate universe still had free access via the e-hatches, four in number, so that any personnel near the ship could find a safe haven from, say, a stellar hiccup. But if you wandered off on a tour and couldn't satisfy *Finity's* cyber watchdog that you belonged where you were, *Finity* could get *very* uncooperative.

And if *Finity* watchcrew had had to call a captain to extricate some of *Rights'* technicians from *Finity's* righteous wrath, it would have taken Alpha's lawyers all day to extricate them from his.

He had nothing personally against Andrew Cruz. Yet. Hewitt was a little further down the well.

The fact they both were Sol-born EC *and* thought that the Company's whim trumped centuries-old understandings wasn't surprising . . . historically-speaking . . . but it did imply a certain . . . narrow-mindedness and, yes, stupidity. He'd never personally met anybody from Sol, but he'd have thought long dealing with the immense distances involved would have adjusted Sol's expectations. Sol early on had issued decrees and made demands as if they could be any use at all six to ten years on . . . but the expectation that

laws made out here should govern *them?* Clearly that
hadn't gotten through to them. Witness the expectation
that had built that ship up on A-mast and nearly ruined the
only station willing to support it.

Would they be better if FTL knit Sol up much closer to
them? The exotic trade would be a decided benefit, especially to these struggling Alpha-based merchanters, but
Sol was immensely populous, numbering in the billions,
and consisted of a hundred governments thinking they
could decide what people who lived lightyears away, under
circumstances they couldn't begin to imagine, should do.

The fact that Andrew Cruz had decided to ignore custom, tradition, and law suggested that what the EC had
consistently done, the EC was still doing—still claiming
right of ownership over every station and ship in space.
The EC had appointed a man who thought it not only a
good idea, but morally *right* to try to bring a force into a
visiting ship by exploiting a centuries-old safety measure—

Said it all, that did. And he didn't believe the station-
born EC Director, Abrezio, had had anything to do with it.

It was worth noting that the persons who had put up the
scandalous picture were rumored to be station residents,
and that one version in circulation had put Cruz's face on
all four of the towel-clad agents.

JR personally wished the picture had never happened.
It didn't make their mission easier.

But the decision to invade a ship? Not their decision.

The actions that had made Cruz less than popular on
station? Not their actions.

He had sent a message to Abrezio.

We deeply regret the confrontation. Our security proce-
dures require a thorough inspection of the equipment
brought aboard our ship. The request for release of the
agents took precedence. The fact that there was a security
breach in the mast lift lobby is regrettable, and the posting
of a picture on the schedule boards was emphatically not
our doing.

The fact that some of Min's crew had been in the crowd
was regrettable, too, and Old Man Jun, Min's father, had
issued a stern reprimand regarding the rowdiness.

Giovanna Galli, however, had her own issues with Customs, and with *Rights*, and what she did was Giovanna's decision.

We have now removed all data and image recording devices from the gear confiscated, and we stand ready to set it outside our access if someone responsible will come to the access and request it.

Probably Abrezio would love to send Cruz, but there was no likelihood Cruz would undertake it. Probably some innocent fellows from Maintenance and Safety would have to go up there and figuratively knock on the door.

We hope that this will close the issue. We have no desire to carry the matter further.

[Signed] JR Neihart, Senior Captain, Finity's End, *Pell Registry.*

Chapter 10   Section iii

There was one more step to take. And Abrezio hadn't slept well. He couldn't hide that part.

"Is something wrong?" his wife asked, finding him in the kitchen far, far too early.

He didn't share everything. Couldn't. Shouldn't. Two of them worried as hell weren't going to improve the situation. He shrugged, poured a second cup of tea, and didn't quite look at her.

"Is it bad?"

"Not necessarily," he said. "Potentially it's good."

"Then why do you look like hell?"

"Worry that it won't be. But," he said, then paused. Callie always steadied him. Her voice brought simple sanity to what was otherwise chaos. And he felt guilty for not having told her what he'd already done. But it couldn't make her happier. That was his reasoning. And it would put a shadow in her eyes, so that friends might wonder. Carrying a deep secret, he'd observed, left such shadows. He had them. Callie put up with his silences patiently, not continuing past a question. And it would be selfish to shift the greatest burden of his career onto her shoulders, even part of it.

"But?"

He shook his head. And lied by changing the subject. "Just trying to mop up the picture mess. And hoping to see these visitors pull out soon—them and their insurance notions. They *are* paying. They've cleared *Firenze*'s debt, at regular exchange rates in materials we very desperately need, *Firenze*'s in the black, and it's good. They've pronounced her navigation system too antiquated to try to fix, and they've got some unified system they're ordering in from Venture, with technicians. That message will go out when *Finity* goes, with the others, we hope, while the Gallis sit and wait. It may take as much as a year to implement, and they'll apparently have that bill paid, likewise."

"So that's good, isn't it?"

Callie could sound so happy, when things weren't, necessarily.

"Well, it's good for our bottom line and it's good for the Gallis, granted it all materializes. And the Gallis will understandably be grateful to whoever made it possible. We *hope* they then stay an Alpha ship."

A frown. "You think these visitors are trying to change that?"

"It seems logical to me that loyalty's going to go where the support is. And for a large reason hanging over A-mast, we can't provide that to our ships. I can't see a Pell-based ship pouring funds into an Alpha-based ship for no reason but beneficence."

"But they can't control them, either. The Gallis, I mean."

He drew a deep breath. "No. That's true."

"The Gallis belong here. I think maybe—what we should do—is invite some of these people socially."

Shocking thought. "Dear, you haven't met Giovanna Galli."

"Perhaps it's time I did. Maybe not here, if that would make her uncomfortable, but we could hold an event at one of the nice Strip restaurants. Not to talk business, but just mingle. Get to know each other." Her bright smile flashed at him. "I think I'd like that. I'm quite enthused."

That—was actually a concept. "Now is not a good time, but after we do shed the visitors, when we have just ours left . . ." Status. Prestige. Of all times in his career, he couldn't be seen to lessen his—with Sol looming on the horizon. "Maybe more intimate get-togethers. Maybe some sponsored events. For the senior captains, maybe. It's not at all a bad concept. Just the administrative office. Ourselves, the Oldfields." There was another problem in her notion. "You've never spent an evening on the Strip."

"I've hardly ever gone there."

"Well, it's gotten no tamer. And lately much more pressured."

"But that will go away fairly soon."

"That will go away." He stood up and gave her a gentle hug. "I'm going in to the office."

"You don't want breakfast?"

"I'll have much more appetite for lunch, I'm sure. I'll meet you then." Callie spent her days in an office at the Industry and Materials Board, which had sensible hours, and a regular lunch. "Noon at the Country Kitchen."

"I'll be there." She gave him a light kiss. "Noon. I'm sure it will all work out, whatever it is."

"Do my best," he said, and left the kitchen, picked up his coat where he had left it last night far too late, and headed out to the office, through a lift system mostly delivering alterday staff home to a deserved good night's sleep. His code guaranteed a private lift car: he had no trouble getting one, and used the brief transit time to put a message into system for Captain Niall Monahan.

See me soonest.

That would probably hit before Monahan got up, but that was all right. He could use the time just to sit in the familiar confines of his office and put his thoughts together, which he'd tried, with mixed success, to do last night.

His world had changed yesterday. Ever since he'd taken

this office, decisions made had had consequences that lay somewhere in the distant future, that time when Sol's appointed representatives arrived on his doorstep and began demanding an accounting of his time in office.

Yesterday . . . from the moment he sent that message down the Stream . . . he'd set a new timeline in motion. A timeline now with consequences as near as twelve years from now, message out, message back; or sooner, if Sol had a ship ready and wanted to risk it.

Whatever resulted, Andrew Cruz . . . had become a distinct problem.

There was a word in ship-speak that Qaribs used to describe Cruz, untranslatable, they said. But *vindictive* seemed apt. He'd never really appreciated it until now. He'd thought a lot about that word last night. He'd remembered an allegation, upon the ill-fated Bryant's run with *Rights* crew and Hewitt aboard, that *Qarib* was carrying banned substances, difficult to prove or disprove. Customs had been involved. *Qarib* had appealed to him, he'd shelved the matter and personally cleared *Qarib* to move with no stain on the record.

Customs. Again.

God knew what attitudes Cruz had held before he left Sol, or how his notions had fermented during a decade of close contact with a pusher-crew—admittedly their own odd brand of humanity—but without question Cruz had come onto Alpha with an exaggerated idea of what he was meant to control and what ought to happen quickly.

Over the years Cruz had gone from assuming he would have *Rights* running before the next pusher arrived, to the realization that, after twenty years, *Rights* wasn't working, and he had no idea why. Sol . . . was not going to be happy, because Sol had this notion that a big ship was a big card to hold, and Sol's authorities believed they'd dealt their boy Cruz unbeatable cards from a stacked deck.

Thinking back, *Rights'* aborted run had not been the turning point. The turning point had been when Hewitt and a handful of his finest had boarded *Qarib* for that run, and come out of it alive, but without that signed document attesting to their competency. Worse, they'd come out of it with rumors on the Strip involving the words 'actions endangering the ship,' which was just about as damning an accusation as *Qarib* could have issued. Hewitt had been furious. Cruz had been much colder and calmer in his reaction. And *Qarib* had been passed over for EC cargo.

Vindictive.

He'd recognized that about the man, on a small scale, and done his best to mitigate the problem, but the balance had shifted in the last forty-eight hours. The exchanges between Cruz and *Finity's End* had escalated matters. Cruz had found a new focus for his anger and frustration, a much bigger target . . . and he was scaling his actions accordingly. *Finity's End* would leave, eventually, but Cruz's sense of entitlement wasn't going anywhere. And for Cruz to watch his one real chance of saving *Rights* leave without giving up its secrets? That disappointment . . . was going to have consequences.

He'd fired off an irretrievable message that *was* going to bring Sol here possibly in less than a decade, if the data worked. Benjamin Abrezio was going to be the man that had sent the data. Solo. No credit to Cruz at all. With luck, he could keep that transmission and what it held secret until Sol just . . . showed up. If not . . . he was going to spend some very unpleasant years as the primary target for that vindictive streak.

What he didn't know, was what allies Cruz, who had started his voyage as a bright young man, might have had in the central office back on Sol Station, and whether *any* of those remained. He doubted anyone had ever thought the project would take as long as it had. Cruz was ambitious as well as vindictive, and whatever committee had appointed him and ordered that damnable ship built—had an objective for it and had their own agendas to protect. But Hewitt was the newer appointee. Those who had sent Cruz out might even have aged and retired, while Hewitt's patrons were still in office.

Everything he'd done was assuming Sol had been building ships all this time, hopefully small, standard FTL ships based on solid, proven tech. Another like *Rights* would do them little good . . . unless their engineers were better than Alpha's. If they had those ships, if they had probes, if those numbers were good . . . if all those ifs were true, Sol could be here within a decade. And when Sol showed up, suddenly operating on an FTL time-scale—and discovered that all Cruz had to show them was a ship that couldn't do what it needed to do—Hewitt would be ever so eager to demonstrate Cruz's shortcomings. Just as Cruz would want to sabotage Hewitt.

But he himself was, like Cruz's backers, not getting any younger. He had responsibilities. Callie was one. He'd fight, for her. And he had made his move to settle the business and not leave Callie the legacy of a problem that had eaten up half his career.

Put Cruz in charge after him? God help humanity.

Damned right he'd fight to hold Alpha and keep Sol from making its habitual mistakes. He'd reached that conclusion long since.

Now—it was beyond any change of mind. The data had flown. But that decade it might take Sol to get that message and respond . . . still gave Cruz time to solve the problem of that ship and get it in operation.

If only, he'd begun to think last night, there were a faster way to get that information to Sol. If only that route were operational, he could get Sol in here in about a year, and have himself *clearly* the hero of the operation. End speculation, put power solidly in his own hands, in the hands of someone who *could* administer Alpha sanely— someone who could deal with Pell rationally and keep everybody safe.

And he'd realized, last night, there might be a way . . . for a high, very high-stakes gambler.

"Early, sir." It was Ames arriving at his usual time.

"Had some thinking to do."

"Tea, sir? Breakfast roll, maybe? Missed breakfast, myself."

"Tea," he said. "Just tea, for me." A breakfast roll meant a trip down the lift to the service bar, but Ames wasn't essential for the upcoming meeting with Niall Monahan.

And on that thought, he added: "Go get a decent breakfast. Take at least an hour."

Chapter 10   Section iv

"So," Monahan said, when he'd accepted the cup of tea and settled opposite the desk. "Your message."

"Yes," Abrezio said. He pushed the buttons that locked the door and cut off communication with Ames' desk: Ames, if he did come back inconveniently, would see a clear *do not disturb*.

"So is there a problem?" Monahan asked.

"No. Absolutely not."

Monahan took a sip of tea. And looked quizzical.

"This is in strictest confidence," Abrezio said. He set his cup down. "Can I rely on you?"

"We made the choice to be Alpha-based, though we've had opportunities elsewhere, and overall, have no regrets. You've treated us right over the years."

"You've been honest. And reliable. We're grateful for the loyalty, and we hope if there are any negatives, we've dealt with them."

"So far, yes, sir. We have no grievance with station."

Plain man, a plain answer. There was always, always stationer and spacer, and that was a wide gulf. But not nearly so wide as the gulf between himself and Andy Cruz. Monahan was *not* Andy Cruz, nor anything like him. He'd be *proud* to share a history-making moment with Niall Monahan.

"Captain, I want you to understand, before I say anything, that you do *not* have to hear this information—but that if you do—you will *not* divulge it. You will not share it with fellow captains or family until I give you clearance. I am about to make you an offer requiring absolute discretion—" It was formula, a legal notice; he had rarely applied it, but he knew it by heart. "If you do not wish to hear that offer, refuse now. If you violate the order of silence you *and* any persons receiving or believed to have received that information in any form will be placed in isolation until the situation you could affect resolves itself. And the situation could be of long duration. I can say that there *is* great advantage to you and your crew in your hearing it. But once you do, consider yourself locked into a contract of silence, breach of which or suspected breach of which, will place you beyond the reach of civil law or legal relief. Violate that trust in any regard and you will, in effect, be detained and isolated. Understand that if you do accept it—you will be given favored status. In effect, we *need* you. We are willing to reward your ship extravagantly. And it involves a voyage of considerable risk."

Lengthy pause this time. Monahan took down the tea sip by sip. Down to empty.

"I'll hear it," Monahan said, "if you'll answer one thing in advance. Does it route us to Pell?"

Guessing, beyond that route, and that contact, was not hard.

"If I answer you yes or no, you're legally committed. Do you want to walk out now?"

A lengthy pause. A sip of tea, and a moment of thought. "I'll hear it."

"Sol," Abrezio said. And Monahan didn't flinch.

"You have the coordinates?"

"We have. As yet, they're untested. It's a risk. It's also the most lucrative run you could ever make."

Deep, deep breath. Two of them. "Well," Monahan said. "How solid is the information?"

"We think very solid."

"You think. There's been a probe?"

"No," Abrezio said. "It's untested. If it works, you'll be back inside a year, year and a half."

"Assuming we get back."

"It's a double risk. A two-hop."

"But you think it's good."

"A scientist thinks it's good. And from the first hop, you

may be able to get optics on the second. His note, not mine."

"Assuming no glitches on the other end. Assuming Sol doesn't think we're a spook from Beta and blast us into the hereafter. We can't warn them we're coming. Also assuming they won't have a long debate about it all and want to hold us ten years for information."

"They have FTL in theory, have had since Pell passed the specs on. It's only logical to think they've been building something. Probes ... without question, to be ready to test any potential jump points they find. Ships most likely, whether mega-ships based on the *Finity* blueprints or something to their own design using the theory. What they *don't* have is information. And the really critical lack— they *don't* have a crew that's not just passenger load on a bot."

Monahan was quiet for a moment, staring into space. Then he leaned back. "Understand, if we take this on, we're not going to do it for free, and we're not going to be held there teaching them what we know. Just like *Gaia*, we're not going to have them messing with our ship or our crew ... not going to have them boarding us."

"I can't guarantee anything the Sol office might take into their minds to do, but *you* will be the ones with those coordinates and if they want them, they'll have to deal with you. You can pick your time to tell them anything and you set your conditions. I'll be honest with you: I've transmitted the data, but you'll beat the message and be back here before they get it. You can also tell them, and I'll be sending communications with you to this effect, that there are serious problems here, with the station and with the project *and* with the personnel they sent, and we *need* communication, back and forth, them to me, to knit up what's not been connected in a long, long time. As is, *you're* how they're going to get that message. You'll be the only ship that can assuredly get back, and you can tell them with some authority that you're their only source of FTL instruction, which can *only* be done at working boards, in transit, and by working crew. Am I accurate, since sims have not rendered

Rights crew competent to manage even a little ship like *Qarib*?"

Monahan's right brow lifted—at that statement, from him. But he wasn't oblivious. He'd heard the talk. Besides the fact that *Qarib* had refused to sign the papers for Hewitt's crew, which pretty much said it all.

"You would be accurate, sir. Sims can keep experienced crew in shape, but first few runs, they'd be safer with a bot in charge. Untrained perception can really mess with your mind *and* your common sense."

"You'll go with a complete report on the *Qarib* debacle, and on the situation with *Rights*, and with Admiral Cruz, and Hewitt, and the delicacy of our dealings with Pell, *not* driving them into the arms of Cyteen—no credit to Enzio Hewitt. Confidentiality is expected on that report, as well. It'll be under my executive seal. Electronic transmission: you won't have any responsibility for delivering it personally. They may ask you your opinion. My advice to them is—deal carefully and respectfully with Pell. They don't want the consequences if it goes the other way. And you can express that in plainer terms with my blessing."

"I haven't said I'll go."

"If I weren't quite certain of your answer, I'd never have asked you here." He paused, then: "That's not quite true. I hope to God I read you correctly. I'm desperate, Captain. I'm responsible for the lives and well-being of everybody involved on Alpha *and* beyond. I'm prepared to do what I have to do to protect them from the future men like Andrew Cruz will bring them. I have one shot and this is it. If not *Galway*, then another ship, and until that's settled, I'm sorry, but deal or no deal, I'd have to keep you in isolation until that information has succeeded—or failed. I had rather you have this opportunity, and succeed at it, and get us an understanding at least as far as *Gaia* got out of Sol. I trust you. I have confidence in you. I had rather have you on your way, and untouchable. In all the risk in this, *that* is a certain safety . . . granted the data is sound."

"I could leave here. Never come back. Sell the information you've already given me to Pell."

"And without the coordinates, it's just one more rumor, and you won't have those until you board your ship."

"Nothing to make me use them."

"Except your honor. Your curiosity."

"Quite." A slight, humorless smile. "And the compensation?"

"Immortality. Reputation. History. You'll be the ship that got through. And in financial terms you'll write your own ticket, for modernizations, cargo, you name it. You'll be our favorite and only son. I know *Finity's* offering you a deal. I'm offering you a riskier one, and I think a better one, with an everlasting name to go with it."

"Everlasting glory. Or its reverse, in some eyes. Supposing we survive the trip."

"If those numbers are good, Captain, it's already inevitable that Sol will come. The information *will* get there, down the Stream. The question is—whether Alpha gets to receive a response during my tenure. I'm not young, and I believe Admiral Cruz sees the entire station as nothing more than the support frame for that damned ship, while Hewitt—is on his own mission. Six-plus years is a long time to keep a secret on Alpha. You understand. If it becomes known, it may become known in such a way that all sorts of political forces get into play, not to the good of this station, which is my deepest concern. Once it hits the Strip— all bets are off, and our ships and our supply and the willingness of Pell to supply us all become a question. I want it done, I want it done fast enough that I will still be sitting here to advise what comes back to us. I want a responsible crew to be able to inform whatever Sol sends us that there is a lot to learn, that we look forward to close and frequent contact, and that we have experience and contacts useful to them."

"And that you aren't Cruz," Monahan said grimly.

"Is that meant positively?"

"Yes, sir, it is. Entirely positively. You aren't Cruz and you aren't Hewitt."

"Will you do it, Captain?"

Monahan stared into his teacup. Finally: "If I say yes,

I'll be wanting something stronger than this. I'll be a fool. But I'm a fool for sitting here in the first place."

"Essential crew. I wouldn't ask anything else." He wanted to plead. He would plead. But Monahan was balanced on a thin edge, yes and no. And the only recourse he himself had was unacceptable—to hand the data to *Finity's End* and Pell and only *hope* the Konstantins decided not to destroy every station between them and Sol, ripping up the whole ancient pathway simply by withholding supply. And only hope that the knowledge didn't immediately tip Cyteen into bitter rivalry with Pell. It was all so delicately balanced. It all depended on a set of personalities in positions to know things, make decisions, and send the whole human race on a course of live and let live, or send it down the old, cold path of suspicion and violence.

"Essential crew only. My shift. I'll expect all the Monahans to be kept here at no charge, and to be sent on to Venture, if we don't make it. We've got contacts at Venture. We have some history there."

"You're a brave man, Captain."

Monahan shrugged. "I'm none of that until I talk to my Family. Them, I'll have to tell."

Abrezio took in a breath.

"Mr. Director, sir, if they won't back me, that's that. Do what you like to us all, and we'll all take a pusher-trip to Sol, if that's your solution—but I'll tell you *my* terms. I'll do it because it's what has to happen. I'll tell my whole Family because that's the way we are. My Family will keep the secret till I'm away because that's who we are. And I'll do it the way you ask, jump with one shift, keeping the secret tight until we leave, because it's asking enough to risk some of us: none of us would risk *all* of us being shipped out to Sol. Anybody can follow us if they like. But we're already fueled: it's the outsiders that have stalled our final process. We're carrying cargo, but it's low mass and that's to the good, on our journey. We've food for the entire family for Alpha to Bryant's to Glory and back, which is also to the good. Should we encounter problems, we'll have enough to keep us until we find a solution. We can be out of here and on our way tomorrow, and nobody to break the secret before we go. Our own won't betray us."

He hadn't been prepared for Monahan to revise the terms on him . . . but Alpha had history with the Monahans, and they'd been honest all the way. Telling the whole Family—as the man said: it was their own safety potentially at risk if word got to wrong places. And shipping a hundred fifty-odd unwilling people on a pusher for a decade was—beyond unmanageable.

"I won't want to be walking around with the coordinates in my pocket," Monahan said further, "and I do want a meeting with *Finity*. I want you to know it. If worst happens and we don't get back—*Finity*'s the one doing this insurance. I want to sign with them, up front and plain. I want my Family inside that agreement—so if we don't get back, there's a means to *get* them on to Venture that won't depend on charity and won't rest on whatever situation might develop at Alpha once *Galway*'s mission goes public. I can't justify my doing this otherwise."

That was an immense risk—any contact with *Finity's End*; but it was a few days; it didn't involve possession of the coordinates; and if it got *Galway* away and beyond reach—hell, there were worse risks to his administration, and the chiefest one was Cruz, with Hewitt close behind. Put the coordinates and the mission beyond Cruz's reach, and he could sleep at night.

"Agreed," he said. "Agreed, Captain."

"Then I'll take that shot of Scotch, sir. I'll be honored to share one with you."

"Liquid breakfast for us both, captain."

"Not my first," Monahan said.

"Nor mine," Abrezio said. "And having agreed, I may take the day off and go home and sleep, which I didn't do much of last night. I'll do no more important business today than this. None in my whole tenure, for that matter." He got up, went to the buffet, and brought back two whiskeys, handing one to Monahan and resuming his desk chair. "To our agreement, Captain. To honesty. To the Monahans, one and all."

"To you, sir, in all respect."

"I'll draw up agreements and a report you'll carry. With any luck you can be back in a little over a year, covered in glory. *Probably* they'll be sending some EC staff that you'll have access to for the duration of the voyage. Give them a good impression of us. Bring them here in a helpful frame of mind. Get them to understand what's gone on and convert them. I hope you will."

"We're a persuasive lot," Monahan said. "We'll do our best."

He had a good feeling about Monahan—an understanding of the needs that drove him. The notion of involving the outsiders—he would have refused, except he trusted that what he'd feared at first, that Pell had somehow found out they had the coordinates—wasn't the case. *Cruz* didn't know, and if nothing had leaked on Alpha, it was reasonable to think that nothing had leaked outside Alpha. *Finity*'s purpose seemed this notion of insuring the Families . . . and it did make sense.

FTL had changed things, sped up voyages, created a multitude of ships that flitted in, drank, caroused, and went their way again without a care in the world for the stations that they visited; and no close relations with stationers at all. Sleepovers between crew produced offspring who could only say their fathers were probably of a certain ship but not necessarily know a name. Stations held to things like marriage, and property, and such—the old values. FTLers owed some of their loose ways to the pusher crews, who were free and easy once they docked; but these matrilineal spacer Families were overall a rougher lot. No respect for anything, stationers were wont to say of them. *Morals of a spacer* was an insult.

But by their own rules, spacers were honest, and they *did* look after their own, and in this situation he was more ready to trust the Monahans than some born and bred stationers he knew, for both honesty *and* common sense.

As for some committee straight from Sol, with all their assumptions of entitlement—

Having Sol come charging in full-scale, with no good concept of the delicate relationship between the Konstantins of Pell and the Emorys of Cyteen—with all the stations dependent on them . . .

Sol had no concept.

With the well-spoken Monahans breaking it to them gently over the course of the voyage that the colonies and spacers had different ways, but were good people—that was not a bad thing.

Reliable trade with Sol, with its resources . . . that was going to send shockwaves through that delicate relationship, but prosperity would follow. As JR Neihart had said in that first meeting, these spacers . . . these rowdy *merchanters* . . . might well be humanity's best hope for a peaceful existence in space.

He began to see the true value of the proposed alliance of merchanters—beyond the obvious value to the merchanters themselves. Properly handled . . . the stations would benefit as much as the ships.

"I rely on you, Captain, to use discretion in dealing with *Finity*. Do I understand correctly that once you've signed, you're free to go anywhere, even Sol, without interference from other ships in the alliance?"

Monahan nodded.

"Very well. The minute *Galway* clears Alpha system, outbound on a Sol vector, the news will break, *Finity* can warn Pell, but they can't do a thing about it. Pell's in a peculiar position—*not* anxious to have their little empire challenged, not anxious to have to deal with Sol, but they'll have to: by the time the news gets to them, if those points prove out, Sol will already be on its way, and *you* will be, with a hold full of exotics. Shipments from Sol will be here in increasing numbers and things will change. For the better, for Alpha, and for Alpha's spacers."

Monahan sipped his scotch, savored it a moment, then: "Cruz absolutely doesn't know?"

"He does not."

"Not going to like you much. And Hewitt's not to trust, sir, absolutely not to trust."

"I'll worry about that. Not much he can do, once you're on your way."

"Theoretically, *Rights* can over-jump us."

"A ship that can't make it to Bryant's? I doubt even he is fool enough to make that move."

"Risk aplenty is in this," Monahan said. "Sim training just isn't enough. Hewitt proved it on *Qarib*. Sol's going to lose ships. Cyteen used azi crew, little more than human computers, and even they didn't risk it past the initial test of the systems. Cyteen leaves FTL to the Families. Cyteen leaves *trade* to the Families. If Sol tries to send untested ships with sim-trained crew through barely mapped points, it's going to be ugly. We'll warn them, but hell if *we're* going to stay and teach them. Hell if we want other ships, company ships, horning in on Sol trade. *Galway*'s not your only loyal ship."

"And I'll do all I can to protect their interests as well. I can't promise you that Sol won't try, but I will urge them to wait and let the points be mapped and fully tested. I'll extend your concerns and insights."

"Can you promise me *Galway* won't get tangled in their authority?"

"I'll give you every seal and document I can produce to the contrary. Rank as an EC officer, representing me, under my seal, and considering what you're bringing them, they'll say thank you, *sir,* to you *and* to me. Outside of that, I'd say—take a page from history and use old *Gaia's* answer when they wanted to put a new crew aboard. Keep them out. And be on guard. If you have to come back empty from this run, do it. We'll prefer you for cargo. Enough for you?"

Monahan drank the last of the glass, set it down. Gave him a direct stare.

"I'll be putting together a crew list. Single shift: we'll be a little frayed, and it will mean some extended downtime between jumps, but we'll run well enough on that. This is assuming the Family gives us leave to go. I'll need that secure meeting space."

Abrezio pushed buttons, produced a code and a room number, a planning room outside the Strip. He handed it across the desk. "Lift right outside these offices can accept this code. Give it to them. Have your meeting. Get me a yes."

"I'll do that, sir. I think I can say with some assurance that I'll have a firm yes by shift-change."

"Captain." Abrezio stood up as Monahan stood up, and reached out a hand. "Bring me an agreement. What's at stake is incalculable."

No choice. No real choice. *Galway* was the best they had.

"Shift-change," Monahan said. "Promise."

It was unprecedented, the all-hands call, bringing all the seated crew, trainees, and seniors not to Rosie's on the Strip, but to the admin offices, and mysteriously so, to a lift in that hallway, which could only take them about ten at a time.

"This is weird," Ross said to Fallan. "This is really weird."

"New one on me," Fallan said, which was something Fallan rarely could say.

Their turn came. They boarded, with Ashlan, Mary T, and others, and the lift raced off a short zig-zag distance to a plain narrow hallway with an open door.

"Spooky," was Mary T's comment.

But it wasn't some blue-coat trap, which was the thought in Ross's mind. Everybody was there. His mother was there. His aunt and two uncles were there, gran, and great-gran, and, looking uncommonly daunted, a very young cousin of his in maintenance.

Niall and Owen were there, and the lift was still delivering cousins. There was seating at a long table, but Niall and Owen were standing up.

So they all stood.

"Is that all of us?" Niall asked. The room had become extremely packed, and only Mary Ruth, who was very pregnant, being encouraged to sit.

"We were the last four from the lift," Ellis's voice called, from the door's general direction. "There was nobody behind us."

"Close the door." And a moment later: "Secure back there?"

"It's closed." Ellis again.

"All right," Niall said. "I'll make this fast. I've talked to Abrezio. We're given this space with Abrezio's promise there's no bugs, and if he's lying, well, we'll hope to be arrested and watch the result. Here's the deal. We leave most of us here on Alpha. Myself and a handful of volunteers, first shift having first call, take *Galway* to *Sol* and back."

It felt as if the oxygen had gone short in the room.

Sol. *Galway.* And volunteers.

"It's a high risk," Niall said. "The jump points aren't tested. We'll be first through, with all the risk in that. We'll be coming back, however, with our kind of speed, with all manner of favor points with Alpha, with Sol; and with finance enough to refit for any sort of docking the future brings. We get special status with the EC; and we assure the saving of the ports we depend on. It's a fair deal. And I'm for it, because—" There had started to be a murmur. *"Listen* to me. Risk *always* exists. And change is definitely coming. *Sol* will be coming, because the Director's already transmitted the data down the Stream. It's six years in transit, and a lot can go wrong in six years, with the whole of space finding out that data's been sent, and Pell and Cyteen alike maneuvering to deal with Sol, not necessarily in a way we'd like. Not to mention the jostling and fuss among the little stations. What *we* can do is get to Sol and back again far faster than those wishing us ill can get organized, make ourselves part of the credit, and set ourselves up proper for the new age that's coming. There'll be trade with Earth, and Alpha can become the trade hub it's been hoping to be. And equally important, *we* get to demonstrate to Sol that Family crews are what can get through with best economy; that they'd be fools to try it with raw crews, cold off sims. We'll show them what a little honest ship can do that this monster modern ship they built couldn't do. Their hired crew couldn't do it; Cruz couldn't do it; and if they ever want cargo moved reliably, now and in the future, it's us that'll move it, so *no hired crews."*

That phrase rang all the way to the bones, quickened the blood and shortened the breath. Ross felt goosebumps.

But going to Sol, Ross thought. An untested point.

"We run a risk," Niall was saying, "a risk of losing the

ship herself. And losing us that make the run. But I've got
Abrezio's agreement that we can meet with *Finity* and sign
up with their alliance, which assures those of us going on
this venture that should anything happen, there'll still be a
Monahan presence up and down this end of space and, by
your determination, there'll always be a *Galway* operating.
We won't lose the name. Whatever happens, they'll *tell*
about us, and either way, if we do this, the Monahans will
be running with the systems we need to compete in what's
coming. What I'm asking for is your approval of me to go.
I've committed us far as saying you'll vote. And I'm asking
you to approve; and I'm asking some of you to volunteer.
I'll be leaving fine skilled people behind, if so happens you
have to carry on without me; but I'm hoping to be round-
tripping from Sol in what time it takes plus a little time to
tell the truth to them that needs to hear it, and after that,
after we're back at Alpha, I'm hoping to take us all aboard
Galway again and get on to Venture for a modern refit,
clear of debt. I'm planning us to be at the head of Alpha
ships that trade with Sol and maybe clear to Pell, ring-dock
and all. Enough of scraping by and hoping things change.
I'm for taking on this run, to hell with Cruz's Folly—and
God bless us all in the voyage. Will you back me? I'm asking for hands on approval, not volunteers yet. I'm asking
for a yes or no from all of you. In the best of my opinion,
this is what we should do. Hands for yes. Voices for no."

Hands went up, tentatively. Fallan's did, straightaway.
Ross put his hand up, and saw all the others, one and another until it seemed everyone's hand was up, though none
happily.

"All right," Niall said. "That's it, then. I'll be asking for
volunteers now."

Hands went up again. Everybody's. No hesitation.

Niall turned aside, stayed standing, hands on hips, shaking his head. Finally he turned back, still shaking his head.
"You're going to have me crying yet, cousins. No, hell, no,
you all can't go. Somebody's got to be here to keep the
blue-coats entertained."

That got a lowering of the hands in general, and a little
obligatory laughter.

"So I'll be asking my own shift first. Who'll go?"

Hands went up again. Fallan's among the first. Mary T and Ashlan. How could *he* not? Ross put up his hand, as other hands were going up, Helm, and Scan, and Com . . . he'd been scared to put it up, and now was scared he'd be told to put it down, himself first shift's trainee, no more than that.

"You don't need to," Fallan said, beside him. "We can manage."

"The hell," he said, looking straight ahead, past a number of hands. "It's going to be sights to see, isn't it? Original Earth. Close up and personal."

"Given we live to see it. This is no easy stroll, Ross. It's feelin' our way through. In every sense."

"So it's also learning," Ross said, rock-steady, now, and no way was he going to lower the hand unseen. "I'd for sure be less loss than *you'd* be."

"Let's don't plan to lose," Fallan said.

"We've got too many," Niall was saying. "Essential ops and maintenance, in case. No services, thank you with all my heart, but we'll be a bare bones run. Whole first shift bridge crew; two seniormost of all other first shift; plus senior medic, thank you, Jack, and senior cook, since you've had the hand up, Charlie, and God bless you both. We're officially full up for this run, and God knows we've no shortage of food. Owen, brother, you'll be in charge stationside. You'll be dealing with Abrezio. He's being reasonable. Extremely. I'm going to have an understanding with *Finity* and her ilk to get you out of here if there's any problem— I'm requesting a meeting with them as soon as we're done here. We'll have an undock party tonight, open to all, and we'll share a drink all round. But I want nobody stupid-drunk, and I want each of us to wear the shore ring on the off hand and watch each other politely, got it?"

The little gold band, engraved *Galway*, was usually worn on the pinky finger of the hand of choice, and those that couldn't wear a ring in their work wore it on a chain, and put it on for occasions. It was a proud, proud thing when a junior-junior picked a trade and put that on his hand.

Wearing it on the off hand meant—remember. Do what you're supposed to do. Whether keep an appointment or, in this case, stay sober enough to know what you're saying, don't get hung over, and don't forget your orders.

"The story's simple," Niall said. "We're making our scheduled run to Bryant's. That's how it all will work. But if somebody forgets, somebody shut the silly sod up. You all keep an eye and an ear to each other. No slips. We can bet Rosie's got bugs. Got it?"

"Yes, sir," came from the gathering.

"So. Tomorrow we issue board call, and you all turn out. *Everybody* pack and check out of the hotel, make it look real. The board call will come when it comes, and you all report to the mast doors as if you're boarding. Don't be too prompt. In fact, take your time and trail in by twos and threes as you usually do. First shift boards as prep crew goes aboard, all of us who're truly going; and at that point we'll shut the hatch. The lot of you just stand and chat as usual until we fire up, and stay standing as if the board call will come, even while we pull out. It'll be clear to everybody in fairly short order that we're not all aboard, we're moving on an unaccustomed vector, and nobody in ops is apt to know what we're about. Once the questions start, you just saunter back down the corridor and back to the Strip as a group, and if anybody asks, say some of us took off to Ireland."

That got an honest reaction. Old joke on *Galway*, for *dropped out of sight*. Ross laughed, and others did, until it came clear that it really was where *Galway* was bound, this voyage. Earth. The Ireland she'd never seen.

"And with that, we're dismissed, cousins."

It hardly seemed real, what was happening; but Niall began to leave the room, and was having a hard time of it, cousins and aunts and half-sibs and all wanting to wish him well and hug him and tell him they were with him.

"You sure about this?" Fallan said quietly, at Ross's side.

"Comes to me I'd feel like hell at this moment if my shift was going and I wasn't."

"Fool," Fallan said.

"All right, cousins. I'm off to tell Abrezio," Niall said, at the door. "We'll be partying tonight as we go up on the schedule boards. We'll party, and we'll be happy, and we won't tell the others what's really happening, got it?"

It was normal as normal could be. Their entry on the schedule boards would change, they'd be listed with a time of departure—sleepover partners might drop by Rosie's for a drink or two, and a wise spacer hoped they all got along.

Ross could envision the party. It was every time they left dock. He had a clear vision of being at the boards for departure. He had been, the last three years.

But he couldn't imagine what it would be for most of his cousins and uncles and aunts to gather up their duffle and go on back to the Strip . . . left behind, trying to get back into the sleepover they'd just checked out of. He was leaving his mother and gran, who might not have participated in his bringing up, but who were especially family; and leaving Peg, who *had* brought him up, who'd stayed six months on Bryant's when he was born, and had viewed him as especially hers, among the nursery lot, and become their minder on station calls. Peg was among the senior-seniors now. He was leaving them all. He wouldn't be seeing them for a while.

"You're volunteering," Peg said when he caught her by the door.

He gave her a gentle hug. "It's my shift, Peg. All my shift. Junior I am, but it's my shift. You expect me back, hey?"

She hugged him back. "Yeah, sure. Already expecting you. Waiting already."

"You take care of Mum and Aunt Lila for me, eh?"

"You say goodbye proper, boy. See that you do."

Mum had left faster than she needed to, and not given him a hug. Which said she was upset.

Lila and Gran had gone with her. His tie with them was thinner than his tie with Peg, but he felt the tug all the same. Mum and her sister Lila were third shift fitters, not as involved with his life as Peg and his year-mates, who'd scattered to other shifts and gone to the trades as they'd grown; but still—she was his mum. And she'd worry about

him. Aunt Lila would. Gran and Great-gran would—
maybe—be proud.

"I'll do that tonight. But we can't use goodbye outside
this door."

"I'll do it now, then." Peg hugged him, kissed him on the
cheek—she had to stand on tiptoe to do that nowadays; and
let him go and left with the ebbing crowd.

Fool, Fallan had called him. And Niall hadn't accepted
him—yet. He was standing in the mostly empty room, a
still stone in the outflow of cousins, when older cousin
Ashlan came up and put an arm across his shoulders.

"So it's us, is it?"

"Yeah," he said. "Yeah. Am I going to see my shift go,
and not be with them?"

"Hell of a chance," Ashlan said, and the arm dropped
away. "I see my brother over there. Got to talk to him."

Chapter 11   Section ii

Ross went on out the door, thinking about Jen, now the
initial shock had passed. He'd hoped that his hookup with
Jen might go on another week, maybe, however long it took
the visitors to finish their business and the departure hold
to lift and life to get back to normal on Alpha. Instead . . .
he just had tonight.

And after that—Who knew? Even if all went well, even
if *Galway* made the round trip and they all returned as
heroes, *Finity's* course was back to the Beyond, and
Galway—if the Luck was with them, *Galway* would become rich, a favorite child of Alpha, with the greatest prize
of all: being main ship on the Sol/Alpha run. Still . . . Fallan
and Lisa Marie had met again, one from *Gaia*, one from
Atlas, when the grand old pusher-ships almost never saw
one another at dock, and when the pushers' converted de-

scendants had taken routes on opposite ends of the inhabited universe.

So he couldn't say never. And partings happened, every voyage. Hearts got broken, promises got made, and people swore to meet again, and at least you could leave messages for each other—hello, I'm at Bryant's, doing well . . . hope to hear from you—messages carried in the black box feeds that every ship sucked up and spat out at every docking. Hi, hello, I'm at Pell, hope you're well . . .

He'd never gotten much mail. A couple of casual letters, Hi there, it's Marcy, hope you're doing well. I'm at Bryant's and I'm bored . . .

He'd be somebody, when he got back from this one, wouldn't he? A long, strange trip. He felt exhilarated and scared at once; and if there was one human being he longed to tell, it was Jen, right now, just to see what she'd say.

But that wasn't the way it was to be. *Galway* had been fueled and loaded when the second and third outsiders had shown up, and station had issued a general hold while they sorted that out: *none* of the locals were allowed to leave, mostly because station wanted live, loyal bodies walking up and down the Strip among the horde of outsiders.

Then *Finity's End* had shown up and station had *desperately* wanted to hang onto its loyal local live bodies.

Now station was letting one ship go—so people might think it was the ebb of the crisis and station was relaxing. *Galway*'s sudden departure appeared as the harbinger of, well, station relaxing its grip, leading to a peaceful outcome.

And then the news would seep out, and excitement was going to roar up and down the Strip.

He'd give a bit to see that, too; but he'd have to get that story from Peg and Mum and the others left safe ashore—when he came back.

Now he had to get into a different frame of mind; and people would drink tonight, but tomorrow they'd be down to business and getting their heads back to work.

Jen would see the schedule board change. And she'd know to come find him tonight. He didn't have to tell her.

He didn't know what the customs were at her end of space, but here, people would know, and Rosie's would be jammed.

Chapter 11   Section iii

"*Galway*'s on the Departures," Fletcher dropped by the room to say, and JR looked up from his keyboard, in as much of an office as he'd been able to fit in a travel case, and as much as he was willing to take onto Alpha. Computer, mostly, a supply of Pell's best try at coffee, and his second-favorite mug, his stationside mug. Its older cousin rested—or floated—in his locker in his much more comfortable, but inaccessible, downside corridor office aboard *Finity*.

JR pushed a button on the flat black box that sat on his desk, and took a sip from the mug, while Fletcher waited for a reaction, and he waited for the green light to come on.

It did. He said: "We've not heard from them yet."

"There's a party at Rosie's come maindark," Fletcher said, standing.

Same custom all the way to Venture, for a departing ship. Pell had put the lid on the celebrations. Pell had too much traffic and too many ships coming in and going out, not the close-knit sort of community Alpha had. The party-goers here would all know each other's names.

Excepting theirs, that had come in as strangers.

"We haven't heard from them," JR said. "*Galway*'s our one holdout, still. Mum's had no word of their leaving dock. Neither has Jen, that she's said. This is a surprise."

Fletcher dropped into the chair nearest the spindly desk. "Jen hasn't said, and she'd have reported it if she'd known. Something else weird. For about an hour there was a stream of Galways headed to the station offices, then out again, and it's not clear what it was about. Whole damn ship's crew in the offices?"

"And now on the boards for departure. Clearly they've been fueled and loaded all during our sit here. Everything's been held, since we arrived. No doubt the station's wanted a friendly population on the Strip, to keep an eye on us. That plan backfired, leaving the crews in dock to hear our proposal. So now they release the only one we *haven't* got, before we've scheduled our departure? If anything I'm wondering if station's been pressuring them. They're the newest ship Alpha's got, among the regulars, and maybe Alpha wants to ensure that loyalty, get them out before they sign. But I'm afraid that minor mystery will have to remain unsolved. It's time we left, too, with or without a decision out of *Galway.* I'm a little surprised, I admit."

"We'll catch them at Bryant's, out of Alpha's direct ob-servation. There's no great gain by taking the whole lot of us to Glory."

"Says sad things to Glory if we don't, however. We've got those unaccounted-for ships to find first, but I don't want any station to get the notion they're written off. If we sent off *Nomad* and *Mumtaz*—Asha's more of a diplomat than Min."

"God, yes. Min takes no prisoners."

"We send *Nomad* off from Bryant's and catch up with *Galway*, where she may be more willing to talk."

"I don't think either Mum or Jen would be too unhappy with that move," Fletcher said. "What I hear, several more of us wouldn't be unhappy to run into *Galway* again."

"I'm wondering why the whole crew met. In admin of-fices, yet."

"All the adult crew, and the retireds. Jen's out and about. Likely she's on it."

"Keep me posted. I think—"

The com beeped. Given circumstances, he didn't let it go. He flipped it open. Message from Jen. 18. 14. 1. 21. He keyed 66. Come ahead.

"*Galway* wants to talk. Fletch, somebody will be com-ing into the restaurant. Bring him here."

"It's kind of a surprise," Jen said, over a beer, "isn't it? Are you for Glory beyond that?"

It was not an easy meeting. Naturally Jen wanted to know what was going on, why the meeting, all of that, and Ross couldn't say. He'd just relayed a message from Niall, was all, Niall wanting to talk to JR, and she'd sent that.

Now it was them. Their business. And naturally Jen was curious.

"Look," he said, "maybe. Maybe someday. I know you need to know, you know I know, and that's all I can say except this is the last night, and I'd like to spend it in your place, if you don't mind. But I've got the undock party at Rosie's. And you're invited. Well, everybody is, but you, especially; and Fallan will be hoping the same for your Fourth, so however it works out, we'll say our goodbyes until someday."

Jen frowned at him in a way he'd learned in such a short time to read, that little moue that meant *you're holding something, aren't you?* He ducked the gaze and stared off at two Santiagos at a nearby table.

Her hand touched his. Warmer than his. And it wasn't all from his holding the cold beer.

"We'll be there," she said. "And for the rest . . . we'll figure it out."

"I do like you," he said. He could be honest about that. "Really a lot." Don't compare your sleepovers, Ashlan had advised him. Never compare. They'll think you talk about them, too. Just say it was great. But the fact was, he'd never felt like this about anyone. And it was hard, not telling her so.

"I like you, too," Jen said, "really a lot. Above and beyond. I want to find you again."

"Mutual," he said. He closed his fingers on hers.

"Your hand is cold."

"The beer," he said. "That's all."

"We can make use of the time we've got," she said. "We can do that, go to your party, come back to the Olympian."

"I'll be needing to get my stuff in order. Soon's that's done, well, I'll be heading for Rosie's." Fact was, he didn't know what state his nerves would be in tonight. "But we'll plan on a next time."

"We could meet at Bryant's."

He tried to say as naturally as possible, "That's true." And took a sip of beer. A lie tasted bad. "Enough of someday. Let's go for what we've got."

Chapter 11   Section v

Fletcher was back. With Captain Niall Monahan. JR stood up, offered a hand. Niall took it, looking solemn and worried.

"We're bug-free here," JR said right off, settling back into his desk chair, as Niall sat down. "I don't know how many places you can say that, but we're pretty sure of our safety to talk freely. Pleased you came, sir. What can I do for you?"

"This insurance you're offering . . . I talked to the Director. I said I was going to come here. He has no problem with it."

"I'm glad if that's the case. Ultimately, it's good for everyone. Coffee?"

Niall shook his head, frowning, looking very much as if there was something else to say.

"Trouble, sir?" JR asked.

Deep breath. "Maybe. Maybe not. Say we had something major happen. How far are we covered in this agreement? And what percentage of profits are we paying in? I can pay a big up-front. All we've got. But can you then cover us?"

It was a question what major thing did Niall Monahan anticipate happening to *Galway*—and when. The man was worried, and there was a specific, definite fear; but it wasn't up for discussion—yet.

"The terms are," JR said, "ten percent of proceeds from all sources, hired-haul and self-owned, per annum, to be reserved within ship's funds wherever a ship has an account—to cover losses; and if you have to use the insurance, coverage is repayable, once that ship is operating again, by an additional five percent atop the ten, interest-free if repaid in good faith and steadily. Once the fund's built—and once older ships are up to standard—it'll be less, we hope."

"Pell's the banker."

"Pell's not. Cyteen's not. Alpha's not. You maintain the sum in your own accounting, and send it on call, if needed."

"The stations, sir, they're not going to want to release ship credit that way."

"It's not their credit. And they don't get to reckon it that way. The ship withdraws it, it's the ship's to send where it likes."

"Because we say so?"

Sensible question. And they were at the bag-end of the universe with most of the work done, unstoppable now. "Members by now will include just about every ship that moves. And as for holding a ship's funds, a station would be ill-advised to claim a ship's own goods, or to cheat on the sale."

Niall nodded slowly. "And if stations are on the outs with each other and aren't dealing?"

"If stations are behaving badly, they might not see trade at all for a time. And precious little they can do to each other with no traffic in or out. They can send messages to each other, but they can't move a kilo of flour. And their messages will take a few years to get there. *That's* how it works. We do have teeth. There is a clause in the agreement that says, quote, on a vote of the members, majority ruling, a station can be embargoed, with the sole exception of humanitarian shipments, as long as the issue remains unresolved."

Lengthy silence, then.

"What happens to this organization," Niall asked, "when Sol comes in and the EC starts issuing orders?"

"That's the clock that's always running on us, isn't it? This is now. If we wait and let things fall as they will when Sol comes in, well, not so good. We are a political interest, the same as any station. And we need to act like it."

Deep breath. The man's face was a study. Apprehension. Desperation. "I'm about to break a trust at such a level—this is not easy, sir. It is not. Can I have your discretion?"

"Not where it regards safety of us and ours. Not where it regards the mission we're on."

"Fair enough," Niall said after a moment. "But discretion as far as you can. When you've heard my argument."

"That I grant."

"Abrezio has the jump-point to Sol."

Disastrous news. It hit like a hammer. "Confirmed?"

"Sure as they can be, but untested. He's transmitted the coordinates down the Stream. They've gone."

"Are they going to send a probe?"

Niall made the apologetic shrug that was common currency on Alpha, for all the shortfalls, all the out of stocks and can't-do's. "Not from here. And the point is—the message has *gone*. It's unstoppable. There's no way Cruz can get ahead of it, no way Cruz can get credit to himself. *Rights* can't move. *Galway* can. So we're elected."

"To test that point? Good God, sir."

"Abrezio has offered the Family his care and his protection, while a few of us make the run; but that's saying Abrezio can stay in office the year with Cruz against him. He's not a young man. He's got no enforcement but the blue-coats, and it's gotten real confusing as to who's an Alpha blue-coat and who's *Rights* crew when it comes to the Strip. And *without* us making the run—it's six and more years, with Cruz and Enzio Hewitt increasingly in charge. That . . . is not a happy picture. We've watched the changes in Alpha. Witness we're sitting here talking in secret because the man's got eyes and ears everywhere. It wasn't always like that. Time was, ships got repaired right and people could speak their minds. Not now. Not ever with Cruz having his way and Hewitt grabbing for what he can get. And right now Abrezio's hit them hard and they don't know it yet. Abrezio will get in a second, maybe fatal, hit, if we go, sent by him, and we tell *Sol* how it is, and how Cruz is, and that the man's a fool and wasting resources, as he's amply proved. We'll know the route. We'll be the guides. And we'll be giving any new Sol authority the word on who's to trust in the process."

It was a clear enough picture. "When did he transmit?"

"Yesterday, is my understanding."

"So around six years for the coordinates to get there, more to probe and test. But granted *you* get through—and prove the route—Sol could be here in force within the year."

"Assuming they have ships, sir. Assuming *Rights*' aborted run wasn't a mechanical that's a fundamental flaw in the design Sol might *also* be using. And assuming their hire-on sim-trained crews are better than what Cruz has put together here."

"Let's assume it," JR said. "All of it. Worst case scenario. We assume they can build far more efficiently than we can, and *some* of that effort will have gone into FTL—anticipating, in all that clutter around Sol, there *is* a way to get here. Whether they've meanwhile gone in any *other* direction—we don't know. But it seems a given that they're interested in *our* direction."

"They still need qualified crews. And that's a worry to us. That's a deep worry on our side. Supposing they listen and take our warnings to heart . . . we'll *not* be devoting *our* lives to training Sol hire-ons, whose sole purpose will be to take away the very trade we've been promised. We'll not be trusting them. Not in the least."

"And we're not going to say the Sol EC can't use hired crews," JR said. "But we can say they'll not be highly favored anywhere up the line from here. Their hired crew can haul the Earth trade up to Alpha from Sol, and Family ships can take it on from Alpha. As long as Earth keeps feeding goods to Alpha, there'll be plenty to haul."

"A point, sir. One to consider. We figure, at the very least, we'll have to ferry their trainees to Alpha, if that's what they want, and we'll spend the return voyage talking to those people and explaining how we work, and why Cruz is a fool. But—and on this I'm down to begging. I've told you what I know. I've given you the warning. I'm asking for that insurance you're promoting—knowing I'm risking my ship. I'm putting my hopes in the alliance you're promoting. And in Ben Abrezio staying in office and talking sense to the EC. I'll be risking us so we can stay in operation and not be put out of business by hire-ons and so that we all get a dose of Earth goods to remind us we're human. And I'm asking you, if nothing else, to take what funds we've got to account—I'll transfer them—and take the rest of the Monahans somewhere they can be safe, and where they can wait for us, safe from Andrew Cruz. Bryant's is distance enough. And if we're not back in the year—if things don't go so well—I'm hoping you'll find some way to take care of them after that. Other Alpha ships'd take us in, piecemeal. In return . . . I can't give you the coordinates. I don't have them yet, Abrezio being no fool. But it's possible *Galway* can transmit them far and wide as she's outbound, so *everybody* knows. I'd do that. If you ask."

To be put in such a position—God, JR thought. Both Abrezio and Niall Monahan. Serious lack of options.

"Once you've signed with us," JR said, "we'll look out for your Family, with or without those coordinates. We'll get them to safety—our four ships can do that, no problem. We'll see them to Bryant's and *if* something untoward happens, I'll personally undertake to get them into the trade as one crew soon as we can. I'll query the membership in line for a build at Venture, see if they'll slip the Monahans into queue—and it's my sense, yes, for what you're trying to bring, they might well." The risk was huge, no question. If they only had time, if they could get Venture involved before *Galway* went, they could build a probe . . .

But the delay—and if Cyteen involved itself, a potent

force with no desire to see Sol and its goods and its influence arrive at all—

In very fact, it was a good thing to have Abrezio as the man who pushed the button, and *not* JR Neihart or any merchanter signatory with them. Not even *Galway. Galway* was doing their best to warn them.

"I'll be in your debt," Niall said. "I'm trusting my people to you. And if ships of your persuasion can possibly make Abrezio look good in the meanwhile—Abrezio didn't ask this. I'm saying it myself. We need Abrezio to survive this . . . to survive the next week, and to stay in charge until we get back and after. You can see his problems. Supply would help, things to keep the residents on *his* side."

And, JR thought, if Abrezio's gamble worked, it could be a short wait. Sol's forces could be here even this year. Which was much too soon.

Damn that part of it. Definitely.

"Time is a problem," JR said. "And we don't know what Sol might have ready to launch, or whether they've gained jump experience in other directions. The organization we're forming isn't complete yet. We were hoping to have it done, and to bring the stations onboard as well, *before* Sol showed up. The *Rights* build, the numbers of enforcement agents here—far more than Alpha needs—I can't swear to what they're planning, but moving a large enforcement presence onto, say, Bryant's, is one step from doing it at Venture. If they're building a military force—so can Cyteen, and I don't think Sol understands that Cyteen can see their bet and raise it. Pell does understand it, but it's far from certain Pell could do a damned thing if Cyteen moves on them except to try to make a deal—and if Sol makes decisions no better than they ever did, Sol is going to meet the rock it can't push—with a lot of casualties."

"I don't see any hope in that situation."

"There is some hope," JR said, "and it's *us.* It's our alliance. Listen. Cyteen and Pell get along—delicately, but they get along . . . because they don't ever meet. Out past Venture, we don't have the EC handing out orders. Merchanters do the talking and negotiating. Cyteen and Pell don't *need* to see each other's faces. Merchanters go between them, goods flow, and they don't bother each other. We don't have 'Pell merchanters' and 'Cyteen merchanters.' We serve a wholly different interest, which is keeping the stations healthy and letting them do what they do best. We don't *let* them argue. *We* say what we haul and when. If Sol tries to disrupt that balance—if Sol thinks they can take over all stations and us as well—they can't. They can't manufacture what we are. If war happens, trade is at risk. And if trade stops, unsupported stations die. Fast. Sol needs to understand that."

"If we don't go," Niall said, "if we back out of the deal, it's six years, maybe a few for Sol to get organized, but all the same—if those jump-points are good, Sol's still coming. And Abrezio may not hold on that long. If *he* goes down—Cruz is in charge. And frankly, *that* scares me more than testing those points." Niall was silent, staring into some middle ground between them, seeing God knew what. Then: "I'm full-loaded with supply. I could stall out there—for one thing, we'll be making conservative jumps: I don't want to enter real space too close to any unmapped mass-point, and it's apparently a two-hop."

God. *Twice* rolling those dice. Three, counting Sol itself.

"And for another, I'd be a fool not to map those points on my way, and before making the return trip." Niall met his eyes squarely. " I can give you two . . . maybe even three years—assuming all goes well. If we're damaged in transit and have to repair . . . you might get even more. We'll be going out of here with just first shift, but stocked for a hundred fifty souls, and our cargo is partly foodstuffs for Glory. So, if all goes well . . . three years before you see us again, likely with passengers, and hopefully passengers that we'll have argued into good sense. If we don't make it, you keep Abrezio in power, get him supply, however you can. He's disposed to support your Alliance. The most of the Monahans will be safe meanwhile, and you get your two years, minimum. Does that bring us even?"

Brave man. Good man.

"It has the organization owing the Monahans a lot if you can do that."

"Refit?"

"Refit?" To get Sol stalled for three, maybe as much as four years? "Damned straight, yes. I don't think I'll even have to argue. You *will* get it. And we'll do what we can to support Abrezio without ruining his credit as a hardnosed EC loyalist. As for Cruz, we've still got a utility pusher we're trying to give back, but so far nobody's shown up to claim it. And guess who's to blame for that? Station's already . . . disenchanted."

That got a slight laugh. A crinkle of humor about the eyes. "JR Neihart." Niall held out his hand. "I'm proud to do business with you. We'll do what we can. Undock's tomorrow afternoon, prep starts in the morning. General boarding's at 0900. My first shift and I are going, and the rest are in your hands. Deal?"

"Deal." They shook hands. JR said, "See you in three years or so. And I'll be buying for at least a week when we do."

"I'll hold you to that."

Niall left, a far happier man than he had come in. Fletcher met him at the door, to see him back through the maze of the Olympian.

JR sat still, staring at the wall and seeing star maps instead, the moving patterns that no ship could alter. Stars and worlds moved and changed relative to each other, the same, but not always the same. Things had shifted since humankind had set out, and kept shifting, and yes, sooner or later Sol would find its way to its old colonies at FTL speeds, the motherworld trying to re-enter what had become a very different environment, with different customs, different issues and different ways of dealing.

The warning and the time delay was the best they could hope to have.

Reality rode wave fronts of information. Right now they knew and Pell didn't. There'd be a time when Pell knew and Cyteen didn't . . . half a year at least . . . during which Pell could make some very bad decisions or some better-thought ones. Best if he delivered that news to Emilio Konstantin personally, and helped that thought process take a good direction.

Hewitt's illicit expedition out to *Finity's End* had, like a high-*V* missile, nudged a lot of situations—spacers' rights, EC infringements, *Rights,* and the station's economic desperation. That towel-clad image now resident on hundreds of personal coms, in various edited versions—continued to circulate. Cruz and Hewitt were at each other's throats and both trying to push past Abrezio. Abrezio had made a move to stop them cold, and extended an offer to Niall Monahan that could upset the whole of humankind.

Had Xiao Min's Com 2 taken that damnable picture? He strongly suspected so. Or it could have been one of the Gallis. Whoever had done it, it was beyond recall now. On such moments—such utterly unpredictable moments—the universe could shift.

He signaled Min, Asha, and Sanjay to drop by, their soonest convenience. They needed to know, first of all.

Sanjay Patel asked the obvious question: "If Monahan betrays Abrezio—will he turn again on us?"

"Is it betrayal?" Min asked. "Abrezio gets *our* assistance, more than he could hope for otherwise, and the numbers still make it to Sol in half the time, *with* a wake-up call regarding the Alpha situation."

"We knew we were running out of time," JR said. "Sol system's outer shell is complex. There had to be something isolated enough and close enough to the old route. And Alpha has pusher records even Cyteen lacks. I'm not totally surprised."

"Our arrival has undoubtedly pressurized the situation," Min said. "The Director may have been holding the data for some time, and push has now come to shove in the situation with Cruz—no love lost there, and the sudden acquisition of the coordinates seems unlikely to be a coincidence."

JR nodded. "I think we're seeing the start of a battle for Alpha, and unfortunately, pessimistically, Cruz is Sol's hand-picked representative, and will have an inbuilt credibility—while Hewitt is far more likely to have living backers, which may make him stronger. Abrezio may have been content to hold Sol a decade out of synch, but now he's risking a ship, his *only* reliable ship. So I agree he's become desperate, and I fear we've made him so."

"*Galway is* an Alpha ship," Asha said. "Built at Venture, but she came back to try to keep Alpha alive. The Monahans are that loyal, is how I read it."

"And trying their damnedest to save Alpha and their own way of life," JR said. "Places and people they know.

They're *far* more tied to this station, this set of stations than we are to anywhere. I don't know whether to respect that or call them crazy. But I think that's the bottom line. I've had a couple of good contacts with them, and that's what I understand."

"They're risking everything," Sanjay said. "trying to save a situation I don't think can be saved."

"Niall Monahan has this vision that if they can keep Abrezio in office and educate Sol—they can win, they can modernize, they can have the best of both situations. Maybe join the modern universe on their own terms, as the conduit for Sol goods." JR drew a long breath. "He wants a refit of *Galway*. I think he sees what we see and I don't think *any* of these people are blind. The Hinder Stars are not viable except as stepping stones to and from Sol. And if there is any hope of moderating Sol's appearance here—it probably *is* Abrezio."

"It's no secret that I have been of the opinion," Asha said, "with Sanjay, that these outlying stations *should* be shut down, to afford no easy bridge for Sol to the Beyond. But many of the ships that serve these places are too small and too old to prosper in the Beyond—and the Families have built something here, different as they are. They *are* different. But undoing everything they have built—there has to be an answer for them."

"Unfortunately," Sanjay said, "it will need to come from Sol. Fortunately—Sol will see the state of things and have to spend considerable resources fixing it before they can use it. But if their answer is hired crews and EC control of shipping, none of these people will thrive. The Gallis are the future they all face if they stay here. Broken ship, broken finance, broken system."

"But not broken, themselves," JR said. "Not yet. *We* can help the ships. We can fit them to serve the situation and make themselves useful to Sol so that, early on, they can out-perform anything Sol brings in. There *will* be a market for Sol's goods, once they're arriving at FTL speeds, and these ships *could* thrive and be in the market for replacement with state-of-the-art ships for these Families. We stick to the fundamental concept: make ourselves the

conduit between potential adversaries, and so doing, keep
them apart long enough for Sol to appreciate the system."

"I think you are overly optimistic," Min said. "Sol will
not understand until we show our teeth."

"That may be," JR said, "but we'll hope sheer distance
and inconvenience is argument enough, so that if we can
educate the ones they send out here, we'll never have to
take action."

"To which end we have at best three years," Sanjay said,
the true pessimist. "Provided by a man who's playing every
side of this arrangement—the EC, Abrezio, and us—for the
best advantage he can get."

"Do not we all?" said Min. "We deal with whom we *can*
deal. Only *we* can cut our losses when we choose, find
other markets, other partnerships. He, unfortunately, is
bound to this station and its options, and he has to come
back here. We cannot predict what may be the situation
here a year from now. Or whether he will come at all."

"Our departure may need to be delayed," JR said, "at
least until we know what best to *do* with the Monahans left
behind. He wants them transported to Bryant's to wait.
He's worried they may be the target of some sort of retaliation. But we cannot move them unless they're willing to
be moved. And wherever they are, we have to negotiate
their sleepover and food allowance. That's our job."

Chapter 12   Section ii

It was like every undock party, and surreally unlike—the
whole family pretending to everybody that everything was
normal and they were outbound to Bryant's—pretending
to everybody that came—and more, pretending to each
other, and to the handful of youngest that came in and left
again. Some of the minders had doubled up their charges
so that Arden could come, being sister to Aileen, who was

a first-shift engee, and going. Arden tried hard to be bubbly and cheerful. Too hard, Ross thought. But Aileen took
her off into a corner, not to talk about what they weren't to
say, but just to talk for a bit and give her a hug and share a
beer.

"Hey," a cousin said to Ross, and punched him in the
shoulder, a congratulations, or encouragement, or whatever more nobody could say. That shoulder had met so
many such encouragements it was getting sore, the more so
as the cousins were several beers on.

Santiagos had come to Rosie's, which was a bar they
frequented anyway. *Firenze* crew was there. And *Qarib*
came early: the Qaribs, in their custom, drank only tea,
mingled for a while, presenting well-wishes and a small
basket of expensive fruit sweets, quickly depleted. Then
they drifted out again, most of them, excepting the Third,
who stayed to talk with their Fourth—old friends, those
two. The Firenzes came in, clearly ready to party to all
hours, happy and loud.

But Jen hadn't shown up. Nor had Lisa Marie. Fallan
had a table, and a beer, on which Fallan was making slow
progress, and he had no dearth of friends to drop by and
wish him well. She *would* come, they both would. Ross and
Jen had spent the whole afternoon in Jen's room, and she'd
talked a lot about meeting at Bryant's, which hadn't made
things easier.

But he'd said nothing to disabuse her of the idea. He'd
said sure, yes, they would, and tried not to sound as if he
was lying. He hoped—desperately hoped—she hadn't seen
through it and gone straight to whoever she reported to.

Maybe she'd gotten a bad feeling about him and she'd
been warned off, or decided on her own not to come tonight. He hoped not. God, he hoped not. He hoped he
hadn't messed up Fallan's relations with Jen's Fourth. He
couldn't forgive himself if that was the case.

None of the visitor ships had shown up. Maybe their
captains had laid down a no-go for some reason of politics.
Maybe they were all upset. Niall had *said* he was going to
sign with their insurance. Niall had gone to meet with JR
Neihart.

Had *they* had a set-to that had reverberated to all the crews, all the agreements?

He cast a look toward Niall, who looked maybe a little solemn, but there was a lot to be solemn about.

And finally he found the chair next to Fallan, vacant for a moment, and dropped into it.

"Dunno," Fallan said without being asked. And shrugged. "Haven't given up. She is what she is. She won't be sitting down to a long drinking session. But if she doesn't come fairly soon, I'll be on my third beer."

"Did everything go all right with Niall?"

"Far's I know it—*There* she is!"

It *was* Lisa Marie, and *Finity's* Senior, with one of the *Little Bear* captains, and behind them a whole flood of the outsiders, streaming in. Lisa Marie took a straight course to Fallan's table, and Ross got up with a little flourish and an offer of the chair straightaway.

He was looking immediately for Jen among the incoming crowd, and saw her headed toward him—not the tallest of anybody, and lost for a moment as she forged a passage through a wall of Firenzes and Santiagos, but she came. Manners didn't dictate a public hug, not at their stage of an arrangement, but she hooked his arm against her and hugged it all the same. "Sorry. We had a meeting." She took his jacket collar and pulled him down to whisper, right against his ear. "We know. First shift. Is that you?"

"Yes," he said. God, it was scary that someone knew. He wondered if it was his fault and he couldn't ask. She held hard to his arm.

"I want a beer. Maybe several."

"I'll get you one," he said.

"God, you." She gave him a passionate kiss right in front of everybody, and hoots followed, and laughter.

"There goes my reputation."

Second kiss. Arms wound around his neck.

"Beer," she said.

"Deal," he said. And *still* couldn't ask her the things he wanted to ask. He had the shore ring on his right hand, telling him the conditions on which they could be here. He took the cheerful slaps on the back, cousins and others cheering the demonstration he and Jen had just produced, everybody in high good spirits, and if it made people laugh, really laugh for a bit, that was to the good.

He made it to the bar, wedged his way in, still with his shoulders stinging. Rosie himself drew two beers and shoved them across the water-tracked surface. "On the house, Galway," Rosie said. "You and the girl. Good luck to that."

He took the beers. He was sure he blushed. He got back to Jen with the beers mostly unspilled, handed her hers, and nodded toward the side of the room.

It was at least less a scrum there. Enough beer had flowed that a little high humor had picked up momentum, especially with the visitor captains and crews joining in.

"We're going to be spilling well out onto the Strip," Ross said. "Hope to God we don't get another blue-coat craziness."

"Hope we don't either," Jen said. She was serious for the moment, dark eyes looking deep into his. "You be good. I'll be thinking about you."

No more about Bryant's. She did know something. And neither of them could say it.

"I'll be thinking about *you*," he said.

"Can you come by after this breaks up?"

"No," he said. "Got to turn in and get some rest. Captain's called all crew curfew at 2300. He'll skin us else."

"He doesn't look that fierce."

Niall looked downright happy, point of fact. Happier and freer than he'd been for weeks. He *could* be a man contemplating getting back to regular runs. He could be a man who'd just made a good deal for the ship—the protection they needed for the most of them.

Ross hoped so. Several captains were together, seeming intent on their own business, and fairly happy about it.

Was it just that a deal *was* made? Or was more going on, that maybe *Jen* knew about, and *Niall* knew about, and not all Niall's shift knew?

What could make Niall happy—in these several captains, aside from the well-wishes of *Firenze, Santiago* and

Qarib? Assurance that the Monahans would be safe? That would be the main thing. And if they gave it to him, then, yes, that accounted for it.

"Hey." Jen reached out her fingers and turned his face toward her. "They're fine. It's fine."

You know something I don't? he wanted to ask her. But didn't. They never knew who was listening. Ever.

The party got crazier. Rosie had to evict a Santiago from the bar top. His mates caught him as he slipped and fell and gave him several tosses before a deadly sober *Santiago* captain stepped in and set them down at a table, the three rowdiest.

Jen held his hand and, her head on his shoulder, told him a story, about her, about Pell docks, about construction at Venture.

Which *Galway* might see again someday. That was a cheerful thought. Maybe they would even call at Pell, if they came out of this financially able.

Ring-dock. So vast and so high there was actually weather up around the lights, Jen said. Clouds formed, and it rained. It might be pipe condensation, but rain was something that happened on planets, and yet there was more rain of a different kind in a project Pell was undertaking—rain coming down on plants, a hydroponics lab that was set to produce food that had nothing to do with yeast tanks and fish farms and Downbelow plants that had to be processed. Green things. Earth things. Seeds that had slept for centuries.

There were young trees growing there. "No taller than I am," Jen said, "but they're set up and braced so they can grow the way they do on Earth."

"For real?"

"Well, trees grow in pusher-time. They're time-stretched, like us, sort of. Naturally."

"That's kind of crazy."

"It's what the keepers say. I'm hoping to see if they've grown any while I've been away. Someday you've got to get to Pell."

"Don't know as they want us," he said.

"Or Venture. We're at Venture from time to time."

"You'll drop messages."

"I promise. So you have to. Messages in a bottle."

"What bottle?"

"It's an old story. People would put messages in bottles and toss them into Earth's oceans. And the oceans have a lot of currents that push and shove, and the bottles would travel, and people would find them clear around the planet from where they started. Messages in bottles. I'll leave something for you every place I touch."

Ships picked up such messages in their black boxes, spat them out everywhere they docked.

"So you have to leave things for me. So I know where you are. Let's don't take as long as Fallan and the Fourth to find each other."

"All right. Deal."

The noise level was getting deafening. Somebody had put on loud music and everybody was overtalking it. They tried to talk, but he half-shouted the last word, near as she was.

"This is crazy," he said then.

"Want to go somewhere?"

"Can't. I'm under orders—stay at Rosie's, stay together."

"Is it always like this?"

"Never seen so many people show up." A second's afterthought. "There've never *been* this many people on the Strip. I think the blue-coats are probably afraid to come in here tonight. But I think we've fractured all the safety codes."

"Captains can move us. We're behaving. No problem."

That was true. For that matter, if Rosie himself said move, the locals wouldn't argue. So they stayed and drank, kept a pleasant buzz going. Jen asked him about Glory. He asked her about Viking and Mariner and what she knew about Cyteen.

Twenty-three hundred hours and Niall stood up, called for attention with Rosie's help—a mug thumped on the bar finally lowered the noise level.

"Twenty-three hundred," Niall called out, "and we've haven't quite drunk Rosie's dry—"

"We're out of ale," Rosie shouted from the bar, "and we're about out of rum!"

"Well, then," Niall called above the whistles and thumps, "let's hear it for Rosie, who's a good friend to *Galway*, and let's let the man go home to his wife and kids. Wish us well, all, new mates and old, and we thank you mightily for coming! Turn in the mugs and stack the chairs, friends! Let's leave Rosie an easy cleanup!"

"Well, that's a nice custom," Jen said as they got up.

"Doesn't leave a mate sleeping in a corner," Ross said cheerfully. "And it helps the bar staff." He freed his chair from its track and upended it on the tabletop, set the clamp to hold it in place. "Get those mugs, would you, Jen? Those go to the bar." He fished a scrip out of his jacket pocket—he'd put the right denomination into his pocket before the evening started. "Lay that on the counter, will you?"

She took the mugs and the scrip up while he stacked the other two chairs. Family took the incapacitated in hand, and with a good deal of shouting back and forth and well-wishes to *Galway*, everybody began to leave.

"I know I shouldn't tempt you," Jen said as they stood in the clearing room. "So I won't."

"You do," Ross said. "But I can't. Got to join my own, now."

She put her arms about his neck, locked her hands behind his head, looking up at him. "You take care. You take *good* care, Ross Monahan."

He gave her a lingering kiss, and a second, and it really was time to go. Fallan and Lisa Marie were standing amid the tables and upended chairs, holding hands, still talking.

"You take care, too," he said. And: "Cousins are off. Got to haul Fallan away."

Last kiss. Quick and light. The ship called. And he had to go.

Jen came trailing in, almost last, downcast, hands in jacket pockets, with none of her usual energy.

"Jen," JR said. He'd waited to intercept her—not surprised she came among the last.

And he was not unsympathetic for the mood, either. Merchanters left places and people. It was the way of things, and partings were ordinary—you'd see a person again, or you might never. Or it might be decades, like Mum and *Galway*'s Nav 1.

But it was a crazy plan the Monahans were embarking on, risky beyond ordinary good sense, and even Mum's rock-steady philosophy wasn't handling the leave-taking as matter-of-course. A crazy plan, a move that no Family ship would undertake, except here, at the stretched edge of EC threat, with a station estranged from most other stations, a station out of resources, with a power struggle in full swing, and a ship and Family heavily invested in the outcome. It was a different mindset here. Of all ships that *should* be capable of breaking out of the downward spiral, *Galway* might—and still she wouldn't relinquish her station attachments. Family ships wealthier, less desperate, would leave the place. But *Galway* was deeply invested here. And saw Alpha as their best hope.

Maybe it was *Atlas's* influence, the old pusher connection. The smaller pushers, locked to a single route—a pair of stations. Venture had built the Monahans a ship that had, twenty, thirty years ago, the potential to leave the Alpha trade, but they'd been sure of Alpha, they'd been invested in Alpha, and they'd gone back to Alpha's service, not foreseeing (who could have?) Sol's decision to divert resources to *Rights of Man,* mad as that was.

Now Alpha rewarded them with this run. If that was the right word for it.

JR gave a nod to Jen, signifying down the hall, to his quarters, and Jen came. JR walked in, went to the desk, flipped the switch that turned on their equipment that apparently did exceed the ability of Alpha to listen in.

"What's your sense of it?" he asked Jen, taking his habitual chair.

Jen sat down, hands clamped on the chair arms. "They're set on the glory of it. And the profit. And most of all—damn it." Jen's voice shook. "They're damn fools. They love the Strip. They love the stationers. They love their lives back and forth to *three damn stations.*"

"Is that the case with young Ross?" he asked. He didn't think so.

"Hard to say. He's curious about the Beyond . . . real curious. But he loves the old man, really loves him, and the old man's lived his life here. He isn't ready to lay it down. Seems the captain's got this notion the Hinder Stars are where we came from, that the Hinder Stars can civilize Sol, the history's written here, and Sol will finally read it."

"Young Ross said that?"

Jen shook her head. "Mary T did. Longscan, who's going. She's the senior captain's half-sister. I don't know who's the source and who's the influence. Fallan—Fallan says he's always wanted to see Sol. Old *Atlas* never went there. And they're all saying they'll be famous. Is that a reason?"

It was a question. "*Finity* already is famous. *Finity's End* sheds that on all of us, and we benefit enormously from her reputation. We behave with a sense of obligation to that. So I don't begrudge *Galway* her moment, her chance to make the name something to respect. And to make Alpha something again. That's not just a word. That's power. And better Alpha have enough of it to keep Sol at bay."

"And then become just as much trouble as Sol could be."

There were things not in Jen's need-to-know. And they

were getting into that territory. But the edge of it—yes. She should know. And understand the why of things that otherwise might divert her attention.

"Sol's already trouble. They sent Cruz. They didn't build *Rights* as a merchanter. She's differently configured. To move people. And when Sol does get here under their own power, they'll have navigators and technicians that may work out the problems with *Rights*. On that day, the day *Rights* leaves this system, more than Alpha may have a problem."

"You're saying—"

"As a merchanter, it's real short of cargo room—for its size. For transporting EC personnel, however . . ."

Jen's brow furrowed. "Police?"

"EC policy, EC rules, EC enforcement. Pell threw them out, Venture ignores them, but they're more evident at Bryant's. Glory has a few, I hear. Alpha has over seven hundred of them, best number I have. It's employing them to do repairs and carry supply, but their training is in tasers and self-defense. And that ship is capable of moving out several hundred of them at a go. *That* is upsetting. It's a long time since we've even considered anything like an armed force. We worry about it, in the context of Pell and Cyteen, but so far nobody's made a move of that sort. *Rights* is a point of irritation—a problem that's been under perpetual construction, that's created other problems, but as for what it's intended to be and what it *may* be, once they work the kinks out—it's not a remote problem. My own opinion is that if Abrezio loses control—if Cruz becomes the style of governance on Alpha, we'll have that ship to deal with. And maybe its cousins, coming in on *Galway*'s trail. Niall Monahan thinks he can lead Sol and Alpha down a different course, *if* Abrezio stays in power. He's offering to stall it long enough for us—but we've agreed to help Abrezio out, amid our other concerns. We can get him supply he needs, better situation here. Quietly. We don't want to create an impression he has Pell backing; but the impression he has connections—would not be a bad thing. And we just hope *Galway* does everything she hopes to do and your young man comes back to Alpha in good form."

"He's not my young man."

"Isn't he?"

Jen frowned. Decidedly. "I don't want a case made of it. It's hard enough. He doesn't *have* to go. He's only a trainee."

"But he wants to, I take it."

"He's going with Fallan. I imagine Mum is upset, too."

"You'd be right. There are some you don't forget."

A silence. "This is one."

"Wishing you the best, Jenniebug."

She'd been missing two front teeth and had her hair in pigtails when she'd worn that name. Her eyes watered. The tears didn't spill. "Yeah," she said. And got up and hugged him. "You and all of us. Captain, sir."

"Go to bed," he said. "Better sooner than later. You're excused to hit the bar on this one. Just this once. You have jobs to do tomorrow, one of which will be to show up, say goodbye, and not to embarrass anybody. Then we've got the Monahans to see to, who're going to be as upset, and they have everything at stake. So go. Don't get hung over. And make morning call dry-eyed and sober."

"Yessir," she said, and patted his shoulder and walked out, straight and proper.

The next generation, she and Ross Monahan. He had to wonder . . . what would happen to them, to the way of life the Alliance sought to protect. Was it too little, too late?

Defense was something people talked about in the Beyond—the Beta Incident still influenced decisions in places of power. Military wasn't a forgotten word, but it was a word from history, not current events, right along with war, and border and country, not applicable. There were the routes, the solar systems, the planets, but *territory* was flexible, the only sure thing, the exterior of a station or a planet's atmosphere. Everything moved at velocities and on vectors that had to be known and figured for, but a border? Where, precisely, was that? And none of those stations, none of the planets, could truly exist on their own. One station's excess was another station's need, right up the chain of supply, their very existence dependent on their ties with merchanters, the willingness of merchanters to visit that port.

The alliance they were forming was dangerously new and untested. They *hadn't* trusted the Alpha merchanters enough yet to tell them all of it, but what Niall Monahan proposed to do was *exactly* what the core of the alliance was preparing to do, should the stations challenge their charter—go invisible, go silent, and wait. There were places in the dark where they were building up supply, places that would signal back if you flashed the right signal. He'd talked about teeth in the agreements; and there were teeth—the ability to stop trade. To embargo.

But with Sol's arrival imminent, with the likelihood that Sol would arrive with its own ships in multiple, not Family nor anything approximating it—there would be a challenge. If those ships arrived to carry blue-coats, they were one kind of problem . . . primarily to the stations. If they arrived cargo-based, they were another . . . to the merchanters.

And it was a serious question exactly what Sol was going to send.

If it was a science and exploratory mission, to establish links to Alpha—good. In that scenario, Alpha gained importance as a crossover point, a transition between Sol's way and everybody else's. They could deal with that and even welcome it—if it signaled a new attitude and a willingness to listen. Unfortunately, no one really believed that would happen. There had never been a period of non-contact: there'd been lag in their communications, with Sol always half a decade or more out of date on its information. Sol knew there was a network of stations, they knew there was trade, they knew human beings had spread out and multiplied—as Sol had spread through its own solar system and established commercial and scientific enterprises.

They knew at least that much. They knew how it worked . . . and had still ordered a massive and economically ruinous ship-build at Alpha, a ship designed to carry people, and sending personnel to take charge of the enforcement arm of Alpha's Earth Company offices—sending Cruz, in fact, as well as a fair number of young, at the time, ECE recruits.

Was Cruz a wild card, gone far off Sol's instructions?

Somehow, he doubted it. Sol had completely changed the nature of the pusher-loads that had used to keep Alpha comfortable. Everything was the ship-build. The station suffered, but there were jobs in the build; and jobs in the ranks of the blue-coats—jobs that earned station credit . . . but with nowhere to spend it. Trade suffered, and Bryant's became much more closely linked, commercially, with Venture and Pell: they'd seen it as they came down the string that led here. One ship from Alpha currently at Bryant's and no further, by the schedule boards; nothing from Bryant's coming here currently, four ships stalled here, one in disrepair, three on hold because the presence of four Beyonder ships scared the locals . . . there'd been a lot wrong here when they'd come in. There'd been no reason *Santiago* and *Qarib* and *Galway* couldn't undock and go— but all processes had frozen. *Santiago* was half-loaded. *Qarib* was awaiting fueling. *Firenze* wasn't fit to move. *Galway* was ready to go—but had sat under hold.

Was it Abrezio who had held them fast? Or had Cruz? Or was it the unease of the whole station, the stationer population that stayed well out of view?

It was Abrezio who had sent the coordinates on to Sol— independent of Cruz. A last ditch attempt, perhaps, to win out over the EC's golden boy.

A lot was going on here. A lot *would* go on when Sol made its appearance here. And given all evidence they'd seen in Cruz and in Hewitt—it wasn't going to be a science mission. It was going to be an arm of the corporation that had issued orders and demanded compliance and accounting, and that viewed itself as the center of human civilization, making decisions for the star stations because they were, well, *Earth*.

And their notions of ownership and rule were going to come smack up against stations and merchanters who had been making their own decisions out here for centuries because they were, well, *separate*. And liked it that way.

One of the biggest risks in Sol's intervention was the tendency of Sol to issue orders before it really had a thorough understanding of what it was dealing with. Some committee on Sol Station met and voted, and there they were. There they *would* be, once the time-lag was down under a year. Bringing Sol real-time with human affairs was assuming that Sol would accept advice.

God. It was going to be a mess.

Tomorrow . . .

He'd given his orders. He wanted to get moving again, leave Alpha and carry what they now knew to Pell and beyond.

But they had to delay to deal with whatever fell out with Abrezio and Cruz—not a happy prospect, once the news broke; and they were obliged to take care of the Monahans left on the Strip, which—God knew—was going to be messy.

He'd distributed problems to the other captains, John, Madison, and Mum—Madison was going to be near the mast-entry to assure there was no difficulty; John was going to be at Rosie's tomorrow after *Galway* launched; and Mum was going to troubleshoot whatever came up.

Himself, he was going to be at Critical Mass, where people could find him at need.

Chapter 13   Section ii

Math. Math. And math. Ross lay abed staring at the ceiling, and then not seeing it at all. Seeing *Galway*'s boards, and going through the checks in his head, sequences, routine and otherwise. He'd shadow the boards, sometimes Fallan, sometimes Ashlan, whichever was on at the moment. In long ops sessions, the boards cycled. The live board ran the operation, the other and the number three served as check on the main, but the computer shunted actual control in a set rotation, twenty minutes on, then rest twenty. He sometimes got main when it was down to routine, and then Fallan or Ashlan was checking his moves, and he was, at such times, sweating, and trying never to have them *have* to override him.

Nav took over from Helm on jumps. Helm initiated, but Nav finished the operation. And he was a long, long way from taking the handoff.

But things could happen. People were fragile. And the knack of coming out of the fog of jump knowing what you'd set yourself to know, mentally fit to snatch control from the computer and deal with it if there was a problem—he was a long, long way from that. He wasn't wholly sure he could do it, but Niall had slid him in when Abel had broken down, had a seizure right at his post, and him only thirty-one ship-years.

He'd liked Abel. Funny. Likeable. And dead at thirty-one, for reasons, their medic said, that he'd been hyping himself on drugs to come up from the drug that tranked you down for jump.

Why do a thing like that? Because Abel didn't want to fail. And his team kept helping him, saying it didn't matter, they were fast up, and he'd overcome it. It was a sluggish metabolism. Some people were slower than others, but Abel wasn't a washout, give it a while.

Abel had given it something else, God knew where he'd gotten it, or what desperation had made him try it, but Bess swore *she* hadn't prescribed it. Abel had left a physical note, saying the name of the drug, which Bess recognized; and saying he thought it would work, and confessing what he hadn't told anybody, that he was seeing spooks in the jump-sleep, and his nightmare was not coming clear of them, that he was finding it harder and harder to come back . . .

God, that was the last thing he wanted to think about on the eve of undock. He'd really liked Abel. Abel had been the silly one, *and* the buffer between him and the real controls. Fallan had taken it harder than any of them. And that was when Niall had set him to watch Fallan, to stay close to him on Glory Strip—which was where it had happened.

And since then he'd tagged close to Fallan, on Bryant's, and Alpha, and Glory, three years sitting Nav 1.3, and almost, Fallan and the others said, ready to take them through a jump.

Not yet. Damned sure not on this one. You don't have

to go, Fallan had said to him, and he knew it was because
Fallan was kind-hearted and because a trainee Nav 1 was
still not stable enough or practiced enough to do them that
much good.

Except to fend off the spooks and be level-headed and
not have Abel's unlucky ghost sitting fourth in their memories. He was himself, Ross Monahan, and not Abel, and
he could, if nothing else, spell them in the quiet times and
fill a seat that was useless empty, and be one more set of
senses trained on a problem.

Let them go without him? He couldn't. Absolutely not
an option.

And the experience—shadowing the boards on the first-
ever FTL to Sol? He could have free drinks off that story
when he was old as Fallan.

He rehearsed the boards until his head hurt. He packed—
he had stored pictures of Jen; and his pocket com gave
them up to a more permanent storage, a little unit he had
that attached to the wall of his cabin and would display those
pictures in a slideshow any time he wanted. He packed
everything he'd brought off the ship; and a few treasures
going back. He had patches from *Finity's End,* from *Little
Bear, Mumtaz,* and *Nomad,* and Jen had given him a few
Alpha had never seen: *Dublin,* notably, the *second* mega-
ship, a longhauler from the far side of Cyteen, the legend-
ary Reillys. It was a collection he'd built from his junior-junior
years, and it had doubled on this layover. If he sold them,
to real collectors, hell, he'd make a small Strip-side fortune, but they were not for sale. He always carried a few
extra *Galway* patches, in hopes of a trade.

And this time—he wondered if ships at Sol had the custom at all. It'd be something to bring back.

Well, *Galway* patches were going to be beyond popular
when they did get back. God, when they did get back, Jen
would hear, wouldn't she? She'd get the rumor, wherever
she was. And Niall and JR Neihart had talked and might
talk again—it was certain the greatest Pell ship would be
interested in what they could report.

So a meeting with Jen wasn't out of the question. It
might happen within a year of their getting back.

Books. A whole library of stored books, to trade about. Some games. He'd picked up two new ones from shops that hadn't seen major new games in years. It took minds off the deep dark, and God knew, it was going to be the deepest and loneliest dark he'd ever visited, out there where you were sure spooks made the pinging on your hull and scan picked up things you couldn't see twice. He'd thought *Glory* was a lonely run.

Excited, God, yes. Terrified? With every reason. But excited began to win out. It was the chance of a lifetime. Of any number of lifetimes.

And he'd have things to tell Peg. And his mum. And Jen. Things to tell every Monahan who'd had to stay behind and every spacer who hadn't made the trip.

No question.

Chapter 13   Section iii

They'd gotten through the undock party. Abrezio, with the monitors showing a tranquil maindawn on the Strip, had reports on his desk that nothing, absolutely nothing untoward had transpired during maindark, despite the considerable consumption of alcohol. A couple of Firenzes had fallen asleep on a bench, not exactly depravity and crime, had moved on when requested; and another couple had shed clothes and gone at it in a section of Spacer's Rest hallway, ignorant of or ignoring the security cameras.

For an undock party—with the visitors in conspicuous attendance and Rosie's spilling out onto the open Strip—it was astonishingly well-behaved. He'd ordered enforcement to stay clear and leave celebrants able to walk to find their own way, and to politely escort or cart those who couldn't to their ship's sleepover. The gathering had broken up at the scheduled time, the Monahans had gone to their sleepover, the visitors had done the same, and only a ragtag of Gallis and Rodriguezes had stayed up to all hours at the one bar he'd allowed to stay open through the night, the Pearly Gate—a moneymaker on such occasions, and a rotating permission with a little risk of untoward behavior.

Unless one counted some damage to a pool table, it had gone very well, and the Pearly Gate wasn't complaining.

The word had *not* gotten out what *Galway* was really up to. The boards listed Bryant's Star, and the clock was continuing to run for an 1100h departure.

At about 0900h the essential crew would board, power up, and *Galway* would pull out, at which point a hundred plus Monahans who weren't going would pick up their baggage, return to the hotel they'd just vacated, and check back in.

Galway, meanwhile, was going to pull out and quietly take a vector that nobody in ops was going to believe when they saw it.

At *that* point, he could look forward to the personal pleasure of informing Andrew Jackson Cruz that *Galway* was on her way and there wasn't a damned thing Andrew Jackson Cruz could do about it. The message had gone. Any message Cruz sent would look like a whining postscript.

Was Cruz going to be happy with him?

Oh, no. Definitely not.

Was Cruz going to use his actions as an excuse to gain control of the station? To try to make himself the hero and Ben Abrezio the landgrabber? Cruz might try. But the fact that the coordinates existed and were on their way to Sol . . . one way or another . . . and that they now had to deal with Bryant's, Venture, Pell and points beyond regarding that imminent arrival—threw the matter into a realm of politics in which Cruz had no credentials, and not even a mandate from Sol. And that, if it did come in the form of EC reps on the return trip . . . would arrive far too late.

Because a hundred and more people left on the dock were not going to keep the secret, and if all of them didn't know, those that did would spill it before the day was done. Once it was out, every crew on the Strip would hear it, and

word would get back to every star-station in succession, a
wavefront agitating every political situation on every station as far as ships had ever gone.

Sol was coming. Maybe not tomorrow, but soon.

It was going to be an interesting evening on the Strip
and in the ordinary corridors and meeting-spaces of the
station. Elation. Apprehension. Doubt. All those things.

Abrezio was planning on a double shift. He might be in
his office through the night, but he was set up to issue orders nicely drawn up, to keep enforcement on the Strip to
a minimum presence, to have the bars open and a discount
on drinks. It was going to be a celebration. The hangover
might come in a day or so when they had to take sober
thought and hold some meetings.

He had a little confidence that JR Neihart was going to
have the Monahans on his hands, and that he *was* going to
keep his word and accept the responsibility—he had no
doubt that he was going to have Neihart arriving at his office before tomorrow maindark, and that there were going
to be demands for the coordinates, data that would be
handed to Niall on his way through the hatch and not before.

He had been asking himself about that one ever since
his bargain with Niall Monahan.

Question was, a big question, did he assume that JR
Neihart *would* be surprised when the majority of *Galway*
crew was left on the Strip? Certainly when *Galway* took
out in a Sol-ward vector, the personnel who'd stayed on
Finity's End despite the rules were going to notice that
fact. Probably there were personnel aboard the three other
ships that would likewise observe it.

But had Niall Monahan already told him? Would Niall
leave his people here without *knowing* he had the support
of this new organization? In Niall's place, he'd be worried
about losing that support, if Neihart could claim it was
made under false pretenses. And if he were Neihart, he'd
arrange some means of getting those coordinates, perhaps
in a coded message prior to *Galways's* jump, as part of the
deal.

So assuming Neihart would know, one way or another,

before he could call him into the office for a meeting . . .
assuming there was a fairly good chance Niall Monahan
would transmit those coordinates to Neihart before leaving the system . . . assuming all that, should he call Neihart
in, explain everything, give him the coordinates as an act
of good faith, if nothing else?

It was a question: How powerful was this organization
of Neihart's and was it or was it not somehow in league
with Pell? Either way, what could Neihart do with them,
other than spread them throughout the Beyond? And that
would be a footnote to the knowledge that they existed at
all. Risk his expensive ship and overjump *Galway* to test
them himself? To what purpose? The EC wasn't about to
deal with a Pell ship directly.

So . . . say he would give the numbers to Neihart, send
them to Pell with his blessing, in effect, could he, in turn,
get Neihart to help broker a peaceful negotiation with the
Konstantins? God knew the man had the skills. If he was
truthful in his aims to help the merchanters and keep all
the stations alive . . .

What, exactly, was *wrong* with easing the contact between Sol and Pell?

Well, a lot of things. Pell would play politics—how not?—
and Sol would counter. Being a broker between the two, he'd
deal with the unhappiness of one or the other. Probably
both. But upsetting Sol by an action Sol hadn't approved was
not a fine prospect either.

And yet, when Sol got into records here, Sol would find
out he and his predecessors had made unapproved decisions every day of every year. Welcome to reality, he'd
say . . . provided he could greet those incoming officials
with a healthy station and profitable trade system.

So: Pell was going to hear. And one thing you could say
about the Konstantins—they were not a committee, they
didn't answer to one, and they made decisions that stuck.

Right now—he'd be acting in his own arena. And while
Cruz could complain, events were bound to run under
their own power until Sol *could* receive *Galway* and organize an expedition . . . a number of fact-finders traveling on
Galway, if they had any sense, to be told in great detail

during a long voyage and a layover that there was a great
deal wrong with Andy Cruz.

But they weren't guaranteed to believe what they heard.
Cruz *came* from Sol. Cruz had been sent here, with a mission, by people backing him. People with their own notions
of what needed to be done out here.

One way and the other, JR Neihart was going to know
and one way and the other, Andy Cruz was going to find a
way to tattle-tale to Sol when they got here that the stationmaster had been colluding with the enemy. Hell, what *was*
the difference, anyway, whether or not he told Neihart?
Cruz had never shown any affection for the truth, and Cruz
already accused him of said collusion. Were it not for the
evidence time-stamped into official records, Cruz would
say anything that advantaged him and disadvantaged his
enemies . . .

Among whom Abrezio numbered himself—quite gladly
lately.

If it were his fate alone, he wouldn't hesitate a moment.
He'd call in JR Neihart, read him the plain facts of the case
he would see in a few hours—and give Captain Neihart the
hint that if Pell *were* to make a gesture in the way of support for Alpha, that Alpha might reciprocate—that Alpha
might soon become a good ally to have, in a universe again
including Sol.

But—he had Callie to think of. His personal savings
were small. A generous pension was what he'd counted on,
and that came in doubt in a situation where Sol decided it
wasn't happy. So many, many things could happen for reasons he couldn't predict or affect.

He owed Callie. It was going to be a hellish year of charges
and coun023charges in the administration—building up to, he
hoped, a relatively realtime contact with Sol, maybe even
within the year. And damned if the support of the Alpha
ships, and their fledgling Alliance, wasn't going to be key to
making that contact favor *him*.

Callie would understand. Hell, Callie would tell him to
stop thinking about her and do what was *right*. And *right*
for Alpha . . . was to call Neihart in the instant *Galway*
jumped . . . and come clean.

And then, in the little interlude before it all started, he'd take Callie out to her favorite restaurant, explain everything to her . . . then go home and really sleep for the first time since the first visitor had docked.

Chapter 13   Section iv

Checkout at the Fortune was cleared: Owen had checked everybody out, paid the bills, deactivated the station account, every action routine for a departure.

Everybody left the hotel, slung duffles onto the trundling flatbed that moved ahead of them and, by custom, cleared the path for walkers. They were all turned out, from minders carrying the two babies, and minders walking with the small cluster of youngsters, to elderly Jennet, Ennis, and Cam, who rode a little transport, too old to hike the distance to the mast entry, midway down the strip.

They couldn't say goodbye, not even whisper it to close kin: they'd celebrated the undock last maindark, and those who knew, the most of the Monahans, were doing their best to do everything ordinary. Ross had his duffle, had his personal jump-packet in his jacket inner pocket, where there was no misplacing it, and he strode along with first shift, with the nav team, with Fallan and Ashlan. Ordinarily it *was* a cheerful procession, everybody already focused on their next port, on a different experience, old friends to meet there, if ships moved in their ordinary way.

This was another sort of thing. The kids weren't going to get an inkling until most of the Family began collecting their duffles to hike *back* to wherever Owen got them lodging—likely right back at the Fortune, while the Fortune was going to be in the process of changing the sheets.

And while word was flying up and down the Strip that everything, everywhere had changed.

He was excited. And scared as hell.

Other people on their own business, headed up or down the Strip, gave cheerful waves, sometimes called out a name, and they waved back, not expected to stop. When a Family headed for the mast, there could be no stragglers, no exceptions. He waved at certain hails—a great number came from Rosie's frontage, where staff turned out, even Rosie himself.

There were occasional outsiders along the way, who also waved in the ordinary fashion. Some called out in their own ship-speak, friendly-sounding, so Monahans answered back in their own—"See you again!" That was a lucky thing to say. And spacers turned incredibly superstitious on setting out—favorite socks, lucky bracelets—he spotted them on cousins who weren't going. The Monahans were calling up all the luck they owned and laying it on the shoulders of first shift, he read that message with no trouble. Peg had her great-great-gran's rosary in her jacket on every undock, and he had no doubt she had it now, and might be "telling the beads," as she called it, in her pocket. He hoped she would. They might be needing a miracle. All along there'd been some special people waiting for a last goodbye; but Jen hadn't been among them; and it wasn't Jen's style, chasing after somebody who then had to hurry to catch up. He'd hoped a little, and dreaded seeing her, because if there was a moment that he still could stall out and lose his resolve, it might be seeing her and having to say goodbye all over again.

But he wouldn't buckle in front of Jen, either. He was resolved on that.

And at last there were the doors to the masts, clear doors, a temperature barrier and a legal barrier and a crowd barrier, not the real division, yet, but final enough. They opened and they went inside, where another barrier screened the working offices—which usually were lighted.

Not today. *Office Closed* was lit, along with instructions for emergencies. Only one stationer administrative type was waiting there, a youngish man in a suit and long coat, the sort stationers wore in cold areas. He offered a hand to Niall, then took an envelope from his pocket and gave it to him, saying something that, in the noise of the heaters and a nearby working lift, Ross missed hearing.

Is that it? Ross wondered. Is that the coordinates?

Niall shook the man's hand, the man went back to the doors, and Niall handed the envelope to Fallan.

"Hmm," Fallan said, breaking the seal, and opened it on the spot, while Niall waited. Fallan looked at it, and everything except the fans fell quiet, the lift fell silent, and everybody was fixed on the envelope. It was a piece of paper, of all things. Not a chip, but a piece of paper.

Fallan nodded, and passed the paper to Ashlan. Who looked at it and passed it to Ross.

Ross looked at it in his turn, took in the coordinates and vector calculations, the mathematical snapshot of the gravity wells and their relation to Sol and Alpha. In his mental map, he tried to make three new territories stick fast and make sense all at once, with Fallan's accuracy. He was Nav, at least trainee Nav. The data halfway clicked, given he'd never seen those numbers before. The vector out of here was something he'd never seen. The destination . . . God, he knew Sol, just because it was tradition; he'd read the pusher charts, because that was where instruction started. But in the route—they were going somewhere slightly off from the pusher route, playing tag with a never-visited point of mass that *had* to haul them down for them to exit hyperspace, a point of mass estimated, but never clearly seen.

"Going to be interesting," Fallan said. "But yes. Doable."

How did you handle the relative motion? Enter at distance was his guess. If the mass was enough. For two skips he stopped being scared of the general situation and started being marginally scared about something far more concrete, like four percent of a solar mass with a relative motion he'd really prefer be much closer to Alpha's.

"Interesting," Ashlan called it.

"Yeah," was Fallan's word for it.

"So we're a yes," Niall said.

"We can do it," Fallan said.

"Then let's go," Niall said. "First shift to the lifts."

"See you," somebody said, and people hugged each other, who were second shift. Second shift's Nav 1 hugged Ashlan, and patted Fallan on the shoulder, and Helm 1's half brother hugged him. Someone grabbed Ross's hand and squeezed it, but he wasn't sure who, because a number of cousins were patting him on the back and wishing him good luck.

He went. Niall was going, and it was just his job to stay with Fallan, that was the only mission Niall had handed him when he'd joined the shift. Stay with Fallan, who was old, and fragile, and who might not make a really rough trip, in which case, God help them. But if you were first into a jump-point, Fallan's hand was the one you wanted pushing the buttons.

Into the lift. It was a pared-down first shift that went with Niall, and support staff crowded in, all of them in one lift car. Niall punched buttons, machinery slammed and hummed into operation, and they moved, going up, so far as the human brain interpreted it.

So far as any observer up in ops might know, it was routine, first shift going up to do what first shift always did: open the hatch, start the warmup, flip switches, check the systems, and generally get processes in motion that could be controlled from the bridge. They did keep a human-habitable level of heat going, an automatic shunting of solar heat here and there to do useful work. One of the steps for an immediate departure was to fold that array down and tuck it in to protect it. Engineering's job, that, along with the checks and tests.

And once they made that point in the checklist, ordinarily, they'd open the lock, exhale warmed air into the boarding tube, and start the boarding of the rest of them who had jobs to do, the two idle shifts pitching in to assist the kids and the minders and the senior-seniors. Ordinarily when they did move out of lock, people would be huddling together in the comfortable warm lounges for a cup of something hot, and they'd move out gently on nothing more than steam, a little waste water from the lines, and then, having moved free of the station—they'd get everybody settled and put a little push on for an hour or so. Ordinarily they'd run a day or two, maybe more, laze along doing housekeeping, getting things in order, attending personal matters and generally getting their mindset back into ops, having had their blowout stationside—and not being in a hurry, comparatively, against the distance they were about to travel. Do it right, was the general mantra.

Only this time they were backing out and turning their bow to a vector only pusher-ships used, and a station admin with its own troubles was about to admit what it had done and *why* most of the Monahans were still on station.

Galway was going to push back, swing round, and run like a bat out of hell, that was Niall's word, passed to first shift moments before they left the Fortune. They'd do a hard accel, get the hell away from the solar mass, and go far and fast, uncatchable, irrevocable, and beyond all argument or threat of retaliation from anybody . . . so the Monahans left behind couldn't be any use as hostages in an argument in Alpha admin. *Finity* was there, *Finity* was a potent argument not to start anything with spacer-folk— but they could at least make it clear they were unstoppable.

Easier on themselves as well. Less time to sweat and worry. Ross was for it. He told himself he was. He was determined not to shiver. But he was damned scared, trying not to think too far ahead, trying not to have any doubts, but his mind kept skittering this way and that into things they had to do immediately, the things *he* had to do, and the thought of Jen, and Sol, and Peg, and the sendoff in Rosie's . . .

Focus, he said to himself, and jammed his hands into his pockets as they went—"up" being defined only by the direction the lift moved: the lift decks were gimballed, an amenity. At Glory, they weren't, and the masts were only stubs. Here, they extended considerably.

And *Galway* was docked a far distance out. Somebody in control could still push a button, stall them out. The lift trip seemed to take forever. *Was* the G-force less than normal?

He gave a twitch, hadn't intended to. It was almost a shiver.

"You all right?" Fallan asked.

"Yeah. Fine. I'm fine."

"Not too late. We can make it with two."

"I'm fine. Intent on learning something this trip."

"Last chance," Fallan said, squeezing his shoulder.

"Hell, no," he said.

"Going to be an interesting jump. You see the relative motion?"

"Yeah. Did."

"Tell you something I've told you before, and I'll tell you again before you go, because this mass is going to talk to us."

"You think?"

"My Lisa Marie—she agrees with me. Can't just ride the numbers, friends, and this time I'll prove it to you, 'cause for this one—there ain't no chart."

"I'll be feeling for it," Ashlan said. "You keep telling me, I believe you, and I keep trying."

"No chart to distract you this time, Ash-me-lad. This is the time you'll be searching with every fiber of your being, and with that squee-angled motion that mass has got, you and nav and all will be *feeling* that mass answering to the ship coming in. We'll be writing a blank page. But we'll do it. Anybody scared?"

They laughed. Of course they were. And then Fallan asked, "*You* scared, Ross?"

Ross said. "I'm not ducking out. But damned right I'm scared."

"Scared is smart, coupled with *aware*," Ashlan said.

"He'll do," Fallan said. The lift was starting to slow, close to their berth, and they were starting to float, weighing a little less. "He'll do right well. Might let you shadow me on entry. Hell, I might switch off and leave your board the active one."

"God, no!"

They laughed. They all laughed, except Ross, who'd had that trick played on him once, when he'd *thought* his board had gone live. You never knew, shadowing, when the number one might play that trick on you. But there was a reason there were three sets of hands on every station during jump: the active board, the one that counted; one whose input advised the active board; and one, like Ross's, that simply shadowed. Ross's *didn't* count. It was pretty good. He was getting it. He was close, but, God, the joke shocked him to silence.

"You're all right," Ashlan said, hand on his arm.

"Sure he is," Fallan said, while Ross's heart thumped hard. And right now his hands on the controls would bring up that red pulse in the corner of the screens that advised everybody third nav had a very elevated pulse. There was no hiding. It would do that when they moved out. It would do that for sure when they went for jump—it would undoubtedly do it when they came in. He remembered his first time to sit third-seat, and Fallan's pulse, first of the four dots, had been a nice steady green, easy as a walk down the Strip.

They made a chain of linked arms, Ashlan anchoring them all by his grip on a takehold, as the lift car came to a stop.

The door opened to Niall's button-push, and let them out in a metal-and-ceramics chamber a little bigger than the lift car, the far side of which was *Galway*'s hatch. Niall, duffle strap over his shoulder, the safe way to bundle yourself and baggage over, made the crossing without a tumble, just sailed neatly to the hatch, uncapped the switch and opened it up.

Niall first, then Nav's three; and then Scan, Longscan, and Com, Engineering and the rest to follow. It was a point of pride to go over quietly, take a grip and, with the footplate, make a nice long glide to the far wall. It was cold as hell's hinges—exposed skin couldn't take much of it, and people hurried, piling up until the lift was empty and the last in, Second Cook Tess, called out, "Last man!" in a clear soprano. "Shutting the hatch!"

The unmistakable sound followed, ending in a solid thump.

"Hatch is green!" Tess shouted, meaning the inner hatch would respond now, and Niall lost no time. Inner hatch opened and lights went on, bringing life to *Galway*'s passages, and warm air followed, at least warm enough to feel the difference, not warm enough for the ice that had formed on hair and clothes and baggage to melt.

They were in. They were home, a mass of floating, frosted bodies working with fair efficiency to hand each other along, clear the airlock, and get that cold shut out entirely. Last Man passed the inner doors, called out a *safe,* and shut the inner hatch.

Then, still adrift, they had the vents overhead blowing air on them that would melt the rime-frost and help breathing get back under control. Everything passed into routine, the echoing voices, everybody anxious to get to stations and start flipping switches and bringing *Galway* alive again—getting the ring moving was among first things, decoupling from the mast, and getting spin started. Ordinarily that waited for the last boardings, the last of Last Men from a sequence of groups.

Not this time. The inward-bound lift wouldn't be bringing up the others and there would be no wait for the off-shifts and kids and seniors to get to quarters. They used the takeholds to drift, a bundled-up procession, rightwise into the bridge. Everything was cold, much as the quick-heat system was doing to give them warm breezes. The surfaces would frost if you breathed heavily on them. Ross reached his own seat next to Scan 1's, and floated his way into it, pulling the belts across to keep him there—everyone was doing the same, until Niall, centermost of the bridge, used a handhold to right himself to what was approximately a standing position. Doc Jack was there with his aide; Mike the cook with Tess, all with takeholds along the bulkhead.

"Thirty-second warning," Niall said. "Anybody got a problem?"

Nobody said anything. Thirty seconds slipped by and Niall pushed the button.

There wasn't a sound for a moment. Then a couple of thumps, multiple lighter sounds, and they were uncoupled. Gradually, gradually *down* began to assert itself, light as a feather's fall at first, currents of air, and the ears' awareness which way was up. It took a bit. Anything anybody had left unsecured would settle. There were mysterious small sounds as that happened here and there, and bodies began to sink into their seats and cushions began to give.

They had systems checks to go. Boards came live. The shift had a cargomaster—they were loaded, a great deal of it foodstuffs, for Bryant's and Glory, and they were not, Niall's decision, going to jettison anything. It made sense, with the unknown ahead.

Nav boards came live, mostly black, with green print crawling upward, informing them of systems waking up. Ross's said, correctly, that his screen was shadow to 1 and 2. He keyed in.

Keying in jump coordinates was a process. It awaited them getting underway, getting the system up and aware of their true bearings.

It began to feel more like normality, these people, these boards, the process. Things were ticking down to moving the ship. Ross drew a long slow breath and let it go, waiting for data to turn up, waiting for the system to deliver them a precise position. His weight was in his seat, his feet were on the floor, and he was, finally, getting a bit warm.

No few people had gotten up to shed coats and take them back to lockers. Jackets were enough, and there were things to arrange. Ross stood up, took his jump packet out of his inside pocket, put it into the little console slot designed to hold it, and said, "Take your coats?" to Fallan and Ashlan, himself being juniormost.

Ashlan had shed his, and started to hand it over, when an alarmed look came into his eyes, a fixed stare past his shoulder, spinward. "Blue-coats!" he said under his breath. Ross turned to look, and Scan 1 shouted the same as a thunder of footfalls came down the ring toward them, a black and blue cascade of uniforms and armor and *guns,* God help them, arriving on the fragile bridge. There was shouting, there were blue-coats coming in among the banks of consoles, threatening with tasers and batons. Niall put himself in the way of several, and Sam H lit into them from the flank, and they were still coming, maybe thirty of them, with, behind the ranks, God help them, Andrew Cruz.

All that hit in seconds, and the dark tide was past Com and Longscan and coming down on them, pushing and hitting as they went. Chains were out, spacers' quick answer to fools, and Ross hadn't one—hadn't been carrying it into security-sensitive places. All he had was his bare hands, and he grabbed the collar of a blue-coat who shoved him aside, spun him around and gave him an elbow in parting. That—before a baton cracked across his forehead and he hit the deck sideways, full length.

"Dammit," he heard. And was stepped on, tripping a man, a cousin or a blue-coat, he couldn't for the moment see. "They were hiding in the lounge, damn 'em." That was Ashlan's voice above him. Ross tried to get up, got to a knee and found a counter with his elbow, but somebody's hand grabbed his jacket and pulled him back down next to a seat base.

"No," Fallan hissed. "No. Get out of here. Come on!"

Out wasn't possible. They'd cast loose from the station link to start the spin. But, "Move!" Fallan urged him, the both of them, crawling and scrambling at the last as Cruz's voice rang out across the bridge, giving orders, telling them he was taking control of the mission, to stop fighting, and what rest he was too busy to hear—he and Fallan had made it out to the entry corridor, where main lights had gone off, leaving dim glow-light and cold.

"Come on," Fallan said, trying to get to his feet. Ross lifted Fallan up with him, had to catch his own balance more than once.

"Where are we—"

Fallan grabbed his jacket sleeve. "E-chute. Come on."

He threw an arm about Fallan and ran with him to the spotlighted blue arrow on the bulkhead. Fallan pulled up the latched cover, Fallan's fingers flew on the enabling buttons, and Ross looked back to the lighted bridge, beyond the stub wall, where blue uniforms cut off the view.

The trap opened under their feet. He hugged Fallan as they dropped. Airbags cushioned their entry, all about them, crushing them together—it was gauged for one, not two; and he'd not done this since he was a junior-junior, on drills.

He heard the hiss of the interface and braced himself. The inexorable sweep of the ring was going to pick up the pod, jerk them along with it—deliver them outside the ring.

Bang. Bump. And a jolt as it shot them out. He held Fallan close throughout, in bitter, bitter cold, air that burned the lungs, froze what was running on his face.

Bang! went the interface, and they lurched forward and stopped, zero-g again at the outer rim of the personnel ring next to the #3 e-lock and its suit-locker, with wan light, with warm air, triggered by their arrival, blasting at them, hot on one side, beyond cold on the other.

"Here." Fallan snatched something from inside his coat and shoved that into his hand. A paper—*the* paper. "Into the jacket. Get suited up and get out of here. Get to *Finity*. She's right below us, end of the mast. Hell, you can't miss her."

"You can't stay!"

"There's one person *knows* those coordinates," Fallan said, and tapped his own forehead. "I know. And we got us Cruz, don't we? So Abrezio's problem's down by one, and *Cruz* has to treat me right. I'll be the one keepin' Niall's promise, because Cruz's fools can't stop me. *Trust* me," Fallan said darkly. "Some'll be slow comin' out of jump fog. Some'll be sick. We'll take 'em, first jump or second. I'm the one that knows the numbers, and if they go hurtin' any of us, or we can't get control back . . . well, I'm the one that has to put in the coordinates, aren't I? Decimal points are killers. Quick and done with. And even when Sol gets Abrezio's message, Sol won't know if that point is real, then, will they?"

Decimal points. "God, Fallan!"

"We'll take care of 'em. We own all the buttons, don't we? The old girl doesn't respond to strangers. We'll be back—on our terms. And one way or another, *Finity* will get her two years. Minimum. You go, Ross. Tell 'em! They got to know. They *need* to know. Get suited. Now! The blue-boys got to hunt for which chute, but they won't be long. Go!"

He didn't want to. He wanted to put Fallan and that paper into a suit and get him out of reach—at which point things would play out with the information available.

But if Cruz was up there, Cruz might know everything—the coordinates and all. And without Fallan, without his abilities to *feel* space—God knew—

Fallan physically shoved him. Drifting, he fetched up against the e-hatch airlock, and he knew he had no option. He wasn't entitled to pick and choose Fallan's orders. *Two years*, Fallan said. And he had no idea what that meant.

"Go on!" Fallan said.

The area was warming fast: the systems did that; but surfaces burned, they were so cold. Something melted on his forehead and dripped down. He swiped it away and his hand came away dark.

God-damned blue-coat.

He pulled himself into the airlock, turned and backed into the hardsuit, using the low overhead to push down into it—a hundred and more drills, best foot, next foot, best arm, other arm, and let it seal as the helmet settled on. The suit fed air, icy at first, then warm, as the circulation started, and the astringent air filled his lungs on too-fast breaths. Danger there. He took a deep one, let it out slowly to still his nerves as the suit checked its seals. The instant the green light flashed on the HUD, he pulled his arms free of the braces, bent his knees and freed his legs, and tried to turn. He saw Fallan, the old man dead serious, as the door warned of closing.

"Give 'em hell, Fal!" he shouted inside the suit, and maybe the speaker was on, and maybe Fallan heard it. Fallan raised a hand and the door shut between them.

In the next moment—no choice of his own—the outer hatch opened and a jet of air blew him backward out the lock into the uncompromising glare and shadow of the mast itself. He had no orientation for a split second, only the vast expanse of *Galway*'s hull, that he never, ever had seen from any vantage—real, and carbon-spotted, and streaked with sulfur traces, rotating slowly past his view.

With EH-3 blazoned in lights on the hatch—plain and near, with large arrows on either side, blinking in sequence, beacons to the safe harbor. His vision blurred; he blinked it mostly clear, and for a moment almost forgot why he was . . . where he was.

Dammit.

He gave himself a mental shake, then used the jet fixed to his left glove: light jet, to stop the rotation, another to reorient, putting the station rings at his back, and a third to stop. And there farthest out on B-mast, part in shadow, part in sun-glare . . .

Leviathan.

Finity's End.

Go there. Go there. Go *there*. Get help, if help can be had. Something about two years. What did Fallan mean, *Finity* will get her two years? Should he know what that meant? Had Niall said? Had he forgotten? What else had he forgotten?

God . . . his thinking was muddled. He tried not to panic, held tight to that order from Fallan. Focused on that problem with every working neuron. Get to *Finity*. Tell them about Cruz. Give them that paper.

Finity. That monster dead ahead. Get there, sure. A tap of a button, and he'd run right into her. Get aboard? That . . . was a whole other problem.

He could call for help. There was a frequency dedicated to emergencies. *Finity* had crew aboard. *Finity* could hear a call.

But so could people he didn't want to notify. Yeah. That was clear-headed thinking.

Station ops might be on that list. Abrezio might be. They might have been double-crossed up one side and down the other. Or Cruz might have gone rogue. God, he hoped that was so. The whole rest of his family, except for those in the ship behind him, were captives on the station.

So . . . Don't call. Aim . . . for an e-hatch.

His head throbbed. That damned blue-coat baton had whacked him a good one. His nose was bubbling: he didn't remember that blow. He sniffed it back, then had to sneeze and that was the worst thing to do. The faceplate was all dark-spotted, and his eyes were blurring, gummy with the tiny drops of free-floating blood. He couldn't damnwell *see* what he *had* to see, the detail on *Finity's* hull, those all-important cycling arrows.

He squeezed his eyes shut, wiggling them around, trying to clear them, waiting for the suit's built-in system to clean the faceplate, trying even harder to sort a mind starting to wander.

Right now, he was drifting slowly in the right direction, but it was a long, long way for a suit-jet. He knew that much. He'd never practiced suit-drill in hard vacuum, let alone in the light of a cranky red sun.

No panic. No. He was tending in the right direction, he was aimed at one very big target. Problem was, that target had a very tiny bullseye. Little corrections now saved big expense of suit propulsion later. He just had to figure where the corresponding e-hatch was in that huge, huge expanse of dark metal, and hope to God *Finity* hadn't taken security measures since the blue-coats' trial of it, and hadn't, God save him, turned off those guide arrows.

Shadow on his glove became blinding ruddy glare. He was confused for a moment, then realized something had moved that had been shadowing him, and that something was *Galway,* moving out away from the mast.

Galway. Fallan. Niall and Ashlan and Mary T and all the others. *Galway* was moving.

With goddamn Andy Cruz calling the shots.

Nose clogged again. He choked, and that made the situation worse. Faceplate clearing wasn't working. He *wanted* to turn and see what was happening over his head, but it cost the little he had from the hand-jet, and he daren't. Sun-glare was all, likely, and the faceplate was cleared in streaks—likely he'd run the risk and still not see a damn thing.

Galway was rotating on her axis, was what. Getting underway. She'd put the big jets on, soon as she'd reoriented.

She was going. Nobody could stop her. Nobody from outside. And the Monahans inside would be depending on that single Monahan outside to get that message to . . . someone.

JR Neihart. Get it to JR. Tell him they'd been betrayed. Warn him. He'll take care of the Family.

Somehow. Between half-choking on his own blood, with his eyes filming and the mask blurring, that *somehow* was growing scarily hard. At the rate he was moving, he might not get to *Finity* in time.

He risked a small boost, toward where he hoped the hatch would be, and in desperation, when he still couldn't find it, he tried a call . . . Abrezio be damned. "*Finity*-com, this is Ross Monahan, outside the hull, needing help. Over."

First call he made with some hope. Second, third, fourth and on—with diminishing belief anybody heard him. He told the suit to change frequency, and deliberately called the station. "Alpha Maintenance, this is Ross Monahan, outside the hull, got an emergency. Over."

Repeated calls got nothing. Alpha's sun, Barnard's Star, cranky old bastard, could be interfering. He tried a third frequency, universal emergency.

Nothing.

The sunglare was on him full now. His suit was pumping coolant to his back, and he had nothing but the immense hull of *Finity's End* in front of him, red-lit by the star, and growing slowly, slowly larger. There was a tiny shadow on it. His shadow, he realized, through the blur. That was how far he had to go.

Undock was complete. *Galway* was moving out. Abrezio watched the event in his office, courtesy of ops channel 1, which, given the fact no Alpha ship had moved this month, was going out to all the screens. It looked like a return to normalcy on Alpha.

A reason to celebrate.

There was an old proverb about calm before a storm. And they were having that. The lift had only delivered a few of the Monahans to the upper mast. The majority would be starting back soon—with the *early* departure of their ship displayed up and down the Strip. They'd be walking back with their baggage, and checking back into the hotel they'd just checked out of, and probably no few of them headed for their bar to talk about it.

On the screen, *Galway* continued its backward push.

The Monahans were going to be drawing attention and questions all along that path. And they would be clear to explain what ops would not yet have figured, that *Galway* was on a course other than the one ops had intended.

Cruz would come storming in on that information front, he had no doubt at all.

He actually looked forward to that.

Slow. Slow. No waste of propellant, no desire for impact
with that massive and uneven hull. Visibility was worse.
Everything blurred. All the exterior lights on the ship were
nothing but fuzzy points in Barnard's direct and ruddy
glare. But there ought to be paint along with the lights.
Arrows, to guide an EVA gone bad to a point of safety and
rescue.

His own shadow had arms and legs now, a shape made
irregular by the troughs in *Finity*'s hull, the projections
folded, tucked out of the way for docking. Craft needed
occasionally to move about on inspection or repair.

Suddenly, his shadow . . . dived, sharply warped by
something sticking out. He wasn't sure of it, in the hazed
faceplate, but to the side, about a quarter of the way across
the blurred faceplate, there was something. He tried to
angle his whole body to bring that area to one of the clearer
spots on the faceplate, near the edge. His eyes were tending to jerk, strain of trying to focus, trying to scan everything through the haze—that and outright terror of trying
not to miss, of having chancy old Barnard's misbehave, of
thinking about what was happening behind his back, up
above him—*Galway* pulling out with God knew what hand
on the controls.

Damn Cruz. Damn them all. Abrezio might have screwed
them. Have told Cruz. Lied to them. Set everything up.

Or Abrezio himself was screwed. And Cruz might *have*
the coordinates, which would screw Fallan's plan.

He couldn't think about that. Couldn't wonder what
was going on on the ship, or what that *plan* was. Two years
didn't matter, only right now. One job. He had one simple
job. Hit the surface of a ship that could practically swallow *Galway* whole, hit it soft enough *not* to bounce off.

He'd need enough propellant to adjust trajectory: contact the surface at an obtuse angle, minimize the force of impact.

He remembered that from training.

And handholds. He needed to find a handhold. Surface should be covered with them.

Find a handhold. And crawl over that surface, trying not to push himself off it, with hands grown increasingly numb, for reasons he dared not ask. Try not to push off, not to use his propellant. Not to miss a man-sized hatch and not to lose his nerve and break down out here.

Beyond *Finity*—there was nothing. Top of the mast, bottom of the mast, no difference out here, just . . . the end of everything. There was ahead of his trajectory, *Finity's End,* and behind, Alpha. Beyond *Finity's* hull was a whole lot of black. Deep black. Forever black.

Couldn't think of that. His half-turn risked losing his orientation to the hull. He got it back, slowly, carefully.

That projection could be a streak on his faceplate. There were a dozen film streaks that changed location and opacity every time the clearing mechanism tried to handle the problem. He didn't *want* to know why it was having so much trouble. He could use propellant and set the most critical course in his life toward that place on the side of the hull. Using it now—used least. If he waited, it might use it down to the last and still not get there.

Damn. He couldn't breathe without breathing down bubbles of whatever-it-was, couldn't get a firm fix on the target, and if he coughed or jerked while he was using the hand-jet, he could throw himself on a trajectory there was no returning from. He had to make a decision, whether it was even there. And what it was.

He was close enough now. If that was the e-hatch, he should see the lights. Or the paint. But there was nothing, only that strange warp of his shadow. Except . . . a memory. A piece of information. The customs inspectors. A utility pusher. Had it damaged something? Drifted up against the hull? Was it maybe *obscuring* the very lights he hoped to find?

Was it *that place* on the hull?

It was at least a place, that projection. It was something he could get hold of. Barring some hiccup from Barnard's Star, a wave of radiation that would cook him despite the suit's insulation, he could last out here a while. Maybe work his way toward a *second* bet, the e-hatch on the mast itself, the location of which was beside every docking port.

He committed. Fired the hand-jet—

And choked and coughed.

Dammit. His greatest fear. He cut the jet off. Fast. And only hoped he'd aimed anything near right. He struggled to see his direction, worried about his speed. If he bumped the hull too hard, with nothing to grab, he'd rebound. Equal and opposite.

He was going faster than he liked. He tried to estimate the lineup with the side of the hull. Still couldn't damned well *see.*

Couldn't see. Couldn't feel his hands. Couldn't swallow, couldn't breathe worth a damn—Didn't want to think what he'd done to himself with that convulsive cough.

But he was still going in the right direction.

Chapter 14   Section iii

It was an uncommon stir on the Strip—the Monahans, together, walking back, carrying their own duffles, the stronger carrying them for the weaker.

Abrezio wasn't surprised at all. He wasn't surprised when the calls began. It was time to release the story to the station feed, rather than let rumor carry it.

He was about to do that—had his finger on the button when his secretary came to the door and laid a physical message on his desk.

It had the *Rights of Man* logo on it. Cruz's signature in facsimile above it, in blue ink, above his name in type.

He unfolded it. It said:

In my capacity as director of the Rights of Man *project, I have commandeered the ship* Galway. *I am on my way to Sol at this hour to personally ensure delivery of the coordinates to the proper authority. Having tracked your secret dealings with the Monahans and the Neiharts, I have every reason to believe that Pell will have advance notice and possibly its agents have the data. Your loyalties have become increasingly suspect, constituting more than sufficient justification for my current actions. I will definitely be reporting that matter, and an assortment of other actions not to your credit.*

Depend on it.

[signed] Andrew J. Cruz

Chapter 14   Section iv

Coming to it, coming to it. The shape *was* the lit side of the utility pusher, and he was going to hit it too fast. It was possible it was just drifting there, not clamped, and hitting it could send it off in one direction and him in another and *neither* in toward the hull.

Worst time for a coughing fit. But another one happened. Ross struggled to suppress it, which only made it worse, and when it finally quit, he couldn't see a damn thing. The cleaner made a pass and gave him a single thin streak of blurred vision.

He saw a bar of some kind. More than just a handhold.

He gave the hand-jet a little burst, aiming for that bar, whatever it was. *Finity.* The abandoned pusher . . . at this point, he didn't damnwell care.

Going too fast.

Dammit!

He put out both hands, blind, and hoped not to rebound.

Contact. He *was* rebounding. A moment of panic . . . then his right elbow caught, stopping him cold, and he wrapped that bar with both arms, hugging it close, gasping for breath as another coughing fit happened. When it was over, he just held there, eyes closed, giving the cleaner a chance to work.

The slit of vision he finally got showed metal, showed a white patch, part of an arrow, the universal symbol for rescue, and he handed his way along the antenna, or rail, whatever it was, to reach the area outlined in white.

Another cough, and even that slit disappeared.

He brushed his hand blindly, felt another bar, a handhold. He pulled himself to it, searched again, and found a depression. At the center was a latch. *The* latch. His chest tightened. Relief, he thought. He hooked his feet in the universal clamps, braced his other arm with the handhold, and pulled.

The area sank inward, slid aside. He felt for a bar that ought to be there, and found it. Pulled. Light flooded the far side of the faceplate.

He hauled himself toward that light, shaking in every limb, no help to his coordination. He tried the suit com again.

"Help. E-hatch. I need help." Not the most coherent message. So hoarse he hardly knew his own voice. "Anybody? I'm inside *Finity's End* e-hatch. I need help."

A red light, just a brighter glow in the general blur, started to blink in three-pattern. The hatch was going to shut.

That was all right. He was pretty certain he had all of him inside. He reached for the lighted button and shoved it with the palm of his glove, still holding onto the handgrip, drifting, otherwise. He coughed. Choked. Things were happening now that he couldn't affect. The hatch had shut. The red light had stopped and the blinker was blue now. Lock was cycling.

Suddenly it was green. He thought maybe he'd been out

for a moment. He wasn't sure. But the faceplate was clearer. Vague shapes appeared. A single small hole of clarity showed a hatch identical to the one he'd left behind.

Then the inner hatch opened, and a man in work blues was there, looking at him, pulling him in by the arm, both of them drifting.

The man said something. He couldn't hear it. "Mike on," he said, and the suit produced the blessed, wonderful sound of a human voice saying, "Where'd you come from, fellow?"

"*Galway*," he said. "Monahan." He choked, another coughing fit, fought for breath. God, had he made it here just to die? He tried to say, thought he shouted: "Cruz is aboard."

"Passed out, maybe," he heard, and: "Faceplate's a mess. Get him into the warm and let's get him out of that rig."

"Cruz," he said again, on a liquid breath. He wasn't sure if they heard him. He thought, dimly, that they hadn't.

They towed him through the inner hatch, and he had the drifting, streaked view of an overhead light, a wall, bodies around him. Somebody steadied him, and somebody worked with his suit to get the helmet up and back.

He saw light and faces then. "Get a towel," somebody said. "Hell, get a towel."

Dark beads were floating around him, escaped from him, from the helmet, he wasn't sure. "Catch that," somebody said. "Here. It's mostly clean."

They applied pressure to his forehead. It hurt. Felt raw.

"Cruz," he said, clear as he could manage. "Andrew Cruz got aboard."

"Aboard *Galway*? You Galway, kid?" And to the side: "What's it say on the suit?"

"Yes," he said. "*Galway*'s outbound. To Sol."

"Good lovin' God," one said. "Call JR."

"Yes," he said, trying to nod his head. "Call. Help. Tell JR . . ."

Somebody left, sailing off elsewhere.

"Are you bleeding anywhere else?" one face asked him.

"Dunno," he said at first. Then, as he thought back: "No."

"He's been breathing it into his lungs," somebody else said. Female voice. "Get him out of that."

"JR," he said, fighting to hold the thought, as another coughing fit threatened. "Got a message for the captain."

"Call's going out." Sam was the name on his work blues, and he held the towel to Ross's mouth until the fit was over. "Easy, kid. Easy."

Hands worked to get him out of the hard-suit, piece by piece disassembly, no automation here, wherever "here" was.

Ross shut his eyes a moment and mustered the sense to say, "I've got the numbers. Nav 1 gave me the numbers." He had an arm and chest free. He patted his jacket, felt the presence of the paper, the paper on which so much depended. "Got it. Got to tell—"

"That's happening right now," Sam said. "Come on, just leave that rig." And as the cloth on his forehead lifted: "Damn. That's clear to the bone. Let's get him up to the offices and get some gel on it. Needs a medic, soonest."

Chapter 14   Section v

Galway was moving out, hard burn, and the first cluster of Monahans was back on the Strip, calling for a transport for their senior-seniors and youngests.

And answering questions. Why? What had happened?

And the simple answer they gave was, in some instances, cheerfully, in high spirits, "They're goin' to Ireland," and in others simply, "First shift's going to Sol. They got the numbers."

Word of that flew by runner and pocket com, like a fire loose on the Strip.

JR's com had messages backed up from *Little Bear,*

Mumtaz, Nomad, Santiago, Firenze, and *Qarib.* But the one from *Finity's End,* all numbers, prioritized its way in.

The codes said major trouble, *Galway,* and security emergency. Send crew.

Damn. No idea what that was.

"Fletch," he sent the call out. "Go to the mast. Code red. Scramble ten."

Then he called Abrezio's office.

Chapter 14   Section vi

"Captain Neihart is on one," Ames said, regarding the call.

Abrezio sat at his desk, staring at the wall, thinking about the bottle of Scotch in the cabinet and telling himself recourse to it was the stupidest response he could make.

There was flatly nothing—nothing—to do, except to try to minimize the shock to Alpha's two constituencies, to keep everybody calm, assuring them it was a known situation and they were working on it.

He'd had calls from ops, calls from scheduling, upset that *Galway* was not observing the schedule. But news was already loose on the Strip, the happy version, that didn't involve Andy Cruz. That was also the version that was hitting the stationer channels so far as he was able to tell.

But Neihart calling—Neihart having his own observers much nearer *Galway* than he was—he feared that was not going to be the happy version.

He picked up. "Captain Neihart?"

"Serving notice we've had a code red scramble to the mast. Something Galway's *done has involved our ship, and* Finity *security is en route. Request station not interfere."*

God, had they clipped *Finity* on pull-back? What in hell was going on?

"Acknowledged, Captain. I'll personally see to it. Immediately." Cruz had hijacked *Galway,* done God-knew-what, and *Galway* had the coordinates. Cruz was going to come back as Sol's golden boy, granted anybody ever came back. And when he did . . .

He had maybe a year to hold office. Minimum. A year to find a way to counter whatever mess Cruz brought back with him.

Give the coordinates to JR Neihart? Right now?

He needed to think.

"Give me a call when you know something," he said. "Keep me informed. Please."

Chapter 14   Section vii

Coughing wouldn't stop. Sam had looked it up and said he *should* cough, having breathed in what he had, but every coughing fit made Ross's head throb, and made him lose track of what he needed to say. They'd applied gel to the wound and a gauze wrap, which didn't stop the hurt, but it stopped the blood running down into his eyes. They said it was nasty. They said he needed a scan and a medic, and they said they were sending him down the mast.

"Got to talk to your captain," he protested. "Got to." He didn't know what *Finity* could do, fast as she was. There was no way to stop a ship without killing people. And he wasn't sure he was making sense to anybody, but getting back to the Strip and getting to *Finity* officers—that was at least the right direction.

"Should we clean him up?" the dark man asked.

"Evidence," Sam said. "Whatever happened, for the record, let 'em see. C'mon, Galway, let's get you down to help."

"Jen," he remembered, as they slung arms about him and towed him toward the exit. "Jen Neihart."

"There's four Jens, two Jennies and a Jennifer," one said. "You got a specific?"

"Security Jen."

"Allie's Jen. Little Jen. Yeah, they got a security unit coming. She might be with them."

"Wrap him up. It's colder 'n hell's hinges out there. He's already shocky."

He didn't have a say in it. They put a thermal blanket around him, arms, head, and all, and he just let go and let them, drifting, sheltered in the dark of the blanket, dark as space. In intermittent moments he thought he was there again, but he heard their voices, and reminded himself, past the beat of his pulse in his skull, he was going the right direction.

"All right, Galway, we're going to move now. We're orienting your feet to the lift, got it?"

"Yeah," he said, and with a crash and a thump, the lift engaged, and there was floor under his feet. He wasn't doing well at balance, but they were holding him. He wanted to see where he was, but it was bitter cold, and the blanket actively gave him warmth—it was all right. A long ride, the whole length of the mast, and a sensation of rising.

Until it stopped, and doors opened, and he needed to walk. He tried, and a helpful hand pulled the blanket from around his face so he could see where he was going. Sounds came and went strangely. Echoed in his head. There were moving figures, a blurry wall of them. His eyes were watering.

"Ross!" a voice said, and it *was* Jen, right near him. "God, what happened?"

"Cruz," he said, one word that explained everything. "Got to tell your captain."

Arms came around him, blanket and all, not enough to hold him up, he didn't think, and he was starting to need that. "Coordinates," he said, and the cough took over. He patted his chest, where they rested. "Here."

Another arm took him up, strong and able. "Get him to the Olympian," a man said, "and don't answer questions. Get him on the trolley. Move."

Hadn't used the trolley since he was a junior-junior. They brought him to it, he shed the blanket, grabbed one of the poles, and sat on the edge of it and Jen sat with him, while the others stood, holding to the uprights. It spared him questions—but not stares. The bandage was conspicuous. His jacket was bloody. He was. His hair was sticky with it. But the trolley outpaced onlookers—dizzying ride, it was. He gripped the stanchion hard, let his eyes shut when the dizziness hit.

Concussed, he thought. Very likely. Lot of blood. He didn't know how much had gone into the hardsuit. He was eyes-shut and wobbly as the trolley braked to a halt and Jen urged him to get up. Somebody else said hold the entry and don't let anybody in.

That was all right. He was having trouble enough staying on his feet. A little motion-sick, he thought. And the hall was tilting alarmingly. But there *was* a down, which was better than none at all, and there was air and light, and somebody was saying *Finity's* medics were going to have a look at him.

"JR," he insisted, and Jen tightened her arm about his ribs and said, "First thing. Hold on, Ross, don't pass out on us. We're nearly there."

Chapter 14   Section viii

It was still not too late to scramble a crew to *Finity* and interfere with *Galway*. They were that much faster. They could, a fact they preferred not to give out, considerably overjump another ship in transit.

Was it a risk they wanted to run, on untested coordinates— if they could get the numbers out of Abrezio—and get them accurately?

There were pros and cons, very serious ones on both sides of the balance.

Galway had sent them, evidently, a message, in the

battered person of their first-shift third nav—and seeing him guided into the makeshift office and set into a chair, the question of next moves was in the balance.

"Cruz," was the first thing Ross Monahan said. "Got aboard. Blue-coats." Coughing convulsed him, painfully so, and Jen hurried to get him water. He spilled a deal of it, drank, got the coughing quiet. "Sir. Fallan said—bring you the paper." He handed the cup to Jen, reached into his inner jacket pocket, fished deep, and came up with a paper, crumpled and blood-smeared. "Coordinates. Sir." Then: "Fallan said—you'll get your two years. Whatever that means. He said—they'll be slow out of jump. There's two jumps. And if there's no choice, Fallan said—he'll screw the entry. This paper—it's the numbers. It's what we've got—" Coughing took over. Water quelled it. "Fal said—we own all the buttons. Said—if he *has* to do it—he'll screw a decimal."

Others had come into the room. Madison. Johnny. Mum. They stood quietly to hear what Ross Monahan said.

Mum folded her arms, took a deep, steadying breath, "He'd do it," Mum said. "Won't write those coordinates down, no. He won't need to." There was a trail of moisture down mum's cheek, nothing in her expression. "They'd be fools to mess with him. Or *Galway*'s Senior Captain. Fallan says he's smart. Station-born crew—never jumped? They'll be puking their guts out."

Silence, then, except Ross's attempts to quiet the cough.

JR looked at the paper. Blood had gotten onto it, but the numbers were clear. He folded it, pocketed it. *Finity*'s nav team could check it out.

The balance was tipped. *Finity* wouldn't break dock. *Galway*'s crew was alive. Was going to fight as canny spacers fought—and do some desperate, very nasty fighting when they came out of jump, while the mental fog was still thick. If *Galway*'s crew won the fight—they'd see each other again. If Cruz and his trainee crew lost Fallan, and thought they were going to jump *Galway* back to Alpha, when they hadn't managed *Rights* or, equally notoriously, *Qarib*, nobody would hear from *Galway* again. An unkind universe didn't give special leeway to fools.

"The question is," Fletcher said, "where does Abrezio stand in all this? Was *Galway* double-crossed?"

"We'll find out. He didn't hesitate when I asked for security clearance for—" JR lifted his chin toward young Ross, who was trying hard to keep his eyes open and focused, but those eyes shifted to him, nonetheless, squeezed tight, and opened again. "You think it was Abrezio?"

"Don't know, sir. Cruz. Hiding back in the crew lounge, what I think." His brow twitched and he winced. "Guns. Came from behind us."

"We'll find out soon enough." JR set a hand on the bowed shoulder, pressed slightly and felt it heave, then relax as Ross's eyes drifted again.

"We've got the numbers," JR said to his crew. "We could catch them, we could try to clip a vane, but that's risking us and them, and God knows what Cruz would try. My bet's on *Galway* crew." Alby had shown up, *Finity's* surgeon, with staff. They were waiting. They *didn't* have facilities in the sleepover for more than sprains and bruises. But they could take privileges at the clinic down the Strip. "Ross." He pressed again, getting the boy's attention. "I have a deal with your senior; and indirectly, with your Nav 1, and we owe you—we owe you and all the Monahans beyond telling, right now. We promised Niall we'd look out for you; and we will, whatever it takes. I want to send you down to the station clinic with our med staff. I'll be calling in the Monahan captains and telling them what's happened, and keeping promises, top to bottom. If there's anything we can do for you else, we'll do it—but best we just get you looked at soonest." Shock was evident, and the bandage was turning pink with blood the gel wasn't quite stopping. "Jen. Go with him."

"Yes, sir," Jen said. "Mike. Lucien."

They got him up. They got him to the door, but it was clear Ross wouldn't be walking to the clinic.

"Get a trolley," JR said.

"We have one waiting," Fletcher said, as Ross and company cleared the door. Fletcher lingered. So did Madison and Johnny and Mum, who quietly took seats.

"Two years," Mum said. "Fallan's got a plan. Depend on it."

"We've got time—I hate to say, whether or not they make it," Madison said. "It won't be any one-year trip."

"He'll do it," Mum said, arms folded, jaw set.

"I'm hoping, with you, these are good numbers. First well's a bit scary—too many unknowns in there—but should be doable. Sol's going to get them in six years, whether or not. But we'll figure two years. And that will be enough. When word goes out Sol's coming—be it in two or three years, or twice that, once we can give them the expectation and the facts, the Beyond will start believing it. And we've got a potent argument for preparedness."

"Rights," John said, "is a potent argument for preparedness. No merchanter, no station, can look at that ship's configuration and say it's been built for cargo. There's no more someday, no more wait and see how it shakes out. It's shaken. It's on us. We organize, or not."

"What's just happened to *Galway* will tip any sane merchanter over the line." Madison said. "No one, *no one* wants to live with the threat of EC pirates commandeering their ship. Infuriating as it is, win or lose on those numbers, she's got her place in history, and it's *not* to the EC's credit."

"Right now, we have work to do," JR said. He glanced at Mum, who didn't want to discuss things, not right now, maybe not for weeks, and at Madison and John. "I have to talk to the Monahans' acting senior, first off and personally. He needs to know, from us. Call Min. He can pass the word where it needs to be, and we're going to have to keep the lid on crews' reactions. I also need to talk to Abrezio. About in that order. Use this office and the adjacent."

"I'll take Min," Madison said.

"*Firenze*," John said.

"Mum, can you take the conn?"

Translation: handle every loose end, deal with the unexpected. Mum gave a nod, neat and sharp. Stab in the heart, that news from *Galway,* but Mum prioritized. There had been days as bad. Some worse. There was still hope in this one.

"I'm calling Owen Monahan," JR said, "and I'll be meeting with the Family. Rosie's is their turf; I'll go there. Then I'll be seeing Abrezio and asking questions. If I don't like what I hear . . ." He looked at each in turn, and didn't bother completing the sentence.

"We're on it," Madison said.

They had one *Galway* crewman in the number one clinic, with a *Finity* medical crew insisting on taking over—it was their right with their personnel. It was another issue, treating a *Galway* crewman, but: "Don't argue with them," Abrezio answered a doctor's query. "This is politics and it's touchy. Only person with more right of way is a *Galway* captain."

"We have one coming," was the answer. "Burning a trail coming here."

"Don't argue, don't get in his way and don't do anything but provide them what they need."

The Scotch bottle was looking increasingly attractive. *Galway* was out of dock, blazing a trail only pushers took, the Strip was a ticking bomb that alcohol could not improve, but shutting their bars down was against custom, against what spacers called their rights, and the last thing Abrezio wanted to do was bring a squad of EC enforcers in to confront the situation.

Galway hadn't gone for jump yet. Ships long at dock did careful shakedowns before that operation, and in that much, *Galway* was behaving normally.

Nothing else was.

He *was* rid of Cruz. There was that one bright spot. Unfortunately he was not *permanently* rid of Cruz, and there were a handful of individuals left here that posed immediate problems.

He had *not* heard from JR Neihart, beyond the code red that had sent *Finity* security to the mast entry, to return with one *Galway* navigator, and there was no more information beyond the fact that the navigator was now in the clinic—a situation with troubling echoes of the prior incident at Rosie's. And at Rosie's, *Galway* personnel were assembled, a gathering that was no longer happy in the least.

"JR Neihart is arriving at Rosie's," Ames reported. "He's sent word he *will* talk after he's had a word with the Monahans. The Monahan third-shift captain is with their man in the clinic, along with *Finity* security and medics. There's also been a dockside meeting between Xiao Min and Sanjay Patel, and rumor is apparently being passed about the situation with Cruz at its core. Whether or not it's all accurate is not clear."

"*We* don't know what's accurate, at this point," Abrezio pointed out. "We just need to keep rumors from becoming riots. Keep airing the statements. New release every fifteen minutes." It at least kept people focused on the information flow, not ranging the halls. "Tell them meetings are in progress."

They were running thin on information.

He made a decision. "I want Bellamy Jameson. Tell him I want him in my office an hour ago. And keep it quiet."

"Yes, sir," Ames said, and Abrezio leaned back in his chair and stared at the doorway, thinking about Callie, thinking about the scary possibilities of domestic breakdown if panic took hold in the station. Release of information was critical. Keeping the Strip quiet was critical, and that meant controlling Strip security. It was a question, right now, who was in charge, whether Hewitt had gone with Cruz or not, but his gut said No. His gut said Cruz would not leave without securing control of the *Rights* project, and Hewitt was the only real candidate to run it.

Hewitt had arrived with orders from Sol to audit the station bank, to "double check the supply records for the sake of the station residents."

A lot of good that had done. It hadn't gotten them a pusher-load of station supply.

Hewitt had also brought in EC security, and assumed authority to control security around the project. He'd ordered all of A-mast devoted to the project. He'd taken over A-mast offices, and the A-mast access in their entirety.

He'd stepped up recruiting EC security from among Alpha citizens, and used a fairly extensive brawl on the Strip as an excuse to declare the Strip a "sensitive" area, thus taking over enforcement authority over both masts and the Strip. On the books, Bellamy was still head of Alpha civil enforcement, and Bellamy still held authority over the rest of the station, its residents, its industrial areas—but the whole space interface had become Hewitt's. And with Cruz out of the picture?

In recent years Bellamy had lost staff, in an economy that had pinched funds even for *lighting* in any warehouse section unrelated to *Rights*. Hewitt had increasingly found *Rights'* concerns in the most damnable places, while his eye on the bank's management of *Rights'* funds also kept a watch on civilian supply and product-printer operations.

Oh, without Cruz, there would indeed still be Hewitt. And, previous orders to Bellamy regarding the Monahans notwithstanding . . . Hewitt was still in charge of law enforcement on the Strip, which was so, so delicately balanced right now. If stationers felt blindsided and uncertain about Sol's now-impending visitation—generally good news, but not for every enterprise—*spacers* were now getting the news of Cruz's takeover of *Galway* and the Sol route. And when spacers were upset, they went to the bars, and when they were truly upset—things could get broken.

And when things got broken—*Hewitt* found excuse to expand his office.

Bellamy Jameson, dammit, had to do some of the same, push *Hewitt* back, and get his own force out onto the Strip before Hewitt's moved in with tasers and batons.

Presumably Bellamy was paying attention. Presumably Bellamy was giving orders, since Bellamy was slow responding to his call, dammit.

He gave Callie a call, just to see how she was doing, how their section was doing, whether things were quiet in the residential corridors.

"I'm watching the vids," Callie said. Her voice had none of the usual cheer. "It's quiet. Mother says it's quiet in *their* section. Dad's gone to the pub to try to get news, but nobody knows anything. Is it true the ship's jumped?"

"Not true. They're still in shakedown."

"They do have the coordinates. And Cruz is with them."

"Yes and yes."

"I have to ask . . ."

"No. I didn't order him. And I'm not sure what the exact situation is on the ship. Yet. Information is still coming in. One of *Galway*'s crew escaped—injured. He's being treated. You can tell your mother that much. She can relay it. You can say where it's from. Whatever happened on that ship wasn't peaceful. You stay in the apartment. Don't answer the door. Don't answer calls you don't recognize. Hear me?"

"Yes," Callie said. And they ended the call.

The clock ran. And he sweated.

The Strip was quiet, most places. Ominously so.

Ames appeared in the doorway. "Chief of Security Jameson, sir. On com."

Abrezio picked up the com. "Bellamy."

"Sir."

"I expected you *here.*"

"Counter orders from Hewitt. Kept me waiting on com-hold, or I'd've answered sooner, and then the bastard just told me to stay on civ-side alert. Do I have an order, sir?"

"Damned right you have an order. I'm officially freeing you from him. We're taking back control. I want you to go to the Strip, take charge, move in civil enforcement. Hewitt's out, you're in. Hewitt's authority is confined to *Rights* personnel, *not* enforcement."

"Yes, sir. I'll need to muster some escort." There was the sound of the lift working, of button-pushes. "Such as we have."

"Don't push the spacers. Regard the spacers as on *your* side and don't let *Rights* throw any weight around. If you have an encounter, defuse it. Hell, offer to buy them a drink and talk it over in a sitdown. And ask politely for their help. Executive order. Cruz's rules are *gone.*"

"Yes, sir, understood."

"Good man. Keep it all low key. Advise me at any time."

"Yes, sir."

Abrezio punched out. He'd just set up an unthinkable confrontation, project enforcement with civil enforcement.

Hewitt was not likely to stand down voluntarily. But there was a certain resentment that had grown up between enforcement, in their blue uniforms, and *Rights* crew, who tended to be young, paid the same, but serving very few duty hours outside their training. And Hewitt's rules didn't touch *Rights* personnel. Oh, no.

Hewitt was a clever man. Cleverness made enemies.

And Hewitt's enemies were all in his contact list.

So was one other.

He called that com himself. He got one of the serving staff, a woman having trouble hearing him in the ambient racket. She passed him to the owner, with a muffled advisement.

"Mr. Rosenfeld," Abrezio said. "This is Director Ben Abrezio. Will you pass on some news to the captains? Cruz is gone. *Out,* along with his rules, along with Hewitt's authority over the Strip. I will be talking personally with ship authorities and working this out. Tell your patrons—tell them the only valid authority is civil enforcement. Bellamy Jameson is back in charge, and we'd appreciate their cooperation with his officers. I'll be back to you in . . . Give me an hour."

A pause. There was a great deal of muttering in the background. "Yes, *sir*," Rosie said. "I copy that. I'll certainly pass that on."

Chapter 15 Section ii

Head hurt. Things were a little blurry, still, but overall, it was a different pain. Ross put up a hand.

Another hand stopped it. Jen leaned into view. "Don't mess with it. They did a first-rate job. You got a dent in your skull and a three-inch patch, which looks real good. A few months on you won't have a scar to speak of."

"*Galway,*" he said.

"Not jumped yet," Jen said soberly, "but no stopping them, Ross. I'm sorry. Captain says trying to clip them, even if we overtake—is just too chancy, for us and them."

"They communicating at all?"

"No. Not a word out of them. And I'd know. Captain would tell me . . . for you to know. He promised."

"God." He shut his eyes a moment, but it did nothing to revise reality. "How's the rest of us taking it?"

"Number two and three are going to be holding session at Rosie's, with a lot of sympathy up and down the Strip. Fourth's been sitting watch over you. What's happened is a rotten deal. But *Finity's* going to stand by you, all of you. The Alliance is."

"That thing you're putting together?"

"That thing, yes. We're going to see you through this, however we have to do it." Jen held his hand gently. "Senior captain and third are at Rosie's, talking with your second and third, Mum's in charge at the Olympian and our second's here, along with our security and our medics, making sure you're all right. Brilliant job you did."

He had to take her word on that. Memory was muddled. A desperate attempt to stay awake, to reach a mammoth ship on the far side of a narrowing gap in a blurry dark sea.

"Your senior got the paper." Fallan's last order, to get that to JR.

"You gave it to him yourself. Remember?"

He didn't remember. And nav, even a trainee, couldn't go blank on things. *"I can't."* He said it with a little panic. "I can't remember. You're sure I did?"

"Saw you. I was there. You'll remember. You'll get it back. What was it hit you? Baton?"

He didn't remember that, either. Just Fallan, saying go. Something about two years. A streaked visor and the view of *Finity's* hull below him . . .

"I've lost stuff. *Two years.* What's with two years?"

"Hush." She bent and laid a finger on his mouth. And suddenly looked toward the door, alarmed.

Bodies slammed the walls of the hallway. People swore and shouted, and something metal crashed over, clanging, followed by thumps. Jen got up, shut the door.

"What is it?"

Jen shrugged, her back to the shut door. "Somebody dropped a tray, I guess."

"The hell!"

Jen touched the earpiece she was wearing, head tilted, and looked at nothing in particular for a moment, then looked satisfied.

"Seems you just had visitors. Fortunately, Fletch and Madison were sitting out there. All settled. We'll be moving you out of here pretty soon, get you back to the Olympian. Or the Fortune, your choice. Either way, you're not going to be bothered by visitors."

"My family," he said. "At Rosie's?"

"They are. Soon's you're cleared, we can move you. We can drop by there on the way if you like."

"I'll walk."

"Hell if you will. Flat on your back, sir."

"Walking. I'm fine."

"Concussion and blood loss. You can ride the damn trolley."

"Sitting up."

"Deal," Jen said. "Seriously, are you up to it? Rosie's, I mean, not the trolley. There'll be questions you may not want to deal with. You're not to stress. Doctor's orders."

Stress. He laughed, not from humor. Winced.

"Headache?"

"All right, all right. Walking's not the best. Just get me cleared out of here."

Chapter 15   Section iii

Mum was holding down the Olympian venue. JR had left her settled in a chair in the lobby, with two of *Finity's* security kitted up and meaning business.

JR and John had two more behind them, on their way

through the crowds outside Rosie's. Security from *Little Bear* and *Mumtaz* and *Nomad* were present, with Min, Sanjay, and Asha Druv.

Julio Rodriguez met them at the door, a calm and very serious Julio Rodriguez, doubtless having gotten the news.

"Captain." Giovanna Galli made her way through, brow furrowed and unhappiness in the lines of her mouth. "What's the plan? Is it true? They're going to Sol?"

"No thanks to Andrew Cruz." He hadn't stopped moving—in the press around them, stopping meant stalling, and his target was Rosie's door, if they could penetrate the crowd there. "We have the coordinates. What value they are, *Galway* intended to test, and for what I know, that's still their aim, but now they've got Cruz on their hands. You can spread that news."

Galli dropped back into a trailing cluster of her own crew as others surged up with questions; but those were too late. *Finity* security moved to the fore, moving people from the entry, clearing a path fairly politely.

"Let them in!" somebody inside called out, and a path developed, people crowding back, giving space where there wasn't much available.

"Captain!" Rosie shouted, from behind the bar. "Back here!"

JR took the offered space. Rosie's bar, securely bolted, and Rosie behind it, was as secure as the place offered.

"Get a little quiet here!" Rosie yelled, and people shushed each other, and quieted the place.

A middle-aged man with a *Galway* patch and a captain's tag shouldered his way to the bar, leaning on it. "Finity! Have we got news?"

"On your man Ross," JR said, "good. He's in the clinic, about to be released. On *Galway*, unfortunately no contact, no message and she's still proceeding. I'm afraid they *are* going for jump. You're Owen Monahan, acting senior."

"Yes, sir, I am." A dozen Monahans had elbowed their way in, and those behind hushed the crowd, so the word passed, in furious hisses for quiet.

"Ross carried word from Nav 1. Fallan's all right, everybody's all right, so far as we know. Cruz and a group of

Rights crew ambushed them on spin-up and took the bridge. Fallan sent Ross out an e-hatch with the numbers . . . on paper. Only copy, so far as we can tell, besides the one in Fallan's head. Fallan's word via Ross was, they're going to Sol and they'll handle Cruz on the way. Considering the shape he was in, Ross did a hell of a job getting down to *Finity*, with *Galway* pulling out. Came in the same e-hatch as the customs lot."

"What's he saying, what's he saying?" was the rising question from the press further back, and JR said, "Get me a chair."

There was some maneuvering and shoving, the chair came right across the bar, and JR set it in place and stepped up onto it as the crowd of concerned spacers crowded close as they could.

"Here's the short of it," JR said. "*Galway*'s away, bound for Sol by two untested jump points, no prior probe. It was a deal made in good faith with stationmaster Abrezio, as one of *Galway*'s senior captains explained to me in confidence, *before* signing with our alliance. He wanted to be certain the Monahans left behind would be covered, under any circumstances."

Expectant silence, *not* from the Monahans, who already knew.

"I assured him they would be, and we discussed the details. The one circumstance we did not expect was Cruz lying in wait aboard the *unlocked ship* itself."

"Whose orders?" someone shouted. *"Abrezio's?"*

"Unknown, as yet. We've reason to suspect Cruz was acting on his own. Abrezio has been nothing but respectful in his dealings with us. I'll be going to his office directly. I'll know more after I meet with him."

A tap on his arm. Rosie. And the big man shouted from below:

"Stationmaster's a good man. Called and asked me to pass to you—Cruz is out and Hewitt with him. Abrezio's taking the station back. Says Bellamy Jameson is back in charge. Asks you to behave yourselves reasonably well and help the man out!"

That got a cheer from the locals, and a few rude suggestions, then shouts to shut up and let *Finity* finish.

JR nodded acknowledgment. *"Galway* resisted, and in the general mixup, *Galway's* Nav 1 sent their third nav out in a suit and down to *Finity's* hatch *with* the coordinates, asking him to report the situation. He was injured in the fight, but he made it to *Finity,* made his report, and he's currently under the care of our medics in the station clinic. So . . . we've got the coordinates, and we'll not be holding them for ourselves, but giving them to the merchanter's alliance, which is *all* of us. There's not a ship here that hasn't signed, and we'll make them available to any and all of you. We're *not* advising any other ship try that route 'til it's proven. *Galway's* taking a big risk—for all of us—and we urge that we *all* wait for their safe return." He wasn't mentioning, out loud, for stationer ears, what veteran spacers knew might happen out there—for fear somebody might contact *Galway* with a warning.

A grim murmur went through the press, nobody dissenting.

"But the future's not all on the Monahans," JR said, into the troubled quiet after. "The alliance we're forming isn't complete. We have a few ships left to sign, and if Sol's coming in, we need *the stations themselves* signed on, assurance they'll deal with *us* and not any hired-crew Company ships. Sol may be coming, but the EC won't take our trade, they won't take our way of life—and they won't come back in as the lords of all that moves, either. No and *hell,* no."

Hell no echoed back, multiplied by a hundred voices.

"Have they got ships?" JR asked. "We don't know. Maybe they've been building a dozen like *The Rights of Man.* Maybe they're all ready to move, and they've been sending out probes to find routes in this direction, but there's no way they're Family ships. They haven't our history, they haven't our experience, and if they want to trade, Sol's goods need to move on *our* ships, because a creature like *Rights of Man* isn't going to be highly welcome at the stations past Alpha, with *no* damn cargo hold and *way* too many EC enforcers aboard."

"She ain't highly welcome *here!*" was the shout from the rear of the crowd.

And a second voice: "But what do we do to stop it?"

"We stand together," JR shouted, "we lay down *our* rules, and we make our own deals with stations—if stations want cargo from places we serve more than they want enforcers out of Sol, which I think they will—they'll deal with us, who know their history, their needs, their leadership, and their people. We have to play fair with the stations: they need us and we need them. What we *don't* need is Sol coming in here and telling us their rules."

"So what's *Pell* going to do for Alpha?" came the same voice, from a knot of Firenzes.

"Nothing," JR said flatly. Pell probably wished Alpha would fold up and quit existing, which was the Konstantins' opinion of everything Sol-ward of Venture, but he wasn't about to say that now. "*Stations* take care of themselves, not other stations. But they'll trade with us, with merchanter ships, with alliance ships, and *we'll* get that cargo to Alpha, because Alpha staying in business is good for *our* business. You signed with us, and that gives you rights to trade where you damned well please to trade, and to be backed by the whole rest of the alliance if any station including Sol—*or* Pell—wants to tell you you can't. We're not a Pell organization. We're *merchanters*. We deal *for* merchanters."

That got a cheer. And the banging of mugs on tables.

"You want to deal with Sol and the EC, you're free to go there. That's your choice. You're still in with us. That's how it'll work. Any ship is free to do what it wants *unless* the alliance for some good reason declares an embargo on a station. Then we ask every ship stand by your allies, supply each other, and hold trade from that station until we say trade. Any station we *have* to reason with collectively will talk to us collectively until the problem is solved."

That was more than they'd ever said on Alpha. And it met sober faces and quiet while people thought that over.

"We have enforcement means of our own," JR said. "We can help a station out—or we can withdraw long enough to

make a reasonable agreement logical. And if *all* of us are
signatory, including the stations, we'll reason with the stations and they'll reason with us and we'll both get what we
need." He paused, to let that sink in. Then: "The EC's had
its day, and *these* are our principles." He ticked them off on
his fingers. "First, station authority can inspect the hold,
but it stays off our decks."

A cheer for that one.

"Second: We plot our routes. We go where *we* choose, not
where some EC official says to go." Silence. Not disagree-
ment, just a lot of hard listening. "Most importantly: We lay
down the law on our decks according to our customs, we
operate each ship as a sovereign nation, we keep records as
we see fit, and we *don't* turn them over to customs."

"Yes!" came from a number of voices. And from others:
"Hell, yes."

"If Sol wants *more* of us to come there, Sol has to bargain
to get us, just like any other station. The merchanters' alliance is no one ship, no single rule-making body of individuals. Any alliance ship may make requests and ask cooperation
from ships in its vicinity. A ship will not make rules and exceptions except by consensus of all ships in reach; three or
more ships constitute a local decision-making body, which
should simply consider the best interests of merchanters as a
whole. If you all agree, there will be procedures to notify the
stations and to notify the rest of the Families. If you have an
egregious situation, word will flow, and the alliance as a
whole may choose to act. Whoever *you* want to take into
your Family is yours, and that's that. When Sol trade comes
in, we'll trade with Sol, we'll back Families that do, if that's
their choice. But we're advising stations beyond Alpha not to
accept hired-crew ships. What Alpha does will be by vote of
the ships that trade here. You locals have kept this whole
region alive. It's your routes, your votes, and those of us from
outside will accept your decisions and work with you, but it's
my sense of things that that ship holding all of A-mast has
done no favors for Alpha or for your trade. Do we on *Finity's
End* view that ship as good for us? We aren't directly interested. Do *you* view that ship as good for you and Alpha?"

"No!" was the resounding answer.

"Then there being a quorum of local trade, we accept that view," JR said, "we'll report it along our route, and we'll hope that the first FTLer to reach Sol will be *Galway, under* the Monahans—"

A cheer for that, loud and clear.

"The Monahan Family, meanwhile, is signatory to the alliance and the alliance will stand by them, looking for the return of *Galway*, and fair dealing from all parties. The Monahans have trusted us, and we'll stand by them for whatever it takes. Captain Owen Monahan, sir, you and yours, we'll be talking with you, and taking account of specifics, whatever we need to do. We'll be meeting with all captains before we leave Alpha, and asking advice from the Families who know this region better than anybody. On the current situation out there, we don't know more than we've told you. We've got our own observers on *Finity* who will tell us when *Galway* jumps, and we will pass that word on. Godspeed to her and all the Monahans."

"Let's hear it for *Galway*," Diego Rodriguez said, banging a fist on the bar. "Cheers for the Monahans and hell's coldest pit for Andrew Cruz!"

That let loose the commotion, banging of glasses and shouting. JR stepped down and let it run.

Owen Monahan found his way to the back of the bar.

"Buy you a drink, sir."

"JR to my friends," JR said. "And I'll gladly take it." He wasn't sure how much Niall's Second knew about Niall's intentions, whether the Monahans in general had all the knowledge Ross Monahan had relayed. It wasn't certain Ross Monahan himself understood all of it.

Two years, delaying out there, whatever was going on aboard—granted that first point itself was not a disaster.

He had to be honest with this man, in due time. Expectations of a return couldn't be ratcheted up and let down again so suddenly. Soon enough that information would leak, and eventually the whole station would find out, stationers as well as spacers.

But full disclosure to the rest of the Monahans had to come *after* the ship had left the system, and in private, he said to himself. It was not news for family to hear shouted across a bar.

If they survived the first jump point, they'd try to take control of their ship, and if they succeeded, Fallan Monahan would put in the right coordinates for the second jump.

If they didn't succeed—Fallan had a choice to make. *Galway* could sit still, with both Monahan navigators refusing to jump back to the known coordinates of Alpha station. He could sit there for two years, with EC crew aboard threatening to take matters into their own hands, and probably not a one of them confident enough to do it. If it got uglier than that—Fallan might make a small adjustment to the second jump coordinates, and they wouldn't survive.

It was going to be ugly, no matter how it went. If the information was wrong—or if Cruz was a total fool and put his own crew in—*Galway* might not survive the first jump, might not survive the second, and the third itself was no cinch. *Sol's* relative position and motion might be known, but first time to a point of mass, even with solid readings, was always risky: you didn't want a novice on nav and you didn't want a novice on helm. No way.

So was there reason to hope? There was. Cruz could not be that stupid. Fallan would be perfectly willing to take them to the *first* jump point.

But one way and the other, it would be years before any news of *Galway* got back to Alpha.

Chapter 15   Section iv

Not the most dignified mode of travel, but, given the dizziness with colorful storefronts and animated displays reeling past, Jen was right to make him take it. Ross concentrated on Jen, walking beside the rolling vehicle, and let the rest go hazy. He wasn't the only passenger. Madison and Fletcher had gone on ahead somewhere. But one *Finity* security guy rode, one walked on the other side.

There was no baggage. God, Ross thought, everything he owned, all his clothes, every trinket and keepsake and reference book—it was all on *Galway*. He had one grossly stained jumpsuit and jacket in a plastic bag, a casual, un-marked jumpsuit some Finity had given him, and a pair of boots that he was wearing. He had his ID. Had his licenses, his ring . . .

Oh . . . and a hospital toiletry kit.

That was it. He'd have to float a loan for the cleaning. Not that Mum or Peg or anybody would begrudge it. It was just—

Just the coming back with *nothing*. Having lost his whole shift, and Niall, and everybody, and worrying about *stuff* was just—easier than wrapping his mind around losing *people*.

Jen said *Galway* hadn't gone yet. It was still in shake-down. Might be for days and days, getting far from Bar-nard's mass. On a chancy run, that was a good precaution. He hoped after the initial set-to that the blue-coats settled down and figured out that this wasn't a sim, and that real stars had their ways. Getting them a little scared—yeah, his team knew how to do that. Get them to realize what they *weren't* trained for, and to figure it out, that their lives didn't ride on *Andy Cruz's* judgment, for which they could be soundly grateful. He'd had Fallan's cold dose of reality on some of his own mistakes, not meant to scare him— Fallan had no nerves. But scared, yes. Damn right.

He had a glimmering what Fallan might do, on that first jump. Just a glimmering. And it could give those blue-coats religion real fast.

God, he didn't want to think about it. His eyes were wide open, but he wasn't seeing the storefronts or hearing anything but the muddled echoes of people on the Strip. He was seeing the nav screens, and watching the lines and knowing the sensors were always lagged, and you had to know how lagged and react . . .

Noise. Lot of people.

"You awake, Ross?"

"Yeah. Thinking."

"We're nearly there. Your head was down."

"I'm awake." He blinked the haze away, looked beyond Jen and saw familiar frontages, turned his head in the direction they were going and saw Rosie's . . . and a crowd of people, the biggest crowd he'd ever seen in his life, so many they were jamming the doors at Rosie's and spilling out onto the Strip, a lot with drinks in hand, and impeding the progress of the trolley, not in an aggressive way, just too many to make room. It was a mixed lot, a scattering of Firenzes, Qaribs, Santiagos, Little Bears, and Mumtazes, a couple of Finitys and then a younger cousin, Allie, with them.

"That's Ross!" she said. *"Ross!"*

"Wait," he said, and reached out and took Allie's hand. "The rest of us inside?" he asked her, and meanwhile the crowd surrounded the trolley, a friendly crowd, and one offered him a drink, which wasn't supposed to be out on the Strip.

"He shouldn't," Jen said. "He's got a knock on the head. Ross, a sip, that's all."

He took just a sip and handed it back, hoping he actually said thanks, not just thinking it. It was Rosie's cheaper brew, but it tasted good after all the disinfectant smells and the condition of his clothing. Somebody laid a hand on his outstretched arm, and others did, not pushing him, just touching.

"My family's in there," he said to Jen. "I can make it all right."

"Here," she said, and offered her arm. "Help him down, all right? He's a little wobbly."

A number of arms assisted, including Allie and Jen, and he was doing fine until the public address sounded a siren and a voice saying, *"This gathering is an unlawful assembly in violation of liquor regulations and safety regulations. Disperse. This is your only warning. Stragglers will be charged with criminal endangerment."*

The crowd was not in any mood to disperse. That was clear in the reaction.

Jen stopped, with a firm grip on his arm. "Ross. We've got to get you out of here."

"No way," he said. It was a visceral reaction, just one push too many from blue-coats and the EC. *"No."*

"Ross," Jen said, and about that much before the siren sounded again and the edge of the crowd met the blue-coats. "Tom! Give me a hand here."

"Not going," Ross said. "No." He hadn't thought there was a charge of adrenaline left in him. But there was.

Then a rush of Finitys and Little Bears and Santiagos made a wall around them, jostling them in the process, but chains were coming out, wrapping fists at the moment, there being no room to swing, and the blue-coats would be using whatever they'd brought.

"Damn disaster!" Jen swore, and pulled out her pocket com. "This is Jen Neihart, Captain-sir, outside Rosie's. We've got blue-coats and there's chains out."

It didn't take ten seconds before an angry rush poured out of Rosie's and swelled their numbers from maybe fifty to way more than that. Tasers snapped. But the blue-coats weren't charging in, not now.

Then the public address cut on again, with, *"This is Director Benjamin Abrezio. All* Rights *personnel are ordered to proceed immediately to the nearest A-mast access office. This is an immediate boarding call for* Rights of Man. *All* Rights *personnel, proceed immediately to A-mast. Do not stop to gather personal items. Enzio Hewitt, proceed to assume command of* Rights *personnel at A-mast access One. Secure the ship immediately. This is an emergency."*

God, were they launching *Rights* after *Galway?*

"Yeah, you bastards!" came a shout in the first edge of silence. "Get the hell out of our faces! Sneaking cowards!"

"Shut it down, there!" *That* was Owen. Adrenaline ebbed. Ross sucked in a deep breath, thinking now that staying on his feet was a hard job, when a moment ago he'd been ready to light into EC Enforcement bare-handed.

Jen took his arm, quick as a thought. "Yeah," she said. "Stand easy, Ross. We're right with you."

"Going to talk to Owen," he said.

"All right," she said. "We're with you. Let us stay with you. Don't hurry."

Jen had firm hold of his arm, lending equilibrium. Ross

moved, headed for Rosie's door, which he could see, thanks
to people moving out of his way. His balance was unsteady,
but a little of the adrenaline came back, now that he had
the door in view; and people *were* getting out of his way.
He heard a strange thing. "Ross Monahan," voices said,
hushed in the ringing quiet. *"That's Ross Monahan,"* as if
that were something unusual.

It was fairly surreal. He headed for Owen, and saw cousins, and Peg. Peg touched his face and said, "Oh, honey,
how are you?"

"A little wobbly. Peg, this is Jen. Jen, I want a beer. A
little one." It struck him he'd been signed out of the bank
and had no scrip whatsoever. "You're buying, right?"

Chapter 15   Section v

*"This is Director Benjamin Abrezio. Alpha Captains, please
cooperate and comply with instructions. Other captains,
please preserve order on the Strip. No charges of any sort
will be filed against ship's personnel. Enforcement will stand
down immediately in deference to ships' executive officers.
Deputy Chief Jameson, contact my office immediately."*

The wonder was, it was working. He'd waited to put that
message out. Waited until he'd been sure Hewitt wasn't
going to counter his orders. But Hewitt's people were
safely inside A-mast and loading onto *Rights* as fast as
their cards could swipe the security reader.

Recalling the man to his own power base was step one.

Then step two. The great prize, Hewitt's dream on a
stick: command of *Rights*. Abrezio was handing that prize
to him, along with an emergency call.

What emergency? had been Hewitt's texted response,
and he'd answered in a single word: *Finity.* Nothing more.
Hewitt's suspicious imagination could handle the rest, and
all interpretations, to that suspicious mind, led to one

result: *Finity* was making a takeover attempt on *Rights*. They needed to defend the accesses.

Urgently.

Whatever got Hewitt and his people off the Strip. And if Hewitt did decide to move *Rights*, judging by its last less-than-glorious performance, it would take the better part of an hour just getting the fourteen lines and the magnetics all uncoupled.

Trying to move *Rights* out of dock risked damage to A-mast, but hell with the risk: station hadn't had commercial use of A-mast in years, and risk to the station itself was minimal: the mast connector assembly was designed to give, to cave in rather than disrupt station stability. Of course *Rights* could get afoul of one of the visitors, which was far more serious, but below the great ring of the station, and its spokes, B-mast wasn't remotely in reach by simple drift. Just detaching and proceeding backward, upward, or sideways would get *Rights* clear of station, and *that* danger out of the way.

Still . . . Abrezio sent an order to ops, simply: "If *Rights* requests to uncouple, refer it to me. They'll need my express clearance."

"Yes, sir," ops said. That was Giorgio Varese who answered. Chief of ops. And *not* one of Cruz's people. And since the Glory Rebellion centuries ago, one of Sol's own ideas, uncoupling hadn't been solely under any ship's control.

It risked *Rights* breaking away and damaging its berth on A-mast, but if Hewitt did that, he'd set himself up in violation of EC rules. And he'd be under arrest with the full weight of station outrage against him.

"Mr. Varese. Report *Rights* activity directly to my office. Don't deter the crew. Don't inform them you're watching. Track check-in. Let me know when they're all aboard and use the cameras to make sure no one sneaks back out the lock."

"Yes, sir."

Ames flashed the com. "Sir. Chief Jameson's here."

"Good," he said, and a moment later Bellamy Jameson walked in.

"I'm here, sir. Sorry about that mess down at Rosie's. Hewitt's goons bowled over us. Wouldn't listen to me."

"We'll take care of that now," Abrezio said, and handed him a new-minted ID, with a potent load of access codes. "Cruz has left, Hewitt's on his way to take command of *Rights,* and *you're* Director of EC Security on both sides of the wall. As of this moment, you're in command of Strip security as well as residential areas, and all Security personnel including any stray *Rights of Man* crew are under your orders. Anybody who contests those orders is to be put under lock and key until we have a chance to sort this mess out. We've got some justifiably upset spacers who've just seen one of their sister ships forcibly coopted by the EC, not to mention the Monahans themselves present. I don't want a riot and I don't want them thinking I put that arrogant bastard up to it."

"Understood."

"You're going to be short-handed. I want all of Hewitt's hand-picked security to stand down. I want them off the Strip, which means bringing in civ-side enforcement. However, I've asked ship captains, local and otherwise, to keep their own folk in order in the current emergency, and I don't think they're any more anxious for a riot than we are. I'd like your domestic officers to do nothing more than man the Strip to get their bearings, and I want them to smile and be pleasant to the spacer-folk. Rules against drunk and disorderly are temporarily suspended. I don't care if they're passed out drunk on the concourse. Just wish them sweet dreams and be nice to them."

Bellamy nodded. "What is Chief Hewitt's situation? Does he know what's going on?"

"No longer Chief Hewitt," Abrezio said. "He's now the acting captain of *Rights of Man,* and on his way to the ship, along with the entire crew, to deal with an emergency."

Bellamy's brow tightened. "What *emergency?*"

"I wonder." Abrezio allowed himself a moment's satisfaction. "Whatever it is will keep them occupied trying to find it for at least an hour, but if you hear rumors about *Finity* taking over *Rights* . . . squelch them. That's the last thing *Finity* wants at the moment, and I'm very sure on that point. As soon as you leave here, I'd like you to put A-mast under lock, nobody to be allowed out, *including* Enzio Hewitt. He is *not* to leave A-mast until I give permission. As for your promotion . . . he'll know soon enough, when his keycard doesn't work."

"Promotion?" Bellamy asked. "Permanent?"

"As long as I'm in office," Abrezio said. "I warn you: you'll be earning your pay raise, just in personnel juggling. I want you to assign your people from civ-side in every sub office, replacing EC Enforcement. If anybody resists that, arrest them under the Station Safety Act. We'll sort them out later, maybe return some to their jobs, but that'll be at your discretion."

"Sir." It took a great deal to shake Bellamy Jameson, but he was looking a bit shell-shocked. "I'm—not—I don't—we don't have that many trained personnel."

"You'll have to give some junior trainees a baptism of fire. Let them handle civ-side and answer questions.—I know it will put you short, but we've got no choice. We *can't* use Hewitt's men. Tell your folk to trust the bartenders and shopkeepers. If they say a person is all right, they're all right. If they say troublemaker, deal with them. We have to trust the station residencies won't break out in crime in the next shift. Skeleton crew there, to take complaints and investigate as they can. Call in both shifts, tell them dress uniforms, and be polite. Walk up and down, smile, and talk to the businesses and the captains. Don't enforce the minutiae. Trust the captains to control their people. We've got no rivalries we know of. Just some people unhappy to hear Cruz has hijacked one of their ships and gone off to Sol. Which there's no stopping at this point."

"It's true then, they got the coordinates."

"Right now everybody including the bar staff up and down the Strip may know the coordinates. Secrecy is out the hatch and done with. Everyone, spacer and stationer alike, needs to vent a little steam and discuss what to do. Let them. It's not hurting us. That ID will get you into any door. Guard that card. Guard yourself: I'd suggest you take over the office out there in Registry and Finance, operate

out of my hallway, and preserve any records you find.
Hewitt's been into those since he arrived. Be careful. Some
of Cruz's people may still be wandering around and they're
not going to be happy."

"Yes, sir."

"Your salary will naturally take a rise. We'll discuss it.
Good luck, Chief Jameson."

"Sir." Bellamy offered a hand. He shook it.

It was a slightly overwhelmed man who left his office.
But he knew Bellamy, that things didn't overwhelm him for
long. Left to his own devices, Bellamy ran a tight ship, so
to speak, and didn't hesitate to move when he had to.

More, the man was honest and believed in station code,
which some legal wits called *lex solis alieni*, the law of another sun, meaning that a twelve-year question and a
twenty-year round trip to enforce it . . . called on stations
to *devise* an answer that worked. Local necessity had to
make binding laws and issue rulings without Sol being involved. *Lex solis alieni.*

In this case, booting that ambitious little EC import
right into the vacancy Cruz had created, and promoting a
fifth-generation stationer up to run security.

God . . . a year, minimum, without Andy Cruz. Hard to
imagine . . .

But damned if he wouldn't enjoy it. Scared? Hell, yes.
Terrified would be more apropos. Granted the numbers
worked, granted *Galway* got through, and took Cruz with
her . . . he still had time to get the station working the way
he'd always dreamed of it working, if *Finity* and this alliance of merchant ships proved reliable.

First things first: keep spacers happy.

He sent out a message to every bar office on the Strip:
Stay open. Start serving food. Free food, on the station,
and a lot of it, to moderate the alcohol. Bellamy Jameson
now appointed Chief of Enforcement. Call *Civil* Enforcement if you have any problem. Report any improper Enforcement activity to this office immediately.

Message to the bank: honor *Galway* scrip and bill it to
station.

Message to the Fortune: *void the* Galways' *checkout and reissue their room keys. Complimentary breakfasts all round, long as they stay. Receipts, however, must be signed.*

Accounting would have a fit, otherwise. And it was hell and away cheaper than repair bills.

Message to JR Neihart. *We still need to talk. Urgently.*

And then . . . he leaned back in his chair, and let go a long, slow breath. He'd had a head of adrenaline. It had almost run out.

He expected a call from Mr. Hewitt. He expected a very irate call from Mr. Hewitt. Benjamin Abrezio had upended the Earth Company power structure without stirring from his chair. He had very probably just lost his retirement—his position—possibly his freedom, if *Galway* made it through—unless Niall Monahan could do some very eloquent persuasion.

At least Callie wouldn't be touched. Divorcing her would protect her legally and financially. It was just an official status. They could go on living together. Their friends would understand. Their friends wouldn't blame him for what he'd done. They'd even be sympathetic. And if he was hauled off to Sol, at least it would be a quick trip. And friends would rally round Callie, for what that was worth.

He had enough savings, maybe, to beg a one-way passage for him and Callie—as far as Venture. But he couldn't leave Alpha to whatever came. He and Callie had friends, had relatives, had lifetimes invested in this place. What he'd just done . . . threatened all that, but only for him. More to the point, what he'd done might just save the station. It damned sure wasn't terrible.

The terrible thing had been building that monster ship in the first place. The terrible thing had been meekly following EC orders. Sinking resources into a design that Pell had modified and modified since the version the EC had lightfingered from an engineer's files. Espionage from Pell had occasionally delivered observations of those changes, and the engineers had said—*his* engineers had said—it was all for the ring-docking. That they were changes for trade, not the necessary mechanics of the ship and its drives. And meanwhile, *Sol* sent a steady stream of demands, and his engineers had struggled to incorporate those changes Sol wanted.

The damned monster was a bodged-up mess, with engineers blaming programmers and programmers telling the engineers to go to hell . . . and nobody had an answer, just a large mass of metal that couldn't perform the most basic task it was designed for.

But now, finally, *Rights* actually had a purpose. It was containing Mr. Hewitt. And it would continue to contain Mr. Hewitt until *Stationmaster* Abrezio had had time to figure what to do next.

Ames appeared in the doorway. "Captain Neihart is coming in. With a number of people."

"I'll see him," Abrezio said. "I'm very *glad* to see him."

"Right on in, sir," the secretary said, and JR, with a nodded thanks, walked into the carpeted office. Xiao Min, Sanjay Patel, Asha Druv, and Owen Monahan were with him, and there were not enough chairs by half.

"Welcome," Abrezio said, rising from his desk. "Thank you all for coming." He stretched a hand across his desk to Owen Monahan. "You are—sir—a Monahan captain."

"Owen Monahan, Second Captain."

"Doubly welcome. You'll find your scrip backed by the bank and your lodgings re-registered. I am beyond sorry. It was not my order that put Cruz on your ship."

"What *is* your position on the situation, sir?" JR asked.

Abrezio looked a little pale of countenance. Sweating, despite the temperate air. "In short: Mr. Cruz and I are *not* allies. We've never *been* allies. Mr. Cruz was sent here to run the project. He has now left. Enzio Hewitt arrived with authority to run *Rights* security, which Mr. Hewitt used first to appropriate A-mast, and has lately expanded to include jurisdiction over the Strip. Since Admiral Cruz has left us—I consider the project suspended. I sent Mr. Hewitt up to *Rights,* as the *least* provocative place I could put him, I relieved him of any duty to patrol the Strip, and appointed Bellamy Jameson, the head of civil law enforcement, which *used* to include the Strip, to handle *all* law enforcement on the station, including directing the ECE. My orders to him, Captain, include cooperation with ships' authorities, quiet on the Strip, and a new attitude."

"Right now things are quiet," JR said. "Is it your intention to pull *Rights* back and give chase?"

"I don't want Mr. Hewitt to do *anything,* Captain. I

don't think they stand a chance in hell of getting that ship out of dock. They certainly couldn't give chase. I only hope *Cruz* has the sense to keep hands off *Galway*'s crew. He's a fool. An unprincipled fool."

"A fool," Owen Monahan said, "decidedly. It's a long trip, for a fool. I have *every* confidence in our senior captain."

Abrezio looked at Owen Monahan and looked very sober indeed. But not outraged. No. *Mr. Cruz and I are not allies,* the man had just said. One could only imagine what Cruz planned to report to the EC about Abrezio, when and if he got to Sol.

"You say," JR said, "that you've dealt with the scrip and the lodgings for the Monahans. A good gesture. It'll be up to the Monahans how long they stay here. Any ship here would give them passage."

"Until *Galway* comes back," Abrezio said. "We've promised that."

JR just nodded, saying nothing of Niall Monahan's planned layover in the deep dark. "We'll stay a little longer ourselves, seeing how it settles. Among the immediate questions—the people on *Rights* at the moment, who continue to pose a threat. I take it they are loyal to this Hewitt?"

"Right now, yes."

"Until that changes, you will have them to deal with. Unfortunately. Do you intend ever to have these people back on the Strip?"

Abrezio sank into his chair. "I am out of ideas, there, sir. The hiring and training of ECE personnel was part of Hewitt's orders. But I will own they are, for the most part, Alpha citizens, sons and daughters of Alpha citizens, and they are our responsibility."

"They have family here," Min said. "And what is their training?"

"The majority?" Abrezio said. "Enforcement."

"And the minority in FTL ops?"

"From the ship's entry security scan," Abrezio said, "a minority, yes. Those missing from that scan are, I assume, with Cruz, though possibly some of that number are holding the number one mast access area. About twenty percent of the entire ECE is trained on the sims. The ones who voyaged with Hewitt on *Qarib* may be with Hewitt now."

"Which means those with Cruz are completely without real-time experience," JR said, and Abrezio nodded. "And they have ops on *Rights*, with Cruz's man Hewitt in charge."

Another nod.

"Am I correct, sir, that *you* have EC authority overriding Hewitt's, with Cruz not even out of the system?"

"Technically," Abrezio said, "I do. But . . ."

"Technically is good enough," Sanjay said with a shrug. "Within the regulations. Not that any of us give much for them, but considering your position. And theirs. If you order them to stand down, and Hewitt resists, he might be placed under arrest."

"I ordered Hewitt and the rest to board *Rights*. That got them off the Strip. But keeping them up there—is another matter. They were provisioned-up for the test run, sufficient to have gone to Bryant's. They can easily stand us off until you leave. And if I can manage to get them sorted out, they may view it's just a matter of waiting. Granted *Galway* gets through, come another year, I may not be in office."

Meaning, in Abrezio's expectation, Sol might be arriving here within the year, with all that meant.

Tell the man? Pell would know. Venture would know. Eventually Alpha would know—and maybe they ought to give Abrezio the information.

But until *Galway* cleared the system and went out of all communication, however time-lagged, they were saying absolutely nothing.

"You've got them contained, at least," JR said. "What do you see happening?"

"I foresee the people on *Rights* trying to get back onto station once they realize there've been changes. Enzio Hewitt has had designs on *Rights* and its crew since he arrived, and he thought he was going to run the Strip. I just put Strip enforcement in the hands of civil authority, the way it *used* to be, before the *Rights* project, and I'm *not* handing it back over to Hewitt. Given the equipment in

A-mast, cutters and such, I'm sure they'll escape that area eventually, not with any good will toward me and my staff, but civil enforcement, answering to the civil court, is going to be the rule on Alpha until Sol officially puts me out of here."

"You'll have the Strip's backing," Owen Monahan said. "We'll pass that word, and we'll back you."

"Thank you for that," Abrezio said. "The problem is the sheer numbers involved."

"You'll have cooperation from us, as well," JR said.

"Regarding that," Abrezio said, his frown deepening, "there is a problem. To get Hewitt and the *Rights* crew to move, I told them that there was an emergency on A-mast, that *Finity* was moving to take over *Rights.*"

JR drew in a deep breath, parsing *that* situation for its problems. Min had a smile he used often for social purposes. This one was small, wicked, and Min didn't say a thing.

"I heartily apologize," Abrezio said, "but at that precise moment, I didn't see another way to get them off the Strip before they came in with tasers."

"A serious problem," JR said, "if they decide to move *Rights* back and spin up."

"We have to give clearance to undock."

"And they have the ability to damage the mast if they ignore that. Is the ship armed?"

"Enforcement has tasers. So far as I'm aware, there's nothing larger."

"I mean the ship itself."

Abrezio slowly shook his head. "No, Captain, I don't think so. I would be surprised. Sincerely. Is yours?"

"Not as such," JR said. "And nothing we would like to use."

"Right now," Asha said, "the ship is using station's power, from the mast. They've not disconnected and not spun up."

"No," Abrezio said. "They have not."

"They pose a problem," JR said, "but the greater one if they have access to utility pushers and construction equipment. Including cutters."

"I'm afraid they will have. And they will get back in. But a few at a time—we can stop that."

"On the other hand, they might pull *Rights* out in the notion *we* have to be stopped."

They might estimate *Finity* could go after *Galway* and stop her—*not* his intention, but Hewitt didn't know that. And the notion of a ship of *Rights'* size and power moving out with mayhem in mind toward ships on B-mast was a threat all on its own.

Invade A-mast to deal with it, hand to hand? Station security against what amounted to a military? No. Not even if they weren't outnumbered. Not even if the merchanters added their numbers to the mix.

But arguing with *Rights* as a separate hull was . . . *extremely* problematic.

A cranky monster in the hands of a sim-trained crew. God . . .

Stop them. Basically *stop* them.

Rights was, aside from internal modifications, a first-generation *Finity's End*. He *knew* its systems. If he was at the helm, trying to cut loose from an uncooperative station . . .

Ship brought live would have a mind of her own. Ship wouldn't spin up the ring until she was free of station. Ship would object to the pull-back with the lines still engaged. But that objection could be overridden. What *couldn't* be . . . the one thing that would stop *Finity* cold . . .

Damn.

"From what we saw coming in," JR said, "you have two ships parked on a level with A-mast, sir. *Firenze* and *Qarib*. And not that far."

"Under bot control," Abrezio said, looking puzzled.

A low grunt, a quickly inhaled breath: the other captains had read the idea. Abrezio might not see it yet.

"I know something about that ship's design, and her failsafes. Its crew may know one override procedure, but with your cooperation, sir, and the Gallis' forgiveness, we can escalate the situation into a no-go condition. That ship *will not* ram another vessel."

Abrezio stared at him. Understanding—yes. Appalled. Yes.

"One of the parking bots maintaining position for the ships you moved off to bring us in—can have a little malfunction. It is a risk—and if this goes wrong I'll owe far more than an apology to the Gallis, but this will create a no-go condition the instant they bring *Rights* sensors live and prepare to push out. I'm thinking *Rights* is probably configured for tests, with all her safeties set tight as possible. She'll be a stickler for the rules. It's possible Hewitt or his Helm know what to do and what buttons to push, but if they don't override the collision alert, they won't move. Period. What you have to do, sir, is get *your* bot to start moving *Firenze* in right now. Sooner we start, the closer we can get before they get through their Pre and try to move, lines or no lines."

Abrezio's face was pale. Sweating. His eyes were unsteady—rapid thinking. "*Rights* did get out of dock on her test run. But she took over an hour doing it. And she needed a pusher to get back in."

"If we're all lucky," JR said, "it'll be a simple no-go to lock *Rights* down. They can't spin up till they back out; so they've got that to go through; and once they get that far, and enter instructions to back out, computer will read the surrounds and spot *Firenze*'s movement and refuse to move. Ultimately, we park *Firenze* inside the critical proximity limit. And that will be another no-go condition. If we're really lucky, nobody on *Rights* will know the major overrides, even better, if the overrides are bio-locked to Cruz. If we're not lucky—"

"They could collide."

"They could. We could easily end up with two damaged ships. In which case there's going to be more exceptions flooding that ship's systems. A storm of exceptions it'll take a senior engineer to sort out."

Owe Giovanna Galli? At very least he'd owe an apology for the risk. At most—a total refit. But take out *Rights'* jump vanes, and Alpha would be years on the repair.

"If we do clear *Rights* for pushback and let go the lines,"

Asha said, "no damage to the mast or the Director's EC record. He'll have cooperated. And *they're* stuck on *Rights* with no station access, once we freeze them in place."

"*If* we can get *Firenze* close enough fast enough," JR said, "yes. I'd take the chance."

Do him credit, Abrezio didn't hesitate. He pushed a button on his intercom. "Ames. I need you. Right now."

Chapter 16   Section ii

The beer was probably a mistake. But the thought of leaving, even to a safe, clean bed, was just not what Ross wanted right now. He sat next to Jen, in one of Rosie's highly sought booths, with the noise swirling about him, coming and going, and friends well-wishing the Monahans . . .

But all the same, they waited for *Galway* to jump out and be gone, and that, he thought, though it could take minutes or days—that was why he didn't want to leave, even with Jen to keep him company.

"Ross, you got to get to your room."

He decided not to shake his head. It hurt. A lot of things hurt. "No," he said. "Not. *Can't.*"

Jen slipped her hand past his elbow. "Then lean on me," she said. "It's all right."

"I'm balanced as is."

"The hell. *Lean.*"

He gave way slowly, and did find it more comfortable. Let his eyes shut from time to time.

He could hear cousins talking. Owen had left their number three in charge, and gone off to talk to Abrezio, along with Jen's senior, and several others, and he didn't know what about, but rumor was, on the Strip, that Abrezio had fired Cruz's lieutenant, Hewitt, and Hewitt's whereabouts was not entirely clear, but that Bellamy Jameson was back in charge on the Strip, and people thought that was good news. Blue-coats had come into Rosie's to talk quietly to Rosie himself, and after that they had just left, past all the crowd outside. Rosie had passed word about Jameson, and said that they wanted the captains to keep the lid on, and apply their own judgement.

Then Rosie started passing out free food, a lot of it, which went the rounds. Ross looked at it, a tray on the table filled with options, and thought it might be a good idea, or then, again, maybe it wouldn't. His stomach just wasn't interested.

Rumors circulated. Runners were going back and forth from the captains in the meeting in admin, and talk was that they were putting pressure on Abrezio, but on what, wasn't clear.

Then a runner came back who delivered messages to several of the captains, and created a little stir close to the bar.

A final bit of adrenaline surged, and Ross sat up straight, thinking that *Galway* might have gone. He was prepared for that.

"I'll see what I can find out," Jen said, and wriggled out of the booth.

Moments later, Giovanna Galli, with a hissed expletive, left in a hurry, with her first-shift crew, shoving roughly past the gathering at the door.

Jen came back and said, her head close to his, "I'm not sure. It's the meeting. They're calling her and her helm and nav.—Got to go talk to my senior."

He didn't figure it. Of all ships potentially involved—*Firenze*?

But then he saw Aki Rahman headed out the door with two of the *Qarib* crew.

Owen was already in the meeting. So were the four outsiders. Of senior captains in Rosie's, only *Santiago* was left; and Diego and Julio Rodriguez likewise got up, two of his senior crew tailing them, and headed after Rahman.

Hell, he thought, and looked to the side as Jen came back.

"Station's requesting *Finity* security to the doors outside the number one mast access," Jen said, "and putting civil enforcement on alert. *Rights* crew has put A-mast doors under lock, and Station wants *Finity* and *Little Bear* to go on ahead to the mast doors, to apply tasers if they have to, but the thinking is to scare any *Rights* crew that's in A-mast out onto *Rights*. They *want* them to undock."

"To do what, for God's sake?"

"To strand them out there," Jen said, with a wicked grin he hadn't seen before.

His brain wasn't parsing information well. Things passed in a haze, and facts wouldn't connect. Giovanna Galli, the Rahmans. *Rights* and *Finity's End* headed for a confrontation, while *Galway* was out there with no knowing what was going on aboard. She was running hard, according to reports from *Finity,* wasting no time getting vector established, climbing further up Barnard's well, all those things—but so much else could be going on. People he loved could be getting killed.

At the very least were under threat.

And nothing, not a damn thing he could do. "How far are they?" he asked, and wasn't meaning the situation in the mast.

"They're at two g and pushing it," Jen said, perfectly well understanding him. "They're showing no sign of aborting."

No sign. He wasn't sure what Niall would do.

Or Fallan.

"Wish I was there," he said. "God. Wish I was there."

Jen squeezed his arm. "I know. But figure Fallan's hoping like everything that you're here."

"Doesn't make that damn much difference what I did. The coordinates are here, on Alpha. Word's going to get to Pell, with or without me."

"Hell if. Not just about the numbers. It's about what Cruz did. Because of you," Jen said quietly, under the general noise in Rosie's. "We know. All of us know and will know. It's the worst nightmare, the EC trying to steal one of ours. The alliance means to make sure that can't happen. And what you did makes a big difference. We know. And station knows. And station can't hold back, now. They've got Pell to deal with because those numbers got to us. Abrezio knows he hasn't got a choice about it, and Cruz won't be his friend. Abrezio's shutting down Cruz's organization—that's what's happening out there. He's shutting down Cruz's whole operation. And I'm betting he'll sign with us. That's a big step. We get all the Family ships lined up, and even if Sol comes in here with their hired crews, no station's going to trade with them. Which is where we *start* negotiating. The Beyond is bigger than Sol. They're going to have to figure that out. So you and Fallan did something, between you, that's changed things for good and all."

"I'm not sure I like to think that."

"Changed, because they have to, love. We know it. They'll figure it out, when they come up against the Beyond. If they have sense, they'll listen to us."

"Would Cruz listen?"

A deep breath. "No," Jen said. "But with luck—he's not getting to Sol."

Chapter 16   Section iii

"Captain Galli's here," Abrezio's secretary reported, and JR got up from his seat in Abrezio's office, not the only one to rise: Abrezio himself stood up. JR had intended to intercept Giovanna Galli outside, to break the news in private, but there was no such chance. Her co-captains were behind her, along with, presumably, her number one helm and nav; and Julio and Diego Rodriguez were, along with *Qarib's* senior captain, Ahmad Aki Rahman, whose standard-speak wasn't the best. Worried. And with reason.

"The one affected," JR began quietly, "is *Firenze.* Captain, operations are underway—time is of the essence—but you *can* abort them, which is why I called you. Your ship is positioned above the station body, at a remove where a diagonal course will intersect *Rights of Man* on pull-back. It should trigger an absolute no-go on *Rights.* We don't believe they have the ability to override. We need to render that ship helpless, and your ship has the mass to damage *Rights* beyond any doubt if *Rights* is managed by fools. I offer whatever it takes—the repair, beyond a doubt. A refit. You write the ticket. Or tell us abort. And we'll find another way."

Giovanna stood there staring at him, and didn't ask the obvious—why aren't you risking *your* ship, Neihart? He said, quietly, "Mass and position, Captain. Best pick. Best chance. And I will—personally—owe you. Big."

"You pay your debts, Neihart?"

"I do. And I will. Even if there's not a scratch on her."

"I'm already betting everything I've got. All that all of us have got. You want more, all right." Lips clamped tight. JR felt it—hardest thing he'd had to ask of any outsider, and this woman had had every bad break there was. "Damn it, Neihart. *Damn* it."

"Damned sure there'll be a *Firenze*, damned sure the Gallis will be top priority, come what may," JR said. "The alliance will see to it."

"Yeah," Giovanna said shakily. "Yeah." She looked around at all of them. "I believe you. I understand the reasons. But I'm *in* on this, I'm in, I stay. I sit."

"Captain, yes, you do. Take *my* chair. We need the door open. We've got more people out there. And this is going to take time."

Abrezio called his secretary in, and gave orders without elaboration. The secretary brought chairs, kept the door open, provided a feed to handhelds, linked to the ones in Abrezio's office.

Giovanna steadied down, sat with arms folded, watching lines on a schematic. *Firenze* was moving under a parking-bot's nudge, and she was on course to enter *Rights'* exclusion zone.

More feed switched in, audio from ops, mostly a quiet mutter about the bot's fuel supply and the station shadow, and the bot's ability to stop *Firenze* at a given point. Acceleration was complete. She was moving as fast as she needed to. And the bot would suffice to brake within the exclusion zone if *Rights* left dock.

JR stood between Min and Sanjay, Asha on Sanjay's side, all of them having chosen to stand and give place to the *Galway* and *Firenze* officers in this office with the larger screens. He was figuring, all the way down those lines, he was internalizing the diagrams, knowing the controls. He'd *been* helm, once, and it didn't leave your awareness. He could only hope, among a number of things he suspected *weren't* set the way they should be, that the exclusion zone was set particularly wide, as it should be during shakedown and testing,

"*Rights* is going for undock," ops said. "Didn't ask permission, sir, just started the procedure."

"Bastard probably expects to use my exclusion of his boss from the infostream to justify it." Said in a tone JR had never heard from Abrezio. "He's welcome to try."

He liked it.

Other than that, no one spoke, just watched those numbers, the graph of *Firenze*'s projected path, the little dot moving along it. Watched ops' readout of *Rights*' undock procedures, the shifting estimate of her estimated push-out and potential intersection with *Firenze*. Disconnect of the bundle was the first. That was a little slow, not having gotten station's cooperation. Disconnect of the passageway was the second, and still proceeding. Disconnect of the grapples would follow. There would be more to follow. Small things that could cause major problems, if not done in order and thoroughly.

Breaths drew in, faces grew tense. Under ordinary circumstances, one of the final procedures should be a handshake with ops, whose sensors should guarantee a clear space and whose officers would be up to the moment to assist, should there be any complication.

In this case, they were going through disconnect on their own, defying Abrezio's authority, and station ops *should* have told them they had a bot pushing a parked and crewless, fairly large merchant ship on a path that was going to cross *Rights*' only path away from its bow-dock with the mast. *Firenze* was not even showing any lights in the move. No transmission. An uninformed bystander might just say the parking bot had had a directional jet stick in "on," one of its small corrections to keep *Firenze* in place just continuing to fire. It was subtle, it was quiet, so far. *Rights'* automatic communication with ops was minimal, proper, unalarmed.

And *slow. Rights* wasn't a confident ship. From the timing, every switch was requiring two and three considerations before engaging.

The passageway uncoupled: all *Rights* crew that intended to board, had apparently boarded. The grapples would be next. Helm was ready . . . probably. He could imagine everyone trying to remember their procedures and get it right—novices, all. Com would be making records: that was automatic. *Rights'* computer talked to ops, confirming the grapple disconnect, and Abrezio told ops: "Let them go."

Scan was *surely* live by now. You didn't handle a megaship like a dockside trolley and suddenly throw it into reverse.

The crew ring began to rotate, finally—*finally.* Good thing it had taken them so long: *Firenze* was not quite into the zone, but about to be. And on *Rights*, there were now feet on the deck, *some* protection against inertia.

Procedures. A lot of procedures. A number of personnel were supposed to move out now, run physical checks and report readiness. Maybe they did, maybe not. There was nothing Family-like about the crew.

Maybe they'd just sit there, JR was beginning to say to himself. They might be satisfied that they'd saved *Rights* just by undocking, confident no intruders were going to get onto their deck.

Ops continued saying, periodically, "Rights *is undergoing checks.*"

Not the check they wanted to see, preparatory to movement. The scan wasn't rotating. Scan hadn't turned on. That was worrying.

Procedures, JR said to himself. Shut his eyes a second, *seeing* the requisite button. He opened them, staring at the screen, willing scan to *find* the problem before helm moved. A mistake could damage the station.

Scan began to rotate. *Rights'* running lights came on,

sparks of light in absolute shadow, light elsewhere drowned in the sunglare.

"Come on," Owen Monahan said. "Undock thrusters, you stupid bastard. *Don't shove the mast.*"

"She's moving," *Firenze*'s Helm said. On the screens, barely perceptible, the assemblage of glare and shadow that was *Rights of Man* began edging ever so slightly away from the mast.

Then opened up *way* hard.

And stopped. But continuing to move. Fast.

"Shit!" That was Giovanna herself. She lapsed into shipspeak.

"Brake," JR said, to his connection to ops. "Brake, all-out, ops 1."

The exclusion zone traveled with *Rights*. JR darted a glance to the numbers in the corner of the image. Accel had spiked and gone null. Stern thrusters were working, *not* under Helm's control, which—JR didn't have to be on the bridge to see it—was bringing relative motion to a sudden zero. Shutdown. And not just shutdown. Collision avoidance.

"She's aborted," JR said. "Galli, *Rights* just aborted. She knows your ship's there. She's not under Helm now. Auto avoidance is active. Bot's braking *Firenze* now. Ops, have you got a projection?"

His contact with ops stayed silent, ops working on it, no question—calculating the propellant the bot had and hoping to hell the reading was accurate. It rarely mattered. Now it did. Extremely. *Rights* had gone to a non-regulation *V* and changed all their figures. Then she'd gone into no-go, and begun to cancel the motion toward the hazard's path. *Rights* under auto had a far better hope of doing that than ops did of stopping *Firenze*'s mass that short with a lowly parking-bot.

The lines predicting the meeting point did not look good. "*Hundred percent on the braking push,*" ops said. They were keeping no reserve in the bot's tanks. When they ran out, the bot would stop braking. It would have to be overtaken in its fuelless course and refueled or pushed, along with *Firenze*.

"Burnout," ops said, deadly calm.

The bot was on its own. *Rights* was still on autopilot, correcting, correcting.

Rights' Helm had no override. The evident solution was to fire the laterals and complicate the motion, away from the predicted intersect, or just speed up. But control didn't rest with Helm. It was all the computers talking to each other. And voting.

Lines were continually adjusting on the overlay. Change and no-change, calculations down to the last hope of avoidance. *Firenze*'s progress was inexorable. *Rights'* progress was a slowly moving number. Giovanna Galli's mouth was a thin line, her face and her Helm's both frozen, stolidly watching.

Come on, JR thought. *Finity* would have sounded an alarm, he would have entered an override, and Helm would have reacted with a solution.

But *Finity* would never be in this situation. That hard burn . . . *damn*, what the hell had Helm been thinking?

There was a blue line. *Rights'* track, and a red one, *Firenze*'s, They were headed for intersect, past and present solid color, showing no future course for either ship past intersect, but transparent circles that could be rebound, and wreckage.

Then the redline, *Firenze*'s track, turned yellow, and a yellow line sprang into existence. Perspective shifted. Yellow was continuing now, and blue advance slowed drastically

"It's a miss!" Asha said. "She's going to miss!"

Giovanna and her Helm grabbed each other's arm, hoping.

"The clearance," ops' cold voice said, *"will be one point three-seven meters."*

A cheer went up. It was still to prove—it was tight. There was a little tractor effect. But ops' computers handled that sort of thing.

"Firenze *is clear,"* ops said finally. "Rights *is braking. Ops will prepare a tanker to overtake and refuel the parking-bot, and return* Firenze *to a safe position beside* Qarib."

"Mr. Director," JR said, above the murmur in the room.

"Suggest you move *Rights* out to park. They may try to contact *Galway* in hopes of a fix for the shut-down. If they get one, we may have them yet to deal with."

"Captain." That was ops. "*Galway* has jumped. She is no longer in the system."

The room fell quiet.

Stayed quiet for a long moment.

When that yellow line had continued, and *Firenze* sailed clear, for a moment everything had been all right. It drew a huge cheer in Rosie's.

The image lasted a full minute. Then the image shifted back to the schedule board. *The Rights of Man* was listed as Departed, but instead of a destination it said Mechanical Hold.

And right under it, *Galway* was listed as Departed System and the destination said Sol.

Ross read it. Took pains to keep expression off his face. Jen was by him. Nearby, Tilby Monahan, Third Captain, was getting a call, and nodding solemnly. Every Galway face in Rosie's, by ones and twos, turned toward Tilby, who listened intently, and a silence fell. Laughter still drifted in from out on the Strip, but there was none inside Rosie's, now.

"Good luck to them," Jen said under her breath. "Fallan's no fool. Nor's your captain. He'll be rid of them first chance."

They'd hoped, through the hours, that somehow they might get a call from *Galway* that it was all settled, that they'd gotten the better of Cruz and his blue-coats. But that call hadn't come.

They'd just gone. Early.

It was even possible they'd gone without telling their passengers to belt in, trank down, take precautions. If so . . . it wouldn't be pretty on the far side.

Adrenaline was still high. Ross's heartbeat was heavy and felt slow. Or time was out of sync for him, and things were drifting past, surreal.

Jen's hand was on his. Somebody else's rested on his shoulder, some cousin, he thought, somebody who wished him well.

He couldn't feel lonely, where he was, among Family, and with friends. But he could feel—left. Lost. And apt to stay that way, maybe for a lifetime. He kept seeing the bridge, and Cruz, and Niall and Fallan, and the blinding red brightness and absolute dark outside the hull. He still coughed, and it still hurt like hell, and he had a sip of beer to try to stop the feeling.

Peg sat down by him, said, "You did right, Ross. You did everything you could. Now it's their turn. Just wish 'em well."

"Yeah," he said, and looked again at the uncompromising screen. "Yeah."

Chapter 17   Section ii

"Paperwork." Funny how, even though hard copy was virtually nonexistent now, the term for filling out forms remained.

And for the Senior Captain of *Finity's End*, ensconced now in his sleepover office, the pile-up was considerable, after recent events.

Little Bear had left. She'd kite through Bryant's, stay for conference at Venture, and dispatch news for Pell via courier.

After which—

JR still asked himself whether Cyteen had always known the route *Galway* was following. But Cyteen still had to be told, and meanwhile *Finity* had to get signatures, virtual or otherwise, on agreements—in which endeavor they had to deal with their opposite number, *Dublin*.

They had Alpha's agreement to the Alliance, made in full disclosure of *Galway*'s revised mission and Alpha's commitment to nudge Glory and Bryant's Star into joining. Not too curiously, Abrezio had seemed relieved at the longer time frame. The more time to get the station in good order and the *Rights* crew sorted out, so he said.

And he was committed to that course. He'd explained everything, and handed over the coordinates minutes after *Galway* jumped. Never mind they already had those numbers thanks to Fallan's quick thinking and Ross's courage; it was an act of faith and good will JR could appreciate.

The standoff of the big ship was working better than they'd dared hope. An in-depth examination of the operational manuals had revealed there *was* no override built into her systems. The stolen plans predated *Finity's* actual build. And there was nothing in the build notes to imply the local engineers and programmers had yet considered the possibility they might need to argue with the ship's alarms and clearances—*Rights* was, granted, still in testing, and her crew was still in training. And she was *stuck*.

He'd had the dubious pleasure of sitting in on the teleconference with *Rights'* acting captain, who had been willing to talk—at length. The man did have a slick tongue. If one believed him, Hewitt had noticed the meeting between Abrezio's office and *Galway*, and when the entire Monahan Family had gathered in a secure meeting room in station offices, Hewitt had known it and made the leap of logic as to what those private meetings had entailed. He'd gone to Cruz, and Cruz—obsessed, so Hewitt claimed—with his place in history, had made the decision to board *Galway* and take personal command of the mission, leaving Hewitt in charge of the *Rights* program.

One could imagine exactly how that conversation had gone, and who planted the idea in whose head.

Hewitt explained the illegal pull-out as a choice necessitated by the position Abrezio had put him in. He'd believed Abrezio's advisement that *Finity* was going to move against *Galway* and Cruz, and now he understood that Abrezio had both distrusted him and misled him, and he was very sorry Abrezio had felt compelled to do that. He now understood what *Finity* was about, Hewitt said, and he wished he had known from the outset, because he would have done differently. His trainee crew aboard were good people, and they were suffering and they wanted to come home.

He would work with Abrezio in the hopes they could present Sol, when Sol did arrive, a healthy merchant trade. He would truly hope, given that Abrezio *had* a working relationship with *Finity,* that he might even get information from *Finity,* possibly the help of *Finity's* captains, in ironing out *Rights'* problems and getting her safely into operation.

He would welcome *Finity* engineers aboard. *Rights* would, after all, be Abrezio's success as well as his and Cruz's.

And he would appreciate it if *Rights* were moved back into dock.

Perhaps, JR had thought, looking at the complete disgust on Abrezio's face, it would be.

When hell froze over.

Abrezio and his staff had begun interviewing offices Hewitt dealt with, and the inquiry, now that Hewitt was contained, was getting a very different story from the one Hewitt told. Seasoned enforcement officers and a vice president of the station bank were now talking about reprisals, inappropriate information-gathering and, not too surprising, exchange of favors with a construction firm, soon to be under investigation.

Hewitt and his crew were to stay indefinitely on *Rights of Man,* parked where *Firenze* and *Qarib* had been parked. They had rotation, but no override code. So *Rights* sat, with a machine's patience, completely stalled and calmly awaiting a code to end the shutdown, which was likewise not in Hewitt's manual. Meanwhile there was food, there was water—*Rights* was amply supplied from her intended run to Bryant's.

And there was an understanding given, that if any enforcement personnel could muster an appeal from someone on Alpha, like family willing to take on legal responsibility, they could be extracted and offered a chance to leave the service for other employment.

And Abrezio, so he said freely, began to hope for at

least three years before Sol EC invaded his station . . . *that* information had breathed life into the man, who began to have plans, definite plans, and who wanted to talk to other stations and to the Konstantins, who wanted time to greet the future as a partner, not a servant.

Finity made a commitment to watch the situation. There was a time-within-which *Galway* was likely to return if she could return: first if they were in safely at the first jump-point but had reason to doubt the next one was safe; and second, if they made it all the way to Sol and came back with mission accomplished.

Finity added Alpha-Bryant's-Venture to her schedule, with a promise of raw materials destined for station repair, goods high on Abrezio's requests in return for his signature on the Alliance agreement. And *Finity's* mission *back* through the strand of stars was to negotiate a station-rights agreement with other stations and sign *them* up as alliance-compliant stations before he approached Pell for the Konstantins' signature.

The Monahans were well set at Alpha, determined to wait for *Galway's* return—and to deal with what fell out. Alpha was, in ways still not completely within a Beyonder's emotional makeup, their home port, a term almost as potent with them as *ship*.

The Gallis were doing well enough—heroes of the action against Hewitt. *Firenze* was back in dock . . . on A-mast . . . and a thorough examination by *Firenze* and *Finity* engineers had created a sizable purchase order that *Finity* herself would see filled at Venture and Pell.

It was, overall, a good result. Even Rosie's plumbing, according to a cheerful message from Jen, had been fixed. He could only hope *Dublin* was having equal luck. Two or three years, station time, was a scary-short window before things might begin to happen.

"JR?" came over his earpiece.

Fletcher was back. He touched a button on the device. "Did you find him, Fletch?"

"Right here."

"Send him on in."

"Not alone."

Why was he not surprised.

"Just him, please. Tell her I promise not to bite."

"She'll object."

"And he doesn't need her doe-eyes on him while he's thinking. She's a persuasive little rascal."

"That she is. Sending him in."

"Thanks."

The door slid open, and young Ross Monahan stepped through. Jen was right behind him, but stopped at the threshold, under JR's warning glare.

The door slid shut and JR waved a hand at the second chair in the room. "Have a seat."

"Sir." Ross sat . . . on the edge.

"You're looking better. Memory back yet?"

"Solid, sir."

"Excellent. Thought as much. Got a copy of your full account." He picked up a data-stick. Laid it down again. "You're a hero, Ross."

He squirmed. "No, sir. My shift . . . they're the heroes."

Not comfortable with the word. That was a good sign.

"We're set to leave in four days."

"Jen said. Sir."

A little wistful, for all he tried to hide it.

"Miss her, will you?"

Ross met his eyes squarely. "A bit."

"Cocky."

"No, sir." Except he wasn't. The two had been pretty much inseparable for days now. Their relationship had become open season for ribbing. He'd met JR's query with the response it damnwell deserved, and JR liked that in him.

"So . . . what will you do? Got a bit of a wait ahead."

"Try to keep sharp. Those sims you gave us will help. We're very grateful."

"When *Galway* gets back, she'll be getting a refit. New engines. The works. You'll be one up on your team."

His brow twitched. "Not by choice, sir. And I won't replace Fallan or Ashlan. No way I'll step up."

"They'll welcome the knowledge. You know they will."

"Yes, sir."

He moved his fingers, taking the sheet of paper with it.

"Sims aren't as good as the real thing."

"Better than nothing."

"And if I were to offer you an alternative?"

That got him a look. Straight and narrow-eyed.

"How would you like to shadow the boards on *Finity* . . . until *Galway* returns?"

Eyes widened. Temptation. Oh . . . the temptation. Then squeezed shut.

"No, sir. I need to stay with the Family. We've got to weather this together."

"Understand, you're not the only one I'm making the offer to. Just the first. Because, no argument, Ross, you *have* earned favor-points on this ship. And there's one of us would be particularly happy if you spent a while."

He sat still, just staring into space. Then: "Does Jen know about this?"

JR shook his head.

"That's why you didn't want her in here."

"Yes."

"I'm tempted, sir, I won't deny it. But . . . I can't see myself going off even for a year. Family needs us right now. Needs to know we're together. And my ship-time . . . if something happened to set me at a gap . . . bad enough my shift going clear to Sol and back without me. There's people right now old enough—they might not be there when I got back."

"Understood. Were our positions reversed, I'd be thinking the same. But we owe you, Ross. We all do. Think about it. It's a gift we can give *Galway*—ahead of that refit. And above all else—don't let Jen make the decision for you. You know how she'd vote. And she lives a lot in the now."

Ross attempted a small laugh. "She's persuasive and she's got an argument, I'll grant you that."

"And you, sir, have only glimpsed her talents." JR stood up, held out his hand. Ross stood up and met it, a firm, dry grip. JR picked up a tag, held it out. "Key to *Finity's* lock, if you will. Take it. Discuss the terms with whoever you want. Make your decision what's best."

Ross took it and slipped it into a pocket. "Thank you, sir. I will."

"This offer isn't for Jen's sake, understand that. And it's not because your presence as eyewitness to what happened on *Galway* won't be useful, though it might well. Don't know how you are on nav, but Fallan picked you, and for nerve that drives the luck, you've got it. You proved that several times over. Our nav look forward to working with you. So: it's an honest offer, but you do what you feel right doing."

"Thank you, sir."

He lifted his chin toward the door. "Go now. Before Jen breaks the door down."

Chapter 17   Section iii

It was an undock party unrivaled even, Rosie's waitstaff said, by *Santa Maria's* or *Atlantis'* departures.

Finity's End was heading out, with *Mumtaz* and *Nomad* following within hours. *Santiago* was preparing to leave in two more days. The bright lights and the music were all shutting down, employees of various sleepovers and eateries going back to other jobs until—well, whatever happened next. The Olympian was shutting down. So were smaller sleepovers, including the Argent, which had housed *Santiago* crew.

But not all the bright lights were going. The Fortune was staying open for the Galways, and the Opportunity, for the Firenzes, though the Qaribs were soon to leave.

There was a sadness about it, the quiet settling in again, but not entirely this time. This time there was something different. There was anticipation for the future—for ships coming back. For change and supply finally coming in.

There was difference for a few Monahans, too—who were packed up, because they were going with *Finity* for a run out and back, *Finity* promising to bring them home better than they went out, trained for systems *Galway* didn't have yet, but would. Ross wouldn't be alone—Ian was going, Helm; Connor Dhu and Netha were going, two of their engees. And they'd get home again: *Finity* promised it. Ross had had to buy everything. His duffle was aboard *Galway,* an inconsequence, against everything else that traveled with that ship. He had new clothes, a jacket with the *Galway* patch . . . and a lot of personal stuff that people chipped in to give him. Most precious thing, his crew ring. *That* had never left his hand.

So he was on the other side of matters, saying goodbye for a time—goodbye to Peg, and his mother, his aunt, and a flood of cousins. Goodbye to Owen and everybody he meant to see again in not so long.

Finity was here, their own sleepover and its bars and restaurants holding their own undock party, but Finitys strayed in and back and forth as they pleased, along with the Mumtazes and the Nomads, so the party in Rosie's spilled over and out the door and freely mingled with parties up and down the Strip. Blue-coats weren't highly visible the last number of days, and the Strip got along right well. Officers were still in short supply—mostly it was crew celebrating at this point, while formalities got done and signatures and scrip were accounted for.

Jen came and went—she had him, no question: they'd see each other aplenty. It was those that weren't going that needed to be seen, and she didn't cling. She just showed up and promised Peg she'd be sure he behaved.

It was at once the noisiest and best-behaved undock party Ross himself had ever seen. Usually there was at least one noisy drunk and maybe a shoving match—but it was a *happy* crowd. It wasn't that easy for the Galways, still—there was a lot of hurt and worry; but in the end, it was why Ross had said yes, he was going—because in them that were going with *Finity's End,* the ship had hope. Hope of allies, hope of promises kept, hope of that refit, hope that out in the deep Beyond there were brothers and sisters in the trade that *weren't* going to leave Alpha to die, and who *would* talk basic sense to the EC when it came, and to anybody who thought merchanters were disposable.

There was an optimism rising. There were expectations. And hopes.

A commotion arose from the doorway, welcoming shouts, not clear the reason at first, and Ross stood up to see. The silver-grey of *Finity* jackets showed in the press of bodies, around a man not so tall as most—JR Neihart, with Madison and Fletcher and a number Ross didn't know. JR came in and mixed crews cheered—no question of these people buying their own drinks tonight. Ross stayed put—he still wasn't up to shoving his way through; but then a hand slipped past his elbow and an arm hugged his.

He didn't need to look to know.

"Damn, you're sneaky," he said.

"That's my job," Jen said. "How are you holding up?"

"I got a chair, is what, and I'm not leaving it." He sat back down, and there was a chair next to his that had been Connor's, but Jen sank into it.

"Good for you."

"Still a little wobbly. But looking forward to this." It was a test of his own commitment, saying that. It felt right—which was a comfort. "You sure you're going to bring us back?"

"Promise," Jen said soberly. "Really promise, on that one. We'll get back here."

"Exit going to be as splashy as your entry?"

"You'll see. Captain's going to have you shadow first shift. You'll get a good view."

Scary prospect, that. But he looked forward to it. Extremely. It began to be vivid to him. It began to be imaginable.

And at that moment came a second entry by that far door, an entry that caused a murmur that swept like a wave across the room, that cleared space for the cause of it.

A plump, grey-haired man in a business suit, holding hands with a grey-haired woman in conservative clothes. Both were neat, looking very out of place, and the man—a familiar face.

"That's Director Abrezio," Ross said quietly, in the general hush. "That's actually Ben Abrezio."

He watched as JR Neihart went to meet the pair, as JR took Abrezio's offered hand, shook it, and then said to the hushed gathering, "This is Director Abrezio. His wife Callie Taylor. They're here to wish us off—in many senses."

General laughter, at that. The departing visitors had put a strain on Alpha. And changed it.

And about that time the schedule board and every screen in Rosie's went bright blue, and on it in huge white letters: "Thank you, Captain James Robert Neihart."

"JR," Jen said under her breath, in a general buzz of spacer reactions.

"Thank *you*, sir," JR said, "but I'm not *that* man."

"A Captain James Robert *founded* this station," Abrezio said, and the buzz went nearly silent. "The first-in knew him. There's a plaque in ops, about the only part of this station that's original. But we're here because of one James Robert Neihart, and we're here now because of another. As Alpha's director, it's an honor to say it, sir, you're in that class on Alpha. Will be, as long as Alpha exists."

"You're stuck, Senior Captain!" a voice called out from the crowd. Madison lifted a beer mug. "Captain James Robert, and an honor to serve the ship with you, brother!"

"Man's earned it," Ross said, feeling goosebumps. It was centuries ago *Gaia's* first captain had set Alpha here. It was something that he'd seen what he was seeing, hearing that name.

The man who carried it didn't ask to carry it. He was a smallish man, looking at the moment as if a weight had come down on him, and he wasn't that glad of it. But people cheered, all around. People saw what they'd been looking for without knowing they'd been looking at all.

There were burdens and there were burdens. Ross thought he'd had one, being left ashore, knowing so much was riding on *Galway,* and the first-shift crew that were the heroes. He'd just been left behind, and when *Galway* got back, he'd still be a nav trainee.

Captain James Robert had a different kind of weight settle on him, something that wasn't going to get smaller.

Even a nav trainee could see that coming. It was scary to think what *Finity* was up to, what they were doing, bringing changes to everything, fast as they could, a wavefront of change rolling in front of them.

Finity's End was the future she was shaping. And he would sit shadow on her boards.

CJ Cherryh
Complete Classic Novels in Omnibus Editions

To Order Call: 1-800-788-6262
www.dawbooks.com

C.S. Friedman
The Best in Science Fiction

To Order Call: 1-800-788-6262
www.dawbooks.com

DAW 17

Tanya Huff
The Peacekeeper Novels

"Huff weaves a fast-paced thriller bristling with treachery and intrigue. Fans of military science fiction will enjoy this tense adventure and its intricately constructed setting."
—*Publishers Weekly*

"Anyone who has read any of Huff's previous books featuring Kerr . . . knows of her amazing ability to combine action, plot, and character into a wonderful melange that makes her books a joy to read."
—*Seattle Post-Intelligencer*

AN ANCIENT PEACE
978-0-7564-1130-5

A PEACE DIVIDED
978-0-7564-1151-0

THE PRIVILEGE OF PEACE
978-0-7564-1154-1

To Order Call: 1-800-788-6262
www.dawbooks.com

Suzanne Palmer
Finder

"A breakneck-paced and action-packed science-fiction adventure featuring an endearing con artist whose current mission to retrieve a stolen spaceship ignites a war.... A nonstop SF thrill ride until the very last page."   —*Kirkus*

"Fergus Ferguson makes an excellent lead in this fast-paced hard-sf repo adventure set in space opera's sweeping scale and balanced on the heart of one very finely wrought character. Suzanne Palmer's writing is delightful."
        —Fran Wilde, author of the Bone Universe trilogy

"Palmer makes short-distance space travel feel as comfortable as riding a bicycle, and concludes this entertaining caper with a clever resolution and a hint of intrigue. Fans of space adventure will find this a fine example of the form."
        —*Publishers Weekly*

"Wicked, fast-paced, and fun. This is a total romp, and I loved it."   —Elizabeth Bear, author of *Ancestral Night*

ISBN: 978-0-7564-1635-5

To Order Call: 1-800-788-6262
www.dawbooks.com

DAW 219